KISSING THE CONQUEROR

What was she thinking? She could not marry him. Being married because a man owed her and her brother a blood debt was nearly as bad as being married off by the king to please some court sycophant. Jolene decided she was letting his fine looks and the way he could make her feel steal away all her good sense.

"Nay," she said softly. "To be married for such cold reasons—"

"Ye think I am cold?"

"Nay, but the reasons you give for this marriage are."

"Then I will give ye another reason."

Before she could protest, he kissed her. She placed her hands against his chest to push him away the moment she guessed his intent, but she never even tried to hold him back. The minute his mouth touched hers, she slid her hands up his broad chest and wrapped her arms around his neck. At the first nudge of his tongue, she opened her mouth to him, shivering with pleasure as he stroked the inside of her mouth.

She truly did like kissing this man, she thought dazedly . . .

BOOKS BY HANNAH HOWELL

ONLY FOR YOU

MY VALIANT KNIGHT

UNCONQUERED

WILD ROSES

A TASTE OF FIRE

HIGHLAND DESTINY

HIGHLAND HONOR

HIGHLAND PROMISE

A STOCKINGFUL OF JOY

HIGHLAND VOW

HIGHLAND KNIGHT

HIGHLAND HEARTS

HIGHLAND BRIDE

HIGHLAND ANGEL

HIGHLAND GROOM

HIGHLAND WARRIOR

RECKLESS

HIGHLAND CONQUEROR

Published by Zebra Books

HANNAH HOWELL

HIGHLAND CONQUEROR

ZEBRA BOOKS
KENSINGTON PUBLISHING CORP.
http://www.kensingtonbooks.com

ZEBRA BOOKS are published by

Kensington Publishing Corp.
850 Third Avenue
New York, NY 10022

All Kensington titles, imprints and distributed lines are available at special quantity discounts for bulk purchases for sales promotion, premiums, fund-raising, educational or institutional use.

Special book excerpts or customized printings can also be created to fit specific needs. For details, write or phone the office of the Kensington Special Sales Manager: Kensington Publishing Corp., 850 Third Avenue, New York, NY 10022. Attn. Special Sales Department. Phone: 1-800-221-2647.

Zebra and the Z logo Reg. U.S. Pat. & TM Off.

First Printing: March 2005
10 9 8 7 6 5 4 3 2 1

Printed in the United States of America

HIGHLAND CONQUEROR

THE MURRAY FAMILY LINEAGE

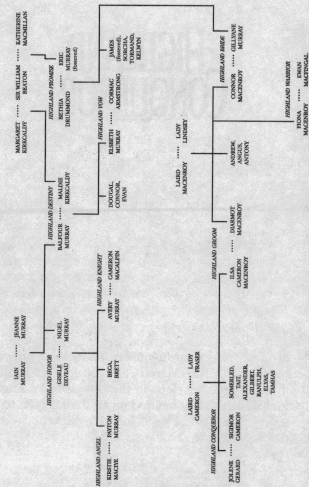

HIGHLAND ANGEL
KIRSTIE ····· PAYTON
MACIYE   MURRAY

IAIN ····· JEANNE
MURRAY   MURRAY

HIGHLAND HONOR
GISELE ····· NIGEL
DEVEAU   MURRAY

MARGARET ····· SIR WILLIAM ····· KATHERINE
KIRKCALDY   BEATON   MACMILLAN

HIGHLAND DESTINY
BALFOUR ····· MALDIE
MURRAY   KIRKCALDY

HIGHLAND PROMISE
BETHIA ····· ERIC
DRUMMOND   MURRAY
(fostered)

HIGHLAND KNIGHT
AVERY ····· CAMERON
MURRAY   MACALPIN

BEGA,
BRETT

HIGHLAND VOW
ELSBETH ····· CORMAC
MURRAY   ARMSTRONG

DOUGAL,
CONNOR,
EVAN

JAMES
(fostered),
SORCHA,
TORMAND,
KELWYN

HIGHLAND CONQUEROR
JOLENE ····· SIGIMOR
GERARD   CAMERON

LAIRD ····· LADY
CAMERON   FRASER

SOMERLED,
TAIT,
ALEXANDER,
GILBERT,
RANULPH,
ELYAS,
TAMHAS

HIGHLAND GROOM
ILSA ····· DIARMOT
CAMERON   MACENROY
MACENROY

LAIRD ····· LADY
MACENROY   LINDSEY

ANDREW,
ANGUS,
ANTONY

HIGHLAND BRIDE
CONNOR ····· GILLYANE
MACENROY   MURRAY

HIGHLAND WARRIOR
FIONA ····· EWAN
MACENROY   MACFINGAL

Chapter One

England—Spring 1473

"Stop staring at me."

Liam Cameron cocked one brow in response to his cousin Sigimor's growled command. "I was but awaiting your plan to get us out of this mess."

Sigimor grunted and rested his head against the damp stone wall he was chained to. He suspected Liam knew there was no plan. He, his younger brother Tait, his brother-in-law Nanty MacEnroy, and his cousins Liam, Marcus, and David were chained in a dungeon set deep in the bowels of an English lord's keep. They needed more than a plan to get out of this bind. They needed a miracle. Sigimor did not think he had done much lately to deserve one of those.

This was the last time he would try to do a good deed, he decided, then grimaced. It had not been charity that had brought him to Drumwich, but a debt. He owed Lord Peter Gerard his life and, when the man had requested his aid, there had been no choice but to give it. Unfortunately, the request had come too late and the trouble Peter had written of had taken his life only two days before Sigimor had led his men through the thick gates of Drumwich. It was swiftly made clear that Peter's cousin Harold felt no compulsion to honor any pledges made by his now dead kinsman. Sigimor wondered if it could be considered ironic that he would die in the house of the man who had once saved his life.

"Ye dinnae have a plan, do ye?"

"Nay, Liam, I dinnae," replied Sigimor. "If I had kenned that Peter might die ere we got here, I would have made some plan to deal with that complication, but I ne'er once considered that possibility."

"Jesu," muttered Nanty. "If I must die in this cursed country, I would prefer it to be in battle instead of being hanged like some thieving Armstrong or Graham."

"Doesnae your Gilly claim a few Armstrongs as her kinsmen?" Sigimor asked.

"Oh. Aye. Forgot about them. The Armstrongs of Aigballa. Cormac, the laird, wed Gilly's cousin Elspeth."

"Are they reivers?"

"Nay. Weel, nay all of them. Why?"

"If some miracle befalls us and we escape this trap, we may have need of a few allies on the journey home."

"Sigimor, we are in cursed England, in a dungeon in a cursed English laird's weel fortified castle, chained to this thrice-cursed wall, and condemned to hang in two days. I dinnae think we need worry much on what we may or may not need on the journey home. There isnae going to be one. Not unless that bastard Harold decides to send our corpses back to our kinsmen for the burying."

"I can see that we best nay turn to ye to lift our spirits." He ignored Nanty's soft cursing. "I wonder why there isnae any guard set out to watch o'er us."

"Mayhap because we are chained to the wall?" drawled Liam.

"I could, mayhap, with my great monly strength, pull the chains from the wall," murmured Sigimor.

"Ha! These walls have to be ten feet thick."

"Eight feet six inches to be precise," said a crisp female voice.

Sigimor stared at the tiny woman standing outside the thick iron bars of his prison. He wondered why he had neither seen nor heard her approach. The word *mine* ripped through his mind startling him into almost gaping at her. The woman standing there was nothing like any woman he had ever desired in all of his two-and-thirty years. She was also English.

If that was not a big enough flaw, she was delicately made. She had to be a good foot or more shorter than his six-feet-four-inch height and slender. He liked his women tall and buxom, considered it a necessity for a man of his size. Her hair was dark, probably black. He preferred light hair upon his women. His body, however, seemed suddenly oblivious to his habitual preferences. It had grown taut with interest. Being chained to a wall had obviously disordered his mind.

"And the spikes holding the chains to the wall were driven in to a depth of three feet seven inches," she added.

"Ye obviously havenae come here to cheer us," drawled Sigimor.

"I am not sure there is anything one could say to bring cheer to six men chained to a wall awaiting a hanging. Certainly not to six Highlanders chained to the walls of an English dungeon."

"There is some truth in that. Who are ye?"

"I am Lady Jolene Gerard."

If she thought standing straighter as she introduced herself would make her look more imposing, she was sadly mistaken, Sigimor mused. "Peter's sister or his wife?"

"His sister. Peter was murdered by Harold. You came too late to help him."

Although there was no hint of accusation behind her words, Sigimor felt the sting of guilt. "I left Dubheidland the morning after I received Peter's message."

"I know. I fear Harold guessed that Peter had summoned help. Harold had kept all routes to our kinsmen tightly watched so Peter sent for you. I am still not certain how Harold discovered what Peter had done."

"Have ye proof that Harold murdered Peter?"

Jolene sighed and slowly shook her head. "I fear not. There is no doubt in my mind, however. Harold wanted Drumwich and now he holds it. Peter was hale and hearty and now he is dead. He died screaming from the pain in his belly. Harold claims the fish was spoiled. Two others died as well."

"Ah. Tis possible."

"True. Such tragedies are not so very rare. Yet, ere that spoiled fish was buried, two of Harold's dogs ate some. They did not die, did not even grow a little ill. Of course, Harold does not know that I saw that. The dogs snatched some of the fish from Peter's plate when his sudden illness drew

Harold's attention. I saw it because I had to push the dogs aside to reach Peter."

"Who died besides Peter?"

"The two men most loyal to Peter. The cook presented the fish as a special treat for the three men as it was their favorite dish. It was claimed that not enough fish was caught to prepare the dish for everyone. They were also served the last of the best wine. I believe that is where the poison was, or most of it, but I can find no trace of it. Not upon the ewer it was served from or the tankards it was poured into. I did not get hold of them fast enough and they were scrubbed clean."

"Did ye question the cook?" asked Liam.

"He has disappeared," she replied.

Sigimor cursed and shook his head even as he hastily introduced his men. "Then I fear Harold will go unpunished. Ye have no proof of his guilt and I am nay in a position to help ye find any. It might be wise if ye find somewhere else to live now that Harold is the laird here."

"But, he is *not* the lord of Drumwich. Not yet. There is one small impediment left."

"What small impediment?"

"Peter's son."

"Legitimate?"

"Of course. Reynard is nearly three years of age now. His mother died at his birthing, I fear."

"If ye are sure that Harold killed your brother, ye had best get that wee lad out of his reach," said Liam.

Sigimor noticed that Jolene only looked at Liam for a brief moment before fixing her gaze upon him again. Liam might not be at his best, being dirty and a little bruised, but Sigimor was surprised that the little English lady seemed to note Liam's highly praised beauty, accept it, and then dismiss it. That rarely happened and Sigimor found himself intrigued.

"I have hidden Reynard away," she said.

"And Harold hasnae tried to pull that truth from ye?" Sigimor asked.

"Nay. I am very certain he would like to try, but I have hidden myself away as well. Harold does not know all the secrets of Drumwich."

"Clever lass, but that can only work for a wee while, aye? Liam is right. Ye need to get yourself and the bairn away from here."

Jolene stared at the big man Peter had hoped could save them. That the Highlander would honor an old debt enough to ride into England itself was a strong indication that he was a man of honor, one who could be trusted to hold to his word. It was certainly promising that not one of the men had yet asked anything of her despite their own dire circumstances, but were quick to tell her to get herself and Peter's son and heir out of Harold's deadly reach. They were also big, strong men who, if set free, would certainly hie themselves right back to the Highlands. Harold would not find it easy to follow them there.

It did trouble her a little that she could not seem to stop looking at the big man named Sigimor. Most women would be breathlessly intrigued by the one called Liam. Despite the dirt and bruises, she had easily recognized Liam's beauty, a manly beauty actually enhanced by the flickering light of the torches set into the walls. Yet, she had looked, accepted the allure of the man, and immediately turned her gaze back to Sigimor. At three and twenty she felt she should be well past the age to suffer some foolish infatuation for a man, but she feared that might well be what ailed her now. The fact that she could not see the man all that clearly made her fascination with him all the stranger.

She inwardly shook herself. There was only one thing she should be thinking about and that was the need to get Reynard to safety. For three days and nights she had heard Harold ranting as he had Drumwich searched and its people questioned. Last night Harold's interrogations had turned brutal, filling the halls with the piercing cries of those he tortured. Soon one of the very few who knew the secrets of Drumwich would break and tell Harold how to find her and Reynard. Pain could loosen the tongue of even the most loyal. It was imperative that she take the boy far away and, since she had no way to reach any of the rest of her family, these men were her only hope.

"Aye, I must get myself and the boy away from here, far away, to a place where Harold will find it dangerously difficult to hunt us down, if not impossible," she said and could tell by the way Sigimor stared at her that he was beginning to understand why she was there.

Sigimor's whole body tensed, hope surging through him. She said she was in hiding, yet she stood there within plain sight apparently unconcerned about being discovered. There was also something in the way she spoke of taking the boy to a place far away, a place Harold would have great difficulty getting to, combined with the intent way she was staring at him, that made Sigimor almost certain she intended to enlist his aid. He noticed that his companions had all grown as tense as he was, their gazes fixed firmly upon Lady Jolene. He was not the only one whose hopes had suddenly been raised.

"There are nay many places in England where ye could go that Harold couldnae follow," Sigimor said.

"Nay, there are very few indeed. None, in truth. Trying to reach my kinsmen has already cost one man his life. That route is closed to me, as it was to Peter, so I must needs find another."

"Lass, it isnae kind to tease a mon chained to a wall and awaiting a hanging." He caught his breath when she grinned for it added a beauty to her faintly triangular face that was dangerously alluring.

"Mayhap I was but trying to get you to make an offer ere I was forced to make a request. If you offer what I seek, I can ponder it, quickly, and accept, telling myself all manner of comforting reasons for doing so. If I must ask, then I am openly accepting defeat, bluntly admitting that I cannot do this alone. Tis a bitter draught to swallow."

"Swallow it."

"Sigimor!" Liam glared at his cousin, then smiled sweetly at Lady Jolene. "M'lady, if ye free us from this dark place, I give ye my solemn oath that we will aid ye in keeping the bairn alive and free in any and all ways we can."

"Tis a most generous offer, sir," Jolene said, then looked back at Sigimor, "but does your lord give you the right to make such an oath? Does he plan to honor your oath and share in it?"

Sigimor grunted, ignored the glares of his men for a full minute, then nodded. "Aye, he does. We will take the lad."

"And me."

"Why should we take ye as weel? Ye are no threat to Harold's place as laird of this keep." Sigimor had fully expected her to insist upon coming with them, but he wanted to hear her reasons for doing so.

"Oh, but I *am* a threat to Harold," she said in a soft, cold voice, "and he knows it well. If not for Reynard, I would stay here and make him pay most dearly for Peter's death. Howbeit, I swore to Peter that I would guard Reynard with my very life. Since I have had the raising of the boy since his mother's death upon childbed, there was no need to ask such an oath, but I swore it anyway."

And there was the reason to take her with them, Sigimor mused. She may not have birthed the child, but she was Reynard's mother in her heart and mind, and, most probably, in the child's as well. It also told him the best way in which he could control her, although all his instincts whispered that that would not be easy to do. None of that mattered, however. He had been unable to save Peter, but he was now offered the chance to save Peter's sister and his son. Even better, in doing so, he could save the men he had dragged into this deadly mire.

"Then set us free, lass," Sigimor said, "and we will share in the burden of that oath."

Her hands trembling faintly from the strength of the relief which swept through her, Jolene began to try to find which of the many keys she held would fit the lock to the door of the cell. Hope was a heady thing, she mused. For a brief moment she had actually felt very close to swooning and she silently thanked God she had not shamed herself by doing such a weak thing before these men.

"Ye dinnae ken which key to use?" Sigimor felt an even mixture of annoyance and amusement as he watched her struggle with the keys.

"Why should I?" she muttered. "I have ne'er locked anyone in these cells."

"Didnae ye ask the one ye got them from which key ye ought to use?"

"Nay. He was asleep."

"I see. Weel, best pray some other guard doesnae decide to wander down here whilst ye fumble about."

"There will be no guards wandering down here. They are asleep."

"All of them."

"I do hope so."

"The men at arms, too?" She nodded. "Is everyone at Drumwich asleep?"

"Near to. I did leave a few awake, ones who might be eager to flee Drumwich once the chance to do so was given to them." She cried out in triumph as she unlocked the door, opened it, then grinned at Sigimor.

Sigimor simply cocked one brow and softly rattled the chains still binding him to the wall. The cross look she gave him as she hurried over to his side, the large ring of keys she held clinking loudly, almost made him smile. He sighed long and loudly when she started to test each key all over again on the lock of his chains and he heard her mutter something he strongly suspected was a curse.

His amusement faded quickly when she stood very close to him. Despite her delicate build, his body was stirred by the soft, clean scent of her. He fixed his gaze upon her small hands, her slim wrists, and her long, slender fingers, trying to impress upon his mind that she was frail. His body continued to ignore that truth. It also ignored the fact that her hair, hanging down her slim back in a thick braid reaching past her slender hips, was black or nearly so, a color he had never favored. Just as blithely it ignored the fact that the top of her head barely reached his breastbone. Everything about her was wrong for a man of his size and inclinations, but his body heartily disagreed with his mind. It was a riddle he was not sure he could ever solve.

"Are ye verra certain Harold's men are asleep?" he asked in an attempt to fix his mind upon the problems at hand and ignore the soft curve of her long, elegantly slender neck.

"Aye. I kicked a few just to be sure." She found it more difficult than it ought to be to concentrate upon finding the right key and ignore the big man she stood so close to.

"Just how did ye do it?"

"I put a potion into the ale and wine set out to drink with the evening meal. I also had two of the maids carry a physicked water to the other men the moment the ones who sat down in the great hall to dine began to drink. Near all of them began to fall asleep at the same time."

"Near all? What happened to the ones who didnae begin to fall asleep?"

"A sound knock upon the head was swiftly delivered. There!" She smiled at him as she released him from his chains, only to scowl when he snatched the key from her hand. "I am capable of using a key."

"When ye can find it," he drawled as he quickly freed the the others. "How long do ye think your potion will hold Harold and his men?"

"Til dawn or a little later," she replied, thinking that six big men chained were a lot less intimidating than six big men unchained, standing and staring at her.

"How long do we have until dawn?"

"Two hours at the most."

Sigimor put his hands on his hips and frowned

at her. "Why did ye wait so long to come and free us?"

"I had to lock a few doors, tend to a few wounds inflicted by Harold, and help those who had kindly helped me to escape from Drumwich. Then I had to collect some supplies to take with us and gather up the things Harold's men took away from you. And, considering that *I*, a small woman, put every fighting man at Drumwich to sleep with the aid of but two maids, I believe your implied criticism is uncalled for."

"It wasnae implied."

"Sigimor," snapped Liam, before smiling at Jolene. "Ye did weel, lass."

"Thank you, kind sir," Jolene responded, returning his smile.

Subtly, but firmly, Sigimor nudged Liam away from Jolene. He might not understand what drew him to this tiny, thin Englishwoman, but, until he cured himself of the affliction, he did not want any other fool trading smiles with her. Especially not Liam who already had half the women in Scotland swooning at his feet.

"How do ye plan to get us all out of here?" he asked her.

"We could march right out the front gates, if you wish," Jolene replied. "I had thought we would leave as quietly and secretly as possible. If there are no obvious signs of our leavetaking, it may be a while ere your escape is discovered."

"Somehow I think Harold will find a castle full of men still asleep or just rousing immediately suspicious."

"Ah, of course. You are right. And, I suppose the missing horses and what I have done in the stables will also alert them."

It sounded as if she was gagging on those words, Sigimor thought with an inner grin. "Lead on then. I want to put as much distance as possible between us and Harold ere he awakens."

As she started out of the cell, the men falling into step behind her, Jolene said, "Aye. The sooner we reach Scotland, the sooner we will rid ourselves of Harold."

Sigimor doubted it would be that easy, but did not say so as he followed her along a dark, narrow passage heading away from the cells. Harold had already committed murder to steal Drumwich. Lady Jolene clearly feared for her life and her nephew's. If the screams in the night were anything to judge by, Harold was using brutal methods to try and find her and the boy. A man like that would not stop chasing her down simply because she had crossed the border into a country that was not particularly fond of Englishmen. Sigimor felt sure of that. Harold would mean trouble for them for quite a while yet. As he watched the gentle sway of her slim hips, Sigimor inwardly cursed. Harold would not be the only trouble he found in the days ahead.

Chapter Two

The sudden flood of light caused Sigimor to blink rapidly as he struggled to accustom his eyes to its sting and see where the little Englishwoman had led them. Until they were outside the walls of Drumwich and riding hard toward Scotland, he would be wise to remain cautious around her. He was not sure what could prove worse than being chained in a dark cell awaiting death, but he would take no chances. If nothing else, he owed the five men who had ridden with him all his strength, wit, and cunning to get them away from Drumwich free and safe.

A soft noise drew his gaze to a bed of blankets and furs upon the floor of the small chamber. He moved closer to stare down at the small boy lying there and staring back at him. Thick raven curls marked him as kin to Jolene, but those big eyes were a clear, bright blue. When the little boy smiled at him, Sigimor smiled back.

"How wondrous," said Jolene as she picked up her nephew. "He is not frightened of you at all."

"Why should he be frightened of me?" demanded Sigimor, scowling at her.

"Oh, indeed, why? Mayhap because you are a stranger built like a mountain and smelling like a privy."

"I do *not* smell like a privy." He accepted his weapons from a grinning Liam. "Where are the supplies?"

Jolene pointed to the seven sacks she had carefully packed. "There. One each. Before he fled, Old Thomas readied the horses and the saddle packs are also packed with all you brought with you and whatever else we could fit into them. Wineskins, waterskins, and bedding are already secured to the saddles." She gave Liam a brief smile of gratitude when he moved to help her secure Reynard in a blanket sling which settled the small boy close against her chest.

The moment they all had their cloaks on, Sigimor gave her a little nudge. "Lead on, lass."

She nodded, and, as Sigimor picked up the sack she had intended to carry along with his own, she grabbed a torch and started to lead them away from her small haven. One of the men behind her had obviously picked up a torch as well and she was glad of the added light. Despite the safety she had found in the passages beneath the keep, she hated them, hated the suffocating dark of them. Only in the little chamber had she dared light enough torches and candles to push back the dark. The only thing that had kept her lurking about in the chill bowels of the keep was her fear of Harold. Having six large men marching behind her did a lot to quell her fears of Harold and of the dark places she had sought refuge in.

When she reached a thick oak door set deep

into the stone wall, she glanced back at Sigimor. "This door leads to a tunnel which will take us to the stables." She frowned slightly. "Twill be a tight fit for men of your stature."

"Nay as tight as a noose," Sigimor drawled and moved to open the door.

Jolene grimaced at the rush of stale air which escaped the passage as Sigimor pulled the heavy door open. Only once, shortly after Harold came to Drumwich, had she checked the passage to be certain it could be used if necessary. It was dark, damp, narrow, and quite low in places. It had also left her shaking and so terrified, she had not returned through it, but risked returning to the keep through the stables. She was not sure the presence of six big men would make the journey any easier. Straightening herself, she stiffened her spine and began to lead the men into the passageway. She shivered, however, when she heard the door shut behind the last man to enter.

The uneven ground made it impossible to hurry, and Jolene constantly fought the urge to run, to escape this place that chilled her to the bone. By the time she reached the door which led into the stables, she was trembling. She felt Sigimor move to open the door, but could not wait for his courteous aid. She shoved the door open and staggered into the rear of the stables, nearly falling into the bales of hay and collection of farm implements that hid the door from view. It took a moment to calm herself enough to realize she was not the only one standing there taking slow, deep breaths. When she saw that Sigimor was already striding toward the horses showing no sign that he had just emerged from a place that felt all too much like a tomb, she had the strong urge to kick him.

"Curse it, Sigimor," grumbled Nanty as he also moved toward the horses, "does naught e'er trouble ye?"

"Aye, the thought of hanging," Sigimor replied.

Sigimor glanced at the two men collapsed on a pile of hay, snoring loudly. Although he had to admire what Jolene had done to help them escape, he found it a little unsettling that one small, dainty woman had been able to render all the fighting men of the keep helpless. He also suspected it would be more than Harold's command which would send these men chasing them down. A lot of the men would want revenge for this humiliation.

Seeing Liam moving to help Jolene mount her horse, Sigimor intercepted him. He grasped her by her slim waist and set her on her horse. After admiring her slender, stockinged legs, he helped her tug down her skirts to cover them. For reasons he could not begin to comprehend, he did not want five other men seeing her legs. Her puzzled glance and Liam's grin irritated him. He did not see that he had just done anything that should puzzle her, and Liam, he decided, saw too much too clearly. Grumbling that they were wasting time, he mounted and led them out of the great stable only to reach for his sword at the sight of two men standing near the open gates.

"Nay!" Jolene cried, riding up beside him. "Tis only Old Thomas and his son." She rode a little ahead of Sigimor and shook her head at the burly, graying Thomas. "You were told to flee this place."

"We will be leaving as soon as ye do, m'lady," said the man. "Just had me the thought that these gates ought to be closed firm behind you and you do not want to be wasting time doing that. Not sure twill gain ye much if all looks as it should, but, at least, with these gates shut tight, them fools will be needing to look about some to be sure ye have all escaped, eh?"

"You are a good man, Thomas. My thanks. Just be sure to get as far away from here as you can and as soon as you can."

"Will do, m'lady, soon as I make sure all was done just as ye ordered in the stables. You take care and, worry not, that bastard will pay for this."

"From your lips to God's ear. Be well, both of you."

As they rode out of the gates, Sigimore asked her, "Just what *did* ye do in the stables?"

"Cut all the saddle cinches and smeared some foul muck o'er the bits," replied Nanty and he grinned at Jolene.

"Clever lass," murmured Sigimor. "That could buy as much as a day, mayhap e'en more."

Jolene nodded. "So we hoped, but an enraged Harold can be very resourceful." She kissed the top of Reynard's head. "And, as long as this boy lives, Drumwich will ne'er be Harold's to claim."

Sigimor slowly nodded as he considered that. "Rage and greed. Both can stir a villain to o'ercome great odds. Best we put as much distance between us and Drumwich as quickly as possible."

He had barely finished speaking when he nudged his mount into a slightly faster pace, the others quickly following his lead. Sigimor cursed the dark for it hindered their flight, forcing them to keep their mounts at a much slower pace than he wanted. A full gallop toward the border was what he craved, but it would be several hours before he could indulge in that urge. Glancing at Jolene and the boy, he knew there would be other times when they would have to stop or go more slowly than he wished. Even if those delays were few and far between, they could quickly devour the lead they had been blessed with. It could well be a hard-won race to the safety of Dubheidland.

With the handsome Nanty's help, Jolene quickly secured a restive Reynard in his sling and remounted her horse. It was only noon, but she already felt the pain of long, unaccustomed hours in the saddle. None of the men complained, but she knew they did not like these stops necessitated by her nephew. This was only the second one and she had worked as swiftly as possible, but the men's need to keep moving was so strong she could almost feel it. She suspected that, if she and Reynard were not there, these men would pause in their race for the border only for the sake of the horses. It was hard to hide her wince when Sigimor immediately led them off at a gallop, obviously deciding that the horses had rested long enough to endure another few hours of hard travel.

She prayed Harold would not follow, but had the sinking feeling her entreaties would be unanswered. Harold could not trust her to leave him alone, to not try to oust him from Drumwich once she found safety and allies. He could not allow Peter's son to live to be used against him, to grow into manhood and come to reclaim his heritage. Jolene doubted he would think twice about slipping into Scotland to hunt them down. The only things in her favor were that he would have to be somewhat cautious once he entered Scotland and he would not enlist any allies for fear of his own crimes being uncovered.

But, she had enlisted allies, she thought, glancing at the six grim-faced men riding with her. Even though Sir Sigimor Cameron owed Peter his life, and now owed her the same debt, Jolene began to feel guilty about dragging these men into her troubles. Harold was vicious, sly, and deadly. She was putting these men at risk for their very lives and she began to wonder if that was fair or right. English lands and English titles meant nothing to them and never would. In fact, she suspected these Scots would be just as happy to see the entire English aristocracy washed out to sea.

Reynard babbled something about seeing a deer, and Jolene sighed even as she replied. It was impossible to give the child much attention when she was caught fast in her own troubled thoughts and riding hard for the border. His brief intrusion into her thoughts reminded her of what this was all about, however. She might ache with a need to make Harold pay for Peter's death, but keeping Reynard safe had to take precedence over that. Reynard was a part of Peter, a living memory of her brother, and the vessel of all of Peter's hopes and plans for the future of Drumwich. Until Harold was defeated, her every step, her every action, and her every thought had to concern keeping Reynard alive and safe.

That knowledge did not completely soothe her conscience concerning the Camerons, however. She sternly told herself that Peter had felt it acceptable to ask their aid in fighting his enemy, therefore she should as well. Then again, she mused, men seemed to have no trouble asking other men to fight with them, to risk their lives. Honor and the glory of a battle for a righteous cause were like food and drink to a man. She suspected they did not long consider the possibility of defeat or death. Unfortunately, she did. The moment she had asked these men to help her, she had taken on the responsibility for their lives, and she was not sure she could bear such a burden. Yet, what choice did she have?

She was still fretting over that question by the time the sun had almost finished setting and they stopped to camp for the night. The painful weariness of her body quickly pushed it aside. Jolene had to cling to her saddle for several minutes after dismounting before she could be sure her legs would hold her up. Since Reynard had fallen asleep right after their brief midafternoon pause, they had not stopped again until now. They had barely slowed the horses when the boy had awakened and needed to relieve himself. Jolene was still a little shocked at how Sigimor had held the boy so that the child could do what he needed to do without dismounting, although Reynard had thoroughly enjoyed himself. He had then kept the little boy with him, however, and Jolene reluctantly admitted that she had been glad for that kindness.

Eyeing the fire Liam had already built, Jolene wondered how good her chances were of getting over there with any semblance of grace. Not good, she decided after she tried to step away from her horse and felt her legs tremble. Slumping against her mount, she wondered when, or if, the men would finally notice that she had not yet joined them, had not yet even tended to her poor, exhausted horse.

"I think the lass may be having a wee bit of trouble, Sigimor," Nanty said as he sat down next to him before the fire.

Sigimor looked at Lady Jolene who had not taken one small step away from her horse since she had dismounted. "Nay used to long rides. I suspicion she has ne'er done more than trot about her brother's lands."

"Wheesht, e'en I am feeling sore. Ne'er have liked spending a whole day in the saddle." When Nanty began to stand up, obviously intending to assist Jolene, his eyes widened slightly when Sigimor clapped a hand on his shoulder and held him down. "Her mount needs tending, if naught else."

"I will see to her. Watch the wee lad."

Sigimor studied Lady Jolene carefully as he walked up to her. She looked exhausted, pale and untidy. Unfortunately, she still looked far too attractive to him. Wan though it was, her face was still lovely. Beautiful, thickly lashed, silver gray eyes, a small straight nose, and a mouth that could tempt a saint with its full, beautifully shaped lips. He wanted to be irritated by her weakness, by her obvious inability to keep pace with them. Instead, he felt an urge to cosset her and a sincere respect for how she had done her best without complaint. Not good, he thought, and frowned at her.

"Ye best walk about some or ye will get too stiff to move," he said and almost grinned when she glared at him.

"Thank you for your kind advice," Jolene replied, unable to keep all of the sarcasm out of her voice. "As soon as my legs feel inclined to do as they should, I shall be sure to follow it." She thought the heavy sigh he gave earned him a good kick in the shin, but she was unable to grant herself that pleasure. "What are you doing?" she demanded when he wrapped one strong arm around her shoulders and tugged her away from her horse.

"Walking ye about." He pretended not to notice when she stumbled and wrapped an arm around his waist to steady herself, although his body quickly tautened with awareness. "Liam, see to her horse," he ordered his cousin as he started to walk Jolene around the clearing they had chosen to camp in.

"I thought I was well accustomed to riding," she muttered once her embarrassment had eased.

"It takes years to grow accustomed to riding for days at a time."

"Days?"

"Aye. Days. Unless the need is dire, we ride straight for Dubheidland. The only allies I have on that route are my kinsmen the MacFingals. If Harold isnae too hard on our tails, we may rest there for a wee while."

"How far away are these MacFingals?"

"Four more days of hard riding, if we and our mounts can endure it."

Four days like this one and Jolene was sure she would have to be carried into the MacFingal keep on a litter. Her legs were finally acting as they should, but now she became all too aware of how badly her backside ached. She heard Reynard giggle and saw Nanty playing a game of tug-o'-war with the child. The sight did not soothe her pain, but it stilled her complaints. That boy was the future of the Gerards of Drumwich. A little physical discomfort was a small price to pay for that.

"Better?" Sigimor asked as they stopped by the fire.

"Aye. Some. Is there enough water for me to wash away a little of this dust?" She was disturbed by how reluctant she was to step away from the man, to put some distance between herself and his big, strong body.

"The angels smile upon ye, m'lady. There is a wee burn nay far from here. Ye can have yourself a bath, though 'tis certain it will be a cold one."

"If 'twas frozen solid, I would chop a hole in the ice just to have a thorough wash."

"Fetch what ye will need then and I will take ye to it."

"You need only to point the way and I—"

"Nay. Ye willnae wonder off alone."

"But, I cannot bathe in front of a man!"

"I will turn my back to ye. Tis the only concession I will make. Ye and the lad willnae be left alone, unguarded, until Harold is no longer a threat." He crossed his arms over his chest and silently dared her to argue.

Jolene opened her mouth to strongly protest, then caught the look in his beautiful green eyes. He would not be swayed. Unlike some men, he was willing to argue with her, but it would be a waste of her time to do so. She had asked for his aid and protection and he obviously had some very firm ideas about what that included. Since he had already proven himself a man of his word, she decided to accept his promise not to look and quickly collected what she would need to bathe away the dirt of travel and the lingering scent of days spent hiding in the bowels of Drumwich. After looking at Reynard to assure herself that he was content in the care of the men, she hurriedly followed Sigimor.

The man had very long legs, she decided, nearly running to keep up with what, for him, was undoubtedly just an easy stride. Long, well-shaped, strong legs, she mused. Although she had never been one to study a man's form too closely, she had to admit that it was pleasant to watch Sigimor's taut backside move as he walked. He was dressed in the English fashion, though not very richly, but Sigimor's clothes fit him a lot more snugly than any other man's she had seen. Either Sigimor was a little vain or he simply had no idea of how tightly his hose fit his legs or how much of his well-formed backside was revealed by the short jupon. Jolene was a little shocked at how much she liked to watch him move. It gave her a strange feeling, one both odd and pleasing.

The moment she had had the light to do so, she had studied him as they rode away from Drumwich. He did not have Liam's beauty, but he was still a very handsome man. His hair was thick, hung just below his shoulders, and was a rich, dark red. He shared many features with his too-handsome cousin Liam, but Sigimor's long, straight nose was a little bolder, his jaw a little stronger, and the shape of his face a little harsher. Liam was heartbreakingly beautiful, in a way that immediately caught one's eye, whereas Sigimor had the sort of handsomeness that took a little longer to cause that stirring effect in a woman. His eyes were a startling true green, set beneath faintly arched brows, and surrounded with brown lashes thick and long enough to make a woman envious. Sigimor also had a very attractive mouth, neither too small nor too big, and his lips holding enough fullness to stir thoughts of kisses. Jolene decided his was a face she would never tire of looking at, then felt a little alarmed by that thought.

When they reached the water, Sigimor just pointed at it, then turned his back. Jolene wasted no time in shedding her clothes, hoping the cool water would be as refreshing as it looked for she was suddenly feeling quite warm. That heat fled the moment she entered the chill water, barely swallowing a gasp of shock. Her bath would be a quick one, she mused even as she began to scrub away the dust of travel. She had been jesting when she had said she would make a hole in the ice just to have a bath, but this water felt as if she had done just that.

Sigimor sternly told himself that it would be ungentlemanly to try to catch a look at a bathing Jolene, then inwardly shrugged aside that pinch of conscience. He had only said that he would turn his back. The urge to see if he could catch a glimpse of the body he craved was too strong to resist. There was always the chance that one good look at her slender form would remind him of why he had always preferred buxom women and cure him of this strange, inconvenient lusting.

Just as he turned his head enough to see her, she stood up in the water. Sigimor caught his breath so quickly he nearly coughed and gave himself away. One look had not cured him. Instead he had to fight the urge to tear off his clothing and join her. Reminding himself that she was a highborn lady, probably a virgin, and that such an abrupt approach would undoubtedly send her screaming into the hills, only tethered his lust a little. He found himself wondering why, and when, he had blinded himself to the beauty of a smaller woman.

Her skin was beautifully pale and unmarred. Sigimor did not think he had ever seen such a small waist. Yet the gentle curve of her hips and the tight, round shaping of her backside was womanly enough to stir his blood. Her thighs were slim, leaving a space at the top that had him aching to nudge into it. Thick ropes of wet black hair clung to the slender line of her back, enhancing the delicate paleness of her fine skin. When she turned slightly, he caught sight of the curve of her breast. It was somewhat smaller than he was accustomed to, but it was perfectly shaped, firm, and tipped with a rosy nipple made hard by the cold water. When she washed her flat stomach, he watched the water trail down to the delicate little triangle of dark curls at the juncture of her thighs and nearly groaned.

Hastily, he turned away. He needed to bring his pounding lust under control. The fashionable attire he had worn for the journey into England hid little and he did not wish to shock her. It took several moments before he felt he had cooled his ardor enough to be seen in a lady's company again. He was glad he had brought a change of clothing for he was going to need a plunge into that chilled water to fully douse his ardor. Since he suspected he would be unable to banish the image of her pale, slender beauty from his mind, he would welcome the looser fit of his breeches and longer, padded jupon. Lady Jolene might be too innocent to notice the all too obvious signs that he was feverishly aroused, but his men were not. Sigimor had no wish to rouse their amusement.

"That was just what I needed," Jolene said as, once dressed, she used the shift she had changed out of to rub her hair dry. "Quite cold, however, but it was worth it."

The way she smiled at him sent Sigimor's desire soaring again and he ordered, "Turn your back," even as he strode toward the water, shedding his clothes as he went.

Jolene gaped at the man, startled by his growled command. Her eyes widened almost painfully and she felt a blush heat her cheeks as she watched him fling off his clothes, but she could not make herself turn away from the sight. She bit her lip to halt a gasp as he bared his torso. His shoulders were broad, his back smooth and straight, and his waist narrow. His skin was not as pale as she would have expected of a redheaded man, but faintly golden in tone. The muscles of his arms were obvious, yet sleek, not bulging somewhat untidily as she had observed on some other men, and there were bands of intricate designs etched into his skin around the top of each arm. Then he yanked off his hose and she felt almost dizzy from the heat which flared to life within her. That faintly golden skin covered his whole body. His backside was as well formed and taut as she had imagined it would be and his long legs held the same sleek strength his arms did.

Suddenly realizing how easily she could be caught leering at him, Jolene turned away, fiercely resisting the urge to try and catch a glimpse of the front of him. The man was turning her into a shameless, wanton creature. Never before had she been so keenly interested in a man's form, or so intensely affected by the sight. It was not comforting to discover that some redheaded Scot was the first to truly stir her womanly interest and desire. She was daughter, sister, and aunt to English earls. To allow her blood to heat and her heart to pound over a Highland laird was pure madness. Her dead kinsmen were probably spinning in their graves.

It puzzled her. How could she go so quickly from having little interest in men to being so keenly interested, so fiercely aware of, a big red-haired Scot? She had had the usual maidenly dreams of a handsome, gallant lover, ones that left her with a faint tickle of delight, but this was no mere tickle to be briefly smiled over and then forgotten. This was a strong feeling, fierce and unbiddable. It was a very poor time to be suffering such a fascination, perhaps even a true lusting.

Control was what she had to strive for. She could be facing many long weeks at Sigimor's side, without the protection of a single kinsman. She would have to guard her chastity herself. That could prove difficult if she was stirred into a witless fever every time she looked at the man. At the moment, Sigimor revealed little interest in her as a woman, as one he might wish to seduce. Jolene decided she must use this time to smother her interest in him. She had spent three-and-twenty years unmoved by any man. It should not be too difficult to cure herself of this sudden affliction.

Then Sigimor reached her side, took her by the hand, and started to lead her back to the camp. The warmth of his hand flowed through her body with every beat of her heart. It was such an innocent gesture, yet it caused her to feel a faint trembling inside. There was no chance to bury those feelings, either. He sat close by her side as they ate, keeping them alive, strengthening them. When she sought her rough bed of blankets upon the ground, Sigimor laid out his bed but inches from hers. If he was going to keep her so close to him, Jolene thought as she struggled to ignore all that attractive male flesh within easy reach, she would never cure herself of her interest in him. It began to look as if keeping Reynard alive and safe was not going to be the only hard, dangerous battle she would have to fight in the days ahead.

Chapter Three

Jolene cursed in surprise when her escort suddenly released a wild, deafening cry and kicked their horses into a gallop. Her mount did not wait for her command, but joined the race. She chanced a glance behind her as she struggled to maintain some control over her horse, but could see no one chasing them. They had moved swiftly all day, but stealthily, avoiding people and towns in the hope of making it difficult for Harold to follow them too easily. This sudden loud exuberance was most strange. Even stranger was the way Nanty and Liam acted as the men suddenly halted. Reining in next to Sigimor, Jolene watched those two men leap from their mounts and kiss the ground.

"Daft fools," said Sigimor, but there was the hint of a smile curving his fine mouth.

"I suppose there is some reasonable explanation for this," said Jolene.

"We are now in Scotland, lass."

"Ah. I see." She wished she could feel as pleased by that as they did, but now she was the stranger and Jolene knew that anyone they met with now would not greet her warmly.

"Dinnae fret yourself. Ye will be safe here."

"Safer than at Drumwich, that is certain." She sighed. "Your welcome in England was not a pleasant one. Tis no surprise that you would be heartily pleased to be back in your own land."

"Few English welcome a Scot with any joy."

"And few Scots welcome the English with a smile, either."

"I dinnae think ye will face much trouble being but a wee lass." He took a deep breath. "Tis good to be back in Scotland. If naught else, 'twill be much easier to ken where our enemy is."

"How so?"

"The moment that bastard Harold crosses this border, he will be watched. Every Scot who catches sight of him will spread the word as to where he is, which direction he travels in, and who rides with him. He and whate'er men ride at his side will also prove a sore temptation to many. He willnae find it easy to hunt us down here. E'en those with no love for a Cameron will wish to trouble him. No one will aid him. Leastwise, none who can truly call himself a Scot."

"Ah, united against a common foe."

Sigimor nodded as he dismounted, then helped Jolene down from her horse. "Tend to whate'er needs ye must now. We will linger here a few moments, then set a hard pace for a while."

Jolene inwardly groaned, but made no complaint as she wandered away to find a private spot to see to her needs and Reynard's. She could still feel the warmth of Sigimor's big hands at her waist. Her attempts to drown her attraction for the man with cold common sense and the need to survive were failing miserably. The best she could do was try to keep it hidden, but that, too, could prove impossible when they spent so much time together. It might have been wiser to try to convince the Scots to take her to one of her kinsmen in England before they fled for the safety of Scotland, but her path was now set. She would have to find hope in the fact that Sigimor did not seem to notice that she was attracted to him, nor did he show any inclination to flirt with her or seduce her. As she set herself to taking full advantage of the few minutes of privacy Sigimor had granted her, Jolene sternly told herself that she would see that as a blessing.

"Do ye think Harold will follow us into Scotland?" Liam asked as he stepped up to Sigimor and offered him a drink from his wineskin.

"Aye." Sigimor never took his gaze from the clump of trees Jolene had disappeared into as he took a hearty drink of wine. "The mon has already killed to get his greedy hands on Drumwich. I dinnae think mere borders will stop him from doing all he can to be very certain he keeps it."

"So, ye think we will have to be killing us an English lordling, aye?"

"Aye. This will be a fight to the death. I think Lady Jolene kens it." He frowned and rubbed his chin. "He willnae trust in her just disappearing, staying out of his way because she fears for her life. Our escape from Drumwich will certainly make him realize she is more than some wee lass he can hold firm beneath his fist. Unless he silences her, he will e'er have to fear that she will find an ally in England, some other lordling with the power to drag him out of Drumwich and make him pay for his crimes."

"Then he will have to hunt down all the servants who fled, too, willnae he?"

"Nay, I dinnae think so. E'en if one of them dared to approach someone with the tale, few lords would take the word of some poor mon o'er that of a laird. That doesnae mean he would hesitate to cut the throat of any of them if he found them, but I dinnae truly think he sees them as a threat."

"Arrogance blinds him. Twas those verra people and the wee lass who rendered him and his men helpless."

"Aye, and that must surely enrage him. He *will* blame her for that humiliation." Sigimor took another drink from the wineskin then handed it back to Liam. "I cannae explain why, but I think there is more, something the lass hasnae told us."

"Why? Because Lord Harold didnae kill her when he killed her brother?"

"Something to wonder on. It would have left him as guardian to the lad, put the heir in his hands to murder at his leisure. Done right, none would question the child's death. Too many children die young. It would have been easy to have her join in the deadly meal served to Lord Peter. I got to thinking on how there was a way he could tighten his grip on Drumwich through her, the dead laird's sister, and the weel loved Lady of Drumwich."

"Marriage?" Liam frowned. "They are cousins, nay too distant ones, either. There is that matter of consanguinity."

"Dispensation could be had and the coffers of Drumwich are full enough to buy it. I suspicion the lass also has a verra fine dowry which might nay stay with Harold if she dies."

"And she is a bonnie wee lass."

Sigimor scowled at Liam as he saw the way his

cousin watched Jolene as she emerged from the trees. "Bonnie enough, aye, for such a wee, thin lass." He ignored the grin his cousin gave him in reply to that. "I am certain that bastard wants the wee laddie dead, the sooner the better, but I do wonder if he is really so verra eager to kill the lass just yet."

"Do ye mean to press her to answer some of these questions?"

"Nay. Not yet. It wouldnae change what we must do. And the lass has the wit to ken that, e'en if that bastard doesnae want her dead now, he will kill her in the end. She would force his hand, if naught else, for she will ne'er cease wanting to avenge the deaths of her brother and her nephew. He may be fool enough to think he can turn her craven and obedient, but she would soon make him see how wrong he is."

"And thus get herself killed. Ye are right. Whate'er else may be happening atwixt those two, it doesnae matter. Varied though the paths may be, they all lead to the grave—hers and the bairn's."

Sigimor was still thinking on the matter as they started on their way again at a steady pace intended to get them through the treacherous borderlands as swiftly as possible yet not exhaust the horses. Reivers ruled this land and Nanty's connections to the Armstrongs might not protect them much. It would be even more treacherous for Harold and that nearly made Sigimor smile. He doubted they would be so fortunate as to have the thieves and rogues so prevalent in the area rid them of their enemy, however. That thought brought all the questions he had to the fore of his mind again and he looked at Jolene who rode at his side.

"Why are ye nay wed or betrothed?" he asked.

Jolene frowned at him even as she felt a start of

surprise over the abrupt question. "I was betrothed once, but the man died when I was but sixteen."

"Naught else was arranged? Ye are now, what, twenty?"

"Three and twenty," she admitted and ignored his raised brows. "Papa died ere he could arrange anything else that suited him. Peter intended to do something about it, e'en attempted it once or twice, but naught came of that. Peter wished the choice to be as much mine as his. Then his wife died and I became chatelaine. Peter was thinking of marrying again so I suspect he may have begun an earnest search for a husband for me."

"But Harold arrived."

"Aye. Peter ne'er liked the man, nor trusted him, but he is blood kin, a cousin." She shrugged. "With no clear proof of treachery, what could Peter do but allow that adder to slither into his hall. Harold explained away the rather large size of the armed force with him by claiming that he had been chasing reivers down. It did not take long for us to realize that we were now prisoners within our own keep, but poor Peter had no time to plan a way to free us. He did not wish to begin an open battle for Harold held all the advantages. Twould have been a slaughter." She sighed and shook her head, grief a hard knot in her chest. "Harold struck quickly, his men in place and Peter dead whilst we all still reeled from the shock of such treachery."

Sigimor nodded. "Clever. And, he used Peter's own honor and sense of kinship against him. He probably kenned that, e'en though Peter didnae like or trust him, the mon would ne'er guess the true depths of his venality. Your brother was a good mon, keen of wit and strong, but he wasnae devious."

"You think being devious would have helped?"

"Och, aye. If he had held a wee bit of that skill, he might have guessed at all that Harold might do, would have been better prepared for such a deep betrayal."

He was probably right, but Jolene felt a need to defend her brother. "He must have guessed something for he sent for you."

"True, but he had already let betrayal into his hall, aye?"

There was no question that Peter had made a serious mistake, one that had cost him his life, but she still felt compelled to turn aside what sounded too much like criticism. "And you would not have?"

"Nay, not with a strong, armed force of men at his heels." He winked at her. "I *am* devious. My first thought would have been on why a mon I didnae like or fully trust needed so many weel-armed men just to visit a kinsmon."

"Peter wondered, but courtesy—"

"Courtesy doesnae require ye invite a mon to put a knife in your back. Or set your heir in the path of danger," he added quietly as he glanced toward where a merrily babbling Reynard rode with Nanty. "Blood kin or nay, I would have made those armed men stay outside my walls and watched them weel e'en then. The mon didnae sit higher at the table than Peter did, so courtesy didnae demand he allow them *all* within his gates."

Jolene was not sure of that, but did not argue. She had begged Peter not to allow all of Harold's retinue within the walls, but he had claimed there was no honorable reason to deny them shelter. There was no doubt in her mind that Sigimor was an honorable man, but he was obviously not as concerned about being the perfect, chivalrous knight as Peter had been. Peter, she decided, had had high ideals. Sigimor had common sense. Peter had had an eye to being renowned as a most perfect, genteel knight. Sigimor had an eye to survival. She had loved her brother dearly, but she wished he had held some of Sigimor's hard-eyed practicality. He might still be alive.

"Ye are devious," Sigimor said, smiling at her.

So enraptured was she by that smile, it took Jolene a minute to grasp what he had said and she frowned at him. "I am not."

"Aye, ye are. The way ye got us all out of Drumwich showed a fine sense of deviousness. Twas a verra clever, sly trick."

"I suppose you think you are complimenting me."

"That I am, but being just a wee lass, I suspicion ye dinnae see it."

There was a look in those beautiful green eyes of his that told her he was goading her. "In England being sly and devious is not something women are encouraged to aspire to."

"And just what are they encouraged to aspire to?"

"Gentility. A woman should be sweet of tongue and disposition, kind to all, especially to those who serve her, skilled at loom and needle, firm and alert in the management of her household, frugal, obedient, and a faithful companion to her lord, giving him peace and comfort in his home." Jolene was not sure she liked the way he was grinning at her.

"How many of those qualifications do ye think ye meet?"

"Quite a few," she said, forcing herself to meet his amused gaze without blushing over that lie.

There was a look in Jolene's eyes that warned Sigimor that it would not be wise to laugh or cry her a liar, and that made him feel even more inclined to laugh. "Weel, I have e'er believed the English could be complete fools. Ha! Save for the needlework, managing a household, and frugality, it seems the English men want their lasses to be much akin to my Meggie."

"Who is Meggie?" Jolene was not sure she kept all of the sudden fierce jealousy she felt out of her voice.

"My hound. Och, weel, I suspicion most of ye at least smell a wee bit better."

Jolene glared at his broad back as he rode away. Her annoyance was added to by the fact that she could not be sure if he had just insulted her by inferring she was not a proper lady, or complimented her for the very same thing. On behalf of all English women, especially those who tried hard to attain that ideal of womanhood, she took umbrage over Sigimor's comparing them to his hound. On occasion, she had thought much the same thing, but that was her right as a woman, one who had to suffer under such rules and beliefs. She told herself that, as a man, his ridicule was hypocritical since he was one of those who tried to keep women cowed, but could not wholeheartedly believe it. Attempting to shake free of her own confusion, she rode up beside Nanty and turned her attention to keeping Reynard happy.

Sigimor looked up from spreading an extra blanket over a sleeping Jolene, then Reynard, to catch Liam grinning at him. "Tis cold and they are too thin to bear it," he grumbled, striding off toward the surrounding wood and cursing softly when Liam followed him.

"She *is* a wee, thin lassie, to be sure," drawled Liam.

"Aye, and a pampered English lady."

"But, verra bonnie. Such fine skin she has. Ye did notice that fine milk white skin, didnae ye?"

"I noticed," Sigimor replied through clenched teeth, knowing he was being goaded, but unable to completely hide how well it was working.

"Weel, 'tis a good thing I ken that ye prefer a buxom lass with fair hair or I might think ye had an interest in the wee lass."

"Ye think too much. Staying with the monks is what did it."

Liam laughed. "Since ye arenae interested in the wee lass, then, mayhap I—"

Sigimor swung around to face Liam so quickly it caused his cousin to stumble back a few steps with a gratifying lack of grace. "And mayhap ye best think on how that winsome smile of yours wouldnae woo the lasses so weel if ye didnae have any teeth. Stop grinning. Ye look like a fool." He started to walk back toward the camp, sighing loudly when Liam kept pace with him.

"Why so irritable, Cousin?" asked Liam. "Where is the harm in being drawn to such a bonnie wee lass? She is your equal in birth, chaste, and nay doubt she has a fine dowry."

"That sounds suspiciously like the qualities one looks for in a wife." It worried Sigimor that he did not immediately and fiercely decry the thought of marriage to Jolene.

"'Tis past time ye took a wife."

"Why? I dinnae need an heir. Dubheidland fair swarms with them."

"True, but that doesnae mean ye dinnae need a wife or bairns of your own."

Sigimor stopped, slowly turned to face Liam, and crossed his arms over his chest. He was strongly tempted to pound his cousin into the mud for putting this idea into his head, if only because it felt right, tugged at a need within him that he was trying very hard to deny. Logic told him Lady Jolene Gerard was all wrong for him, but everything else within him kept saying *mine*.

"Ye did notice her size, didnae ye? And my size?" The fact that his deeply sarcastic tone of voice had no apparent effect upon Liam truly annoyed Sigimor. "If I put a bairn in her 'twould probably tear her apart."

Liam also crossed his arms on his chest and gave Sigimor a look of utter disgust. "That is nonsense and weel ye ken it."

"She is English. 'Twould probably be illegal to marry her."

"Mayhap in England, though that law comes and goes as often as the tide. I suspicion ye wouldnae be able to claim any lands she might have, but ye wouldnae want them anyway, aye?"

"Why have ye set your teeth into this whim?"

"Mayhap because this is the first lass of good birth ye have e'er shown an interest in. Dinnae try to deny it for, although she may be too innocent to ken it, the rest of us can see that ye want her. Ye fair stink of it at times. Ye are two and thirty and have ne'er done more than indulge in an occasional tussle with a buxom whore. Ye have ne'er e'en taken a leman. Ye, Cousin, are a mon who should marry."

Sigimor knew Liam was right, but would rather have all his toes broken than admit it. He had a hearty appetite for fleshly pleasures, but did not often succumb to those needs. While he enjoyed the occasional tussle with a well-rounded tavern maid, it never fully satisfied him. He was always too aware that it was coin that put the woman in his bed and that another man's coin was just as welcome as his. The few times he had tried to woo a better-born lass, he had failed. Such women either feared his size, revealed an unkind amusement over his character, or just did not feel *right*. It was not something he would ever confess to because it seemed nauseatingly romantic, but he liked the idea of having a woman who was his alone, one he could talk to, a companion who would share the burdens of home and family. He wanted a mate. Only once, ten years ago, had he thought he had found one only to be gloriously proven wrong. It was why he was cautious now, would prefer not to be feeling all he was feeling for the delicate Englishwoman.

"And what makes ye think this lady is a good choice?" he asked, inwardly cursing the curiosity that prompted the question.

"She watches you."

"Probably wants to be sure I dinnae stumble and chance falling on her for fear I would flatten her into the ground."

"Idiot. She *watches* you. She shows no interest in any of the rest of us save as companions in this wee crusade."

"Nay, not e'en ye," Sigimor murmured, recalling his surprise over that.

"Nay, not e'en me. She isnae intimidated by your size and your manner. If the way she was glaring at ye earlier today is aught to go by, she also has the spirit to stand up to ye. What did ye say to her, by the bye?"

Still caught up in the pleasant thought that Jolene watched him, Sigimor made a dismissive gesture with his hand. "She was telling me what qualities an Englishmon likes in his women and I told her it sounded as if the fools were thinking to breed a hound, nay a woman."

"Nay wonder she looked ready and eager to gut ye. I was hoping ye kenned how to flatter the lasses, but I begin to fear ye dinnae."

"I did tell her that I suspected most Englishwomen smelled a wee bit better than a hound."

"Tis a wonder she didnae swoon with delight," muttered Liam and then he shook his head. "Ye do it apurpose, dinnae ye? Ye just have to keep poking at a person, waiting to see what will happen."

"Tis part of my charm." Sigimor paused at the edge of the camp and his gaze immediately settled upon the slim form of a sleeping Lady Jolene. "Let it rest, Liam. There may be something there between us, some mutual attraction, but I am nay sure it should or could go any further than looking and thinking. She is an English lady and I am a Scottish laird. A greedy mon wants her and the lad dead. That wee lad is an English lord and she is verra nearly his mother, bound to him by blood and love. Aye, and I still believe she hasnae told us everything, that she holds fast to a wee secret or two. Tisnae a simple matter in any way. Twill go as it will go. One can but wait and see." He started to collect his bedding, fully intending to spread it out at Jolene's side.

"Fine, wait and see. Just be sure ye keep both eyes wide open. Aye, and your mind and heart."

If the last few days were any example, Sigimor mused, he could do nothing else. His mind and heart would not let him.

Sigimor woke with a curse as a small, hard fist slammed into the side of his head. As he hastened to fend off further blows, he realized the woman at his side had not suddenly turned into a virago intent upon murdering him, but was caught fast in a nightmare. Reynard began to cry and Nanty quickly appeared. Sigimor told the man to take the child to his bed, then set his mind to pulling Jolene free of her nightmare before she did him a real injury.

It took him longer than he felt it ought to get her thrashing body pinned firmly beneath him, but he was trying hard not to bruise her. He was a little surprised at the virulence and the variety of the curses she spat out while she fought against the enemy haunting her dreams. The blind panic that briefly twisted her delicate features when she finally opened her eyes struck him to the heart. In a soft, calming voice he had perfected over the years of raising his siblings and many of his cousins, he repeatedly told her who he was and where she was.

The moment she calmed, he became all too aware of the intimacy of their position with her slender legs pinned beneath his and their groins pressed close together. His body's reaction to that suggestive delight was immediate and fierce. Sigimor was not surprised to see her eyes slowly widen and the hint of a blush shadowing her cheeks. Even as a voice in his head told him not to do it, he brushed his mouth over hers, finding her lips soft and sweet.

"What do you think you are doing?" Jolene asked, shivering over the strange tingling warmth his lips had left upon hers.

"Kissing it to make it better?" Sigimor lifted his head only a little until they were nose to nose.

"Tis already better for I am now awake." Steeling herself against the shockingly strong urge to rub herself against that hard length pressing so impudently against her, she gave him what she hoped was a very stern frown.

"What haunts your dreams, m'lady?" Having heard her curse Harold in her dream, he had a suspicion or two, but wondered if she would answer truthfully.

Even as she wondered how the featherlight kisses he brushed over her face could make her insides tremble so, Jolene replied, "Peter's death." It was not a complete lie for there had been glimpses of that horror mixed up with all the other fears and terrifying memories.

"Ah, so that is why ye were cursing Harold, aye?"

"Aye."

"I begin to think ye arenae telling me everything, lass, and for that I have decided ye must pay a forfeit."

"A forfeit?"

Jolene had barely finished muttering the words when he kissed her. This time it was no gentle tease of a kiss, but one that made her toes curl. She tried to fight the feelings tearing through her, but she lost that battle completely when, suddenly, his tongue was stroking the inside of her mouth. How it got there, she did not know, but, when it left, she immediately wanted it back. Instead, she was abruptly free, Sigimor lying on his side next to her with his back to her. He grumbled something about Nanty keeping Reynard with him, then said no more. Jolene stared up at the stars, felt a strange, gnawing ache inside of her, and wondered why she wanted to kick the man senseless. She could forsee a great deal of trouble in the days ahead and not just from that murderous usurper Harold.

Chapter Four

"Harold is in Scotland."

Liam's announcement sent a chill through Jolene, a cold that settled into her very bones. Up until that moment she had been riding beside Sigimor idly wondering if she should scorn him for daring to kiss her last night or try to get him to do it again. Now she was brutally recalled to the reason why she was with Sigimor and his men, why she had fled to Scotland. Unthinkingly, she tightened her grip on the reins and caused her horse to shift about in nervous confusion.

Sigimor reached over and patted her thigh without taking his gaze off Liam. To Jolene's amazement, she felt calmed by that touch. It was a silent reminder that she was not alone. She still felt the pinch of guilt over dragging them into her troubles, but it was fading. Whenever the men spoke of Harold there was such anger and hatred in their voices that she realized they, too, hungered for revenge. They had, after all, come very close to dying at Harold's hands. Jolene had no doubt that these men would never hesitate to help a woman or child in trouble, but they also intended to make Harold pay dearly for imprisoning them and plotting to hang them.

"Are ye sure?" Sigimor asked, reluctantly removing his hand from Jolene's slim thigh once she was calm again.

"Aye. He is being verra brazen in his pursuit." Liam smiled and shook his head. "He is asking about us. He tells all he speaks to that he is hunting an errant wife, that his lady ran off with ye and taking their bairn with her. The fool probably thinks to stir outrage o'er such a crime thus gaining aid in hunting us down."

"And has he?"

"To his face—aye. Behind his back—nay. He is English and many think that reason enough to deceive him. The fact that an English lordling lost his lady to a braw Scot only delights most of those he speaks to. I just dinnae ken how long he will remain the fool."

"Longer than he should, but not, I fear, long enough." Jolene smiled faintly when both men looked at her. "Harold scorns all who are not highborn and not English." She grimaced. "He considers the Scots all ignorant barbarians."

"Aye, he made that opinion verra clear as he tossed us into his dungeon," said Sigimor.

"Howbeit, he is not a complete fool. He *will* soon realize he is being made mock of and change his tactics."

Sigimor considered that for a moment, then nodded. "Aye, he will. He might possibly go to ground."

"Do ye think he can?" asked Liam.

"Enough so that we may nay find it so easy to

ken exactly where he is. If he has brought some coin with him, he may e'en buy himself a mon or two to aid him, e'en to do his talking for him. Some men will do anything for a full purse, e'en help an Englishmon. How many men ride with him?"

"I dinnae ken exactly, but my guess, from all I have heard, is about a dozen."

"Enough to be a threat, but nay enough to rouse concern about a dangerous raid or an English attack. Since he must ken where we ride to by now, he doesnae need to keep close to our heels, either."

Jolene frowned as she tried to think of when or how Harold would have learned exactly where Sigimor was from. "Are you certain he will know where we journey to? I do not believe Peter would have told Harold for, by the time he sent for you, Peter was already deeply suspicious of the man."

"E'en if Harold doesnae ken exactly where we are from or where Dubheidland is, it willnae take him long to find out," replied Sigimor. "We may nay be rich or powerful, but most all ken who we are and where we are from."

Sigimor had turned his attention to Nanty before Jolene could ask exactly how or why they could be so well known if they were neither very rich nor very powerful. She could not believe it was for anything particularly shocking or evil. Men who lent aid to a woman and child, especially ones from a country most Scots probably cursed daily, could not be evil. Since she had been with them not one of the men had treated her with anything less than the greatest courtesy, aside from that one kiss Sigimor had stolen. Surely scandalous men did not treat a woman in such a gentlemanly way. Yet, Sigimor had sounded absolutely confident that the Camerons of Dubheidland were well and widely known. Glancing at her six guardians, she idly wondered if the unrelenting handsomeness of the men of Dubheidland was the cause of their fame. Her idle musings were abruptly ended by what Sigimor was saying to Nanty.

"I think we need to spread the word that Harold is ahunting us and that we would prefer it if he didnae catch us unawares," Sigimor told Nanty. "How far from here are the Armstrongs of Aigballa?"

"Ah, I see." Nanty smiled briefly and handed a sleepy Reynard to Jolene. "Nay far. Nay far at all."

"Good. Ride and tell them of our troubles, of how we need a close watch kept on that bastard."

"Ye dinnae want him routed?"

"I would like naught better, but 'tis best if no one else stains their swords with the blood of an English laird. If Harold is fool enough to stay on our trail, to push this to a confrontation, we will meet him and bury him. We at least have the right to do so, if only because he threatens us. We dinnae want this fight to spread too widely."

Nanty nodded in agreement. "If I take the right path I can spread the word to others. Mayhap the Murrays, and certainly to my brothers. Where shall I rejoin you?"

"I mean to stop a night or two at Scarglas with my cousins, then ride on to Dubheidland."

"If I dinnae catch up with ye at Scarglas, I *will* join ye at Dubheidland."

Jolene had barely joined everyone in wishing Nanty a safe journey when Reynard began to fuss. The child whimpered Nanty's name and kept his gaze fixed upon the departing man. She felt a brief pang of jealousy, then told herself not to be such a fool. Reynard liked all the men and, after all the poor child had been through since Harold's arrival at Drumwich, it was not surprising that he would be distressed to have any one of them leave. It was a little harder to quell that sting of jealousy when Sigimor took the child from her arms and Reynard immediately quieted.

"Nanty has a verra important job to do," Sigimor told the boy as he settled him in front of him on his saddle. "When he completes that chore ye will see him again."

"Nanty is my friend," Reynard said.

"That he is," agreed Sigimor as he nudged his horse into an easy but steady pace, "but he is also a mon with work to do. Sometimes a mon's work means he must leave friends and family for a wee while."

"Like Papa did."

"Aye, just like your papa."

"But Papa has not come back."

"Nay, he must work for the angels now."

"When will the angels let him come home?"

"Och, laddie, the angels cannae send him home." Sigimor stroked the child's thick black curls. "There is nay coming back from Heaven, I fear, but your father is watching o'er ye and listening. He will always be watching and listening to see how ye grow up into a fine, strong mon and take care of his people and his lands."

"And kick Cousin Harold out on his arse 'cause he stoleded Drumwich and sent Papa to the angels."

Sigimor almost grinned at the shocked look that briefly crossed Jolene's face. "Aye, laddie, 'tis exactly what we shall do."

Jolene stared blindly into the distance, away from Sigimor and Reynard, fighting back the tears that swamped her eyes and formed a hard knot in her throat. Reynard understood more than she had realized. He had obviously overheard a few less than genteel remarks as well. Even more moving was the gentle way Sigimor explained Peter's loss to the small child. He was a big, strong man with no fine courtly manners who often said the most outrageous things, yet he was kind and gentle with the little boy, willing to help in the care of him, and astoundingly patient with him.

In fact, all the men riding with her were very good to Reynard. Although none of the men at Drumwich had actually been mean or abusive to Reynard, only Peter and the two men murdered with him had actually taken any time with the boy. She ruefully admitted that Peter and his friends had not revealed the great patience or understanding these men did. Why, they were almost motherly, she mused, and nearly grinned, knowing they would probably fall from their saddles in horror if she ever said such a thing.

It was how Sigimor acted with Reynard that caused her the most astonishment, however. This was a man who compared the ideal English lady to a hound, yet he spoke to a child of angels. What worried her was how that made her feel. It strengthened all the inconvenient feelings she had for him, softening her toward him when she wanted to harden her heart. The man stroked Reynard's curls and spoke of angels, for sweet Mary's sake. How could she harden herself against that?

"There is a village a few hours ride from here," said Sigimor as he rode closer to her. "There is a clean inn there. We will stop there for the night."

Shaking free of her meandering thoughts, Jolene frowned slightly. "Will stopping at an inn not mark our path too clearly?"

"Aye, if Harold follows us to that village, but I believe it doesnae matter much. Now that I realize he can and will discover where Dubheidland is, I see no reason why we cannae indulge ourselves with a wee bit of comfort when 'tis so close at hand." He glanced up at the sky. "Aye, especially as there is a storm brewing."

Jolene looked up at the cloudless sky, but decided not to question him about his prediction. "A clean bed and, mayhap, a hot bath?"

"Aye. Tempted?"

"Mightily. Howbeit, I would not wish my comfort to bring Harold to our door and put Reynard in danger."

"As I said, lass, Harold will soon be at our door nay matter how clever we are. If he is determined to find us, he will. And, wheesht, where did ye come by the idea that I was thinking of *your* comfort?"

She glared at his back as he rode away, taking the lead next to Liam. The man was going to drive her utterly mad. One moment she was feeling all soft and warm toward him; the next she wished she was a big, hulking brute so that she could pound him into the mud.

The Twa Corbies Inn was indeed a clean one, and rather pretty despite its odd name. A very tempting smell was wafting through the inn from the kitchens and Jolene felt her stomach clench with anticipation. The only thing wrong that she could see was that everyone was staring at her with a mixture of horror and amazement. It might have been better if she had remained silent and let Sigimor request a bath for her.

"By the saints, 'tis an Englishwoman," muttered

the innkeeper before he scowled at Sigimor. "What are ye thinking to bring a bloody Sassenach into my inn? And where did ye come by her, eh?"

Sigimor crossed his arms over his chest and stared down at the much shorter, much rounder innkeeper. Jolene could almost feel sorry for the innkeeper, but he was being excessively rude. Glancing at the other four big, strong men with her, she did wonder how Master Dunbar could remain so obstinate. The strength of those frowns should have turned Dunbar into a quivering puddle of obsequiousness. Master Dunbar had obviously not noticed how thin the ice was that he was treading on. Although the others in the inn were still looking at her with a distinct lack of welcome, they at least had the sense to remain quiet. Jolene felt a little hurt by this reaction to her mere presence and hoped Sigimor would not take too long in putting Master Dunbar into a more accommodating mood.

"Aye, she is English," drawled Sigimor. "A wee, too thin, puling Sassenach lass."

Then again, Jolene mused, maybe she would just kick him.

"I hadnae realized so many braw laddies would be set to quivering with fear by her presence." Sigimor shrugged. "Howbeit, since she has set all your bowels to clenching—"

"Of course she hasnae," snapped Master Dunbar, speaking loudly so as to be heard over the angry grumbling of his patrons. "A wee thing like her be no threat to a mon. Be she yours then?"

"Aye." Sigimor was torn between the urge to grin at the cross look Jolene wore and to slap some courtesy into the innkeeper. Unfortunately, satisfying though such actions would be, neither would get him the soft bed and hot bath he wanted.

"Couldnae ye find a nice Scottish lass? Ye look a braw lad."

"I am, but I was bound by a blood debt. Her brother saved my life."

"He asked a high price."

"Aye, he did." Sigimor kept a subtle watch on Jolene as he continued, "Tisnae all bad. The English train their lasses weel. They train them to be sweet of tongue and disposition, kind to all, skilled at loom and needle, firm and alert in the management of a household, frugal, obedient, and a faithful companion to her lord, giving him peace and comfort in his home."

"Saints! Do the fools think they are training hounds?"

"One does wonder."

Jolene gave into the urge to kick Sigimor in the shin and ignored his exaggerated grimace. It only added to her annoyance to catch everyone in the inn grinning at her. She hoped it was because she had shown some spirit, but had the lowering feeling it was because a perfect English lady had just been compared to a hound—again.

"I dinnae think she learned all her lessons," murmured Master Dunbar.

Sigimor bit back a laugh over the way Jolene was eyeing Master Dunbar's shins. He draped his arm around her slim shoulders and kept her close by his side as he and the innkeeper settled the matter of rooms, baths, and price. As they followed a plump maid to their rooms, he idly wondered when Jolene would realize he would be sharing her room.

After checking the bed to see if it was as clean as it looked, Jolene settled a drowsy Reynard on top of the thick coverlet. It was going to be nice to spend a night under a proper roof and in a proper bed.

She had removed her cloak and draped it over the end of the bed before she realized Sigimor was still in the room with her. He leaned against the closed door, his arms crossed on his chest, watching her with an expectant look that made her decidedly uneasy.

"The room is quite acceptable, m'lord," she said. "There is no need to linger. You may seek your own chambers now."

"These *are* my own chambers," Sigimor replied and smiled.

Jolene blinked slowly in shock, then shook her head. "That is quite unacceptable. I cannot possibly share a room with a man. It would be highly improper."

"And sharing a camp with six men is acceptable, is it?"

Of course it was not, but Jolene suspected she would rather have her feet roasted over hot coals than admit that. She certainly could not tell him the real reason she did not want him sharing her bedchamber. The very last thing she wished him to know was that she had been looking forward to this time alone, time away from his side, to try to tamp down the growing attraction she felt for him. It was odd, but she felt as if sharing a bedchamber with him would be far more intimate than sleeping next to him on the hard ground had been.

"There is only one bed," she said and wondered crossly why simply saying that word should make her blush.

"Aye, but dinnae fret. Tis a big one."

Before she could respond to that a knock at the door announced the arrival of her bath. Jolene wanted to continue discussing the matter, but instinct warned her not to do so in front of the maid and the two lads helping her. It quickly became obvious that she was thought to be Sigimor's wife and Reynard their son. When Jolene recalled the somewhat belligerent welcome she had first received, she decided that misconception was probably for the best. When the maid set up a privacy screen before the rough wooden tub, Jolene fought the urge to scowl at it and Sigimor. She had the distinct feeling he did not intend to leave the room even as she bathed.

The moment she and Sigimor were alone again, she put her hands on her hips and frowned at him. "Well?"

"Weel what?"

"Should you not leave now to have your own bath?"

"Ah, weel, there is only this one. The lads will bring up another bucket or two of hot water for me in a wee while. Liam and the others wished to bathe, too, and the inn only has the two tubs." Sigimor moved to sprawl on the bed next to Reynard and then cocked a brow at Jolene. "Weel, set to it, lass. Dinnae let the water cool too much. Oh, and try not to make the water smell like flowers."

Jolene opened her mouth to vigorously argue, then closed it. Every instinct she had told her the man would not be moved and the hot bath she craved was waiting. Casting him a hard glare, she collected her lavender-scented soap, picked out some clean clothes, and then stepped behind the privacy screen. The screen was better protection than trusting him to turn his back as he had at the stream. This journey was proving highly injurious to her sense of modesty.

Despite her annoyance, she gave a hearty sigh of pleasure as she sank into the hot water of the bath. For a few moments she just sprawled indecorously in the soothing warmth, but then her innate sense of courtesy and fairness reared its troublesome head. The man deserved to find the water cold, she thought crossly as she began to wash, but she would have to be satisfied with thoroughly scenting it with lavender. Her mood was much improved by the time she had bathed, dressed, and rubbed her hair with the drying cloth until it ceased to drip. She sniffed the bath water, and was still smiling over the scent of lavender rising from it as she stepped around the screen.

"I smell flowers," Sigimor said as he picked up the buckets of hot water the boys had just delivered and moved toward the bath.

"French lavender," Jolene replied as she sat before the small fire to comb her hair dry. "A very fine soap."

Heaving a loud sigh, Sigimor set the buckets down by the tub then stepped closer to her and held out his hand. "I have no soap."

"I left mine to dry on the small stool by the bath." She met his scowl with a sweet smile, biting back the urge to laugh.

Once behind the screen, Sigimor added one bucket of hot water to the bath, leaving the second to rinse the soap from his hair. He stripped off his clothes, stepped into the bath, and sighed again as the soft scent of lavender wafted all around him. If he did not avoid his brother and cousins until the scent faded, he was certain he would have to knock a few of them down to silence the teasing. He cursed when he picked up the soap and noticed how strongly scented it was, then nearly cursed again when he heard Jolene's badly smothered laughter. As he bathed he made a vow to himself to always carry his own soap, manly unscented soap.

By the time he finished his bath, helped Jolene bathe Reynard and rinse out their clothes, their meal was brought in. Sigimor gave Jolene one hard look to silence any jests, then sat on the bed with Reynard as the bath was cleared away. It proved impossible to tear his gaze from Jolene as she nimbly braided her damp hair. He had never favored dark hair on a woman, but Jolene's thick, shining black hair made him ache. He wanted to see it spread beneath her slim body upon his bed linen as she welcomed him into her arms. Liam was probably right. He probably did stink of wanting her. The desire to make her his was proving too strong to fight.

Concerned that his arousal would become too obvious, Sigimor turned his attention to Reynard. He helped Jolene feed the boy and settle the child on the small bed the innkeeper had provided, then turned his attention to his own meal. Just when he felt himself in control again, he looked across the small rough table to see Jolene lick a drop of wine from her lips. He inwardly groaned as his desire returned in full force.

"Did Liam happen to say just how near Harold is?" Jolene asked as she began to peel an apple with a particularly ornate dagger Peter had given her on her eighteenth birthday.

"Closer than I would like," Sigimor replied.

"Oh. We have lost our lead then, have we?"

"Most of it. The fool must be near to killing his horses or he is changing his mounts all along the way." He watched her pale and admired the way she kept the fear he could see in her eyes under control. "Dinnae look so stricken. I suspected that, if he followed us, he would follow hard. We cannae keep such a brutal pace."

"Because of me and Reynard."

"Mostly Reynard. If 'twas just ye, I would tell ye to gird your wee loins and suffer silently. Reynard is a strong, healthy lad, but still too young to endure a hard race to Dubheidland."

Jolene looked at a sleeping Reynard and sighed. The boy was already very weary. It was but one short step from there to a fever for a child. She would like to race far ahead of Harold, but Sigimor was right. Such a small child could all too easily suffer from such a travail.

She was trying to think of some compromise when the maid arrived to clear away the remains of their meal. It was time to sleep and Jolene was sharply reminded of the fact that there was only one bed. The look upon Sigimor's face told her there would be no compromise here, either, but she felt compelled to make her objections known to him.

"You could bed down on the floor," she said.

"When there is a clean, soft, big bed at hand? Nay," he replied, then shook his head when she looked ready to argue. "Harold is nipping at our heels, lass. Ye and the bairn cannae be left unguarded. Nay, nor can ye be left unguarded in this place where all ken ye are an English lass and are nay too pleased about it. Now, get into bed. Ye need your rest, as do I. I will sleep on top of the bedcovers and ye can sleep safely beneath them."

Although she was still displeased with the arrangement, she walked to the bed and stripped down to her shift. It was very modest, revealing little more than her gown, but she still felt a blush heat her cheeks as she scrambled beneath the covers. Modesty, she told herself sternly, had little place under such circumstances. Until they got to Dubheidland, Sigimor and the other men had to stay close to her and Reynard. Bowing to a woman's well taught and, perhaps, excessive modesty was a foolish thing to expect of them.

She inwardly grimaced and quickly closed her eyes when Sigimor stripped down to his braies. Seeing him in nearly all his strong, male glory only reminded her of the real reason she did not want to share the bed with him. The temptation to touch the fine body was strong. Giving in to that temptation would bring her a whole new set of problems. She was just wondering if this was some sort of divine test of her morals when she felt him move close to her. Jolene opened her eyes to scold him only to find him leaning over her, his handsome face very close to hers. There was a look in his rich green eyes that caused her insides to clench with what she very much suspected was lust.

"Was there something you needed to tell me before we sleep?" she asked, pleased at how calm and polite she sounded.

"Nay. I will just take a wee goodnight kiss first." He grinned when her eyes widened, then kissed her.

Jolene put her hands against his shoulders, intending to push him away, only to be distracted by the feel of his smooth, warm skin beneath her palms. She started to curl her arms around his neck, feeling a little desperate to hold him close, when he pulled away. He gave her a brief smile, wished her a good sleep, then turned away onto his side with his back toward her. It was a lovely back, she thought as she struggled to ease the pounding of her heart, cool the fire in her blood, and cease panting. Broad, strong, and unmarred. When she saw how it moved as he breathed evenly and calmly, she decided that, at this precise moment, that beautiful, manly back would look even lovelier with the hilt of her dagger protruding from between his shoulder blades.

Chapter Five

A yawn so mighty it caused a twinge in her jaw and made her eyes water escaped Jolene as she stumbled through the trees and brush in search of a place to relieve herself. It was all Sigimor's fault she was so tired. After giving her a kiss that had made her feverish, he had turned over and gone to sleep. Tense with needs she did not fully understand and all too aware of how blithely she could give the man the virtue so well protected for three-and-twenty years, she had been unable to sleep until close to dawn. Jolene doubted she had gained more than a few hours of sleep before a far too cheerful Sigimor was rousting her out of bed. She did not understand how the man could stir her hitherto unawakened passion one moment and, in the next, have her fondly thinking of how many ways she could torture or kill him.

After seeing to her needs, she looked around and felt a tickle of alarm. She could neither see nor hear the Camerons. Worse, she had been so tired, so thoroughly caught up in her thoughts, she had neglected to watch where she was going, or how far. Glancing up at the sky, she tried to recall Peter's lessons and guess which way was north. Since they were riding into the Highlands, Jolene felt north was the direction to go in. Praying she had chosen correctly, she started to walk.

It was a long while before she accepted the fact that she was going in the wrong direction. The trees were growing thicker, but the wood had been sparse where she had left the others waiting for her. Taking a deep breath to calm her growing fear, she moved on, telling herself that she must have gone deeper into the wood than she had realized or, perhaps, was only a little off the path she had taken.

Just as she began to think it might be wise to stop walking and start bellowing for help, the trees began to thin out. She heard the faint jingle of a horse's harness and the low murmur of men's voices. Relieved, she hurried toward the sounds, ignoring a voice in her head that warned her to be cautious. That warning grew more strident as she trotted toward the clearing she could see just ahead of her, but she refused to heed it. It was just the remnants of her fear of having gotten lost, she told herself. A faint smile curved her mouth as she thought that her unease was probably caused by the thought of the lecture Sigimor would surely give her for having taken so long.

The smile on her face disappeared abruptly as she trotted into the clearing. She should have heeded her instincts. Some part of her had obviously been alert enough to notice that there was something wrong, something alarming about the voices she had been running toward. They were English.

Later, she told herself, she might be able to laugh

over the way she and the three men in the clearing gaped at each other in astonishment. She had a brief, inane thought that someone needed to teach a few Scots how to count. There were only two men with Harold, not twelve. Then the frantic call to flee that howled through her mind finally reached her body. Cursing, she bolted, but Harold and his men had obviously shaken free of their shock a heartbeat faster than she had.

Jolene had the strong feeling she could not win this race, but she had no intention of surrendering meekly. She intended to make Harold sweat hard for his prize. Her only consolation was that Reynard was still out of Harold's reach.

Harold and his men proved to be a lot quicker than she would have guessed them to be. They kept blocking her chosen route of escape or turning her away from it. Jolene soon found herself doing little more than running in circles. Then, for one brief moment, she saw a clear path into the wood. Just as she charged for it, Harold threw himself after her. Jolene cursed as his body slammed into hers from behind. She hit the ground so hard she was surprised she was still concious. She wanted to throw off Harold, but found herself struggling to breathe instead.

"I cannot believe you simply walked into my hands," Harold said as he took her dagger from its sheath at her waist and stumbled to his feet.

Unconcerned with her dignity for the moment, Jolene flopped onto her back and drew in several deep breaths of air. "It was not quite that simple," she managed to say.

"Where is Peter's little bastard?"

"Peter's *heir* is well out of your murderous grasp."

Her breathing more normal at last, Jolene slowly sat up.

"Is he? I have you now. That will make it much easier to deal with the problem of the boy." Harold grabbed her tightly by the arm and yanked her to her feet. "Where are your cursed guards?"

"Do you truly think I would be here if I knew? I got separated from them, lost in the woods." She gave him a cold smile. "Shall I call for them?"

"You do and it shall be the last sound you ever make for I shall cut out your sharp tongue. In truth, 'tis something to consider, for, although I could certainly find some pleasurable use for your tongue, permanently silencing you holds a great appeal."

The chill of that threat would take a minute to shake off, she thought as he dragged her toward a small fire. He pushed her down and she bit back a curse as her backside hit the ground hard. Two rabbits roasted on a spit over the fire and Jolene realized the men had intended to pause in this clearing for a while. That could prove to her advantage for she felt certain the Camerons would soon start looking for her.

"M'lord," said one of the men, a tall, thin man with a badly pockmarked face, "should we not move from here?"

"Why?" asked Harold as he sat down close to Jolene.

"Those Scots cannot be far away."

"Far enough and we will hear them if they approach. We will wait here for the rest of my men as was planned."

"M'lord—"

"We will wait here. Jesu, Martin, we hold the woman. E'en if those fools stumble our way before the rest of the men arrive, we have her as our shield. Now, fetch me my wineskin."

Jolene breathed a silent sigh of relief. Martin was silenced, his reasonable concerns ignored. She was heartily thankful for Harold's arrogance for it would keep her settled in one spot making it easier for the Camerons to track her down. Now all she had to worry about was Harold's other men and Harold himself. She prayed Sigimor and the others would find her before either of those became too great a threat to her.

"She has been gone too long," Sigimor muttered, glaring at the woods Jolene had walked into.

"Women take longer," Liam said as he offered Sigimor a drink from his waterskin.

"Nay this long." Sigimor took a deep drink of water, handed the waterskin back to Liam, and idly scratched his chin as he continued to scowl at the trees.

"She might be, weel, ill. She did look a wee bit pale. And, verra tired." Liam eyed Sigimor closely.

"Why are ye looking at me like that?"

"Ye spent the night with her in a room with but one bed. Did ye—"

"Nay! I shared the bed with her beneath the blankets and me above. Nay more."

He tried not to think about how much *more* he had wanted and still wanted. Sharing a bed with her had been a torment he was not eager to repeat. At least, he thought, not until she let him beneath the covers with her. And they were both naked. He would touch that beautiful skin, feast upon those perfect breasts—. Sigimor quickly pushed those images from his mind. It had not been wise to give into the temptation to kiss her again. Not only had it made him so aroused sleep had been a long time in coming, but all day he had been tasting her on his mouth. His only consolation was that he was almost certain she shared his passion.

That thought made him frown and increased his concern for her. Jolene was a well-born virgin and, if the innocence of her kisses was anything to judge by, unaccustomed to desire. Could she have fled from that, feared it so much that she would try to get away from him? A heartbeat later, he shook aside that thought. Jolene might be innocent, but she was no weak-spirited, easily frightened maid. If she did feel the desire that flared between them as strongly as he did, she would fight it or accept it, not run away from it. Nor would she leave Reynard behind or risk putting either of them into Harold's grasp. Something was wrong. Sigimor was certain of it.

"Why didnae ye bed her?" asked Liam. "Ye want her."

Sigimor turned his scowl on his cousin. "She is an English lady and a virgin. I may nay be the wondrous, chivalrous courtier ye are—"

"Why did that sound like such an insult?" Liam murmured, smiling faintly.

"But," Sigimor continued, ignoring him, "I do ken that 'tisnae verra gentlemonly to seduce a lass like her. In truth, seducing a lass has ne'er been something I much liked. A bit devious, I am thinking. Unkind, too."

"Mayhap. There are certainly enough lasses about willing to bed a mon just for the pleasure of it or for a wee bit of coin to keep most men satisfied. Then again, some lasses just like to play the game."

"Jolene wouldnae like such a game."

"Nay, she wouldnae. She is a lass one marries."

"Right now she is a lass who is missing. I am going to look for her."

"Ye could embarrass her if ye stumble upon her at an ill-chosen moment."

"She will recover. I cannae stand here fearing to offend her modesty when she could be lost, ill, or worse."

Sigimor was pleased when Liam gave him no further argument. He ordered his cousins David and Marcus to stay with Reynard and the horses. With Tait and Liam, Sigimor started into the woods to look for Jolene. It would indeed be embarrassing if they caught her still tending to her personal needs, but he was willing to risk such an uncomfortable confrontation. Every instinct he had told him that something was wrong.

The worry, even fear, he felt surprised him. It was strong and it ran deep. It was born of far more than his debt to Jolene's brother, or to her, or even a natural need to protect a woman. They had known each other for only a few days and yet she had obviously become important to him. He could understand feeling an immediate desire for an attractive woman, but this was a little puzzling. He felt he ought to have known her longer, more thoroughly, and more intimately to cause him to feel such concern and fear over her safety and well-being.

It was also puzzling that he felt no need to try and cure himself of this strange affliction. He certainly felt no urge to put some distance between them before it got worse or more complicated. From the first moment he had seen Jolene, he had felt possessive of her. Small, dark, and impertinent though she was, he had thought *mine* and still did.

She felt *right*, even when she was glaring at him, fury enlivening her silver-gray eyes.

Once he got her back by his side, safe and hale, Sigimor knew he was going to have to think more deeply about what lay ahead for him and Jolene. It was easy to see all the complications, such as her being English, but it might be time to start studying all that was right, such as the knee-trembling desire she could stir within him. He had never felt the like before and he should stop trying to ignore the importance of that. And, he *would* get her back, he vowed as he scowled at the trail she had left.

"The fool lass left here and walked off in the wrong direction," he said.

"Do ye think she means to walk back to England?" Tait asked, only partly joking.

"To Harold? Nay, she has simply gotten herself all turned about. She probably didnae watch where she was going carefully enough and is now lost." Sigimor looked at Liam. "How close to us was Harold?"

"Too close and drawing closer," Liam replied. "Yet, I wouldnae have thought he was already breathing down our necks."

"But he could be and she is walking toward him, isnae she?"

"So we had best nay just start bellowing her name," Tait murmured as he joined Liam and Sigimor in continuing to follow her trail. "Might be why she isnae bawling like a lost lamb."

"Could be pure, stubborn pride, too," Sigimor said. "I have watched her go the wrong way, turned her about, and had her try to convince me that was the way she wished to go if but for a wee moment. As we left the room at the inn, she turned left instead of right toward the stairs. When I pointed out the right way, she told me she was just satisfying her curiosity about how many rooms were on that floor." He exchanged a brief grin with his companions. "Nay, she is lost and I fear she has wandered a long way refusing to admit it. I but hope that is the only problem."

Following Jolene's trail was not easy for she was obviously possessed of a light tread, leaving only the faintest sign of her passing when she left one at all. Time was slipping away and each minute that passed in which Jolene was not safe at his side, Sigimor felt his fear grow. There were other dangers out there beside Harold. He finally sent Liam to scout the area up ahead of them to be sure they were not walking into any trouble as they searched for her. Although it was somewhat satisfying to know his companions now shared his concern, Sigimor found little comfort in their increasingly grim expressions. He promised himself the privilege of lecturing Jolene until her head throbbed, then turned all his attention back to hunting her.

Jolene glanced up at the sky and inwardly cursed. The day was fading fast. All too soon the sun would be setting. Escaping into the dark would certainly make it difficult for Harold to chase her down. Unfortunately, it would also make it difficult for her. She had managed to get herself lost in the full light of day. She would have little chance of finding her way back to Sigimor in the dark. With her abominable sense of direction, she thought ruefully, she could end up in Wales.

The real trick would be getting away from a very alert Harold and his equally alert men. Jolene refused to think that it was impossible. All she needed was one small chance, one tiny miracle. Even if just Harold's two men were thoroughly distracted for a moment, escape might be possible. Then she could strike Harold with the rock tucked under her skirts and make a run for it. One thing she could do was run fast and she had the stamina to do so for a long time. Just one little chance, she silently prayed.

"The moment we return to Drumwich, we shall be married," Harold said, watching her intently as he spoke.

Obviously her prayers were to go unanswered for the moment, Jolene thought. "You make a poor jest, Cousin."

"I ne'er jest and we are but distant cousins. It was not very hard to get a special dispensation since our blood ties are so very thin."

"And some bishop was so very greedy."

"Tsk, so little respect you have for our esteemed clergy. I but made a gift to the church out of gratitude for their help and understanding."

Jolene rolled her eyes, then scowled at him. "You are very free with coin that is not yours by right."

"I hold it and Drumwich, thus 'tis all mine."

"It all belongs to Reynard, my brother's son, his heir."

"For now." Harold took a drink from his wineskin and then offered it to Jolene.

Thirst overcame her urge to spurn his offer, but Jolene pointedly wiped clean the mouth of the wineskin before taking a drink. The way Harold narrowed his pale blue eyes told her she was stirring his formidable temper, but she doubted she could keep too firm a rein upon her tongue. Simply being so close to the man who had Peter's blood upon his hands roused her hate and anger to a near-feverish pitch. The knowledge that he would kill Reynard, too, if given the chance, and do so without remorse, only hardened those feelings.

"What do you mean by that?" She hated to ask, but felt compelled to as she handed his wineskin back to him.

"Such young children are very prone to dying, are they not?"

"You would actually stain your hands with the blood of an innocent, helpless child?"

"Not if I can help it. I was actually planning to have him proclaimed a bastard. Although I was willing to take the easier, swifter path, if the boy fell into my grasp, making him illegitimate will work as well."

"That would still leave you with nothing. You are not the next male in line."

"But I am named Peter's heir after Reynard."

For one brief, horrifying moment, Jolene thought he was telling her the truth, but then she saw how intently Harold watched her. He was waiting to see if she was fool enough to believe him. It was something he habitually did when he lied, something she had noticed years ago. She was disgusted with herself for forgetting that.

"Nay, Peter would ne'er have named you his heir," she said firmly. "He would have hesitated to disrupt the proper line of succession, but, even if he had, he would ne'er have chosen you. If naught else, he ne'er fully trusted you. He would have chosen Roger whom he loved as a brother and trusted in all things."

When she saw the fury which darkened Harold's face and saw him slightly raise one fist, Jolene braced herself for a blow. It surprised her when he controlled that urge. Harold never resisted the urge to strike those who displeased him. In a strange way, Harold's newly acquired ability to control his fury made him seem all the more dangerous to her.

"I *will* hold Drumwich and I *will* hold you," he said between tightly clenched teeth.

"Nay, you will *never* hold me."

"I will marry you, securing my hold upon Drumwich, and I will bed you, thoroughly."

The very thought of Harold's bloodstained hands touching her made Jolene feel cold and ill. The way he flushed told her that she had done a poor job of keeping her revulsion hidden. He had to be mad to think she would submit herself to a man who had her brother's blood upon his hands and would be perfectly content to add her nephew's to that stain.

"The bride has to say she is willing," Jolene said. "You must know I will never mouth such a lie." The way Harold smiled gave her such a chill, she actually shivered.

"I have been most careful in my choice of the priest who shall marry us. Once wed, I can claim your very healthy dowry and use your place as my wife to try and get Reynard back in Drumwich."

There was such a calm, firm certainty in his voice Jolene felt unable to argue his plan. It was all too easy to believe a priest would just ignore her protests and denials. The man did not even have to be corrupted by a heavy purse. Too many men of the church felt a woman was too weak-minded to know what was best for her. Harold could even threaten her life and she was not sure she would choose death over even a short time as his wife. If he had the wit to know he would lose, too, if he killed her, she knew he could use pain to bend her to his will. Jolene knew she was no coward, but her endurance had never been tested before. It took only one small crack in her will, one whispered *aye*, and she would be married to Harold before God and the laws of England. She would be trapped. And, he was right to say he could get Reynard through his marriage to her. The laws of both lands would demand it and the Camerons could pay very dearly if they tried to keep Reynard, tried to hold him safe with them.

Jolene sternly pushed aside the sense of defeat creeping over her. She might weaken, might slip deeper into Harold's grasp, but that did not mean she had to stay in his hold. Nor did Harold's plans have to go as he had laid them out. It might not come now, but a chance to escape *would* come. She had to believe that or all hope was lost.

"Am I to get a chaste bride?"

His abrupt question startled her out of her thoughts and she stared at him. Suddenly she thought of Sigimor's kisses and felt herself blush. The rage on Harold's face frightened her, but, again, he managed to bring himself under control. He probably did not wish to drag a badly beaten woman before a priest, she thought cynically.

"So, you have let that bastard Scot touch you, have you?" he demanded.

"Which bastard Scot do you refer to?" she asked sweetly, wondering what possessed her to goad him so.

"Would you have me believe the too-proud lady of Drumwich has become naught but a common whore?"

"Common? Nay, ne'er common. Yet, such lovely, big, handsome men—" she began.

"Filthy Scots! You dishonor the Gerard name and blood!" Harold took several deep breaths to calm himself. "I do not believe you," he said after a few moments, the tremor of rage still lingering in his voice. "Nay, you would never demean yourself so, not with one of those Camerons. Barbarous lot. Infamous. They are known throughout this cursed land for their tempers, for their proclivity to breed only redheads, and for their eccentric ways. Tis how I know where the fool is taking you."

"At least they are not infamous for murdering their own kinsmen because of greed."

"Twas bad fish that killed Peter."

Jolene ached to scratch the smug look from Harold's face. "Twas poisoned wine."

"That can ne'er be proven. No one will heed the claims of a disobedient wife against her husband, the lord of Drumwich. Once we are married, your word will count for naught against mine, and there is no one to stand with you against me."

"My kinsmen will heed me."

"You best pray that they do not, not if you wish them to live."

"You cannot kill them all."

"I can silence enough of them to put the fear of God, or me, into the others." He grabbed her by the chin. "And, if you cause me too much trouble, even the pleasure of having your soft body at my command will not stop me from silencing you. That would be unfortunate," he murmured, stroking her cheek, then scowling when she pulled away from his touch, "for I would prefer to hear you cry out in pleasure as I bed you. The two of us could make the Gerards of Drumwich the greatest power in all of England."

It did not really surprise Jolene that Harold had plans far beyond the stealing of Drumwich. Far beyond his capabilities as well, she mused. Then again, he had learned to control his rage, to harness that urge to blindly strike out. If he has learned caution and subtlety, he could be a threat to far more than her, Reynard, and Drumwich. The mere thought of Harold gaining any real power, power over more than Drumwich, was frightening. She had to put an end to this man's plans.

Jolene was just considering a blind attempt to flee, praying surprise would aid her, when one of Harold's men shouted in alarm. His cry was followed by a panic among the horses. Both of Harold's men were suddenly, fully occupied in trying to keep the horses from fleeing. One of the men cried out something about an adder. It seemed her prayers were about to be answered. Although Jolene thought a snake a strange savior, she took immediate advantage of Harold's distraction.

Clutching the rock she had kept hidden beneath her skirts, Jolene leapt to her feet. Harold turned back toward her, but he only had time to shout one curse before she struck him in the side of the head with the rock. He was still crumpling to the ground when she retrieved her dagger and started to run.

Chapter Six

"Run, lass!"

Jolene did not hesitate as she ran through the woods. She had the wild thought that it was odd how her heavenly guardian sounded like a Scot. Then Liam was at her side. He moved to keep just far enough in front of her to lead her, yet be near enough to immediately help her if she needed it. She wanted to tell him that all she needed was someone to point the way, but decided she had better save her breath for running.

Liam stopped her only once. He gave the call of a blackbird. Jolene was just about to compliment him on how perfectly he did that, when it was answered. Knowing that meant other Camerons were not too far away, she did not really need his signal to start running again. She suspected that, if she knew where to go, she would run right on past Liam, so anxious was she to get back to Sigimor and the others.

Her first sight of Sigimor was him scowling at her. Jolene did not think she had ever seen a more beautiful sight. She gave into an urge she did not fully understand and ran straight for him. To her relief, he opened his arms and caught her, holding her almost too tightly against him. She wrapped her arms around him and let the feeling of being safe again flow through her.

"Trouble?" Sigimor loosened his hold on Jolene slightly, but took due note of the fact that she did not ease her tight grip upon him.

"Harold," Liam said as he caught his breath.

"Following ye?"

"He will be soon."

Sigimor eased Jolene's grip on him and looked at her. "Can ye run a wee bit farther?"

"Aye," she replied. "Just point the way."

"We can discuss this further when we put some distance between us and Harold."

As they ran toward the clearing where the others waited, Jolene suspected Sigimor's *discussion* would consist of a lot of awkward questions concerning Harold. That would probably come after the lecture, she mused, which might give her enough time to think of what to say, something she hoped would not tell the full truth yet not truly be a lie.

Then she caught sight of Liam and groaned. She was now certain he was the reason she had been given the opportunity to flee. There was a chance he had heard many of the things Harold had said and he would not hesitate to tell Sigimor every word. When they finally stopped running, she hoped she still retained enough wit to *discuss* things with Sigimor. She was not sure what the man would do if he found out all of Harold's plans, but Jolene suspected it could mean trouble for her, something she already had a bounty of.

Sigimor used only a few curt words to get everyone moving the moment they reached the others. He secured Reynard snugly against his own chest and Jolene made no protest. He was the better rider and the weight of such a small child would not hinder him at all, as it occasionally did her. She inwardly groaned when she mounted her horse, but made no complaint. She fully agreed with Sigimor's plan to use what little was left of daylight to put as many miles as they could between them and Harold, and as swiftly as they could. There would be time later to pamper her bruises and recover from her ordeal.

The murky gray of late twilight finally stopped them. Jolene fought the urge to collapse as she dismounted. She took Reynard from Sigimor and saw to the little boy's needs. When he fell asleep within moments after he had finished his meal, she envied him. Not only was he able to achieve the deep, restful sleep of the innocent, but he had enjoyed the comfort of being pressed against Sigimor for the duration of their hard ride, the man's big, strong body undoubtedly protecting Reynard from the worst of it.

Jolene wished she could have been pressed so close to Sigimor's chest. It was such a lovely chest, she thought as she started toward some trees and thick bushes at the far edge of their camp hoping to take a private moment or two to see to her own needs. Broad, strong, and smooth. She sighed as she thought of how nice it would be to rest her cheek against that warm skin, to smooth her hands over that chest, especially if he wrapped those long, muscular arms around her to hold her close and—. She frowned as she realized there were soft footsteps echoing hers from behind. Jolene turned and directed her frown at Sigimor who was close on her heels.

"I am slipping away for a moment of privacy," she said, but Sigimor did not move.

"Aye, I ken it," he replied. "I am escorting ye."

"How can I be private if you are with me?"

"Ye can be private on one side of the tree, or bush, whilst I stand on the other side."

"But, well, you will be able to hear me," she nearly whispered, her voice weakened by shock.

"I believe I can bear it."

His eyes were bright with laughter and Jolene's shock quickly changed to annoyance. She might as well toss what few scraps of modesty she had left to the four winds. Jolene actually ached to yell at him, to vigorously argue this infringement upon her privacy, but she did neither. Not only did she feel sure he would not be moved in this, but her personal needs were becoming almost painfully demanding. She muttered a curse and marched off toward a big tree with a thick tangle of bushes at its roots.

The moment she squatted behind the tree, Jolene knew this was not going to work. The urge was still there, sharp and demanding, but nothing was happening. She was simply far too aware of how close Sigimor was, of how a man she was deeply attracted to was near enough to hear her let water. Although her embarrassment lingered, anger over her own foolishness and the awkward situation he had put her in pushed it to the side for a moment.

"You are going to have to make some noise," she snapped. "Sing."

"Sing? Och, nay, lass, ye truly dinnae wish me to do that."

She could hear the laughter in his deep voice

and she gritted her teeth. "Do it or we could be here all night and I will probably do some permanent injury to my innards."

"Why dinnae ye sing?"

"Sigimor! Will you just do it, please?!"

"Dinnae say I ne'er warned ye."

He started to sing and Jolene was so stunned, she had finished her business before she even realized she had started. Using a small square of linen, she tidied herself, then used a little water from the waterskin she had brought to wash her hands. She then hastily straightened her clothing, raced around the tree, and put her hand over his mouth. The way his lovely eyes gleamed with humor even in the dim light told her she did not have to fear insulting him. Then she felt the tip of his tongue stroke her palm. Heat flared up her arm, and she yanked her hand away.

"I did warn ye, lass," he drawled, studying the slight flush upon her cheeks and wondering if it was caused by anger, embarrassment, or, as he hoped, a sudden flash of desire.

Jolene forced herself to concentrate on that noise he had made, one that seemed to have startled every living creature in the wood into silence, and not on what that odd little caress had made her feel. "I do not understand how a man with such a fine speaking voice could sound like that. You have no sense of tone or tune, do you."

"None at all," he said cheerfully as he grasped her by the hand and led her back to camp.

As she let him tug her along with him, Jolene stared at their joined hands and wondered if Sigimor was some sort of sorcerer. It was a strange thought, but no stranger than the way he made her feel all warm and shivery inside simply by clasping her hand.

She did not believe she had ever felt that way before, but she could not, at the moment, recall any other man touching her hand.

Sigimor stopped, drawing her attention. They had reached the camp. Jolene saw that the other men were frowning at Sigimor. Out of the corner of her eye, she saw him point at her, causing all four men to look accusingly at her.

"Ye *asked* him to sing?" demanded Liam.

"Well, at that precise moment, it seemed like a good idea," she murmured as she and Sigimor moved to sit by the fire.

"It is ne'er a good idea to ask Sigimor to sing."

"He is kind enough to ken the pain it inflicts upon the innocent," muttered David.

"Oh. I see." Jolene laughed and looked at Sigimor. "You are taking this criticism very well, I must say."

Sigimor shrugged. "Tis but a wee failing." He looked at her sternly. "Nay as big a one as getting lost because one wanders too far away and, as a result, gets taken up by one's enemies."

Jolene could see by the look upon Sigimor's face, and those of the other men, that she was about to be informed of all she had done wrong and what rules she would now be expected to follow. She helped herself to a bowl of the rabbit stew one of the men had made. There was no doubt in her mind that she would need the strength the food would give her, if only to keep herself from arguing or getting angry. In her heart, she knew she deserved the scold. She had been careless and put them all at risk. She just hoped she could remember that, she mused, as Sigimor began a somewhat scathing account of all her mistakes. He proved far more skillful at delivering a lecture than her brother

Peter and she often had to bite her tongue to keep from defending herself.

"Now, Liam, ye can tell me exactly how much trouble the lass got herself into," Sigimor said, satisfied by the way Jolene was glaring at him that she had heard and understood every word he had said.

"Weel, Harold had captured her," replied Liam. "He and two of his men—"

"There were only three men with her?" Sigimor scowled at Liam when he nodded. "We ran from only three men? Did ye nay think it would have been a fine time to put an end to the fool?"

"I did think on that, but they were waiting on the rest of their men. I didnae have time to go and see if those men were near enough to be a threat as weel. We wouldnae fare weel in the killing of Harold if near to a dozen of his men suddenly crept up behind us. I thought it best to just get the lass out of there."

"Aye, aye, 'twas best. Once ye did that, we lost all chance of surprise anyway, and we were all split up, too. So, how did ye get her away from him?"

"An adder set amongst the horses and the two fools guarding them." Liam briefly smiled his approval at Jolene as he said, "The lass was quick to seize her chance. She hit Harold upside the head with a rock and ran. The mon was so full of his own plots and boasts, he hadnae e'en tethered her."

"What plans and plots?"

"Oh, all of his devious, traitorous plans to hold fast to Drumwich, of course," Jolene said quickly, before Liam could reply. "There was naught said which would necessitate you changing any of your plans." She tried to look calm, even innocent, beneath his steady gaze, but the way his eyes narrowed told her she was probably not entirely succeeding.

"What did ye hear him say, Liam?"

"He is after Lady Jolene to wed her, secure his hold upon Drumwich through her, and use her to help him turn the law full against us and get Reynard back," Liam replied. "Ye were right to think Harold has heard all about us and so will ken exactly where we are headed. Calls us barbarous, infamous, possessed of a proclivity to breed redheads, and eccentric. He threatens our lives as weel as hers and the bairn's. Oh, and for a moment, he wondered if she had taken one or all of us as her lover, then convinced himself that she would ne'er do such a thing. Is that all of it, lass?"

Jolene sent Liam a look that cried *traitor*, but nodded. Since Liam had heard all of that, he must have heard about her dowry as well, but had not mentioned it. Either he had somehow missed Harold's talk of her healthy dowry, or he simply did not consider it an important fact.

"I suspected he wanted her for more reasons than Reynard and what she might ken about Peter's death." Sigimor looked at Jolene, an idea forming in his mind that surprised him, but did not disconcert him in the slightest. "So, ye either wed with him or ye die."

"Aye," she replied. "It seems Harold has obtained his dispensation, and has a priest at the ready, both men made very amiable by the generous use of Reynard's fortune."

"He cannae believe he can keep *ye* sweet and silent by wedding ye, can he?"

Jolene fleetingly wondered if there was an insult hidden in that question. "Nay, but he would give it his best effort, which would probably involve the giving of a great deal of pain. I believe he also contemplated cutting out my tongue, but I cannot be entirely sure which he was favoring during the last round of threats—death or mutilation. Of course, I would still be able to write down my accusations, but, if he caught me, he would probably have my hand struck off."

"Weel, one of them anyway." Sigimor was chilled by the images she painted of her possible fate in Harold's hands.

"Nay, both. I can write with both hands, though 'tis more legible when I use my right hand. I can write with my right foot, too. Bless me, I could end up as naught but a tiny stump of a woman." The way the men stared at her made Jolene all too aware of what she had just blithely confessed and she blushed.

"No one can write with their toes. Ye cannae grip a quill with toes. They are too short."

"Most are. Mine are not."

"Show us."

"I most certainly will not."

"Och, weel, we dinnae have a quill and paper anyway. We will see the trick later. Tis nay important now," Sigimor said before she could argue with that plan. "Now we ken why Harold willnae retreat, willnae give up and go home. Tisnae just the lad he wants. Tisnae just fear that ye may yet get someone to help ye make him pay for his crimes, either." Sigimor frowned at Jolene. "Ye should have told us he had a thought to marrying you, to using ye to secure his claim to the title, the land, *and* the lad."

"Since I have revealed no urge to meekly fall in with his plans, I had rather hoped he had given them up."

"A mon caught tight in a lusting for a lass doesnae

give it up easily. Aye, he kens ye are a threat to him, but he also sees that ye could be verra useful alive, at least for a while. He will take all he craves until ye prove too troublesome. In his eyes, ye are nearly as important and rich a prize as the laddie. Depending upon how fierce his lusting for ye is, mayhap e'en a greater prize."

"Harold has lusted after near every female he has seen since his voice deepened."

"And I suspicion he has been trying to get ye for nearly as long."

Jolene really wanted to argue that, but could not bring herself to tell such a big lie. Since Sigimor's *suspicion* was probably born of things she had said during her nightmare, it would be a waste of time and effort anyway. Harold's interest had settled upon her the year she had begun to change from a child into a woman and had never wavered. The few times he had cornered her still haunted her dreams. Her only salvation had been the fact that so few of their mutual kinsmen either liked or trusted Harold that she had seen very little of him over the years.

She wished Liam had not heard and related Harold's plans. It complicated matters even though none of it either changed what she needed or what she wanted to do. No matter what nefarious plots Harold dreamed up, she still had to keep Reynard and herself out of his grasp. Whether he forced her into marriage or not, Harold was still a threat to her and Reynard and would be until he paid for his crimes. She did not understand why Sigimor looked at her as if she had lied to him. She had only neglected to mention a few sordid details.

Yet again she regretted never telling Peter about Harold's pursuit of her, of the attacks he had made upon her. She had been ashamed, had not wanted to cause trouble or, worse, put Peter at sword's point with Harold, and a hundred other excuses she now saw as mostly foolish. If she had told Peter the first time Harold had cornered and mauled her, Harold might not be the threat he was now. Jolene felt sure Peter would never again have let the man into Drumwich.

Quickly, she buried those thoughts which always brought her grief and roused a strong sense of guilt. There were so many ways this trouble could have been avoided, she would make herself dizzy thinking of them and it would gain her nothing. Jolene also knew she really had nothing to feel guilty about. Harold was the guilty one, the only one truly at fault. If she repeated that often enough, she mused ruefully, her heart might finally accept it.

"Are ye done pondering the matter?" Sigimor asked.

Jolene started and looked at him, then recalled that he had been waiting for her to respond to his remark. "Aye, Harold had been a bit of a problem from time to time."

"Yet Peter didnae kill the mon?"

"I chose not to trouble him with the matter." She sighed. "I was just thinking that things might have been very different now if I *had* told him."

"Aye, they would have. Peter would have killed the bastard years ago."

"Thank you most kindly for offering me that comfort and absolution."

"Twas but the truth." He had to fight a grin over the way she glared at him and was pleased that he had banished the sadness from her eyes. "Ye need no absolution. Naught ye have done put your brother's life in peril, or the blood upon Harold's hands. Tis his own greed, nay more. Only Harold is guilty in all of this."

The man was definitely going to make her go mad, Jolene thought. One moment he would say something that made her ache to hit him with a large, blunt object, and look as if he enjoyed making her so angry her eyes crossed. In the very next breath, he would say something to banish that anger, even make her go all soft and warm inside. If that was not enough to make a woman tear out her hair, she did not know what was.

"That is what I told myself." She grimaced. "It is somewhat alarming that Harold has drawn so close to us."

"Irritating, certainly. In a day or so, depending upon how swiftly we can travel, we will be able to stop at Scarglas. We can rest there for a wee while until I can plan a way to get round Harold and regain some of our lead ere the fool realizes we have left the safety of Scarglas."

"Ye still willnae ask help of our cousins?" asked Liam. "They could easily help us put an end to that threat."

"Nay doubt. Old Fingal would like naught more than having a chance to put the fear of God and several inches of his sword into a few Englishmen," Sigimor said. "Howbeit, as I have said before, I would as lief nay draw anyone else into this conflict. Aye, a helping hand, but nay more. *We* have a right to cut the mon down, a right I mean to make e'en more clear by forcing him to come after us at Dubheidland. If the death of an English laird causes trouble, let it come to only our gates for we can show that 'twas just and fair."

"Surely 'twould be just and fair if 'twas a kinsmon who dealt the blow for us?"

"Mayhap, but the English dinnae always see things as we do. Aye, the Sassenachs are quarreling amongst themselves now and may not e'en care that one of their own has gone missing. So, too, has the bastard crossed the border, armed and ready to fight. Yet, we dinnae ken how high his allies sit at the king's table or how strong those alliances are. There is e'er the chance Harold's death could bring a loud outcry and I dinnae want any others caught up in that trouble."

Liam sighed, then nodded. "Fair enough. We also have proof that Lord Peter requested your aid."

"We do. And, we have the Lady of Drumwich who begged our aid."

"Begged?" Jolene muttered.

Sigimor ignored that interruption. "She has allies of her own." He looked at her and cocked one brow. "Aye?"

"Aye," Jolene replied. "I have allies. Unfortunately, Harold knew who they were and had planned well to halt all and any attempts to reach them. You were the only one he did not know about. Saving the life of a Highland lord was not a tale Peter was inclined to relate to many people, and the few times he did tell it, he did so in a vague way, naming no names. He only told me about you after he had already sent for you. Harold was not the only one taken by surprise when you arrived. I tried to send word out that Peter was dead, but Harold worked swiftly to keep that news from spreading."

"And we didnae speak to many once we entered England. In truth, we did all we could to be little seen and little heard, thus aiding Harold in his secrecy."

Accepting the wineskin Sigimor held out to her, Jolene took a drink from it, then passed it along to Tait who sat on her left. "That was wise. We may not be at war, precisely, but memories of past raids by the Scots are still fresh. I suspect many between Drumwich and the border have suffered some loss in some wild raid." She sighed. "As many of your people have suffered at the hands of mine. Sadly, Harold appears to be eluding those who might hunger for a little English blood."

"Aye, it does seem as if my countrymen are suffering a plague of restraint, curse them. E'en those border rogues let him be. If I had kenned that, I would ne'er have sent Nanty off as I did. Harold is moving more swiftly and with greater ease than I had anticipated. So, we must plan ways to thwart him, ways to deny him what he seeks e'en if he manages to get his filthy hands on ye and the boy."

Jolene waited for him to say more, to begin to put forth a plan or two, but he remained silent, watching her closely. She glanced at the other men only to see that they, too, watched her closely. It was as if they all knew something she did not and that annoyed her. The men had obviously discussed other plans at some point in their journey and neglected to share them with her. Since this trouble intimately involved her, that seemed grossly unfair. In their great manly wisdom, they probably decided such secrecy was necessary to protect her delicate female sensibilities, she thought crossly.

"Well? Do you intend to share this plan, or plans, with me?" she asked finally.

"Mayhap we should wait until the morning," said Sigimor, "after ye have rested."

Taking a deep, slow breath to calm her rising temper, Jolene smiled sweetly at him. "Tell me now."

He did love her temper, Sigimor mused, as he fought the urge to grin. Women rarely stood firm against him or showed him their displeasure. It saddened him, but many women found him imposing, even frightening. A lot of men did as well, but he considered that a good thing. Not this little Englishwoman, however. She did not hesitate to give him a look that clearly said she would like to beat him senseless when he goaded her. Sigimor suspected a lot of men would think him half mad, but he found that intensely attractive.

"I truly think it might be best to wait until the morrow when your head isnae so clouded by exhaustion."

"The only thing my head is clouded with at the moment is a rising fury. Tell me now. Please," she added in an attempt at courtesy which was utterly ruined by the way she spat the word out from between tightly clenched teeth.

Sigimor shrugged. "As ye wish. The plan is—ye and I will marry."

Chapter Seven

"I beg your pardon?"

"Ye and I will marry as soon as I can find a priest."

He did not look insane, Jolene thought as she struggled to break free of her shock. Yet, something had to have disordered his wits for him to say such a mad thing. Worse, he said it in much the same tone he might use to ask someone to pass the salt. Ask? He had not *asked*, he had stated it as if it was an already agreed-to fact.

Beneath her shock stirred anger, an anger roused by a hurt she did not really understand. Jolene told herself it was just pinched vanity, ignoring the voice in her head that heartily scoffed at that pathetic explanation. There was no romance here. It was more a battle maneuver, something meant to block Harold. Later, she might consider it a most gallant gesture, but, at the moment she saw it as no better than being offered marriage for her lands or her dowry or her bloodlines. A sharp distaste for such alliances was one reason she was still a maid at three and twenty.

"That is quite unnecessary," she said, "and I do not see the need for it."

"Nay? Harold seeks to marry you. Tis one of the reasons he is chasing us."

"Aye—*one* of the reasons. Marrying me will not make him turn back."

"It will protect ye if he gains hold of ye again. He cannae force ye to wed with him. E'en a priest eager for coin will hesitate to join a mon with a lass who already claims a husband."

"A marriage between us may not be legal in England."

"A mon of the church will feel compelled to make certain of that, especially if we are wed by a priest. So will Harold if he has plans to breed heirs to keep Drumwich in his grasp e'en after he is dead."

All he said was true, but Jolene shook her head. She was not exactly sure what she was denying— that truth or the inexplicable urge to fall in with his plan. Although she had always wanted a husband, a home of her own, and children, she needed more than he offered, more than a union formed only to thwart Harold's plans. The fact that she was so strongly drawn to Sigimor made that *more* of an even greater necessity. Jolene could all too easily forsee a bleak future where her emotions grew and deepened while his never did.

Bleak, painful, and full of bitterness, she mused. She had seen what happened when one person in a marriage loved and the other did not. Her family was riddled with such marriages. Her own mother had become a hard, bitter woman after years of loving Jolene's father, a man who could not give her what she needed. It was one reason Jolene had wished to have some choice in a husband. There was still the chance of failure and heartbreak when one chose one's own mate, but, she had always hoped, not so great a one. From all she had seen, marriages made for money, land, or alliances rarely proved to be happy ones. She doubted a marriage made to annoy one's enemy would be any different.

"Nay, 'tis a bad plan," she said, then gasped softly when Sigimor stood up and pulled her to her feet to stand beside him.

"We need to talk about this," he said.

"I thought we were talking about it. I do believe I heard myself say *nay*."

Jolene cursed softly as Sigimor ignored her and strode toward the surrounding wood, tugging her along behind him. Obviously the man did not know how to accept a simple *nay*. He was going to try to talk her into an *aye*. The fact that he was taking her away from the others to do so made her a little uneasy. She could think of a few ways he might cause her to grow so witless she would agree with his mad plan.

She would be strong, she told herself. He could coax her all he wished, ply her with blood-stirring kisses, bewitch her with those beautiful green eyes, and seduce her with his fine voice, but she would not waver. Jolene reminded herself that she was a Gerard and they were famed for their resolve. Some unkind people called it blind stubbornness, but she felt that would serve her just as well.

A gasp of surprise escaped her when Sigimor pushed her up against a thick, moss-coated tree trunk. He placed a hand either side of her head and stared down at her. Jolene knew he could easily pin her in place if she tried to move. She tried hard not to meet his gaze, all too aware of the power of those eyes, but failed. It was terribly unfair that he did not appear to be so easily bewitched, she thought crossly. Using every ounce of will she had, she forced her face into an expression of calm disinterest and prayed he would not be able to perceive how big a fraud it was.

Sigimor looked into her upturned face, studied her cool, remote expression, and felt a stab of doubt. Then he looked into her wide eyes and began to relax. The turmoil clouding the silvery gray depths of her eyes was not easy to decipher, but it proved she was not as cold or distant as her expression implied. Jolene could not completely hide her feelings. Her lovely eyes were the windows to her heart and mind. He intended to do his best to learn what was reflected there. This time he would not be fooled, would not remain blind to what a woman truly thought or felt. Sigimor was determined to understand Jolene, or, at least try to get as close to understanding a woman as any man could get.

A little voice in his head told him that Jolene was no deceiver, that she was not a woman who would toy with a man just to feed her own vanity and pride. He intended to remain cautious, however. Everything within him told him she was his match, his mate, and did so more loudly and fiercely with each passing hour. For that reason alone, he would convince her to marry him, but he fully intended to be the one leading the dance this time. Ten years ago he had followed and found himself led straight into a humiliation that still stung. Although he could not make himself believe Jolene would do the same, he would force himself to remain wary.

"Ye have some objection to taking me as your husband, do ye?" he asked.

"Nay, not to *you,* but to your reasoning," she replied.

"And what is wrong with my reasoning? Harold seeks to tie ye into marriage, to use ye to tighten his grasp on Drumwich, and pull wee Reynard into his web. If ye are wedded to me, he cannae do that, now can he?"

"Nay, but he cannot do it if he cannot get hold of me, either."

"He already has once."

Jolene inwardly cursed. It was difficult to argue with such cold, hard logic, especially when all of her arguments were based upon emotions. In her experience, meager though it was, emotional arguments were either scorned or ignored by men. Anything based upon one's feelings, no matter how sound or reasonable, was considered unworthy of consideration. She did not think Sigimor would be quite so harsh in his judgment, but she doubted her words would sway him. Nevertheless, she would try. It might help if he at least understood why she said *nay.*

"Then we shall have to be very careful not to let that happen again."

"Lass—"

She pressed her fingers over his lips to silence him, then hastily removed them. It astonished her that such a hard man could have such soft, warm lips. It astonished her even more that that warmth seemed to have seeped into her body through that brief touch. Jolene quickly shook off her bemusement and forced herself to concentrate on this very important discussion.

"Did you not wonder why I am still a maid at three and twenty?"

"Ye said your betrothed died when ye were sixteen. And, Englishmen are fools. Everyone kens it."

A blush heated her cheeks at that gruff flattery, but she said, "That may be. Howbeit, I am not wed because I did not wish to be married for my dowry, for my bloodlines, or for reasons of alliances and politics. I certainly do not wish to be married simply to annoy Harold."

"Ah. Ye have your head full of fanciful thoughts of love, romance, and all that those minstrels caterwaul about."

"There is no need to sound so scornful. Why should I not wish to have my husband see me as something more than a full purse, a deed to some land, or a treaty signed?"

"Oh, I see ye as more than that," Sigimor murmured, looking her over.

The heat in his gaze as he surveyed her from head to toe and back up again made Jolene's toes curl in her boots. She had never experienced lust, but she was sure that was what was coursing through her veins right now. The man was able to stir that feeling inside her with an alarming ease. She prayed he did not know for she suspected he would take quick advantage of it.

"Lust is not a good reason to marry, either. Lust can be a fleeting thing, but marriage is forever."

"Lass, I owed a blood debt to your brother. I couldnae repay it, could I? So, I will do so by keeping ye and the laddie safe, by making Harold pay for his crimes, and by seeing that Peter's son keeps all that Peter left him."

"There is no need to give away the rest of your life to accomplish that."

Sigimor frowned at her. "Give away the rest of my life? I dinnae see it that way. I am two and thirty.

Tis true I have no need for an heir, but I would like a bairn or two of my own. Need a wife for that since I want my children to be legitimate. Being that ye are unwed and dinnae have Peter as guardian now, I suspicion ye will be finding yourself married off once ye return to England."

The truth of that nearly made Jolene curse. A man would be named as Reynard's guardian and, without doubt, be given rule over her as well. Even Peter had begun to think that she should be married, that she had dragged her feet long enough, and had been considering arranging something. It would be the first thing a new guardian would do. What Sigimor was unaware of was that she was an heiress. There was a very good chance that the king himself would grab control of her and her dowry in order to marry her off to some court favorite or needy kinsman. It gave her chills just to think about it.

"Now, ye ken weel that I am nay after any of those things ye mentioned," Sigimor continued. "Whate'er dowry ye may have willnae be handed o'er to me, will it, and there isnae any alliance to be made. Since your bloodlines are English ones, they willnae gain me verra much here, will they?"

"Oh. Nay, I suppose not."

"Now, I dinnae mean to fail in keeping ye and the lad safe or in sending Harold straight to hell, but Fate can be a capricious thing. The mon already captured ye once and, if he hadnae been such an arrogant fool, could have had ye half the way to England by now. Aye, and wedded, and bedded." He nodded when she paled. "By wedding me ye can end that threat, or, at the verra least, weaken it. Twill also give me the right, by the laws of both of our countries, to chase the bastard straight into the halls of Drumwich if need be."

He watched her closely as she thought over all he had said. Sigimor hoped some of those less encouraging emotions he saw flash across her very expressive face were stirred by thoughts of Harold and not him. As he idly toyed with a thick curl of her hair that had slipped the bounds of her braid, he thought about what other arguments he could use if she still hesitated. He would talk all night if he had to. This woman was his match. The moment he had thought her lost to Harold, he had lost all doubt of that. Since he was sure he would sound like a fool if he told her he wanted to marry her because she felt *right,* he would have to convince her that it was a logical, practical thing to do. If all else failed, he could always seduce her, he mused, and smiled faintly in pleasure at the thought.

Jolene wondered what amused the man. From where she stood, there was nothing to be amused about. He had weighed her down with arguments there was no disputing. Harold intended to marry her to help him complete his theft of Drumwich, so she should take that weapon away from him by marrying Sigimor. Practical, logical, and, she realized with some surprise, hurtful. He gave her not one word of love, affection, or passion. Since they had only known each other for a few days, it was foolish to think a proposal from Sigimor could be anything but practical, yet she wanted it to be. He was giving her calm reason when what she wanted, needed, was wild romance.

For a brief moment, she savored the image of Sigimor proclaiming his love for her, pleading with her in the most romantic way to make him the happiest of men by marrying him. Utter nonsense, she told herself, no matter how pleasant an image it was. Sigimor had not known her long enough to conceive some great passion for her. If he tried to claim such a thing, she would probably doubt his word. There was also the simple fact that Sigimor Cameron was not a man who possessed a sweet, flattering courtier's tongue. Nor could she see him pleading for anything. If she married him, she would have to accept the fact that he would never be the knight of her girlish dreams. He would not be giving her gifts of flowers, whispering tender words in her ear, or sitting by her feet singing her love songs. Recalling his singing, she decided that last was probably a blessing.

What was she thinking? She could not marry him. Being married because a man owed her and her brother a blood debt was nearly as bad as being married off by the king to please some court sycophant. Jolene decided she was letting his fine looks and the way he could make her feel steal away all her good sense.

"Nay," she said softly. "To be married for such cold reasons—"

"Ye think I am cold?"

"Nay, but the reasons you give for this marriage are."

"Then I will give ye another reason."

Before she could protest, he kissed her. She placed her hands against his chest to push him away the moment she guessed his intent, but she never even tried to hold him back. The minute his mouth touched hers, she slid her hands up his broad chest and wrapped her arms around his neck. At the first nudge of his tongue, she opened her mouth to him, shivering with pleasure as he stroked the inside of her mouth. She truly did like kissing this man, she thought dazedly. When he ended the kiss, she noticed that he had wrapped his arms around her, lifted her off her feet, and gently pinned her against the tree.

"Was that cold, Jolene?" Sigimor kissed the pulse point on her slender neck and almost smiled at the rapid beat he could feel beneath his lips.

"Nay," she gasped, then sternly told herself that she must put a stop to this. "You have proven your point. You may cease now."

"May I now."

He kissed the hollow just behind her ear and felt her tremble in his arms. She was so beautifully responsive. His whole body ached to continue this seduction, but he fought for control of his desire. Taking her virginity up against a tree with his men only a few yards away would not be wise. It would give him great pleasure, but he suspected the aftermath could be bitter. Jolene could easily see it as no more than him exerting his power over her to get what he wanted. Sigimor straightened up and slowly lowered her until her feet were back on the ground. He kept his arms around her even as she slumped back against the tree. There was a flush upon her cheeks, she was almost panting, and her eyes had darkened to a tumultuous gray. Those vivid signs of her passion made it even harder for him to rein in his own.

"There, now, lass. There is a fine reason to marry that isnae cold at all, aye?"

"Quite." She moved to pull free of his hold, but he did not release her. Jolene decided it would be too undignified to struggle, so she would relent, and heard an inner voice scornfully accuse her of lying to herself. "Howbeit, I believe I have already mentioned that lust can be a fleeting thing and thus 'tis a poor thing to marry for."

"Ye may be an innocent—"

"May be?" she muttered, feeling a hint of outrage.

Sigimor ignored her and continued, "but I am not."

"I have noticed that, although men demand boundless chastity in the women they choose to marry, they feel it quite acceptable to rut themselves blind until the wedding. And, sometimes after it as well. There is a word for that. I believe it is hypocrisy. Men—"

"Aye, aye, but we can have this argument later. Mayhap some night when we are warming our toes before the fire in my bedchamber."

The thought of being in Sigimor's bedchamber made Jolene feel quite warm. She shocked herself when she realized she was trying to envision him naked as they sat before this fire. She was certain Sigimor had bewitched her. It was the only explanation for how, in only a few days, she could change from a woman who rarely thought about men, to one who was trying to picture this particular man naked. Sipping wine. Perhaps holding her on his manly lap and kissing her ear. Jolene gave herself a sharp mental slap in hope of putting some scrap of wit back into her befuddled brain. This was a poor time to indulge in such scandalous thoughts.

Then again, she mused, perhaps it was exactly the right time. This man stirred feelings within her that were as intriguing as they were disturbing. She had endured a kiss or two before this, but they had only made her want to hit the man giving her the kiss. Sigimor's kisses made her want to push him down onto the heather and jump on him, even if she was not quite sure what to do with him once she got him flat on his back. If she married him, she could discover the answer to that puzzle. She could freely explore this lust he brought to life in her and it would even have the blessing of the church.

It was a mad idea, but she could not easily dismiss it. That annoying little voice in her head kept saying why not? She could not deny that she was fiercely attracted to the man and she had never been attracted to any other. He was a good man, even though he was quite rough around the edges. He was also handsome, young, and strong. Jolene doubted the king or whatever man was named her guardian would present her with such a fine specimen. She certainly did not want to find herself trapped in a marriage with Harold.

"Ye are nay heeding me, lass," Sigimor said, amused at how completely she had become lost in her thoughts.

"Oh." She blushed. "I beg your pardon. I believe you were about to entertain me with tales of your lecherous youth." When he scowled at her, she smiled. "Do go on."

"I think ye may be confusing me with that rogue Liam," Sigimor grumbled. "Howbeit, I have had enough experience to ken that what stirs to life between us is as rare as it is fierce. Neither am I fool enough to think it will always be so fierce. Ach, 'twould probably kill us in a few short years if it was. If ye think that I will then be sniffing about some other woman's skirts, ye had best think again. I will be saying vows afore a mon of God, e'en God Himself, and ye will be my wife. I dinnae take such things lightly. Nay, nor do I have a great need to be having any lass who smiles at me. Ne'er have really."

"You are saying you would be faithful?" She hid her surprise when he looked insulted by the question.

"Aye, 'tis what I just said, isnae it? If ye dinnae kick me out of your bed, I see no reason to go looking for another to crawl into. I ken that many men betray their wives and wives betray their husbands, but it has ne'er made much sense to me unless the marriage has gone as cold as a loch in February. My uncle was ne'er faithful, nay to any of his wives, and has bred himself an army of bastards, but he was ne'er happy. Few of these adulteries are matters of some great, blinding passion or undying love. Vanity, pride, e'en some game played, but most men babble on about a mon's needs. And I say, if the wife allows ye into her bed and it isnae a cold one, then your needs are taken care of, arenae they. Skipping about from bed to bed only causes trouble at home, which should be a refuge from trouble, and breeds bastards who often have a verra hard row to hoe."

Jolene blinked. This had to be the most unromantic vow of fidelty any woman had ever been given. There was also a hint of scorn in his voice when he spoke of great, blinding passion and undying love. Did the man possess none of the softer feelings?

Then she thought of all she had learned of the man from the others. He had become the laird at barely twenty years of age, but the loss of his father and becoming a father of sorts to all of his younger siblings had been only a small part of the burden set upon his shoulders. A fever had cut down many of the adults in the clan leaving him the laird over a large number of widows and orphans as well, many of them little more than babes. Sigimor had taken in many of the orphans and had never hesitated to help the widows in any way he could. She thought of how he was with Reynard and knew he had done far more for the children than give them food and shelter, had given them more than duty and a sense of responsibility. There was a heart in this rough man, and probably a very big one indeed, but he would undoubtedly grow as prickly as a hedgehog if she suggested such a thing. Jolene also wondered how good her chances were of finding a place for herself in that heart.

It would be a big chance to take, she mused, to try to turn a marriage made for such practical reasons into a true bonding. There were immediate benefits, however. It *would* thwart Harold's plans, and mean that she did not have to worry about being used by the king or some appointed guardian for their own gain. There would also be this lusting to thoroughly explore. And, if it all proved to be some horrible mistake, once Harold was defeated, she could return to England and seek an annulment. She was not sure if Sigimor had considered that possibility, and, for reasons she did not wish to explore too closely, she did not intend to mention it to him.

Sigimor gently took her chin in his hand and rubbed his thumb over her tempting mouth. "I am of good blood, my purse and lands rich enough so that ye will ne'er suffer want, I will do my best to see that no one and nothing ere causes ye harm, and I take my vows verra seriously." He gently kissed her. "So, will ye wed with me, Lady Jolene?" He kissed her again, a kiss that strongly hinted at his need for her. "Do ye nay wish to see where this will lead us?"

"Aye," she replied in a husky voice she barely recognized as her own.

"Aye to this, or aye, ye *will* marry me?" he asked as he teased her lips with light, chaste kisses.

"Aye. I *will* marry you."

He pulled her into his arms and gave her a kiss that seemed to melt her very bones. She was still reeling from it when he set her away from him, grabbed her by the hand, and started back to their camp. Jolene wondered how the man could go from hot to cold with such ease. There had been passion behind that kiss. She was certain of it. It irritated her that he could regain control so easily while she remained dazed and heated.

"We will be hunting down a priest on the morrow," Sigimor announced the moment they rejoined the other men.

Jolene had barely mumbled a few distracted thank yous for the congratulations the men offered when Sigimor dragged her toward the place where someone had laid out their bedding. "What are you doing?" She quickly looked for Reynard and found him fast asleep on his rough bed in the midst of all the other blankets laid out for Sigimor's kinsmen.

"Ye need your rest. I dinnae want ye to be too weary on the morrow."

Realizing why he wanted her well rested, she blushed furiously, but he was already walking back to his men. She removed her boots then huddled beneath a blanket as she stripped to her shift. Glancing at her plain, modest shift as she tried to get as comfortable as she could when only a blanket separated her from the hard ground, Jolene found herself wishing she had brought something more delicate, then cursed. The man turned her wits into warm gruel. Closing her eyes, she decided that it might be wise to think a little harder on what she had just agreed to.

"There is a priest but a half day's ride from here," Liam said as Sigimor sat down by the fire.

"Good," said Sigimor as he reached for the wineskin that was being passed around.

"Eager, are ye?"

Sigimor did not bother to reply as he took a long drink, his gaze fixed upon the slim woman he would soon call his wife. In less than a day he would have the right to crawl beneath that blanket with her. Eager was a mild word for what he felt.

Chapter Eight

Warily eyeing the short, round priest Sigimor was talking to, Jolene moved closer to Sigimor's side. Rousted out of bed when dawn was only a meager promise, they had ridden hard to this tiny village. As a result, she had had no chance to speak to Sigimor, although she had done a great deal of thinking. If she did not know better, she would think that Sigimor had done his best to make sure there would be no further discussion concerning the marriage. They would talk about it now, she decided, and tugged on his sleeve only to have him grasp her hand and keep talking to the priest—in Gaelic, a language she did not understand.

Odd, she thought suddenly. Why would they speak in Gaelic now when the priest had greeted them in what Jolene considered the Scot's own peculiar, and very attractive, form of English? Was Sigimor trying to hide something from her? She quickly cast aside that twinge of suspicion. Not only was it a poor way to think of a man who was doing his best to keep her and her nephew safe, but she could not think of any sound reason for him to be so secretive. He had asked her to marry him, she had said she would, and he was arranging that marriage with this priest. No need for secrets there that she could see.

What she could see a need for was a little private talk with Sigimor. No kisses, no pressing that fine, strong body up against hers, and no licking her neck. Just talk. Jolene had come up with a plan she felt he ought to consider. It was one that would satisfy his need to marry her to keep her out of Harold's clutches, yet insure that he was not tied for life to a woman he did not love.

Staring at the small stone church they stood in front of as she waited for Sigimor to finish speaking, she tried to strengthen her resolve. She just hoped she did not lose her courage in the end. It had taken a great deal of effort to decide to present him with her plan. A loud, somewhat hysterical voice in her head was crying out in shock and denial. If Sigimor did not hurry up and finish his talk with the priest, Jolene feared she would falter, that she would take what she wanted, never telling the man her plan to save them both from being trapped in a marriage neither of them had freely chosen.

Sigimor could almost feel Jolene's impatience, but he kept his attention fixed firmly upon his cousin William. What good was it to have a priest in the family if the man could not do what he wanted, he thought crossly. When Liam had told him that the priest they were riding to meet with was a kinsman, Sigimor had been delighted. He had forseen getting Jolene married to him and thoroughly bedded before her clever little mind could think of any alternative to his plan. Instead, he was wasting precious time arguing with a cousin who was proving to be inordinately fond of following the rules.

"There are rules that must be followed, m'laird," William said, then glanced at Jolene. "And she is English."

The way William stared at Jolene as if he feared she would turn into some warty demon right before his eyes was beginning to irritate Sigimor. "I did notice that."

"There are banns that must be called out, signed agreements from her kinsmen—"

"Her kinsmen are dead save for the fool chasing us with murder on his mind. Aye, and if he gets his filthy hands on her, he will drag her back to England and wed her. He will make her life a pure hell on earth for a while, then he will kill her. And, he will *not* be told he has to wait to marry her, either."

"Corrupt priests," snapped William. "England is ripe with them. Do not try to tell me this is all some noble gesture on your part, either. You lust after her. Well, you can just wait a few weeks."

"Or, I can throttle a priest in the next minute or so."

"Sigimor," Liam said sharply as he stepped up beside him, then gave William a friendly smile. "Cousin, it may be true that Sigimor's reasons are not all noble," he said in Gaelic, "but that does not change the truth of what he has told you. This Harold intends to marry himself to the woman to tighten his grip upon all he has gained by murdering her brother. Once he has removed the child from his path, he will certainly be rid of her. If she already has a husband, however, it will put at least a short halt to his plots. That way, if he gains hold of her, we will have time to rescue her. Come, are not two innocent lives worth a little bending of the rules?"

"But, rules are set out for a reason—" began William, although doubt now clouded his expression.

"Aye, to keep some rogue from grabbing an heiress and marrying her against her will. Such is not the case here. Sigimor will not gain much of anything from this marriage for her dowry will surely be held fast in England. Handfast will not protect her. The marriage needs a priestly blessing. Now, if you feel you must obey the rules, call the banns three times, just wait only a few minutes between each one. We can also write up a marriage agreement and we have witnesses right here."

William hesitated another moment, then nodded. "I will do it. I shall wait seven minutes between each calling. Liam, you can help me write up a marriage agreement," he said even as he started toward the church.

"Sigimor," Jolene said the moment the others left them, "I have come up with a plan. I have been thinking—"

"I was afraid of that," Sigimor muttered.

She decided to ignore that remark. "I do not dispute any of the arguments you put forth yestereve. Howbeit, this marriage need not be so final. If 'tis left unconsummated—" She squeaked softly as he started to drag her toward the apple orchard just behind the church. "Where are we going?"

"To some place that is private so that I may say a few things I dinnae want the others to hear."

That sounded ominous, Jolene thought, but did not offer any protest. If they were about to have an argument over something as private as consummating their marriage, she did not want them over-heard, either. Hers was a very good plan, but, when they stopped just within the orchard and Sigimor yanked her into his arms, Jolene strongly suspected he was not going to agree with it. She wondered why she did not feel dismayed by that possibility.

"Did ye really think that I would agree to nay bedding my own wife?" he asked.

It was a little difficult to maintain any order to her thoughts when he held her so close to him, but Jolene persevered. "Marriage, once consummated, is forever. We have known each other for but a few days and most of that time was spent running from Harold. We may not suit each other at all, but once we, er, share a bed, there will be no turning back." That was not exactly true, but she would rather face walking away from an unconsummated marriage than leaving a man she had been intimate with.

"Aye, I ken it. Why would ye think we wouldnae suit?"

"'Tis possible. We really do not know each other well. As I said, we have only been together for a few days and most hours of those days were spent on horseback. A fortnight from now you may well regret this most heartily. Why not wait a while ere you make this a true and binding marriage?"

"This is why."

The moment he lifted her off her feet, she wrapped her arms around his neck to steady herself. She opened her mouth to tell him to put her down and he kissed her. It took but one stroke of his tongue in her mouth and she lost all urge to protest. By the time he ended the kiss, Jolene was clinging to him like the most tenacious ivy. Even as she tilted her head to allow him better access to her throat, she struggled to regain her senses.

"E'en if ye refuse to marry me, lass, I will have this." He traced the shape of her small ear with his tongue and felt her tremble. "Aye, and I think ye ken it."

She did and wondered why she did not feel shamed by that admission. The rules were most clear. A lady clung tightly to her virtue until she was married. She did not stand in orchards and cling tightly to big, strong Scotsmen. Yet, she could not deny the truth Sigimor spoke so bluntly. Married or not, she would share his bed. She did not have the strength of will to keep turning away from what he could make her feel. At least if they were married she would not be sinning, she thought as he gently detached her from him and set her back on her feet. There was still that possibility of fleeing back to England and having the marriage ended there, she reminded herself.

As she met his steady gaze, saw the desire darkening his eyes, she decided to stop worrying about it. Why not grasp a little delight for herself? Why not savor the pleasure she knew he could give her for as long as she could? If the passion he offered proved to be a shallow thing, if there proved to be nothing else to bind them together, she had a bolt-hole. At least she would have some very fine memories to cling to if she had to return to her old life.

"Very well," she said.

The words had barely left her lips when he grasped her by the hand and towed her back to the church. A few sweet words or gentle assurances that all would be well might have been nice, Jolene muttered to herself as she struggled to keep pace with him. Sigimor did seem to be somewhat inept at wooing, except for his ability to kiss her senseless. She doubted it was solely due to the fact that they were running from Harold and that gave a man little time for a proper courtship.

Sigimor was just about to march into the church when the priest opened the door and beckoned them inside. Jolene was vaguely aware of the others standing behind them as they knelt before the priest. She felt a touch of sorrow over the fact that the only member of her family to witness her marriage was Reynard who was too young to understand the importance of the occasion. She also buried an attack of guilt as she said her vows, speaking the sacred words even as she held fast to the plan to end the marriage once Harold was defeated. Jolene tried to ease the fear that she was lying to God by telling herself she would only flee if she foresaw absolutely no hope of a good marriage.

Once the vows were spoken and the blessing given, Sigimor led her to a small table set against the wall. "Tis the marriage lines," he said and pointed to the bottom of the document. "Put your mark here."

Jolene nodded and began to read the paper.

"What are ye doing?" asked Sigimor.

"Reading this document," she replied, a little surprised at how simple it was.

"'Tis in Latin." Sigimor frowned at her.

"I did notice that."

Once over his shock that she was a learned woman, he felt a pinch of insult over how carefully she was reading the document. "There is nay reason to read it so carefully or do ye think I mean to trick ye in some way?"

"Nay, of course not, but Peter was always adamant that one should read a document most carefully before putting one's seal to it. He said that, no matter how honest the man, no matter how much you trust him, it takes but one error in spelling or one awkward phrasing to alter the whole meaning of the agreement. He also said that, although you and the other man may ne'er take advantage of that error, there is no trusting what someone else may do with it."

Her immediate assurance that she did not suspect him of any trick soothed Sigimor's pride. He also had to agree with the lessons Peter had taught her. The way both Liam and William had murmured their agreement told him he was right to think Peter's advice had been wise. She could not know how precise Liam always was in his writings. When she began to sign her name, he leaned over her shoulder to watch and his eyes widened.

"Jolene Ardelis Magdalen Isabeau deLacy Gerard Cameron? Wheesht, the name is bigger than ye are," he muttered.

"Mother felt compelled to honor a vast array of her family," Jolene replied. "Poor Peter was also so inflicted." She briefly smiled at Reynard. "He made sure his wife did not succumb to the same impulse. Reynard is named after his two grandfathers and no more. So, he is Reynard Henry Gerard. A few of our kinsmen disapproved, feeling that such a short name was, well, almost common. Peter would always reply that few would find it common when Reynard reached an age to add Earl of Drumwich after his name, along with Baron of Kingsley, which he already holds claim to."

Sigimor watched the little boy idly skipping around the men gathered in the church. "Tis a lot of weight the wee lad carries upon his shoulders."

"Aye, and it will only grow heavier for his mother's

family holds several other titles and, unless someone breeds a son soon, they shall fall to him."

"But Harold cannae claim them if the boy dies, can he?"

"Nay, for he holds no blood tie with the mother's family. I am not sure he knows of all Reynard might claim. It could change his mind about his dark plans for the child. As guardian, he would have access to whatever wealth there is within those estates. Then again, he may know a little about how important Reynard is to his mother's family for he was as careful to stop me from sending word to them as he was in keeping me from contacting any of my own kinsmen."

"Reynard's guardian will have to be verra carefully chosen."

"Aye, but I fear I will have little say in the matter."

"Weel, there is no use worrying o'er it now."

She nodded and watched Sigimor take the priest aside for a moment. It was a little difficult to accept that she was married. No rings had been exchanged and there would be no celebration. In a few minutes they would all be back on their horses to ride until the sun set. She was not even sure her wedding night would be spent in a proper bed.

Then Sigimor's brother and cousins encircled her, welcoming her to their family and helping themselves to some rather hearty kisses. Their good humor began to banish her confusion and that touch of sadness she had been unable to shake. Just as Liam took her into his arms and placed his lips against hers, she felt a strong arm curl around her waist. She yelped in surprise as she was yanked out of Liam's embrace.

"Keep your lips off my wife," Sigimor said as he took her by the hand and led her out of the church.

"I was but welcoming her to the family," replied a grinning Liam. "Tis an old custom to kiss the bride."

Sigimor made a very rude comment about what Liam could do with that custom. Jolene blushed even as she felt like laughing. Her new husband was obviously feeling possessive. It was no real indication of any deeper feelings, but, added to the desire he felt for her, it caused Jolene to feel a glimmer of hope for their future.

After helping her settle Reynard into his blanket sling, Sigimor set her on her horse, then took her hand in his and scowled at it. "A bride should have a ring."

"It matters not," she said. "With Harold nipping at our heels such things become of little importance."

"Ye will have one as soon as we reach Dubheidland."

He kissed the finger a ring should have been resting on, then strode away to his horse. Jolene inwardly shook her head. She never would have thought Sigimor would be troubled by such a thing, yet it was obvious that he was. And everyone thought women were difficult to understand, she mused as she nudged her mount into a pace to equal Sigimor's. As they rode, Jolene hoped that she could think of enough complicated problems to fully occupy her mind. If she was very lucky, she would not spend every minute from now until they halted for the day fretting over her wedding night.

* * *

Jolene stared at her new husband and tried very hard not to swallow her tongue. They had stopped in a village when the sun had only just begun to set. Sigimor had been very efficient in getting them a room, a bath, and a meal, as well as in enlisting his brother Tait to care for Reynard for the night. They had bathed and eaten their meal, then she had undressed to her shift and climbed into bed. Now Sigimor stood beside the bed prepared to join her beneath the covers and he was completely naked.

She was not sure where to look. There was an awful lot of Sigimor to see. Having never seen a fully naked man before, she did feel curious, but that did little to soothe her nerves. This particular naked man was about to climb into bed with her and consummate their marriage. Jolene dearly wished she knew exactly how that was done. She had the feeling it concerned that rather large protrusion at his groin and she found that thought a little alarming.

He was beautiful though, she admitted as she looked him over while carefully avoiding his groin. All taut, smooth muscle and a well-proportioned body. There was very little hair upon his broad chest. A small feathering of dark red curls there, then a little line of hair starting at his navel and leading down to a thick nest of curls around that protrusion. She quickly looked at his long, well-shaped legs and noted the rather light covering of hair on them. Jolene forced her gaze back to his groin and blushed furiously. It had not seemed quite so intimidating when she had felt it pressed against her as they had embraced, but then they had been fully clothed. Surely men did not walk about with it like that all the time? She was certain she would have noticed it before if they did.

Sigimor sighed even as he felt himself harden even more beneath Jolene's gaze. He had known she was a virgin and that he would have to move slowly and gently when he bedded her. It was apparant, however, that she was also a highly sheltered virgin. He had the sinking feeling he might even have to explain what was about to happen. That could require a great deal more patience and delicacy than he possessed. The prize was worth it, he told himself firmly as he slipped into bed beside her.

"What is this?" he asked as he began to unlace her shift.

"A shift," she replied. "Something a woman wears beneath her gown. You claim some worldly experience. Did you ne'er take off—" She was unable to finish for he was pulling her shift over her head.

"A wife doesnae need to wear her shift to bed," he said as he tossed it aside. "Wives come to their husband's bed naked."

"Then why do some women spend coin on night shifts trimmed with lace and ribbons?" she demanded.

"I have ne'er understood that. To let their mon ken they are interested, I suppose. Then, they both get naked."

Jolene found it all rather astonishing. She was lying in bed, naked, with a very large, naked man and she was trying hard not to giggle. Sigimor was being outrageous and the gleam in his eyes told her he knew it. She refused to encourage him by laughing.

"Lass," he said quietly, and brushed a kiss over her mouth, "I willnae hurt ye." He grimaced slightly.

"Weel, mayhap a wee bit, but 'tis as nature intended. I can do naught about that. Howbeit, 'tis only the first time. Do ye understand?"

"Not one word." He looked so dismayed she had to smile. "I am sorry. I think, mayhap, I was kept very, very sheltered. Since I was ne'er close to being wed, no woman was sent to tell me what happens in the marriage bed. I think the best solution may be for you to just set about it. I will follow where you lead."

"That sounds a fine plan."

Sigimor wanted to just look at her, to study and savor the sight of her slim body. He wanted to taste that soft, pale skin from her lips to her toes and back up again. There were a lot of things he had dreamed of doing once he got her into his bed, but fulfilling those dreams would have to wait. This time he would have to bow to her innocence, would have to be as mindful of her modesty as he was of the need to stir her passion. He could only hope that he could stir her passion until it was hot enough to make the breaching of her maidenhead of little consequence.

He kissed her and kept on kissing her until she was clinging to him. Sigimor silently thanked God that his little wife was so responsive, that her blood was so quickly heated by his kisses, and he took ruthless advantage of that. Slowly, he began to caress her, giving her another kiss whenever he sensed even a hint of tension in her body. By the time he judged her ready for the next step, he was praying that he could find yet another thing that stirred her passion swiftly and fiercely for he was not sure how long he could play this game.

Jolene threaded her fingers through his thick, soft hair as he kissed his way toward her breasts. She was surprised that such a big man with such strong hands could have as gentle a touch as Sigimor had. There did not seem to be a single part of her body that did not tingle from the stirring warmth of his caresses. A few parts ached and she knew it was because they too craved his touch. When he licked the spot between her breasts as he stroked them, lightly rubbing his palms over her nipples, Jolene heard herself make a noise that sounded very much like a moan.

"Sigimor," she murmured, hearing a plea in her voice, but not sure what she was asking for. "Should I ache?"

The feel of her soft skin beneath his hands, the taste of her upon his mouth, and the soft sounds of pleasure she made were pushing Sigimor to the limits of his control. He was not sure he was capable of having a conversation, let alone of answering questions, especially not after discovering that her beautiful breasts were so sensitive. Lifting his hands, he stared at the taut rosy nipples adorning her breasts, and felt a shudder go through him at this further sign that he could stir her passion.

"Aye, ye should ache," he replied, "as I ache. And I ken for what."

Jolene's eyes widened almost painfully as the moist heat of his mouth enclosed the hard tip of her breast. Her whole body arched up, seeking his. The feel of his tongue caressing that aching spot had her clutching at him. When he began to suckle her, she felt every tug of his mouth deep inside her. The gruff words of flattery and encouragement he muttered against her skin as he feasted upon her breasts were nearly incomprehensible to her passion-fogged mind, but they stirred her almost as much as his kisses did. She wriggled with delight as he stroked her belly. She tried to return caress for caress, but somehow he eluded her touch whenever she attempted to move her hands away from his back and arms. There was a fine tremor going through his body and the knowledge that she caused it only heightened her desire.

Then he slid his hand between her legs and her whole body stiffened in shock. "Sigimor?"

"Ah, my wee wife, 'tis permitted. Can ye nay feel how your *belle-chose* welcomes your husband's touch?"

Sigimor felt her open to him as he caressed her, and he slowly eased a finger inside her. It was almost his undoing. The hot, wet feel of her nearly caused him to spend himself on the sheets like some untried boy. He tightly grasped the fraying ends of his control and kissed her as he plied her with his fingers, seeking to prepare her for him as quickly as possible. He thanked God yet again that his wife was proving to be a very passionate woman.

Praying that he had judged her readiness correctly, Sigimor slowly began to join their bodies. He gritted his teeth as he fought against the painful need to just thrust himself deep inside her. The way she wrapped her lithe body around his was swiftly rending his control. He felt her maidenhead give before him and held himself still, allowing her body to adjust to his intrusion. So consumed was he by the need to restrain himself, it took him a moment to realize that her body had yielded its innocence rather easily, that she had only gasped softly and barely flinched.

"Are we done?" asked Jolene, sincerely hoping there was more for the ache in her body, that strange craving, was still there. "You said it would hurt, but I only felt a small pinch."

If he had the strength, he would have laughed. "Nay, not done yet. Ye are fortunate, wife. Your body's gates of innocence werenae locked verra tightly."

He began to move inside her and Jolene lost all urge and ability to talk. She clung to him, quickly catching his rhythm. Jolene felt all those aches and cravings he had stirred up inside her begin to twist themselves into a tight knot at the place where their bodies joined. Just as she was about to demand he do something about that, the knot snapped, sending waves of blinding pleasure throughout her body. She was vaguely aware of Sigimor pounding into her a few times, then bellowing out her name as he stiffened, shuddered, and bathed her womb with heat. Blindly she held him close as he slumped against her, his body trembling almost as badly as hers was.

She was still so dazed, she barely flinched when, several minutes later, he rose from her arms and then returned to bathe her nether regions with a cool, damp cloth. When he climbed back into bed and pulled her into his arms, she snuggled up against him. The way he stroked her back made her sigh with sleepy pleasure.

"Consummation was not the ordeal I thought it would be," she murmured as she felt the need to sleep creep over her.

Sigimor grinned and kissed the top of her head as he felt her body go limp against him. He was pleased beyond words that he had brought her such pleasure at her first bedding, but, not an ordeal? Breaching his little wife had been the most arduous, most exhausting thing he had ever done. It had also provided him with the greatest pleasure he had ever known. As he joined her in sleep's embrace, he prayed she healed quickly. His wife was soon to discover that he was going to prove to be a very greedy husband indeed.

Chapter Nine

Jolene woke up alone. She glanced around the bedchamber, but saw no sign of Sigimor. For a brief moment she wondered if she had dreamed the events of the day before, and the night. Then, as the last wisps of sleep's fog cleared away, she almost smiled at her own foolishness. A faint ache in her body was proof enough that not only was she really married to Sigimor, but she was well and truly his wife.

And, she should have awakened to her new husband's kisses instead of a cold bed, she thought a little crossly as she slipped out of bed and donned her shift. It was a fleeting annoyance, however. Good sense returned as she stepped behind a battered privacy screen to relieve herself and have a thorough wash. With Harold chasing them down, there was no time for whatever little niceties or coddling a husband might offer his new bride. Allowing her to sleep past dawn was gift enough, especially when she knew how determined Sigimor was to get them all safe behind the walls of Dubheidland.

Picking up her shift, she wrinkled her nose as

she caught the faint scent of horse on it, and decided she could not put it back onto her newly washed body. She quickly rinsed it out in the large bowl of water she had used to wash herself, then draped it over a small stool before the fire. Just as she started to pull a clean shift from her bag, she heard the latch on the door move and dived into bed, yanking the sheet up to her neck as Sigimor stepped in carrying a tray of food and drink.

"Ah, now that is what a husband likes to see," Sigimor said as he shut the door behind him and moved to place the tray on a rough, scarred table near the bed. "It pleases him to find his wife naked and waiting in bed for him."

A hint of anger stirred to life in Jolene, but was quickly banished. She was learning to look for that certain gleam in his eye when he said such outrageous things. It was certainly there now. She suspected there was a lot of truth behind his words, but she knew he said them to goad her and was waiting to see what she would do.

"Well, this particular naked wife is more interested in that bread and cheese you have brought her," she said.

"Aye, 'tis best if ye eat something. Ye need your strength." He set the tray on her lap.

So much for trying to best him at his own game, she mused as she helped herself to some bread, then nearly choked on it as he started to undress. "What are you doing?"

"Getting naked, too."

She took a deep drink of cider to wash down the bread that seemed to be lodged in her throat as she watched him shed his clothes. "You have no modesty at all, do you?"

"Verra little. Weel, enough so that I dinnae flaunt

meself afore the world and its saintly mother. Ye did notice that I dressed ere I left our bedchamber, didnae ye?"

"Very considerate of you. Of course, I suspect the women of the village are disappointed by your restraint."

It was difficult not to smile when she saw the faint hint of color on his cheeks. Sigimor's lack of modesty was obviously not due to vanity. He should be vain, she thought as she looked him over, ignoring the blush that burned her cheeks as she did so. Sigimor was a fine figure of a man. Fixing her gaze on his groin as he tossed aside the last of his clothes, she decided even that was not so shocking as it had seemed to be last night. This morning it was just slumped there, resting she supposed. Jolene was just deciding that nerves must have made her see it as far more imposing than it really was when it began to grow. Her eyes widened as it quickly reasserted itself, returning to the size that had both alarmed her and intrigued her last night.

Sigimor bit back a laugh at the look on her face as he hardened beneath her gaze. "Hold the tray steady, wife."

Shaking free of her fascination with his body, Jolene grabbed the tray as he climbed into bed. The linen sheet she had so carefully tucked up under her arms was yanked away as Sigimor arranged his share of the bedcovers over his lower body. Jolene was sure he had done this on purpose, but she felt her long hair provided her some measure of covering and fought back her sense of embarrassment. The crooked smile he gave her as he helped himself to some bread and cheese earned him as severe a frown as she could muster. He might not suffer from the pinch of modesty, but she could not easily cast aside the teachings of a lifetime. Jolene suspected many people would be shocked by the fact that she and Sigimor were naked in bed together, even if they were properly married. She began to think it was probably for the best that she had not been given advice by some matron before her wedding.

"When do we leave?" she asked.

"Later. After the noon hour," he replied. "I sent the lads out to see if they can find where Harold is lurking now."

Jolene had to smile over the way Sigimor referred to the tall, strong Camerons as *lads*, but then she began to worry about her nephew. "Where is Reynard?"

"With the innkeeper's bairns and David to keep a watch o'er him, and our backs as weel. David isnae as good at tracking as the others, but he has a fine eye as a guard. Tis oft said he can scent danger on the wind."

Sigimor rested on his side, propped up on one elbow, and slowly ran his finger down Jolene's spine. He smiled when she shivered and little bumps appeared upon her soft skin as if she was chilled. Moving to sit behind her, he grasped the hair trailing down her back and draped it over her shoulders. He kissed the back of her neck as he stroked her sides, pausing briefly to test the smallness of her waist. As he spread his kisses over her back and shoulders, savoring the taste of her smooth skin, he slipped his hands beneath her hair and ever so gently kneaded her breasts. Using his fingers and palms, he toyed with her breasts until the tips were hard and pressing against his hands, something that happened with a gratifying swiftness.

Jolene sighed a protest when he released her,

then blinked in surprise when he was suddenly in front of her, moving the tray back to the table. "Tis the morning," she said as he pushed her down onto her back and stripped away the sheet.

"Aye, and I have a fierce craving to see all of ye in the morning light," he said as he crouched over her.

The heat of embarrassment soon turned to the heat of desire beneath his gaze. She knew she was a small woman, lacking in the full curves men seemed to desire. Yet, the way Sigimor looked at her made her feel sensuous, desirable, even beautiful. She gasped with pleasure when he bent his head and kissed her stomach. As he kissed and licked his way up her body, she caressed his back and shoulders. Her breasts ached for his kisses and she heard herself cry out as he began to feast upon them. One night in his arms had turned her into a shameless wanton, she thought, in dazed amazement.

When he slid his hand between her legs to intimately caress her, Jolene flinched only briefly, then welcomed his touch. The feelings he stirred within her were both fierce and wondrous. It was also a little alarming for, although he was her husband, she had known him for just a matter of days. Then he slipped his finger inside her and she no longer cared how long she had known him. He made her feel wild and free with his touch, and she was soon arching into his hand, her body silently pleading for the joy it knew he could give her. Jolene realized she wanted their bodies joined again, wanted to feel him inside her, but she could not think of the words to say so.

"Such a responsive wife ye are," Sigimor said as he teased her mouth with short, nibbling kisses. "So hot, and wet, and inviting."

"You seem rather slow to answer that invitation," she said, her voice husky and unsteady. "You toy with me, I think."

"And myself, but anticipation makes the pleasure keener."

"I am not sure I could survive *keener*."

"Neither am I."

She cried out in delight and a touch of surprise as he abruptly thrust himself inside her. He pressed his forehead against hers and closed his eyes as he held himself very still. Jolene wondered if he, too, was simply savoring how it felt to be one. She wrapped her body tightly around his and he opened his eyes to stare into hers. The passion darkening the brilliant color of his eyes made her desire for him soar.

"Ye were made for this, my Jolene," he said as he began to move within her. "Ye were made for me. A perfect fit," he whispered against her lips, then kissed her.

The way his tongue moved inside her mouth matched the way his body moved within hers and it made Jolene crazed with need. She slid her hands down his back and clutched at his taut backside. With the arching of her body and the grip of her hands, she silently urged him to go deeper, to move faster, to do something to ease the ache growing inside her.

Sigimor felt her body convulse around him. The sound of her passion-thickened voice crying out his name, the feel of her heels drumming against the back of his thighs, and the way her tight heat clutched around him sent him tumbling into passion's abyss but a heartbeat after she did. He collapsed against her, keeping a little to the side so as not to put all of his weight on her.

The passion she gifted him with was astonishing. Despite how much he had desired her and how she had responded to his kisses, he had never expected the pleasure to be so intense or the satisfaction so great. He had certainly never expected her to respond with a passion as fierce as his own. When he had awakened this morning, he had begun to question what they had shared in the night, attributing the intensity of it to her virginity, to his knowing that he was the first man to possess her, and even to the days of waiting for that moment. Now he knew otherwise and his feeling that they were a perfect match grew stronger. Sigimor was just not certain if Jolene recognized the importance of what flared between them. He was going to have to give some serious thought to how he could make her understand the rarity of what they shared and what it meant, he decided as he slipped out of bed to fetch a cloth to bathe them with.

Jolene's body was so weighted with the lingering warmth from their lovemaking that she barely blinked when he gently washed between her legs. When he climbed back into the bed and pulled her into his arms, she sprawled on top of him. She was not sure it was a good thing that he could recover so much more quickly than she did. Although that could be because he was so much bigger and stronger than she, and more accustomed to desire, she could not banish the fear that he did not feel the passion as deeply or as completely as she did. When he kissed her and touched her, every part of her responded—heart, mind, and body. She hated to think that only one part of him responded, no matter how much pleasure that particular part gave her.

"I cannot believe we did that in the light of day," she murmured.

Sigimor grinned. "In the light of day, the dark of night, under a full moon, on the floor, on the table in my great hall, in a chair—oof." He caught her small fist in his hand and kissed her knuckles. "Ye worry o'er naught. I thank God now that ye didnae ken a thing about what happens betwen a mon and his wife, that ye didnae have some sour woman fill your head with nonsense that would ensure your marriage bed would be as cold and empty as hers probably is."

"Do you think that is what some of them do? It seems most unkind."

"And I may be unfair, but when I think of what some lasses are told, I cannae help but think I am more right than wrong."

"How would you know what they are told?"

"From my sister Ilsa. She got an earful when one of her friends was to be married. The woman instructing her friend felt that Ilsa should hear it all as weel. Said she would ne'er hear such sound advice from her kinsmen. Woman told her that we were all lecherous swine who would tell her lies if we told her anything at all. Weel, Ilsa didnae appreciate the woman calling us that, and she didnae believe we would lie to her about it all."

Jolene considered that for a moment and nodded. It was difficult for her to imagine what it must have been like for a girl to be raised with, and by what she began to suspect, was a vast horde of men. Yet, having come to know some of these Camerons, she could understand the girl's sense of insult and her certainty that they would not lie to her.

"So, she came to me and asked about it all," he concluded.

Lifting her head from his chest, she stared at him in shock. "She asked *you* about such things?"

"Who else would she ask, eh? I have had the raising of her since she was but a wee lass. Nine or ten. Aye, and ere that in many ways as her own mother died and my father's next wife wasnae much interested in the bairns other women had borne him. Truth tell, my father had poor luck with his wives. Buried four, and, although they were good at breeding, they werenae verra good at mothering."

"Oh. That is rather sad. Although I recall little of my mother, I cannot say that what memories I do have are particularly bad. She was more concerned with what my father was doing or not doing than with the care of me."

"Some women believe that is what nursemaids are for, aye?"

Thinking of women she knew and how their children were cared for, Jolene had to agree. "So, what was this advice that so troubled your sister?"

Idly stroking her back and enjoying the way his desire started to flicker to life again, Sigimor replied, "The woman got right what went where, and all, but nay much else. Since she was raised with so many brothers and male cousins, Ilsa wasnae as sheltered as ye were, ye ken. It was all else the woman spoke of that puzzled her."

Jolene placed her hands on his cheeks and stared at him. "I begin to think you are reluctant to finish this tale."

"Weel, I am nay sure I want ye to hear these rules. Ye may take them to heart."

"A bit late for that, I think. Howbeit, you have now roused my curiousity. What else?"

"No getting naked."

Since her modesty was so deeply set in her heart and mind, Jolene suspected she might have tried to obey that one, but, considering how much she enjoyed being skin to skin with him, she would surely have broken it. "Nay, blush though I do, I rather like being naked with you. Next?"

Sigimor began to relax, his fear that she would begin to think what they shared was wrong fading away. "No touching above or below the waist." He slid his hand all the way down her back and gently kneaded her backside, liking the way it filled his hands and especially liking the way she wriggled against him when he caressed her there. "It should be verra dark and one should remain beneath the covers. It might be best if she also closes her eyes so that she doesnae risk seeing her husband's flesh. A few kisses may be allowed, but she must keep her lips sealed as ladies do not allow the common, uncouth practice of using one's tongue."

"Oh, for heaven's sake," Jolene muttered, not even wanting to think of how much she would have missed if she had ever tried to follow such advice. "Just what *is* the wife supposed to do?"

"Endure."

Jolene shook her head, half in disbelief, half in denial. If that was the sort of advice that was given to new brides, it was no wonder so many marriages never became more than a cold alliance of wealth, land, and power. She briefly felt a little foolish for wanting so much more than passion from Sigimor. At least they shared that. Then, she inwardly shook her head again, throwing off that thought. There was no harm in wanting the richest union possible or hoping that her husband would feel as she did. Jolene was afraid that she already felt a great deal indeed for this man. It would certainly explain how he could make her feel so crazed with desire that, even if she had been raised with such restrictive rules, she knew she would have broken them all. She felt nothing but pity for all the women who had lived by those hard rules for, although their piety and modesty may have been preserved in the eyes of others, they had lost far more than they ever gained.

What the older women, those women who were supposed to be so much wiser, should tell young brides is how to hold fast to their husband's passion and respect, how to win his love. That was certainly what she could use some advice about. The fact that she was so anxious that Sigimor care for her, even love her, told Jolene that she was already caught tightly in his snare, even if she did not put a name to what she felt.

"Weel, lass, are ye feeling inclined to endure a wee bit?" Sigimor asked as he kissed her throat.

Pleased to be distracted from her thoughts, she hummed her pleasure as he nibbled her ear. "If I must," she said in a tone of voice worthy of a martyr.

"Ye did vow to obey me."

"I believe I mumbled that part, making the words as unintelligible as possible."

Sigimor was about to argue that point when there was a pounding on the door and David urgently called his name. He was impressed by Jolene's swift reaction. She was out of bed before he had even begun to push her aside and raced behind the privacy screen, grabbing her belongings on the way. Sigimor yanked on his braies and told David to come in.

"Harold is on his way," David announced as he strode into the room. "Liam, Tait, and Marcus just brought the word."

Cursing viciously, Sigimor began to get dressed. "How close is the mon?"

"Liam is readying our horses as the others grab our belongings."

"Go," ordered Sigimor. "The rest of ye take the laddie and go now. Ride for Scarglas. Jolene and I will meet up with ye there. I said go," he growled when David opened his mouth to speak.

Jolene stumbled out from behind the privacy screen still lacing up her shift as she heard David run off. "Sigimor," she began.

"Nay, lass, dinnae argue o'er this. E'en if we rush, we will be several minutes in the leaving. The fact that Liam returned and immediately started preparations to leave means that Harold is verra close. If the rest leave now there is a chance they can flee the village without being seen. There is no time to find out how near Harold is or why Liam is so urgent. I suspicion Liam's urgency is also born of the fact that Harold has *all* of his men with him now. If we are lucky, we, too, can leave without being seen. If not, we can draw Harold away from the others at least. Aye, he can weary himself and his horses chasing us about whilst the wee lad is brought safe to Scarglas. Harold willnae get round my cousins the MacFingals." He moved to help her finish dressing.

"Are you certain of that?" she asked, fighting her fears. "Harold has proven quicker and more clever than I e'er thought he would. Oh, I knew he had cunning and all, but I did think we could at least outrun him."

"And we will." He braided her hair as she laced up her gown. "Trust me about the MacFingals. There isnae the time to tell the tale now, but my cousins have learned weel how to watch an enemy. As for cunning, few can beat them. Wheesht, they could steal a body out of a coffin whilst the poor soul's kinsmen are still carrying it to the grave."

"I am not sure such a recommendation makes me all that eager to meet them."

Sigimor grabbed their belongings, took her by the hand, and started out of the room. "Aye, they can be a wee bit odd, but they are fine men for all that."

The innkeeper's wife waited at the bottom of the stairs and handed Jolene a waterskin and small sack of food. "Your horses are ready and waiting just outside of the kitchen."

"If the mon asks after us," began Sigimor.

The woman crossed her arms over her expansive bosom. "Och, as if I will be telling some puling Sassenach how to catch such fine, braw laddies. Get on with ye. That bonnie lad of yours has already paid me most handsomely. Off with ye now." She waved her apron, shooing them toward the rear entrance of the inn.

Sigimor pulled Jolene along at a near run, and she did her best to keep pace with him without stumbling. The horses were waiting just where the woman had said they would be. Sigimor secured their belongings to their saddles as Jolene mounted her horse. She braced herself for the hard ride ahead of her. She was a good rider and felt confident she could keep up with Sigimor. What she was not confident about was her ability to endure a long hard ride. Even after days of travel and the hardening she had gained from it, she worried that she could slow Sigimor down if they had to try and outrun Harold for too many miles.

After mounting his horse, Sigimor led her on a winding, stealthy route out of the village. She caught him carefully looking all around as they rode and she realized he was keeping watch for Harold and his men. It was as they reached a spot where the only choice left them was the road that ran straight through the village that Sigimor moved close enough to the road to be able to get a clear view either way. The soft curses he uttered told Jolene that he had been wise to send the others off ahead of them.

She edged up beside him, looked in the same direction he was, and almost repeated his curses. Harold and his men were not far away. Even if he had not had a dozen heavily armed men with him, he would have been impossible to miss. Jolene had seen enough of Scotland and its people to know that Harold proclaimed himself a stranger in both his manner and his dress. He also looked very, very English. Until her time with the Camerons, she never would have realized how clear the difference between the people was. In fact, if he had not had such a large force of men with him, Jolene was sure Harold would have been attacked, robbed, and, perhaps, killed days ago.

"Weel, we have no choice," said Sigimor. "We will start out slow, act as if we are but ordinary travellers or e'en villagers just going about our business."

Looking at the big man beside her with his colorful hair, Jolene had no doubt that the plan would fail. With her cloak to conceal her in so many ways, she might be able to slip away unnoticed. However, a six-foot-four-inch redheaded man was impossible to ignore or miss. Since Sigimor was not stupid, Jolene knew he was aware of how slim their chances were, so she silently followed him as he rode out onto the road.

"If the chase is on, lass," Sigimor said, "keep your eyes on me. Dinnae look back. Twill only slow ye down, and, mayhap, e'en cause ye to falter."

"Do you believe we can outrun them?" she felt compelled to ask.

"Aye. I ken this land far better than he does, or

any of the men with him do. He loses sight of us and he will have to slow to find and follow our trail. I also ken a place or two to hide if need be. If he doesnae guess that we may go to Scarglas, all the better."

Jolene did not have as much confidence in that last statement as she did the rest of what he had said. Harold had stayed close upon their heels with a remarkable tenacity. Since he had obviously learned where Sigimor lived, she suspected he had learned a great deal more about her husband as well, including the fact that Sigimor had kinsmen at Scarglas. She found herself hoping that Sigimor's kinsmen were as sly and dangerous as he said they were.

They rode along undisturbed for several minutes and Jolene began to think fate was smiling upon them. As if that same fate decided to punish her for such vanity, a cry went up from behind them. Jolene froze as she heard Harold bellow her name and then hurl vicious threats against Sigimor. She suspected Harold had recognized the Cameron laird first as, thoroughly wrapped up in her cloak, she was absolutely sure there was nothing recognizable about her or the plain cloak she wore. Pushing aside that inconsequential puzzle, she looked at Sigimor only to catch him making a rude gesture at Harold. When he caught her looking at him, he grinned and Jolene got the feeling that, in some ways, Sigimor was enjoying this.

"Stay close, wife," he said as he spurred his horse into a gallop.

As if she had any choice, she thought, spurring her horse to follow him and struggling to ignore the sound of Harold and his men chasing them.

Chapter Ten

The chill of the steady rain was beginning to seep into Jolene's bones. They had been most fortunate in the weather since fleeing Drumwich, although she suspected some farmers were ill-pleased with almost a sennight of no rain falling upon their newly planted crops. She supposed that, with her ill luck of late, she should be surprised that they had not spent the whole time knee deep in mud. The only good thing about the wretched weather at the moment was that Harold and his men suffered as well.

Her husband, on the other hand, seemed almost oblivious. He sat tall and straight in his saddle, the thick woolen plaid he had draped around himself the only hint he gave that he had even noticed how cold and wet it was. It annoyed her if only because she would soon have to tell him that she could no longer endure it, that she needed to rest, to get warm and dry, before she could continue. Her hands were growing too stiff with the cold to skillfully use the reins.

They had pulled far enough ahead of Harold to be out of sight, but she knew they had not lost the man. Every now and again she caught the sounds of pursuit. For Harold to continue on in such miserable weather indicated a frightening tenacity, and, perhaps, a touch of desperation. Her cousin might well share Sigimor's feeling that once they reached Dubheidland, they would be safe. Harold would certainly be at a great disadvantage then. Jolene hoped both men were right to believe the walls of Dubheidland meant safety for her and Reynard, if only for a little while. She would be in need of a rest, or in need of a place to recover from the lung fever she would probably contract after today.

She suddenly thought of Reynard and prayed that her nephew was safe. Harold might not be hunting the boy right now, but such dismal weather could be as great a danger to the boy. Jolene pushed aside her fears, knowing they were fruitless for she could do nothing for Reynard now. She also trusted the Cameron men to take very good care of the boy.

Peering through the rain, she saw that Sigimor had led them deep into the hills while she had been lost in her thoughts. She could also see that, if he did not go very carefully, they would soon be out in plain view. Even with the rain, she suspected two riders on a barren hillside would be visible. Despite a pinch of doubt over where he was leading her, Jolene said nothing, however. Questions could all too easily ring of criticism and he did not deserve that after all he had done to keep her and Reynard safe. He undoubtedly had a plan. She was just too cold and weary to guess what it was.

Sigimor signaled her to stop and she looked around as he dismounted, but she could see nothing except the rocky hillside. When he helped her dismount, she had to cling to him for a moment before her cold, shaking legs would hold her up. She wanted to curl up in his arms, but, since he was as wet as she was, she doubted she would find much warmth there at the moment.

"Ye will have to walk now, lass, and lead your mount," Sigimor said.

"The path ahead is too treacherous to ride over, is it?"

"Aye, tis a rough path, but twill lead us out of this rain." He kissed her on the forehead, then returned to his horse and grabbed the reins. "I am thinking ye will be pleased with where it will lead us. Tread warily. The ground is rocky and slick with rain."

Inwardly cursing, Sigimor led Jolene along the narrow rocky path. He cursed Harold and he cursed the weather. Jolene had made no complaint, not even after the rain had begun to fall, but he knew she was very near collapse. When he had kissed her, the skin beneath his lips had been icy cold. She was a lot stronger than he would have thought by looking at her, had proven herself so time and time again, but he knew she was at the end of that strength now. He was bigger, stronger, and more accustomed to such weather and even he felt chilled to the bone. His wife had felt dangerously cold.

He led them into a cave, the entrance well hidden by the curve of the hillside and a thick growth of brambles. The dark was nearly inpenetrable. Reaching into his saddlepacks, Sigimor extracted a candle and flint. Once he had it lit, he brought it closer to Jolene and looked her over.

She was soaked through to the skin and, even as he took note of that, she began to shiver so badly he could hear her teeth click. He was sure it was not just the poor light that made her look so ghostly pale. Knowing the dangers of such a chill, he felt a rising alarm, but quelled it. What she needed was to be put into warm, dry clothes, set before a roaring fire, and given hot food, but he could give her none of those things until they reached Scarglas.

Locating a small niche in the rock wall of the cave, Sigimor dripped some wax onto it and secured the candle in it. He then turned his full attention to his wife. Ignoring her muttered protests, he stripped her out of her wet clothes. Pulling a shirt from his pack, he used it to dry her off, rubbing vigorously to try to warm her. After dressing her in dry clothes, he wrapped two blankets around her and urged her to sit down near the candle. Despite her first attempts to protest his aid, she had succumbed meekly to his care of her and that worried him.

Sigimor led the horses to the far back of the cave and made them as comfortable as he could since he did not dare remove the saddles. He then changed out of his wet clothes. Although he dared not light a fire until he was certain Harold was not near enough to see any light it shed or smell the smoke, he checked inside the oiled leather sack tied to his saddle to reassure himself that the peat he carried was still dry. Unpacking his blankets, he hurried back to Jolene's side, sat down next to her, and wrapped his blankets around them both. When he pulled her into his arms, he was pleased to find that she was not shaking as badly as she had been.

"I hope Reynard is well," she said as she wrapped her arms around him and pressed as close to him as she could.

"The lads will take good care of him," Sigimor

replied. "Without the need to shake Harold off their trail, they would have ridden straight for Scarglas and ridden hard. I suspect wee Reynard is warm, weel fed, and safe by now."

"Do you think Harold will find this place?" Now that she was feeling a little warmer, Jolene felt her fears begin to reassert themselves.

"I dinnae think so. Tisnae an easy place to find e'en in the full light of day. My cousin Ewan showed it to me last year after the breach between our families was healed. It isnae always peaceful here and he wanted me to ken all the wee places a mon could hide from an enemy."

"Mayhap we should snuff the candle."

"Nay. Tis but a weak light and soon I will move ye and it to the back of the cave near the horses."

"And then what do you plan to do? You are not going back out there, are you?" She was afraid he might be thinking of risking his life in such a way and, she was ashamed to admit, she was also afraid to be left all alone.

"Nay, there is too great a chance of becoming separated from ye just when ye might need my help. I but mean to stay close to the front of the cave in the hope of seeing or hearing something to tell me where that bastard is now."

"I cannot believe he has clung so tightly to our trail. The moment the rain began, I truly thought he would give up, would seek some shelter, at least for himself. This is most unlike him. Harold hates getting wet or dirty. Always has."

Sigimor nodded. "Men like him dinnae like to dirty their own bonnie soft hands or muss their fine clothes. They prefer poison and slipping a dirk in a mon's back, or paying someone to do it for them. But, we draw near to Dubheidland. He kens he

could lose this game if we reach it. Aye, and he has
to fear that some of your kin may have learned of
Peter's death, of your flight from Drumwich with
the lad. He has the wit to ken that the longer ye
and the boy elude his grasp, the greater the chance
of finding your kinsmen are hunting him. He needs
ye and Reynard to shield himself against that threat."

"And he needs to be back at Drumwich to hold
fast to it. I doubt he fully trusts his men to do that."

"I doubt Harold trusts anyone." He stood up,
then helped her to her feet. "Come, ye had best
settle yourself in the back here. As soon as I ken
where that fool is, we may e'en be able to light a
fire."

"That would be nice, although I am much warmer
now."

"At least your teeth have stopped their chatter-
ing."

He secured the candle on a new rock, then made
sure Jolene was completely wrapped up in the blankets. At her insistence, he kept one for himself,
wrapping it around his body as he moved to the
front of the cave. Since she had ceased to shiver
and he had felt the warmth returning to her skin,
he was no longer quite so concerned about her
health. Now he worried about Harold finding them.
If he stumbled upon their hiding place, it could easily become a trap.

As he listened intently for any hint of Harold's
approach, Sigimor tried to think of ways he and
Jolene could escape if cornered. Although he could
think of many, only sheer, dumb luck would make
any of them work. They could not simply mount
their horses and make a run for it as the trail was
too narrow. Even though the entrance to the cave
was so slender only one man at a time, perhaps

two, could attack, Sigimor did not think he could hold out against a dozen or more men if they attacked with any real persistence, or one managed to push him back far enough to let the others into the cave. He was probably somewhat vain about his skill as a fighter, but even he found the odds of twelve against him a little daunting. He could not even draw Harold away from Jolene so that she might flee to Scarglas. Not only did Harold know Jolene was with him, but, considering her abysmal sense of direction, Jolene could easily walk right into her enemy's arms. She had done it once already.

Sigimor began to think he had made an error in judgment that could cost them dearly, then banished that doubt. There had been no choice. Jolene had been dangerously cold. She had said nothing, but her hands had felt so icy, Sigimor suspected she had clearly begun to have difficulty handling the reins of her horse. At least now, when they had to travel on, he did not need to fear that she would collapse.

The faint sound of harnesses jingling made Sigimor tense. He looked back at Jolene who appeared to have fallen asleep. He worried about that until he recalled how easily she could be roused from a dead sleep. Although he was not too sure she had completely woken those times he had pulled her from her bed at dawn, she had followed orders well and quickly, which was all that really mattered. It was probably for the best that she got a little rest, he decided as he turned back to face the front of the cave and eased his sword from its scabbard.

As the sound of men approaching grew louder, Sigimor silently urged them to keep on going. He inwardly cursed when the sound stopped only a few feet from where he sat. They were too close for comfort. The noise they made, as well as the sound of the rain, might not be enough to hide any noises his horses made and he could not go back there to try to keep them quiet. He was startled when he heard a man speak. His unwanted company was barely a yard away, obviously sheltering beneath a slender outcrop of rock there. Sigimor waited tensely for some hint of Harold's plans and any hint at all that the men had discovered his and Jolene's hiding place.

"M'lord, we must find shelter," said Martin as he huddled beneath a very small ledge of rock next to Harold.

"I know they came this way, Martin," Harold snapped, glaring at the water falling steadily from the ledge.

"They could be but inches away and we would still miss them. The rain is bad enough, but 'tis now sunset. What little light there was is fading rapidly. The men are chilled to the bone and weary, as are the horses."

"Weaklings, the lot of them. What about the two Scots? Those fools must be accustomed to this."

"Just because a man is accustomed to such weather does not mean he wishes to be out riding in it, or that he does not suffer from it. There is a small cottage back down this trail, at the foot of these hills. It looks as if it has been empty for quite a while, but it will offer us some shelter from this rain. We can pass the night there."

"Can we now? And what do we do when the morning comes? Our prey will be long gone and there will be no hint of a trail to follow."

"There is little to follow now save for the occasional horse droppings," snapped Martin. "And what does a trail to follow matter? We know where they are heading and we have men to lead us there."

"And then what? Lay siege to the keep with but a dozen men? And what of this other place those Scots said Cameron might go to? This Scarglas? Did you hear *all* they said about the men who live there? We will have no chance of pulling that little bitch and the boy out of there. Jesu, we may suffer if we e'en just ride by the place, simply continue on to this Cameron oaf's lands. There are some dark things said about those MacFingals and they are Cameron kinsmen."

"Do you mean all that idiocy about witchcraft?" Martin said, his voice weighted with scorn. "Rumor, no more. I would not be surprised to discover that the men of Scarglas let such tales fester because they keep people away."

"I, for one, do not wish to risk my well-being upon what *you* think. That was why I was setting such a hard pace. Curse it, I almost had her this time, her and that bastard with her. There was e'en the chance I could have captured him. His clan would have quickly given me the boy to get their lord back."

"You have been saying that you want him dead."

"Well, I did not say I would actually give him back to his people once I had the boy, did I? Or give him back alive? If I planned well, I could get all I want—Jolene in my bed, the boy in my hands, and Sir Sigimor Cameron in the dungeons of Drumwich again. And there would be no swift death for that interfering bastard. Nay, I would have him die very slowly. In fact, I might even be able to use him to make Jolene do as I say. He is her champion, and more, if I am to believe that cursed priest. I doubt she would be able to ignore his screams of pain for very long. That haughty bitch would soon be eager to bargain with me."

Martin vainly tried to wipe the rain from his face with the sleeve of his dripping jupon. "Why not just kill her? She will cause you naught but trouble. Jesu, Harold, no woman is worth this. You should have killed her along with the others right at the start. If you had, we would be sitting comfortably at Drumwich with both the boy and the keep firmly within our grasp."

" 'Ware, Martin," Harold said in a cold, hard voice. "You presume too much upon our long association. I am but one small boy away from being the earl of Drumwich."

"Fine, *my lord.*" Martin was too miserable and weary to fear Harold's anger. "Keep the bitch alive to play with, if you must, although I do not understand the why of it."

"Because she has scorned me once too often," Harold nearly shouted, "and I mean to humble her. I will make her my wife to secure my claim to Drumwich and fatten my purse, and then I mean to make her pay for every *nay* she gave me. I will destroy that pride of hers. I will use her body in every way a man can use a woman until she is bent with shame. Aye, I might e'en let you have a taste or two. I will make her bleed for each and every indignity she has caused me with this flight into these wretched lands."

Thinking of the things Harold had done to women in the past, Martin could almost pity Lady Jolene. "And if she has taken Cameron as her lover or more?"

"She will pay for that as well." Harold glared at the rain. "I know they are close, Martin. I swear I can almost hear them breathing. Howbeit, it now grows too dark. Where are my men?"

"Since you rode far ahead of them, I suspect most of them are still near the bottom of the hill trying to convince the Scots to lead them o'er this trail. Considering how long it has been since we left them behind, many of them have probably taken shelter." Martin peered through the gloom. "Ah, I misjudged them. They are just a few feet back, but they cling to the rocks as we do."

"If you cannot e'en see our own men behind us, then 'tis time to give up the chase. I doubt we shall have another chance like this so I best begin to think of ways to get at her behind the walls of Cameron's keep."

"Why not when they are at Scarglas?"

"If the chance arises, I will surely take it, but I doubt it will. Those Scots said the MacFingals have been surrounded by enemies for years and ne'er been beaten or had their walls breached. They did not say the same of—of—" Harold cursed, "whatever that redheaded fool calls his keep. I need to finish this and return to Drumwich ere those puling kinsmen of mine catch wind of what I am doing. They might actually find the backbone to try and find Jolene and Reynard."

"Do we watch for the Camerons at Scarglas?"

"Aye, for they are sure to go there. The boy was taken on ahead and they will seek to shelter him from this rain. We will linger near at hand to try to catch them as they leave there. Now, let us get off this cursed rock."

Sigimor listened closely to the men carefully making their way back down the trail. Despite having heard more than two men coming up the trail, he had briefly hoped Martin had been right to think he and Harold were alone. He had readied himself to slip outside and kill them, only to have to cast aside that plan. Although he was still tempted to take the chance that he could end Harold's threat on these rain-soaked rocks, he could not risk it. He felt sure he could have taken down Harold and Martin, and probably a few others, but there was no guarentee that Harold's men would flee if the man was killed. The plan carried too great a risk of his getting killed or injured and leaving Jolene unprotected.

He ached to kill Harold, however, and knew the urge would not fade simply because the man was now out of reach again. The plans Harold had for Jolene made Sigimor's blood run cold and he wanted to end all chance that the man might get his hands on her. Just the thought of that man touching Jolene made Sigimor's innards clench with fury, a fury that had become nearly blinding as he listened to Harold speak of all he wanted to make her suffer. For the first time in his life, he contemplated killing a man coldly, and in a way that would inflict the most pain. He probably ought to be concerned about such a feeling and his utter lack of remorse for it, but he was not.

When the sounds of the men's retreat had completely faded, Sigimor made his way to the rear of the cave. Jolene was still asleep and he was glad she had not heard any of Harold's sickening plans for her. She was still so innocent in many ways. He did not want that tainted by the sort of filth Harold had spouted. She had enough to fear and worry about already.

He sat down and slumped against the wall, his

gaze fixed upon Jolene's face. She looked rather childlike when sleeping, much younger than her three-and-twenty years. She was also beautiful, far too beautiful for a rough man like him. Too rich of blood for a minor laird such as himself and, he suspected, too rich of purse. He was sure it was only Peter's willingness to allow her some choice in who she married that had kept her a maid for so long.

It was too late to turn back now. He may have reached too high, but, now that she was his, he had no intention of letting her go. She was his mate in so many ways, from her wit to her passion. The way she burned so hot for him was a wonder he doubted he would ever become accustomed to. The times he had bedded down with a woman had not been completely cold unions where only he had gained satisfaction, but they were all pallid, easily forgotten interludes compared to what he shared with Jolene. He had never had a woman respond to his kiss or his touch as she did and he was determined to hold on to that pleasure.

Somehow he was going to have to bind her to his side in such a way that she would never even consider leaving him. The passion that flared between them was certainly one way, and he intended to work on those bonds whenever he could. Yet, if his sister spoke true, it was more than that which bound a woman to a man, more than the pleasures of the flesh no matter how sweet. According to Ilsa, a man could only truly bind a woman to him by winning her heart. Sigimor was not sure how one went about winning that organ. If conquering her heart required pretty words and the like, he was in trouble.

Pushing aside that puzzle when he saw that night

was upon them, Sigimor gently shook Jolene awake. The way she smiled at him as she woke, and the soft look in her eyes, made him eager to join her beneath the blankets she was wrapped in. He quickly banished that urge by reminding himself of the need to get her far away from Harold.

"We have to leave here now, wife," he said as he helped her untangle herself from the blankets and stand up.

"Did you find out where Harold is?" Jolene asked.

"Aye. For a wee while he was but feet from me." He took the wineskin from his saddle and handed it to her.

Jolene took a deep drink of wine to calm herself, beating down a rising fear. Sigimor was too calm for there to be any immediate threat from Harold. She was glad she had slept through it all, however.

"He gave up?" she asked as she handed the wine back to him.

"Aye." Sigimor took a quick drink then returned the wineskin to his saddle. "He and his men went back down the trail to seek shelter. The rain and the day's ending defeated him."

"Was that your plan?"

"More or less. That and keeping him too busy to go after Reynard."

"It must be hard for a warrior like you to do naught but run from your enemy."

Sigimor rather liked the sound of *a warrior like you*. It was good that she saw him as a fighter despite everything he had done since Drumwich. She obviously saw herself and Reynard as the reasons he acted as he did. They were, but many women would not so easily recognize that.

"Nay, it doesnae gall me. Aye, I would like a chance to fight, to end this game, but I am nay troubled by the tactics I have chosen. With the two traitorous Scots Harold has with him, the fight would be a wee bit uneven, aye? Fourteen or fifteen against six? Careful planning could win it for us, but, dinnae forget, my men arenae the hired swords that Harold's are. They are my blood kin. Each time I face a battle, I must consider the fact that, at the end of it, I may have to bury a brother or a cousin. That not only makes me think hard about the worthiness of a battle, but carefully consider *all* my choices."

"So, 'tis not just me and Reynard who hold you back?"

"Not completely, but my first thought is almost always where would I put ye whilst the battle rages? My second is to wonder what would happen should Harold win the fight. Tis why we race to Dubheidland, though, if I could find a way to reach the bastard and end his wretched life, I would do it."

Jolene nodded in complete understanding. "I have thought the same. I want him dead and I have ne'er felt such a thing before. That he would make me feel that way only makes me hate him all the more. Now I not only want him dead, I want to spit upon his grave."

Sigimor grinned as he handed her the reins to her horse and took up his own. "Tsk. Shocking. Is that what a proper English gentlewoman ought to be thinking?" he asked as he led her out of the cave, pleased to note that the rain had eased up a little.

"Nay," she replied as she followed him in leading their mounts along the narrow, rain-slick path. "Proper English gentlewomen do not think fondly of kicking hulking great Scots off mountains, either."

"Good thing, too. Without this hulking great Scot to lead ye, 'tis certain ye would get lost."

She really had no argument for that humiliating truth, so she asked, "Did you learn anything about Harold's plans?"

Too much, Sigimor thought. "Enough to ken that he has learned of Scarglas as weel as Dubheidland. We will still rest a wee while at Scarglas. My kinsmen will then have themselves a wee bit of fun turning Harold round in circles whilst we flee to Dubheidland. If Harold is fool enough to face us there, ye will soon get your wish."

"Which one?"

"The chance to spit upon his grave."

Chapter Eleven

"Jesu! She is English!"

Sensing that his wife was about to kick his uncle, Sigimor wrapped his arm around her shoulders and pinned her against his side. He could understand her annoyance. This response every time she spoke was getting tiresome. It was even more so when they had only just arrived at Scarglas and stood in the great hall in dripping-wet clothes. Sigimor glared at his brother and cousins who sat at the head table in the great hall grinning at him.

"Didnae ye tell them?" he demanded of them, not particular about who answered.

"Actually, nay," replied Liam. "We have only just sat down. When we arrived, we were hurried off to bathe, put wee Reynard to bed, and all of that. Took a wee rest, too, although David stayed awake to watch for ye."

"Weel, I am glad ye didnae allow your grievous concern o'er our fate to keep ye from having a much needed rest." The way his kinsmen met his sarcasm with wide grins made Sigimor want to hit them, but he fixed his attention upon his scowling uncle instead. "Aye, my wife is English. She is a wee, black-haired Sassenach. A wet, cold, hungry Sassenach."

"Aye, where has your sense of hospitality fled, Fingal?" scolded a small, fair-haired woman with stunningly beautiful violet eyes as she hurried to Jolene's side and slipped her arm through hers. "Ewan, see to Sigimor ere he starts pounding on someone," she called to a lean man with black hair who was as tall as Sigimor. "Come, m'lady. We shall tend to a bath for ye and some warm, dry clothes. It shouldnae take long and then we may all return here to have something to eat whilst my husband's father beats ye senseless with questions. I am Lady Fiona MacEnroy MacFingal, or Cameron, if ye prefer. Laird Ewan's wife."

"I am Lady Jolene Gerard of Drumwich, m'lady," Jolene responded as Fiona led her out of the great hall, then she grimaced and cast a quick, guilty look back toward Sigimor. Fortunately, he was busy arguing with the older MacFingal. "I mean I am Lady Jolene Gerard Cameron."

"Wheesht, dinnae look so fretful. Nay matter how married one feels, it takes a while to recall that one's name has changed."

Jolene quickly felt at ease with Fiona who led her to a room where a bath was already being filled for her. Explaining that she had had everything at the ready for her and Sigimor's arrival, Fiona helped Jolene undress. The moment Jolene sank into the hot water she began to feel better. She washed herself with the lavender-scented soap Fiona gave her as the woman saw to setting out some clean, dry clothes for her to wear. All the while Fiona talked about the strange history between the MacFingals and the Camerons, soon joined in that chore by an older woman named Mab.

"Here, Jolene, drink this," Fiona said as she handed Jolene a tankard filled with something dark and aromatic.

Cautiously, Jolene accepted the drink and took a very small sip. To her surprise it was very pleasant and she finished it as Fiona and Mab stood by nodding in approval. "Was that some special physic?"

After setting aside the empty tankard Jolene had handed to her, Fiona helped her rinse the soap from her hair. "Aye. Mab and I arenae sure how it helps, but it does seem to keep fevers and coughs away after one has suffered a chill and a wetting." She held up a drying cloth. "How long have ye been married to Sigimor?"

"One night," she replied and blushed when both women grinned.

"Weel, we willnae ply ye with questions here. Ye will have enough asked of ye once ye return to the great hall."

Jolene found herself efficiently dried off, dressed, and her still-damp hair neatly braided in a very short time. Mab and Fiona took turns telling her about the many MacFingals as they worked. If their aim was to help her relax concerning the coming meeting, they were only partly successful. She still felt a little nervous as they escorted her back to the great hall.

Sigimor, his hair still damp from his own bath, was waiting for her at the door of the hall. Jolene was not sure how he managed it, but suddenly he was at her side, her hand in his as he led her to the lord's table. She heard Mab and Fiona laugh softly before they hurried away to take their seats.

The moment Jolene and Sigimor sat down the questions started. Once she noticed that Sigimor had the admirable ability of being able to eat and answer questions at the same time without spitting food around, she left him to it and concentrated on eating her own meal. After the time she had spent with the Camerons, she was able to ignore the occasional lapses into arguments between Sigimor and his uncle. Lady Fiona and Mab had also warned her about the old laird's tendency to argue with anyone about anything. Considering Sigimor's apparent love of arguing, Jolene felt she would be able to enjoy a hearty meal before anyone decided to ask her a few questions.

She subtly studied the MacFingals, noticing that many of them studied her as well. Lady Fiona was quite beautiful even with the faint scars upon her cheeks. Her husband Ewan was big, lean like Sigimor, and as dark as Sigimor was fair. In truth, when placed so close to their dark kinsmen, the Camerons looked almost too bright. Lord Ewan was quite handsome in a dark, rather harsh way, with no hint of softness upon his scarred face unless one caught him looking at his wife. A great many of the men in the great hall shared those looks, although some had slightly softer features and some had blue eyes. The old laird had certainly been a very busy fellow, she mused.

It was all a little overwhelming and Jolene feared she would find Dubheidland much the same. The fact that most of the men in the great hall were Sigimor's cousins was a little difficult to grasp. Her family, on both her mother and father's sides, was small and most of her relatives bred very few children and even fewer sons. Many of her countrymen would be green with the sin of envy if they saw how well the Camerons bred sons. Tall, strong sons who, she had little doubt, were probably all skilled warriors.

"And ye havenae yet killed this bastard? What ails ye, lad?"

Jolene was unable to ignore the insult the old laird gave Sigimor and frowned at him. "He was thinking of keeping me and Reynard alive and safe," she snapped. "'Tis what he vowed he would do. One can hardly pause to engage in a battle with a woman and child close at hand."

"I dinnae see why not," said Fingal.

She suspected he did, but was just being contrary. "Oh? Would you have him tuck us up in a tree or the like whilst he had this battle?"

"Ye are just as impertinent as this lass," he said, jabbing a finger toward Fiona before turning back to Sigimor. "So, ye cannae just cut this bastard's throat and be done with it, then. But, did ye have to marry her to keep her safe?"

"It will certainly help," Sigimor replied. "E'en the Sassenachs would frown on a mon stealing another mon's wife. And, if he does get his hands on her again, he willnae be able to go through with all his plans, nay for a while, leastwise."

"But, to wed a Sassenach." Fingal shook his head. "Twill weaken our good Scot's blood, lad."

"I beg your pardon!" Jolene was getting very tired of the implication that Sigimor had committed some grave crime against his country and clan by marrying her. "I am the daughter and the sister of an earl. I hardly think Sigimor has lowered himself in the wedding of me."

"An *English* earl."

"Enough," Ewan said quietly, but there was an impressive note of command in that one word. "She is Sigimor's wife, thus one of our family now, and I will hear no more insults given her."

"I wasnae insulting her," protested Fingal.

"Ye were treading o'er some verra thin ice. I would prefer it if Sigimor didnae start feeling honor bound to kill ye, thus forcing me to fight him o'er it. If ye feel the need to rant against the English, go find the bastard who seeks to kill a wee lass and a bairn just so that he might claim what doesnae belong to him." Ewan turned back to Sigimor. "Ye havenae asked us to join ye in this fight."

"Nay," replied Sigimor, "and I willnae. Aye, twould be verra fine indeed if we could all ride out to meet him, sword to sword, then kill him so that my wife can spit upon his grave."

"Sigimor!" Jolene hissed in protest, embarrassed by the revelation of her unladylike sentiment.

Sigimor ignored her. "Howbeit, I decided twould be best to keep this fight between me and Harold. I have just cause for killing him, e'en more so now since he hunts my wife."

"If ye have just cause, then, as your blood kin, so do we."

"We cannae be sure the English would see it so. I had no time to study my enemy. I dinnae ken who his allies might be, if he truly has any, or how powerful they are. There could be an outcry when he dies here. If so, I must be the only one caught up in that tangle for I can claim several verra good reasons for killing the mon, ones e'en his allies will have difficulty arguing, e'en if they do have the king's ear."

"Ye fled England with an English lady and the heir to an earl's seat, Sigimor. Then ye kill the mon who came after ye to retrieve them, a mon who claims a kinship with them. Are ye sure your *just causes* are weighty enough to ease the anger that might arise?"

Sigimor nodded. "I hold the missive Peter sent asking for my help, one that makes clear Peter's fear of betrayal and his fear for his son. Harold threw me and my men into the dungeon, chained us, and was about to hang us despite the fact that we entered Drumwich with our swords sheathed and at the invitation of its laird. Jolene wasnae promised to anyone and is now my wife so I can certainly use Harold's attempts to take her as justification for anything I do to the mon. If he follows us to Dubheidland and continues his threats, that, too, is cause enough to kill him."

Ewan nodded. "Ye *have* thought this out weel."

"There is one other thing to consider. Jolene's kinsmen could always be called upon to speak out against Harold."

"Aye," agreed Jolene. "I have been hoping that, with Harold away from Drumwich, someone may have been able to go to them to tell them what has happened. None of them trust or like the man, but they all respected and liked my brother."

"So, ye willnae be allowing us to kill any Sassenachs, aye?" asked Fingal.

"Not unless they try to kill a MacFingal," replied Sigimor.

"Weel, I think we could come up with a way to make that happen yet nay put any of my lads in danger. Then, once swords are drawn, we can kill them."

Sigimor stared at his uncle for a moment, then looked at Jolene. "Mayhap ye best go and sit by the fire or the like. My uncle wants to argue about killing

Harold and there could be a few things said that ye willnae like."

Having finished her meal, Jolene readily agreed. "You wish me downwind from the insults that will soon be heaped upon the English, I suppose."

"Aye, wife. They could get fierce."

She just rolled her eyes and made her way to the high-backed benches arranged before a massive fireplace at the far end of the great hall. To her relief Fiona quickly joined her there. If nothing else, it eased the appearance of her being sent to a corner like a naughty child.

"Fingal just loves a good, rousing argument," Fiona said as she sat facing Jolene, "and Sigimor likes to oblige him."

"He would. I have noticed that the Camerons do seem to enjoy arguing. Sigimor can be particularly contrary at times. I have not known him long, but I have felt the urge to beat him o'er the head at least a dozen times already."

"Only a dozen times? He must be on his best behavior." Fiona shared a brief laugh with Jolene, but then grew very serious. "His sister is married to my brother Diarmot. I have kenned Sigimor and his family for a few years now. He is a verra good mon."

"Oh, aye, he is."

"And ye love the fool, dinnae ye?"

Jolene was so startled by what Fiona said, she blurted out the truth. "Aye, I believe I might, but it might be better if I did not."

"Why do ye say that?"

There was something about Fiona that made Jolene feel she could confide in the woman and, more important, trust her with those confidences. "I am English and 'tis increasingly clear that having an English wife is not something Sigimor will be praised for. I have only known him a few days, less than a sennight. Such a short acquaintance to risk a lifetime upon. Especially when that time has been fraught with danger, something I fear might well cause some confusion about what one might truly feel."

"I didnae ken Ewan for verra long before I was certain he was right for me, that he was my mate. At the time, we both had enemies, but it didnae confuse me that much about all that I was feeling for my husband. Most people would have thought me utterly mad to choose him for he was seen as a hard, cold mon. Somehow, I just kenned, deep in my heart, that that was simply the face he showed the world. It took time for him to believe in me and for me to find that hidden mon."

The message within Fiona's tale was easy to read, but Jolene was not sure it really applied to her and Sigimor. "I do not think Sigimor hides all that much of himself, although I do believe what he does hide is the very thing I want."

Fiona nodded. "His heart. In matters of the heart, men can be such cowards, although I would ne'er use that word to their faces. I ken my brother Connor was and so was my husband. E'en my brother Diarmot to some extent. The men shielded their hearts, their softer feelings, as if they were sheltering the king's treasure. Then again, to the women who love them, tis as rich a prize. Sigimor is akin to them in some ways, but I dinnae think the walls he has built are quite so high."

"Probably not, but the real question is whether or not he will allow me to scale them. And yet, it might be best if I do not even try. Failure might be worse than not trying at all. He married me to keep me out of Harold's grasp. Why are you shaking your head like that? You heard him say so himself."

"I did and I dinnae doubt his word. What I dinnae believe is that it was the only reason."

Jolene blushed. "Well, he did mention one other."

"Passion, of course. A mon doesnae have to take a wife to find that." Fiona smiled at the boy who brought them each a tankard of mulled cider and sipped at hers until she was certain he was out of hearing distance again. "As I said, a mon doesnae marry a lass just because he is lusting after her. He either finds himself some willing lass to ease the need or he seduces the one he really wants. And, if Sigimor didnae want ye as his wife, but still felt ye were in need of a husband to protect ye from Harold, he would have tried to have one of his brothers or cousins marry ye. Nay, he wanted ye for his wife. The hard part will be in trying to find out the *whys* he isnae telling ye."

As she sipped her drink, Jolene thought over all Fiona had said. There did seem to be the hint of more than passion and a sense of duty within Sigimor. He had shown distinct signs of possessiveness, even jealousy. He also worried about her and saw to her care in ways that surely went beyond simple duty. She sighed, realizing that she was grasping at any reason to believe he had some strong feeling for her. That was a dangerous path to tread, full of pitfalls.

"I do not know what to think," she finally said. "I also cannot forget Reynard's importance in all of this."

"Ah, aye, the boy." Fiona smiled briefly. "A fine lad. He is bedded down with all the other young lads, mine and some of the brothers' children. Tis a weighty responsibility ye carry. I ken ye will be faced with some verra hard choices once Sigimor ends the threat Harold poses."

That was something Jolene was trying hard not to think about only to realize that that was not only foolish, it was cowardly. Those hard choices would not miraculously disappear simply because she tried to ignore them. The sensible thing would be to keep them to the forefront of her mind, to accept that everything she did now would affect them. Once she made her choice, there would be no turning back, and it would be best to gain as much knowledge as possible before that time came. The reasons to stay with Reynard were clear. The reasons to stay with Sigimor were not. Not yet.

"Is there someone ye would trust to raise the lad, someone who would care for him as if he were his own bairn?" Fiona asked.

Jolene immediately thought of her cousin Roger and his wife. "Aye, but I cannot be sure the guardianship of the boy would fall to him. My cousin Roger and his wife are young, but childless after ten years of marriage. Roger and my brother were also very close. He is a good, honest man as well. 'Tis just that our king may take a hand in the choosing of a guardian."

"Bah, kings." Fiona rolled her eyes. "Meddling where there is no need. Indeed, that could be a problem. Ye can be fair sure the king willnae think only of the child when he makes his choice. Didnae your brother e'er set down his preferences?"

"I suspect he did, but Harold has probably gotten rid of all such documents since he would not want anyone to see them and use them against him. The best I can hope for is that one of my kinsmen whom I like and respect has the ear of the king, but I do not know who might have that sort of power. If there is one, I do not think Harold knows him, either." Jolene shook her head and took a deep drink of her cider to quell the sudden urge to cry. "Tis too much to sort through, I fear. Too many uncertainties."

Fiona reached over and patted the hand Jolene had clenched tightly in her lap. "Aye, I suspicion there are, and pleased I am that I have ne'er had to face such choices. Now, myself, I would cast aside my worries about Reynard. Ye ken what he needs and what he must do. The only uncertainty there is who will be standing at his side. Ye cannae do anything about it now, mayhap ever, so set it aside. Simply pray that whate'er mon steps forward is one ye want and wee Reynard needs."

"Very reasonable," Jolene said, duly impressed. "Do you know, I used to be a reasonable person, too, but reason and calm good sense have abandoned me of late."

"The curse of love, I fear. Love enters your heart and your wits leak right out your ear." She shared a laugh with Jolene. "Ah, and that time when one doesnae ken if one has any hope of *being* loved is the worst. The second part of what I wish to say is that ye must now fix your thoughts upon your husband. Ye must decide what ye want from him, then look closely to see if ye have any chance of gaining the prize."

"And how do I gain that prize? What did you do?"

"I loved him. Simple, aye? There really isnae anything else ye can do. All else tastes a wee bit too much like trickery and trying to change yourself to better suit what ye think the fool might like is also fraught with peril."

Simple, indeed, thought Jolene, if one did not

have the restrictions she did. There was Reynard to consider. Even if she approved the one chosen to be his guardian, could she really turn away from the child? Knowing that some day Peter would marry again, Jolene had tried to hold fast to being just Reynard's aunt, not allowing the boy to think that she was his mother or ever could be, but the bonds between them were strong. He was just a small child who had already suffered so much, losses he probably did not fully understand. Could she really ask him to suffer yet another? Fiona was right to say she could do nothing about it now, but she doubted she could completely stop worrying about it.

In many ways the question of Reynard's future had a lot to do with her future with Sigimor. She did want more than passion and duty from him, but would it be fair to try and get it? Knowing that she had won a place in Sigimor's heart, could actually have the sort of marriage she had always wanted, would indeed be wonderful. Yet, when she still might have to leave him in order to stay with Reynard, Jolene could not help but think it might also be cruel. Watching Sigimor and Ewan walking toward her and Fiona, Jolene knew she was already doomed to suffer heartache if she chose to remain with Reynard. It did not seem fair to try to win Sigimor's love only to make him suffer the same pain.

"Ye are looking verra serious, wife," Sigimor said as he sat down beside her on the bench and draped his arm around her shoulders.

"We were discussing all her troubles," said Fiona. "Och, the greed of men has e'er been a source of woe."

"If ye didnae want me to ken what ye were talking about, ye could have just said so," Sigimor drawled. "Although I must admit that was a finely worded diversion." He grinned when both women glared at him.

"Ewan, Sigimor just called me a liar," Fiona said, frowning at her grinning husband. "Ye should be defending my honor."

"Sigimor, dinnae call my wife a liar," Ewan said dutifully.

"E'en when she is telling lies?" Sigimor asked.

"Aye, e'en then. Ye should just smile and pretend ye believe her. 'Tis what I do. Ye are a husband now. Tis best if ye learn these things."

"What I am learning now is that ye are but one word away from being soundly beaten."

The way Fiona was scowling at her husband nearly made Jolene laugh. She felt envious of the open affection between the pair. They were the perfect example of what she wanted in her own marriage. Feeling the weight of Sigimor's arm around her shoulders and the idle caress of his hand on her arm, she wondered if they would ever gain that special bond Ewan and Fiona so obviously shared. Just love him, Fiona said. Jolene was not sure it was that easy.

"Ah, lad, there was something I needed to tell ye," said Fingal as he walked over to stand in front of Sigimor. "There was a woman asking after ye, oh, twa days ago, I believe. She sought shelter here for the night. Lady MacLean?"

"That name doesnae sound familiar," Sigimor said, although he felt an unpleasant memory twitch to life inside of him.

"Lady Barbara MacLean? She said she used to

be a Forbes. Aha, I can see that ye recall her now. She said ye would."

"Aye, from years ago whilst I was nay much more than a lad. I dinnae ken why she should be asking after me."

"Got curious when she heard we were kin to the Camerons of Dubheidland."

"Naught but trying to make pleasant conversation o'er a meal, I suspect, and we all ken how difficult that can be," said Fiona as she stood up. "But, 'tis late, and Lady Jolene has had a verra long day. Come, Jolene. I will show ye where Reynard sleeps, then show ye to your bedchamber." She held out her hand.

Jolene had no choice but to take it and let the woman lead her away. "Why can I not stay and find out who this woman is and just why she is asking after Sigimor?" she asked as Fiona led her up the narrow stairs to the bedchambers.

"Poor Sigimor was stunned by the news, Jolene. 'Tis best to wait until he isnae."

"You mean until he can think of a good answer."

"Aye, in a way. Dinnae think he will lie. He willnae. But, with men like Sigimor, 'tis sometimes best to give them a few minutes to set their thoughts in order. Here is where young Reynard sleeps."

Biting back all the questions she had, Jolene quietly followed Fiona into a large chamber with at least a dozen children in it. She smiled faintly as she watched her nephew sleep for a few minutes, before looking at the older boy Fiona called her son. It was not until they left the room that Jolene fully grasped the fact that the boy Ciaran was too old for Fiona to truly be his mother. She was still struggling with a way to politely gain an answer to that puzzle when Fiona answered the questions Jolene dared not ask.

"Ciaran is my husband's son, born of a woman he kenned weel nine years ago."

"You are trying to give me a lesson I think. Unfortunately, my mind has fixed itself upon one thing. Or, rather, one name."

Fiona laughed as she nudged Jolene into a large bedchamber warmed by a big fireplace, animal skin rugs, and thick tapestries. "I understand. I had the same problem only mine was named Helena, Ciaran's mother." Fiona walked over to the big bed that dominated the room and pointed to a night shift laid out on top of it. "This is your answer."

Jolene touched the finely woven linen which felt as soft as silk. "This is what a woman wears to tempt a man. Tis not what I thought to greet my husband with."

"I ken it, but a club laid upside his head will just annoy Sigimor." She laughed with Jolene. "Nay, put this on to greet him when he slinks in. Tis good to remind a mon of all he has now when something from his past slithers up to try and tempt him. Ye will get the answers ye seek and, if there is any warm or fond memories tickling his tiny mon's mind, ye will heartily banish them. And, may I suggest that ye stand by the fireplace as ye begin this interrogation?"

Knowing full well that would make her body clearly visible through the thin linen, Jolene tsked. "You are shameless."

"Aye."

"And very clever." She met Fiona's smile with one of her own, one she knew was just as smug and faintly lecherous as Fiona's.

Chapter Twelve

"I suppose ye would kill me if I kissed your wife, Ewan," Sigimor said as he watched Fiona drag Jolene away.

"If your wife didnae do it first." Ewan exchanged a grin with Sigimor, then joined him in scowling at Fingal. "Did ye e'en pause a minute ere ye trotted o'er here to tell him about Barbara in front of his new bride?"

"Aye, I did." Fingal crossed his arms over his chest and scowled right back at them. "I thought on how this Barbara is a bonnie Scottish lass, one with some meat on her bones."

"She is married," said Sigimor, telling himself not to get angry with the man. Fingal was what he was and would never change. "She has been married for nigh on ten years. I dinnae have aught to do with married women."

"Then ye will be pleased to learn that she is now a widow."

For a moment, Sigimor searched deep within himself for some flicker of pleasure over that news and found none. There had always been a faint ghost of Barbara in his heart, one that occasionally teased him with a passing thought of *what if?* He could not even find that now and he was certain he owed that to Jolene. It was impossible, and foolish, to linger on a faint *what if?* when one held a passionate little wife in one's arms every night.

"Nay, I am nay pleased. Nay much of anything, in truth. Dinnae ken why ye think I should care."

"The woman claimed to have been *verra* close to ye ere she married. Aye, and a few times after that, so I dinnae ken why ye act so pious now."

"She lies." Sigimor shrugged, appearing calm even as he savored the vision of Barbara's throat in his hands. "The woman is verra good at lying. Always has been. Aye, I have seen her once or twice since she married her rich old laird, but nay more than that and only when it couldnae be avoided." He glanced around the great hall. "God's truth, Fingal, she is a liar and more. I doubt she left Scarglas ere she had sampled a MacFingal or two." He almost laughed at the way Fingal briefly glared around at his men, many of whom were his own sons. "And now ye have gone and set my wife to thinking I am some lustful rogue with lasses scattered all about the country. For what? Some lying whore who has probably spent all of her husband's money and is looking for a new mon's purse to empty?" Sigimor could tell by the sharp way Fingal looked at him that he had let his anger seep into his voice.

"I was thinking of getting ye a fine, bonnie lass, a Scot, and one who has enough meat on her bones to bear your weight."

"Och, weel, Barbara is verra skilled at bearing a

mon's weight, true enough. I believe I will keep the wife I have."

"But she is English!"

"That she is. The sister of an English earl, a mon who saved my life, may God rest his soul. And, a lass who has ne'er borne the weight of any mon save me, and ne'er will." He watched Fingal walk away grumbling to himself about young idiots. "I didnae think so many would be so troubled o'er her being English. Can they nay see that she is naught but a wee lass?"

"Nay, but they will. And, she is a Cameron now," Ewan said firmly, then grinned at Sigimor's grunt of agreement. "Tis but a passing irritation, nay more. She is a bonnie lass and Fiona likes her. I will admit, the fair-haired, buxom Barbara did seem to be more your sort."

"Used to be. I am a big mon so thought I needed such a lass." He winked at Ewan. "I suspicion ye ken how I thought and how wrong I was, aye?"

"Aye. I also understand that ye will have to make some explanations now."

Sigimor grimaced. "I ken it. She had that look. Dinnae really want to speak on that old folly, though."

"We all have our old follies, Cousin, and wives tend to discover them. Ye ken mine weel enough."

"But yours is dead and buried. Mine seems to be hunting me down."

Ewan laughed. "She did seem most eager to learn all she could about you. At least she isnae bringing ye a child ye bred on her." He nodded when Sigimor winced. "I love the lad and so does Fiona, but it wasnae easy and my hesitation to tell Fiona about Ciaran didnae help. Best just spit out the truth and get it o'er with. Think on what may happen if ye dinnae and Lady Barbara gets a chance to tell the tale her way."

"Jesu, I could find myself sleeping in the stables."

"One thing I have discovered is that, if the woman in your past did ye an ill turn, your wife will most like turn her anger upon that woman. That is, if ye can tell her that woman means naught to ye now, get your wife to believe it, and, more important, mean it."

"Oh, I will mean it. Wholeheartedly." Sigimor stood up and took a moment to brace himself for the confrontation to come. "Aye, Jolene will have no doubt that I mean it. The only trick will be how to tell the tale without making myself look the complete young idiot I was." He left Ewan laughing and started out of the great hall.

As he approached the bedchamber he was always given upon his visits to Scarglas, Sigimor felt uncertain. Even though he did not like it, he was prepared to explain Barbara to Jolene. What troubled him suddenly was the possibility that she would *not* ask for an explanation, that she did not care enough about him to feel concerned, possessive, or even a little jealous.

Annoyed by this unaccustomed lack of confidence, he strode into the room. He would tell her about Barbara and, depending upon how Jolene acted, he just might tell her in such a way that it would goad her into some telling show of emotion. His wife could don a very calm, almost cold, look from time to time, but he knew she could not hold fast to it. Sigimor looked to where Jolene stood by the fireplace, then slammed and bolted the door behind him, and leaned against it as he tried to catch his breath.

Jolene stood haloed by the light from the fire and she was wearing what looked to be little more than a wisp of light fog. The thin lace-and-ribbon-trimmed shift hid very little of her lithe form. The light from the fire only made it look thinner. Her dark hair hung loose, its thick long waves doing little to shield her. She was as good as naked and, yet, the fact that she was not, only excited him more.

Then he noticed that her hands were planted firmly on her slim hips. There was a scowl upon her face rather than a warm, welcoming smile. Glancing down at her feet, he noticed that she was tapping one bare foot on the sheepskin set before the fire. He also noticed that she did, indeed, have long toes.

"Who is Barbara?" Jolene demanded, hiding the delight she felt over his reaction to her appearance.

"Barbara?" Sigimor forced his gaze back to her face and struggled to clear his mind of the thought of tossing her down onto that sheepskin. "Ah, Lady Barbara MacLean. Just someone I kenned, oh, ten years ago or more."

"I see. So long ago as that, hmm? She has a very tenacious memory then."

"Weel, I am a verra memorable fellow."

Sigimor moved to sit on the edge of the bed and remove his boots. Jolene was acting just as he felt a wife should when hearing about some woman from his past, a woman who did not seem to want to stay there. A brief sideways glance at her revealed that her hands were now clenched into fists and her eyes had narrowed. It occurred to him that, if he wanted to be allowed to answer the invitation her attire offered, if might be wise not to goad her too much.

"A woman does not show such interest in a man without reason, especially not in one she has not seen in ten years or more. E'en you are not that memorable, Sigimor."

He wondered if there was a compliment hidden within that last remark, then forced himself to concentrate on explaining exactly who Barbara was. "It hasnae been exactly ten years. Despite my attempts to avoid her, I have seen her a few times since then. The woman is asking about me because she is now a widow."

"She is hunting you for a lover?"

"My guess is that she is hunting me for a husband, that her own probably left her penniless. I saw the mon but two years ago. Drunk he was, and talking most freely. He said the only good thing he got from marrying Barbara was his two sons. He e'en said he wasnae all that certain the second lad was his since his wife was having an affair with his nephew. Decided the blood of the boy was that of a MacLean so it wasnae so bad. Also complained that the woman would leave him poor as dirt if she could, but that he had finally shut the money chest on her greedy fingers and swore that she would ne'er get any more out of it. I think he held to that vow."

Those were not very loverlike words, Jolene decided, and relaxed a little. "Why would she think you would marry her?"

"Because ten years ago I was a fool of a lad, lust-crazed, fair blinded by it, and, aye, flattered by the attention of such a bonnie, highborn lass. I was about two and twenty, but nay as worldly as I liked to think I was." He pulled off his shirt and pointed to the bands of design on each upper arm, the marks that would be with him until he was dust in the ground. "I had this done to impress her. Near killed me for it festered and a fever set in. Ye see, I had heard her remark upon such markings, ones she had seen upon another mon and I wished to hear her speak of me with the same admiration. She has ne'er seen them."

Jolene was beginning to wish she had not asked about Barbara. That he would do such a thing just to hear the woman speak well of him implied an intensity of emotion he had never revealed to her. Perhaps what she had judged as unloverlike words were actually ones of anger and a lingering pain. It was possible to soothe a wounded heart, but she was not sure she had the skill or the time, especially not if this Barbara was intent upon winning him back.

"I find them very attractive," she said, feeling foolish until he smiled at her. "She chose another man?"

"She had already chosen him, and held to that choice e'en as she played her games with me. Old Laird MacLean, a mon thirty years older than she, looking for a young wife to give him a son, and with a verra full purse. She just wanted to enjoy a few young men ere she was married."

"A few?"

"Aye, a few. I went to see her once I had recovered from my fever and these markings had healed. Thought to send her word that I wished to see her, but decided I would surprise her. I did that. Surprised the mon on top of her, too."

"Oh, dear." It was a little difficult to imagine Sigimor as an unworldly young man, but she could easily sympathize with anyone who found their lover in the arms of another.

"Fortunately, that moment of surprise didnae come until I had heard enough to ken what a fool

I had been. She spoke of her marriage to MacLean come the morning and was assuring the braw laddie in her arms that it wouldnae change what was between them. Her first words when she saw me were demands that I say nothing to Laird MacLean. I told the mon with her to carry on, spat out some insults about nay wanting such a weel used lass, and left. I did think on telling MacLean, but I couldnae find the mon, leastwise nay until I was sick unto death of the whole matter and decided to return to Dubheidland. A few times o'er the years she has tried to catch my eye, but, e'en if I was a mon who could cuckold another, I wasnae interested."

Which made Barbara even more determined to have him, Jolene mused. She had thought to make herself feel better, to bury that flare of jealousy over this woman, but this talk had failed to fully accomplish that. It had not even truly clarified what Barbara was to him. He spoke of lust, not love, but men did seem to be wary of that word. If he had felt something more than lustful and flattered, there could be some real trouble ahead for her. Barbara did not sound like a woman who would give up if she wanted something, and it appeared that she now wanted Sigimor. Jolene was pulled from her thoughts when a now naked Sigimor stepped in front of her, placed his hands on her shoulders, and kissed her cheek.

"Dinnae frown, wife," he said. "She is naught but a bad memory of a lad's foolishness."

"Is she?" Jolene felt herself blush over the way he was looking at her from head to toe. "She is looking for you, Sigimor. From all you have just told me, she is not the sort of woman to give up a hunt."

"That doesnae mean she will net her game. I am nay longer that lad, unworldly and blind to her faults. Now, where did ye get this wisp of naught made to tempt a poor mon?"

"From Fiona. Tis one of those things you said you saw no reason for."

"I think I may be about to change my mind."

Glancing down at the stout proof of his arousal, Jolene murmured, "I can see that."

A little hesitantly she reached out to touch him there. He uttered a soft groan, but the way he moved his hips, pushing himself more snugly into her grasp, told her that was a sound of approval. Jolene wrapped her fingers around him, intrigued by the feel of him. He felt so hard and hot against her palm, yet silken soft as well. He also seemed to grow harder and bigger as she stroked him. Jolene was still slightly amazed that he could fit the thing inside her.

If Barbara was the wanton Sigimor's tale seemed to imply, Jolene suspected the woman recalled Sigimor's manly attributes very well indeed. She had seen enough younger men to know they still had a boyish softness to their looks and that many of them had not yet reached their full breadth and height. Since Sigimor did not look like a man carrying thirty-plus years, she was sure he had looked more youth than man ten years ago. A woman like Lady Barbara had probably seen his potential and was now looking to see if he had fulfilled it. In fact, if it had not been very long since he had last seen the woman, she might already know. Sigimor seemed to think Lady Barbara sought a new husband with a fat purse, but Jolene suspected the woman also had a few more earthy reasons for hunting him down.

Jolene decided that, if the woman came to

Dubheidland, she would find her hunt was not an easy one. Although she was still unsure of what the future held for her and Sigimor, right now he was hers. Being Sigimor's wife gave her a lot of advantages over any interloper, and Jolene intended to make full use of each and every one of them. This passion she and Sigimor shared was definitely one of those advantages.

Sigimor savored the touch of Jolene's slender fingers for as long as he dared. When she slid her soft hand between his legs, however, to gently caress his sac, he knew he had to put a halt to her play. If he did not, there was a good chance he would be spending himself in her hand like some beardless virgin lad.

"Enough, wife," he said as he gently tugged her hand away. "Nearly too much."

"I should not do that?" Jolene suddenly feared she had been too bold, or, worse, had caused discomfort instead of pleasure.

"Ye can do it whene'er ye wish. Tis just that the feel of your soft hand is a pleasure I cannae enjoy for too long." He smiled faintly at her look of confusion. "I would be done, lass, ere I had given ye any pleasure at all."

"Oh." She blushed as he began to unlace her night shift. "Should we not move to the bed?"

"Nay. I have me a craving to love ye right here on this soft sheepskin before the fire."

She felt a shiver of anticipation go through her body as he carefully removed her shift. Sigimor and the passion they shared were swiftly stripping away her reserve, her uncertainty, and even her modesty. Although her blushes still burned her skin, she felt no more hesitation whenever desire stirred within her. When he pulled her into his arms and kissed her, she moved against him and savored the feel of his warm flesh against her own. She realized that, not only did she no longer feel any hesitation, she was more than willing to go wherever he led her. She was even beginning to have a few ideas of her own.

When he ended the kiss, she was not surprised to hear herself murmur a protest for she did love his kisses. It quickly changed to a murmur of pleasure as he kissed his way to her breasts, all the while caressing her body with his big, strong hands. The feel of his mouth upon her breasts made her tremble, her need growing with every flick of his tongue and each tug of his mouth as he suckled.

The feelings he could stir within her should frighten her, but she found them exhilarating. With each kiss, each caress, Sigimor gave life to an unfettered wildness within her. Jolene decided she liked that part of her, welcomed that woman who let her desire run free. That woman saw no boundaries and heeded no rules. She reached for the pleasure Sigimor offered with both hands and reveled in it. She also tried to return it to her man in full measure.

For a brief moment, she was puzzled when Sigimor knelt before her instead of pushing her down onto the sheepskin. That confusion faded as he kissed her middle and gently kneaded her bottom. Jolene closed her eyes in pleasure as he slid his hand between her legs. She parted her legs slightly to welcome his caress. She opened her eyes quickly, in shock, when his lips replaced his hand.

"Sigimor?" She called his name in uncertainty more than protest.

"Hush, wife," he murmured as he kissed her inner thighs. "Gift your husband with this pleasure. Twill be returned to ye twofold, I promise."

He had not even finished reassuring her when all of her hesitation vanished, that wild sensuous woman within her kicking it aside. Jolene opened herself to his intimate kiss, curling her fingers through his thick hair to steady herself as she trembled beneath the strength of the pleasure washing over her. She cried out for him as she felt her desire begin to peak, but he held her steady, his hands firmly grasping her by the hips, as he drove her to those blinding heights with his mouth.

Jolene was still shaking from the strength of her release when she found herself flat on her back on the sheepskin. A heartbeat later, Sigimor was thrusting himself into her. Her waning passion burst to life once again. She wrapped herself around his strong body, welcoming the ferocity of his love-making as he forced her back up that blissful peak. This time when she shattered and cried out his name, he was with her, his cry of release blending with hers.

It was not until Sigimor had hastily washed them both off and set her in their bed, that Jolene fully regained her senses. That wild, sensual Jolene had fled to parts unknown, leaving plain old Jolene to suffer from an intense bout of mortification. When Sigimor got into bed and pulled her into his arms, she pressed her blush-seared face against his chest. She could almost feel him looking at her, but could not muster the fortitude to meet his gaze.

"Ah, my poor wee wife," he said, grinning down at the top of her head. "So wild and free when your blood runs hot and so embarrassed by that when it cools, aye?"

She was not sure she appreciated how accurately he had judged her feelings. "Well, how else should I feel after such a gross lapse in proper conduct?"

"Pleasantly sated? Warm and happily drowsy? Grateful that your mon is such a wondrous lover he can make ye scream?"

"I did *not* scream."

"Och, aye, ye did. My ears are still ringing. I think there were a few *mores* and *dinnae stops* as weel as my name."

That was more teasing than anyone ought to have to endure, Jolene decided. She reached down and pinched him right where his leg joined with his body, one of the very few softer spots on his body. His grunt of pain pleased her. There was no denying that he could make her crazed with his loving, but there was no need of his boasting about it.

"Cruel mistress," he said and began to trail his fingers up and down her back as he savored the remnants of desire still lingering in his sated body.

Jolene was so passionate, so easily enflamed by his loving, she inspired him. He would never admit it to her, but he had never been a particularly adventurous or creative lover. Most of the women he had bedded had been the sort a man bought and paid for. He would reach a point where hunger for a woman drove him to seek one out and he would do so at the nearest inn, tavern, or alehouse. He would select a woman who was both buxom and relatively clean, then bed her. Although he had felt obliged to give her pleasure, he had done only the barest minimum needed to accomplish that. Those women had been no more than a warm body to him in many ways and, selfish though it was, most of his interest had been in gaining his own release from the need that gripped him. If he had not learned that that satisfaction was better if there was some warmth in the woman, he doubted he would have afforded their pleasure what little attention he had.

But Jolene truly inspired him in so many ways. Every gasp she made, every shiver he felt go through her slender body, made him want to enhance her pleasure. The way she yelled his name and how every part of her body seemed affected by her release, inside and out, only made him want to bring her to those heights again and again. In fact, if he could gain a tighter control over his own needs, he would enjoy spending a night seeing how many times he could make her scream. For a moment, he savored the image of loving his wife with his hands and his mouth until she pinned him down and threatened him into riding her hard so that they both found that bliss, together.

He had never used his mouth to bring a woman pleasure before, but he had obviously done it right. Sigimor suspected that knowing he was the only man to ever make love to her added to his enjoyment of pleasuring her in such a way. There were other things he had never done, too, and he was eager to try them with Jolene. There were also a few things he would like her to try on him. His body hardened at the thought and he grinned. Not only was Jolene inspiring him to become a great lover, she was also turning him into a greedy one.

Unfortunately, his greed would have to go unsatisfied, he realized when he looked at her. She was sprawled on top of him like a blanket, sleeping soundly. Considering what they had been through that day, he was not surprised. It was probably only the need to find out who Barbara was that had kept her awake long enough for him to get some loving. He counted himself lucky indeed that she had not fallen ill.

The way she had behaved upon hearing that some woman from his past was hunting him pleased him mightily. Sigimor recognized her sense of possession and had seen the glint of jealousy in her eyes. She was settling down to being his wife, to fully accepting him as her husband. A man ought to be able to build on that, to use a sense of possession and fierce passion to breed love, or, at least, a binding affection. It troubled him a little that he wanted that so badly, but he did, and he was determined to get it.

Keeping one arm around Jolene and crossing the other beneath his head, Sigimor thought about Barbara. Although he had not been a virgin when he met her, she was his first true lover, the first who had not been some common wench bought for an hour or more. She had been the first woman to stir thoughts of love and marriage. Her betrayal had struck him hard, but, he realized, it had really only hurt his pride and struck a nearly killing blow to whatever vanity he had had. It had also driven him back to the sort of woman who wanted to see a man's coin first, a crude but honest business deal. The occasional thoughts he had had of Barbara had been no more than the musings of a man who slept alone far too often and had, for a brief time in his youth, thought he had found his mate. He kissed the top of Jolene's head. This time he had no doubt. He just had to make her see it, too.

And Barbara could cause some trouble for him in that endeavor. Sigimor had the strongest feeling that Jolene was not secure in her womanhood, in her ability to keep her man satisfied. A woman like Barbara would sniff out that weakness in a heartbeat. She could easily destroy whatever advances he had made in binding Jolene to him in heart and mind as well as body.

He could only hope he was wrong in thinking that Barbara was hunting him, but he feared he was exactly right. Sigimor yawned and closed his eyes. If Barbara still had all the ties she used to have, if she was still accepted by all her kinsmen and allies, it would be unwise to refuse her his hospitality if she arrived at Dubheidland's gates. It might not hurt to try and find out ways to reassure a woman when a past lover tries to whisper poison in her ear. Of course, he could just keep Jolene in his bed until Barbara gave up and went home. Sigimor fell asleep still smiling with pleasure over that plan.

Chapter Thirteen

"Harold is still lurking about."

Jolene sighed and looked at Sigimor as he strode into the solar where she and Fiona played with the children. She had enjoyed the past two days of peace, false as it was. It did not surprise her that Harold had followed them to Scarglas, but she had hoped his inability to reach them would discourage him. Either that or the constant harrassment of the MacFingals. No one told her exactly what they were doing, but they certainly seemed to be enjoying themselves.

"Mayhap that is because he is short of horses upon which to ride away," she said, settling Fiona's infant son Ahearn more comfortably in her arms. "Those *were* his horses I saw brought in yestereve, were they not?" She watched in some amusement as Sigimor was suddenly besieged by Reynard, Ciaran, and several other little boys.

"Aye, lass, they were," he replied, then turned his attention to tickling and wrestling with the boys.

Watching him, Jolene realized he loved children

and they loved him. He would be such a good father, she thought as she rubbed little Ahearn's back, and felt a strange new hunger stir to life inside her. She had always dreamed of having children and now she badly wanted to have Sigimor's child. Her life just kept getting more and more complicated, she thought ruefully. Harold, a new husband, a woman from Sigimor's past hunting him down, and, now, a sudden craving for a child from a man she was still not sure she could stay with.

Reynard's happy laugh caught her attention. He was so blissfully unaware of how much danger he was in. The child was thoroughly enjoying the other children and she realized he had never had much chance to play with other children. As the heir, he had been kept apart from the servants' children as much as possible. Peter would have been appalled to see his precious heir playing with the bastard children of the old laird MacFingal and his sons, many of them born of common women. In his way, Peter had been a little too proud of his place in the world. He had bred three children among his tenants and servants, yet had never allowed them near his son, just as their father had kept his bastard children away from them. She was ashamed that she had accepted that, seeing it now as grossly unfair. Reynard would obviously have loved having other children about, and who better than his own siblings, illegitimate or not. If she had any say in Reynard's life when this was over, she would see that that changed.

When Fiona came to collect her sleepy child, Jolene reluctantly handed him over. The brief look of sympathy Fiona gave her told Jolene that the woman understood the sudden need she felt. As Fiona left with the baby, several of the boys trailing after her, Jolene crossed her arms in a vain attempt to lessen the feeling of emptiness she suffered.

Sigimor shooed the boys away and turned his attention to Jolene. He wondered at the fleeting look of sadness he caught on her face before she smiled at him. The mention of Harold usually brought a look of fear.

"So your cousins have not managed to drive Harold away?" she asked as he joined her by the fire and sat down in the heavy oak chair facing her. "I assume that was their intention."

"Some of it," replied Sigimor, smiling when the boys suddenly hooted with excitement and ran out of the room. "Off to conquer new lands, I suspect."

"Reynard is enjoying the company of other children. I suddenly realized that he was kept very much alone, yet 'tis clear he likes to be with other boys, to play with them, and get loud and dirty."

"There werenae any other children at Drumwich?"

"There were, but none were equal in birth. Peter had three other children, but he did naught for them save make sure they did not starve and always had a roof o'er their heads. My father did the same with his bastards. I was just chiding myself for simply accepting that arrangement."

"I doubt ye could have changed their minds."

"Probably not. Your uncle is a very odd fellow," she began.

"Ye will hear no argument about that."

She briefly smiled, then continued, "Odd and clearly without restraint. Yet, one cannot fault him on how he cares for his children, *all* of his children. Most lords ignore those children bred outside of the marriage bed, or, as Peter and my father did, toss a few coins their way and think themselves most generous. Yet your uncle gathers them all in, raising them right along with his legitimate sons, and offering them a chance at a better life. He does it with those people who have been cast aside, too."

"Aye, my uncle collects the lost and the outcast. Always has. He also makes more enemies than friends which is why Ewan is the laird now. Poor Ewan thought his father somewhat mad until Fiona pointed out that he wasnae, that he was simply a spoiled child in a mon's body." He grinned when she laughed, but then quickly grew serious again, reaching out to clasp her hand in his. "We will slip away tonight, lass."

"Ah, I had wondered if that was why you had sought me out and spoke of Harold. After all, he has been about for the whole time we have been here."

"Aye, I was hoping a clear opportunity would present itself, but it didnae. E'en so, we must leave ere Harold brings our fight to these halls."

Jolene nodded, knowing he was right, yet reluctant to leave Scarglas. She had been a little overwhelmed at first, but that had faded quickly. For two days she had felt safe, been comfortable, and had found a good friend in Fiona. All that despite Harold's presence. She hated to give that up, to return to the wearying chore of eluding Harold until they reached Dubheidland where she would have to confront another large group of strangers.

She grimaced faintly as she thought of Reynard. He would not be pleased to leave his new friends and the fun he had playing with them. It did not help that he was really too young to fully comprehend the necessity of leaving.

"Ye will like Dubheidland, lass," Sigimor said, trying to sound more confident than he felt.

"Oh, I am sure I will. I was just thinking that Reynard will not be pleased with this news."

"Ah, there is that. Do ye want me to speak with him, lass?"

"That would be cowardly of me," she said, resisting the urge to immediately agree and send him off to see to it.

"Nay. Why should ye want to give him bad news, and that is how he will see it, especially when it will be verra hard to make him understand. Tis my plan, so I will tell him. And, I will make sure Ciaran and a few of the other lads are about when I do."

"How will that help?"

"With the other lads there he will be wanting to take the news like a mon."

"Like a man? He is barely three years old!"

"Doesnae matter. He willnae want the lads to think him naught but a wee bairn. And, the older lads will ken that this is how it must be, far better than he will. Reynard is a verra clever lad, better spoken and able to understand a lot more than one would expect of a child his age. Howbeit, sometimes children can get another child to understand things better than any adult can. So the other lads will tell him the truth as they see it after I leave them."

"In a language he can understand," Jolene said and nodded. "Then coward I shall choose to be. You may tell him."

Sigimor sprawled back in his seat and grinned at her. "Ye still look a wee bit guilty. Dinnae thrash yourself o'er it. Ye have had to give the lad a lot of bad news of late and get him to do a lot of things he didnae want to or understand. More than your share. No harm in taking a wee rest from it."

"I suppose not, though it did not trouble me so

much before. I think, 'tis just that it has been a peaceful two days and he is so happy right now."

"Aye, most like. Now, why did ye look so sad when Fiona took her bairn and I came to sit with ye?"

Caught up in her thoughts of all poor Reynard was being forced to bear because of Harold, Jolene spoke the full truth without thinking. "Ahearn felt so nice in my arms. I am three and twenty, childless when most women my age have already borne a few children." She blushed as she began to realize what she was confessing. "It was nothing important."

Sigimor stood up, leaned over and lightly kissed her. "'Tis important if 'tis making ye feel sad. Ye were just feeling a natural, womanly craving for your own bairn." He winked at her as he started out of the room. "Dinnae worry. Ye will be holding your own bairn soon. Aye, I will give ye as many as ye want."

"Boastful fool," she said, but he just laughed.

She sighed and looked around the now empty room. Upon her arrival, she would never have thought she would be so reluctant to leave in only two days, but she was. Jolene knew some of that was because she could not be sure she would ever see any of these people ever again. If she told anyone she knew in England about Scarglas and its people, they would think she was insane for wanting to stay, yet she had felt safe here. And welcomed, despite the old laird's constant grumbling about her being English. She was especially going to miss Fiona, the first true friend she had ever had. They were like souls and had known it instantly, a rare thing that she was loathe to give up.

Then she thought of Sigimor's boastful promise

to give her as many *bairns* as she wanted and nearly wept. Although she had only just acknowledged that craving, it had already settled itself deep into her heart. Yet, she was still not certain she could stay with him and so she dared not dream of such things as little redheaded babies. Even as common sense told her to put aside such thoughts for now, however, the craving remained. So did the sorrow over the chance that she would have to walk away from such dreams.

Afraid she was thinking herself into a deep melancholy, Jolene got up and went to pack her things. This was all Harold's fault, she told herself, grasping for a cleansing, righteous anger to banish her heartache. If not for his greed, she would still be at Drumwich, still have Peter, and be preparing herself for some acceptable marriage. She would not have met Sigimor or Fiona. She would certainly not be grieving over the loss of redheaded babies she had not even conceived yet. By the time she reached her bedchamber, she was pleasantly enraged, her sorrow forgotten, and her mind filled with thoughts of all the ways Harold could be forced to pay for his crimes.

"Ye best keep that one," said Ewan as he moved to stand beside Sigimor in the torchlit bailey.

Sigimor took his gaze from his wife and Fiona saying their farewells in the damp predawn, and frowned at Ewan. "Why wouldnae I?"

"Matters arenae fully settled, are they? E'en when ye put an end to the threat Harold presents, the future of that wee lad is still in question. Because of the promise your wife made to her dying brother, that means her future is uncertain, too."

"Her future is with me. She is my wife."

"She is also guardian to that bairn, although no law would recognize her as such. Howbeit, that is what her brother made her when he set the life and welfare of his heir into her wee hands. Dinnae close your eyes to that hard truth."

"She and I will face what needs doing when the time comes," Sigimor said and ignored Ewan's soft curse. "Our two lasses became close verra quickly, aye?"

"Aye," Ewan replied, accepting the change in subject. "Fiona says they are like souls or some such thing, and saw that in each other almost immediately. She also says that, although your wife doesnae see it, she was verra much alone for most of her life. Fiona then told me that Jolene found this pack of fools a bit overwhelming, so ye had best be prepared for her to feel the same when she first sets foot in Dubheidland. She and the lad were kept apart from others, or so Fiona believes. Her brother was obviously verra blood proud, keeping the lines between the laird and all others verra clearly drawn."

Sigimor nodded. "Jolene said as much earlier today. Tis a wonder that she isnae tainted by that, isnae haughty at all." He shrugged. "Mayhap that is why she was alone. She was set in a place she didnae really fit in."

"Could be. Weel, she fits now, eh? And Fiona wanted me to tell ye that, if ye dinnae keep this one, she will do ye an injury. Of course, I told her that, if ye lost this lass, she wouldnae have to trouble herself, that ye would be bloodied enough already."

A little troubled by his cousin's insight, Sigimor just grunted. He did not want to think of what would happen once Harold was dealt with. He had a plan and he would concentrate on that for now. Jolene was his mate and she *would* love him. It was not until he heard Ewan chuckle that he realized he had spoken that last thought aloud.

"A good plan, Cousin," said Ewan, "and I wish ye luck with it." He looked at Fiona and smiled faintly. "If ye do get her to say she loves ye, try to get her to say *always*. Your sister's mon agrees with me. Tis something ye dinnae ken ye want 'til ye hear it. Aye, get her to say *always*."

Sigimor opened his mouth to ask why, then quickly closed it. The word had already settled into his mind and heart. He *would* hear Jolene say she loved him and he *would* hear her promise him *always*.

"Heed me, Jolene," said Fiona, holding both of Jolene's hands in hers, "think verra, verra hard ere ye make your choices. Aye, that wee lad is verra important, but so is what ye have with Sigimor."

"I am not sure *what* I have with Sigimor," Jolene said.

"And ye may nay be sure when the time comes to choose, either. Sigimor is like my Ewan and my brother Connor. My brother Diarmot, too, in many ways. They fought love hard, though they couldnae let go of the women who stirred such unwanted feelings within them. Aye, and sweet words arenae their way, either. Ye have to look at what they *do*, how they act."

"But, how can I trust my own judgment? I could very easily see only what I want to see, not what is truly there."

Fiona smiled in complete understanding. "It *is* difficult, but nay impossible. And, if a mon like

Sigimor gives ye his heart, 'tis yours forever. When such men love a lass, they love her hard and ne'er waver. They mate, and 'tis truly for life. Few highborn lasses such as we are so blessed in their marriages."

"Oh, Fiona, how I would like such a marriage, but—"

"Nay, dinnae think on why he said he was marrying ye. The beginning isnae important. They are usually lying to themselves about the why of it all anyway. Now, when the time comes to make your choice, ask yourself some questions. Is the passion fierce and shared?" Fiona nodded when Jolene blushed. "I thought it was. I could see it in Sigimor's eyes when he looked at ye."

"Tis just lust."

"Sigimor isnae so verra different from my Ewan. He fed the need when it grew strong, but nay more than that. He would buy himself a tussle now and then. He had no lemans and didnae woo the better born lasses. He slept alone. Save for what was a young lad's idiocy with that Lady Barbara, he has ne'er done elsewise. Yet, he cannae seem to keep his hands off ye. Dinnae excuse that as just lust.

"Now, it looks as if Sigimor is ready to leave, so I had best spit out the rest of the questions ye must ask yourself. Does he do all he can to see to your comfort? Does he seem possessive and suffer from jealousy? Does he talk with ye? Does he bristle at the verra hint of an insult to ye? Does he explain himself if ye ask him to? Does he listen to ye? Does he ken your moods and ask ye the why of them? Is he at ease in your company and does he laugh with ye? And, does he hold ye in his arms throughout the night?"

"These things are important?" Jolene asked even as she committed the questions to memory.

"Verra important. I wish I could tell ye more, but promise me that ye will ask yourself these questions ere ye make your choice between the lad and the mon, and that ye will think verra hard on the answers."

"I swear."

Fiona hugged her, then looked at Sigimor as he stepped up beside Jolene and draped his arm about her shoulders. "Ready to slip away?"

"Aye," replied Sigimor. "Fingal says the lads have Harold and his men weel occupied."

"It seems unfair to put them at risk," murmured Jolene. "'Tis my trouble, not theirs."

"They arenae at risk," said Ewan as he stood behind Fiona and wrapped his arms around her. "They but taunt and tease, turning that Sassenach about until he is dizzy. Aye, and they will do so until the dawn. Ye ought to have a fine lead on the fool by then."

"Aye," agreed Sigimor, "and then he will have to find himself some new horses."

The fact that the men heartily enjoyed that circumstance caused Jolene to roll her eyes in disgust. She saw Fiona do the same, revealing yet again, how in harmony they were. Then Ewan surprised her by moving away from Fiona and giving her a brief, but not very brotherly, kiss. The moment he stepped back, Jolene found herself hurried over to her horse and tossed up into her saddle by a fiercely scowling Sigimor. Ewan and Fiona stood arm in arm, grinning widely at what Jolene could only see as Sigimor's jealous reaction to that farewell kiss from Ewan. And, Jolene thought, she would not be at all surprised if Fiona and Ewan had planned it just to see how their cousin would react.

As they started to ride out of Scarglas, Jolene looked back and saw Fiona hold up one finger. Jolene could only smile as she waved, then quickly turned her full attention to keeping up with the Camerons. She supposed she did now have the answer to one of the ten questions Fiona had insisted she ask herself. That had been one of the easy ones for Sigimor had revealed such possessiveness before. However, Jolene suddenly realized that the answers to the ten questions would draw her a very adequate picture of what her husband felt for her. She had promised Fiona she would consider all ten questions simply because the woman was a friend, but Jolene knew that she would do so for her own sake now.

The stealth used to leave Scarglas reminded Jolene very strongly of the threat to her life and Reynard's, however, so she put such puzzles aside. Sigimor had set Reynard with Liam just in case something went terribly wrong and they had to ride hard to shake Harold off their trail. Another strong sign of the uncertainty that surrounded them, and would continue to do so as long as Harold lived.

"Stay close, lass," Sigimor said as he slowed a little to ride by her side. "The sun willnae rise for a few hours yet and ye dinnae want to lose us in the dark."

"Nay, I will be sure to stay close," she assured him. "If I think I am falling behind, I will tie my reins to your horse's tail."

"And if ye do lose sight of us?"

"I will stop and not move another step," she replied, reciting the lesson he had repeated to her over and over again since she had fallen into Harold's hands that one time. "Mayhap sing a little."

"Ah, and ye do have some sense of tune and tone, do ye?"

"Some." She grinned at him. "More than you, leastwise."

"A toad has more than me." He winked at her when she laughed, pleased to see her sadness easing away. "Ye liked Fiona, aye?"

"Oh, aye. Have you ever met someone and just known that you were a perfect match?"

It was on the tip of his tongue to say that he had indeed and that it was her, but it was the wrong place and the wrong time. "Aye. Ye mean someone ye ken is a friend from the moment ye meet him?"

Jolene nodded. "Exactly. The sort of person who makes ye realize that most of the people you know and refer to as friends are really not much more than pleasant acquaintances. That is what I felt with Fiona, a true bonding. I realized that I had never truly had a friend before." She grimaced. "That sounds rather pitiful. After all, I did have Peter."

"Peter was your brother and the earl. Aye, I dinnae doubt ye were close, but 'tisnae the same. My brother Somerled is my twin, my womb brother, and I dinnae think any two siblings can be closer than that. I also have a verra big family and we are close. Yet, I ken what ye mean by that occasional one ye meet whom ye immediately feel a bond with."

"And you have met someone like that?"

"Twice. Liam, though he is a cousin, and Nanty. Actually, I must include Ewan as weel. I felt it, but with the breach between the families and the way he got his hands on Fiona, I had to be wary. It did mean, however, that, e'en though he had taken Fiona hostage and had married her without e'en meeting her kin, I didnae just kill him."

"Very good of you, m'lord. I suspect Fiona was pleased."

"Aye, although her brother Connor was a wee bit disappointed that I didnae at least bruise the fool a wee bit."

"Oh, dear. He did not do so, did he?"

"Nay, for Fiona had already written to him about the mon, that she had chosen him."

"Ah, and, of course, the possibility that Fiona would hurt you if you hurt Ewan had no part in your restraint."

Sigimor laughed. "Och, aye, she would have, too. Nay doubt about it." He saw her glance behind them, narrowing her eyes as she tried to peer through the pre-dawn gloom. "Nay, lass, he isnae following. S'truth, I suspect we will be safe at Dubheidland ere he can e'en take up the hunt again. If naught else, he and his men will be on foot until they leave MacFingal lands."

Jolene smiled faintly and shook her head. "It feels as if he has been holding a knife to my throat for months instead of but days. He has proven far better at this than I would ever have thought him to be."

"At first he just wanted to catch ye both because of all his grand plans. Now, I think he has grown desperate, needs ye and the lad to protect himself. He must ken that, as each day passes, there grows a greater chance that your kinsmen have discovered his game and might already be hunting him."

"Oh, I do hope so."

"Heed me, wife, if Harold discovers he is being sought by your kinsmen, your life may be in even greater danger."

"How can I be in greater danger? The man wants to kill me."

"But nay right away, aye? He has been thinking of using ye to tighten his grip on Drumwich. Howbeit, if he kens that your kinsmen have learned of his crimes and seek to make him pay, marrying ye willnae save him. Then, lass, his thoughts will turn to revenge. I have nay doubt at all that he will blame ye for all of his failures."

"Reynard, too?" she asked in a near whisper, fear for her nephew stealing the strength from her voice.

"From all he has done and all ye have told me about the mon, I believe I ken weel the sort of devil we deal with, and, nay, not Reynard as weel. Once Harold thinks he has lost this game, he willnae e'en think of the boy unless he comes up with some plan to buy his life with that of the boy's. Nay, he will want ye. Ye are the one who eluded him, the one who took the boy and fled Drumwich, and the one who has kept him running o'er this country until he lost whate'er chance he might have had of gaining all he covets. I suspicion ye will be seen as the cause of every ache, every bruise, every moment of discomfort, every coin spent, and every humiliation and indignity."

If she did not know better, Jolene would think Sigimor had known Harold for years, so accurate was his judgment. Harold would indeed blame her for everything that had gone wrong since he had murdered Peter. He would want to make her pay dearly, to suffer for his own mistakes. It was a chilling thought and even the knowledge that Harold's attention would be pulled away from Reynard did not ease that chill much.

She quickly shook aside the fear that seized her. It was a poor time to falter. One way or another, the end of their trial drew near. Jolene knew that she and the Camerons had done, and were doing, all they could to keep her and Reynard safe. She also had boundless faith in Sigimor. If he could not defeat Harold, she doubted anyone else she might have chosen could, either. She would fix her thoughts only upon the battle to come and not fret over all the possible outcomes.

"You are right," she said. "He will want to make me pay. Harold was always best at blaming others for whate'er went wrong. But, we are almost to Dubheidland and then it will be his turn to look over his shoulder."

"Aye, wife, it will be. Tis why I am eager to get ye there." He reached out and patted her leg. "Tis why we will be riding from now until we reach the gates," he said, then quickly moved away to rejoin his brother Tait.

Jolene sighed and tried not to think of how her backside was going to feel at the end of this ride.

Chapter Fourteen

"Jesu! She is English!"

Jolene glared at the man Somerled who looked so much like her husband. She had just spent almost two days in the saddle for Sigimor had pushed them hard. She was tired, dirty, sore, and hungry. The appalled look the man wore, one reflected in the faces of all the other Camerons gathered around, was more than she could bear.

"Aye, I am English. A Sassenach. In fact, I am the sister of an English Marcher lord. What of it?" she snapped and angrily shoved a stray lock of hair off her face.

Although he was tempted to laugh, Sigimor forced himself to be serious. It was hard. His kinsmen now looked more startled than appalled, as if a mouse had suddenly grown fangs and leapt at Somerled's throat. Jolene did look a little inclined to kill someone.

"Ah, now, Jolene," he began in as soothing a voice as he could muster.

"What?!" She briefly glanced at him, before returning her glare to Somerled. "I am very, very tired of seeing this reaction every time I meet someone on this side of the border. You would think I was a plague carrier. What about all one hears of Scottish hospitality, hmm? This is just *rude,* that is what this is."

"Ah, here is Old Nancy," Sigimor said, gently pushing his furious wife toward the plump, graying woman who stepped up beside Jolene. "She will see ye to your chambers where ye can have a hot bath and put on some clean clothes. We can finish the introductions later, after ye have had a wee rest, mayhap? Aye, a wee sleep ere we dine is just what ye need."

"Do not talk to me as if I am crazed, husband," she hissed at him. "Where is Reynard?"

"The lad was asleep, so Liam took him up to the room where the children are bedded down."

"Good." She curtsied to the gathered men, took a grinning Old Nancy by the arm and started out of the crowded great hall. "Mayhap by the time we gather to dine some people will have found their manners."

Sigimor watched carefully until he was sure she was out of earshot and then started to laugh. Chuckling to himself, he moved to the head table, sat down, and poured himself some ale. By the time he had soothed his dry throat, his brothers were all seated at the table and his cousins were crowded around behind them.

"Mayhap I was, er, rude," said Somerled, "but, curse it, she is English! What were ye thinking to take to wife an Englishwoman?"

"That I wanted her as my wife!" Sigimor sighed when his family just stared at him and then he told them the whole story from the moment he had ridden through the gates of Drumwich until he had arrived back here at Dubheidland. "Any questions?"

Before anyone could say anything, Liam strolled into the great hall. He grinned at all the dour faces as he walked to the head table. Nodding a greeting to everyone, he sat down, leaving the chair he usually took on Sigimor's left empty for Jolene.

"Have I missed the customary *Oh, m'God, she is English!?*" he asked as he helped himself to some ale.

"Aye," replied Sigimor, "and the whole tale of our wee adventure."

"Weel, I had to speak to Nanty. He returned but a few hours ago thinking we would be here already. He said most everyone had heard of the Englishmon and that he was traveling hard and fast. They would, however, keep watch. Nanty said he would tell ye all about it in the morning. He was asleep ere I left the room."

"E'en though Harold isnae within their reach, 'tis still good that they were warned. If the bastard gets hold of Jolene or the boy, he will flee to England. Then they will all be a great help."

"Aye, 'tis what he thought."

"Ye have no concerns about him marrying an Englishwoman?" Somerled asked Liam.

"Nay," replied Liam. "Why should I object to a wee lass who saved me from rotting on the gallows?"

"She saved ye so that ye could help her."

"Oh, I think she would have done it e'en if she hadnae needed our help or if we had refused it for she kenned that her brother had sent for us. She also kenned that we had done no wrong."

"But, to marry a lass, any lass, just to keep her from having to marry another doesnae seem a verra wise thing to do."

"Weel, 'twas a wee bit more than that," said Sigimor, ignoring the small snort of laughter from Liam. "She is a bonnie wee lass, of good blood, stronger than she looks, and good company." Sigimor could see that his twin ached to press him harder on the question of why, but he held his tongue.

"She has a temper," Somerled said and several of their kinsmen murmured their agreement.

"Ye insulted her, didnae ye. S'truth, ye are lucky she got angry, nay hurt, or twould be my temper ye would be dealing with now. She doesnae understand why everyone acts so appalled and neither do I."

"Mayhap they are appalled that a laird would wed an Englishwoman, nay one of our own. If they kenned she was kin to a Sassenach Marcher laird, they would be e'en more so."

"Best *they* get o'er it," Sigimor said, casting a hard look at all his kinsmen. "She is just a wee lass. Aye, a wee lass who saw her brother die screaming in pain, who grabbed that bairn and spent three days hiding from her brother's killer in the bowels of her own home, and who spent part of that time listening to the screams of her people as Harold tortured them, trying to get them to betray her. And, a wee lass who saved my life, as well as Liam's, Tait's, David's, Marcus's, and Nanty's."

"True, but she wanted something from you."

"Aye, she did. She wanted us to help her get that bairn away from Harold, out of his murderous reach. She ne'er asked for more than that. And I agree with Liam. She would have freed us anyway. I have no doubt of that. I will see Harold dead because I want to, because he killed a mon who once saved my life and wants to kill a woman and bairn for naught but greed. I married the lass because I wanted to. Harold's plots just gave me a good reason to drag her afore a priest, one she found hard to argue with, though she *did* try.

"So, heed me, *she is my wife*, a Cameron now." He was pleased to hear Liam second that claim. "All I care to hear about now are some plans concerning Harold The Usurper."

In the taut silence that followed, a boyish voice said, "We are going to kill the bastard ere he touches our lady."

Sigimor looked at his youngest brother Fergus who was not quite thirteen. Tall for his age, and nearly bone-thin, Fergus was the only one of his brothers, aside from Somerled, who looked most like him. When he saw how the boy began to shift nervously in his seat beneath the scowls of so many of his kinsmen, Sigimor gave him a broad smile. The boy's quick acceptance of Jolene touched him deeply. He would make sure that none of the others made the boy pay for that.

"Weel," muttered Fergus, encouraged by Sigimor's smile, "she *is* just a wee lass trying hard to keep that bairn alive."

"Exactly," said Sigimor as he stood up. "I need to bathe, rest a wee bit, and find some clean clothes ere we gather for our evening meal. Mayhap by then ye will have set aside your fool prejudices and have a few suggestions about how I can keep my wife and that bairn out of the hands of their enemy."

Somerled fixed his gaze on Liam the moment Sigimor was gone. "Ye truly find naught to trouble ye about this?"

"Nay," replied Liam. "Watch them for a wee while and ye will see why I dinnae."

"Keeping her out of another mon's hands is still a poor reason to wed a lass."

"Aye, unless, of course, ye grab that reason with both hands to get a lass to say *aye.*" Liam smiled crookedly at a still-frowning Somerled. "Remain wary, if ye must, but ye will see that all is weel. Cease trying to make Sigimor see his choice of wife as a bad one. Old Fingal has beaten that to death, e'en tried to turn Sigimor's eyes toward Lady Barbara MacLean, a widow who has been asking about Sigimor, a Scottish lass. At the moment, Harold is the darkest shadow o'er their marriage. He will be sniffing about on Dubheidland lands verra soon."

"And he will die for it," said Somerled, most of his kinsmen loudly agreeing with him. "Ye outran him, did ye?"

"Wasnae difficult. The mon seems to have lost his horses whilst on MacFingal land." Liam laughed along with the rest of his kinsmen.

Harold sipped at the tankard of bitter ale the plump serving maid had brought him. Everyone in the dimly lit tavern part of the inn watched him and his men warily, unwelcome carved deep into their hard expressions. He could not fully blame his men for not wanting to linger here for long. If not for the desperate need to get more horses, he would not have stopped.

"M'lord," said Martin as he hastily sat down on the bench across from Harold, "we may have trouble."

"May? May?" Harold took a deep drink of the ale to still the urge to scream. "We have had to enter this nest of barbarians. We were robbed of our horses and supplies by those filthy MacFingals. We are being robbed again and again as we try to get more horses and more supplies. Oh, and every man in this place would take great pleasure in slitting our throats. And, *now* you say we *may* have trouble? What, by the devil's foul breath, is *this?*"

"A minor annoyance if what I hear is true," Martin replied calmly as the serving maid set a tankard of ale in front of him.

"Have the Camerons finally decided to face us like men?"

"Nay, but someone is hard on our trail. Word has it that we are not the only Englishmen riding toward Dubheidland."

Harold propped one elbow on the scarred table between him and Martin and rested his forehead in his hand. He swore, softly and profanely, for several minutes. Everything was falling apart. He had taken over Drumwich and rid himself of Peter. It had all been so remarkably easy and it should have been enough. Instead, he was dragging himself and his increasingly mutinous men all over this cursed country, paying as much for a toothless mare as he would for a well-trained destrier, and paying a king's ransom for oats and cheese. Harold knew who was following him now, knew that somehow the other Gerards had discovered what had happened at Drumwich. One brief taste of all he had dreamed of for so long was obviously all he would ever have and he knew exactly who to blame.

"I will kill the bitch," he whispered in a voice hoarse with fury. "Slowly."

"Ah." Martin nodded. "The lusting has finally burned away, I see."

Sitting up straight again, Harold finished his ale and signaled the maid for more. "Nay, 'tis still there." He fell silent until the woman filled his tankard, collected her coin, and left again. "I must make some plans. That bitch has ruined everything. I held it all and would have kept it save for her. God's bones, she has set me in the shadow of the gallows, but I will at least thwart her in that. Aye, and use her hard ere I cut her throat."

"These Englishmen may not be after us. There are other reasons for their presence and the tales told may be wrong."

"You know they are not and you know as well as I do that they are after me. If not me, then Jolene and the boy. E'en that will only gain me a short respite for she will quickly send them after me. Now what?" he grumbled when there was a disturbance at the door which quickly drew everyone's attention.

Harold's eyes widened when a woman strode over to the fire he and Martin sat near. She yanked off her cloak and threw it to the slender young man close behind her. She was the first pleasing thing he had seen in this country. A little taller than most women, she was voluptuous in a way that made a man immediately hard with lust. Her hair was a pale blond, her features were perfection, and her eyes were a clear, startling blue. Judging by the richness of her deep blue gown and the jewels she wore, he suspected that she was no common wench. He was suddenly very glad he had indulged himself with a bath and a change of clothes while his men sought out the horses they needed.

"We can probably get a room here, then get a fresh start in the morning," said the young man. "Twill be good to return home." He hung the woman's cloak on a hook near the fireplace.

"We will make one more stop, Donald," she said as she held her hands before the fire to warm them.

Donald cursed and glared at her. "Will ye nay give up this foolish quest? The mon isnae rich, ye ken."

"Richer than I am."

"*I* am richer than ye are now."

"We will ride to Dubheidland, and that is final. I need a husband, Donald. Verra soon I shall need a roof o'er my head. And, if *I* do then so shall you."

"Nay, I shall go to my sister. She will let me stay with her for as long as I wish." Donald shook his head. "Ye can just cease looking so hopeful, Barbara. After ye bedded her husband, my sister will only savor the thought of ye begging in the streets. I cannae see Sigimor Cameron welcoming ye with open arms, either, not after the way ye treated him. From all I have heard of the mon, he isnae one to forget a betrayal. Aye, and ye didnae have much luck catching his eye the few times ye have seen him o'er the past ten years."

"Remind me again of why I am suffering your company."

"Because e'en *ye* ken that 'tis verra unwise for a woman to travel about unchaperoned."

"We are going to Dubheidland. As soon as I am warm again and have eaten, we will travel there. We should make it there ere the sun sets and so willnae have to spend coin in this wretched place."

"Sigimor Cameron will close the gates on us."

"Nay, he wouldnae do that." Barbara smiled and brushed some dust from her skirts. "He will recall some of the ties I have and to whom and willnae wish to risk offending any of them."

"Ye dinnae think he will ken that ye have broken near all those ties? The mon isnae a hermit, Barbara."

"He *will* let us in. I just have to think of some way to make him allow us to stay for longer than a night."

"Mayhap I may be of service, m'lady," Harold said, causing the couple to look at him in shock.

"But, ye are an Englishmon," Barbara said. "How can ye help me? And why should ye e'en want to?"

"Because I, too, seek something at Dubheidland."

"What?"

"Sir Sigimor Cameron's wife."

"He is married?" Donald shook his head. "Weel, that puts a sure end to all of your plans, that does."

Barbara ignored her cousin, recognizing a cunning in this Englishman that matched her own. "Are ye sure we speak of the same mon? That Sigimor Cameron, laird of Dubheidland, is married?"

"For now." Harold sipped his ale, giving her time to think over his words, before standing to introduce himself and Martin. After she introduced herself and her cousin, he said, "Shall we talk, m'lady?"

Harold smiled when, after another brief moment of thought, she nodded. Her cousin obeyed her command to get them each a seat, then joined Harold and Martin at their table. He knew he could make use of this woman, that she was one who was willing to do anything and sacrifice anyone to get what she wanted. For the first time since he had learned that Jolene had married the lord of Dubheidland, Harold felt some of his rage ease. Even beating that priest near to death had not accomplished that. Through this woman, Harold knew he would gain some measure of revenge against Jolene for all she had lost him.

Jolene's eyes widened as she looked at the gown Old Nancy held out to her. It was a beautiful deep green. She knew it would look good on her and even looked like it would fit her well. Then she frowned as she began to wonder where Sigimor had gotten it and for whom.

"Where did you find that?" she asked, knowing her suspicions tainted her voice for Old Nancy grinned.

"Jealous, are ye? Good." Old Nancy ignored Jolene's muttered denial. "This belonged to the laird's sister. After she gave birth, she returned to being as slim as she e'er was, but there were a few subtle changes in her body. They were just enough to make this gown and a few others nay fit her as weel as they once did. She left them here for she felt there might be some use made of them and they would do if she had naught else to wear during one of her visits."

"Tis beautiful," Jolene said, marveling at the softness of the wool beneath her fingers.

"And ye will look verra beautiful in it. Ye will be a pure treat for our laird's eyes and set the rest of the fools back a step or twa as weel."

"Mayhap I should have my meal here. That would allow Sigimor's kinsmen more time to become accustomed to the idea that Sigimor is married now, *and* to an Englishwoman." Jolene looked around the sparsely furnished bedchamber and nearly grimaced, for the only real touch of softness in the room was the sheepskin rug on the floor before the large fireplace.

"Aye, it needs a woman's touch," Old Nancy said as she tugged Jolene off the bed. "Most of Dubheidland does."

"The furniture is very finely made." Jolene reached out to smooth her hand over one of the thick, finely carved bedposts. "Odd that the mothers did not make much of a mark."

"Ye will find their touches in the solar, the kitchens,

and the herb hut. The rest of the keep they left to the lads. Oh, and a wee bit in Ilsa's bedchamber. Tis now used for her and her husband when they come to visit, or if some lady comes here. Few have. This has been a mon's place for a long time. E'en most of the lasses and women who work here, dinnae sleep here. Mayhap a few will now that there is a lady of the keep. Come, let us get these clothes on ye. The laird slipped in to dress ere ye woke and he will be waiting for ye."

Jolene was pleased with the diversion. She had begun to feel intensely guilty as Old Nancy had spoken of what she might accomplish as the lady of Dubheidland. Even though she knew it could mean an abrupt end of her time with Sigimor, she suddenly wanted this trial to end. She wanted Harold dead and buried. She wanted to know who would be chosen as Reynard's guardian. She wanted her choices set before her so that she could make them and be done with it. There was heartbreak ahead of her no matter what path she chose and she wanted that blow struck so that she could cease fearing it.

"Now, m'lady, no need to look so worried, aye?" said Old Nancy as she efficiently braided Jolene's hair, pinned it up, and attached a pale green veil to her head to modestly cover Jolene's hair. "Ye look verra fine. Ignore the scowls and grumbles ye might hear this eve. They are all good lads, but they dinnae like surprises. And, they all worry about Sigimor though he would probably beat them all soundly if he kenned it."

Although she knew the woman was only trying to put her at ease, her last statement only darkened Jolene's mood. As Old Nancy escorted her back to the great hall, Jolene realized she was about to meet a horde of Sigimor's kinsmen who would certainly hate her soon if she chose Reynard over their laird. At the very least, Sigimor would be somewhat humiliated when his new wife left him to return to England. She would not only be heartbroken, but would have to accept that there was a veritable army of Camerons cursing her name. Undoubtedly, the MacFingals would join in the chorus. Just thinking about the fury she could stir up made her want to go back to bed.

Then she saw Sigimor waiting for her at the entrance to the great hall. He wore a plaid, a rich blend of red and black, a white shirt, and soft deerhide boots. Jolene barely stopped herself from sighing in appreciation like a moonstruck girl. He looked so big, so strong, and just a little uncivilized. If she had to leave him in the end, she knew this would be how she would see him in her memories for the rest of her life. Jolene suddenly doubted she would ever be able to remember him without feeling the pain of loss.

Sigimor looked at her and she nearly preened beneath the appreciation he revealed in his smile. That strengthened her waning courage and she stepped up to him, slipping her hand into his. It faltered again when he looked at her head and scowled. A little nervously, she touched the light veil shielding her hair.

"What is that on your head?" he asked. "Why are ye hiding your hair?"

"A wedded lass is supposed to cover her hair," said Old Nancy.

"Nay this one." Sigimor quickly removed the veil and thrust it into Old Nancy's hands. "I dinnae like it." He was not sure he much liked the way Jolene's hair was all coiled up on her head, either, preferring the long braid she had worn before, but decided to leave that argument until later. "Ye can explain it all to me later," he said to Old Nancy when she began to sputter in outrage. "If 'tis some custom a wife is expected to follow, mayhap Jolene can do so if we have to go to court or the like. She doesnae have to do it here. Nay amongst family. This is Fergus the Last," he introduced his youngest brother who lurked at his side. "The bairn of the family." He winked at Jolene when Fergus glared at him. "He has asked to sit next to ye."

"I would be honored," Jolene said, smiling at the beardless boy who was nearly a head taller than she was.

As she walked with them to the head table, Jolene calmly answered Fergus's questions about Reynard. He was especially fascinated by the fact that such a small boy was both an earl and a baron. As she talked she studied the men in the great hall. It appeared that their shock had faded, but wariness had set in. The one that interested her the most, however, was Somerled, Sigimor's twin. He stood up as she approached and was all that was polite as she was seated on Sigimor's left, but she sensed that he did not approve of her, of her place as Sigimor's wife.

The friendly smiles and greetings from Liam, Tait, David and Marcus calmed her only slightly. She could not count on them to gain her the approval most of Sigimor's family now withheld. When she thought of how they would feel if she left Sigimor, her mood quickly grew dark again.

She struggled to eat the food Sigimor piled upon her plate and ignore the watchful gazes fixed upon her. Talk of all that had happened while Sigimor was gone swirled around her as she studied the great hall. It was well furnished, the chairs, benches, and tables all of the sturdiest oak. There were quite a few chairs, she realized, far more than she had seen in even the finest English hall. The better plates, eating utensils, and tankards were not just at the head table, either. Some weaponry decorated one wall, most of it of the finest quality, and a large, rich tapestry depicting some battle hung over the massive fireplace at the far end of the hall. Jolene began to think that the Camerons of Dubheidland might not be considered wealthy by English standards, but they were far from poor.

Just as Somerled fixed his gaze on her and Jolene tensed, preparing herself for a confrontation, there was a commotion just outside the doors to the great hall. For one brief moment, Jolene was pleasantly relieved. Then a beautiful, voluptuous blonde was nearly carried in by two men. One quick glance at the look on Sigimor's face, an odd expression of dismay and fury, told Jolene that the woman was Lady Barbara MacLean. Suddenly, dealing with the cautious mistrust of an army of Camerons did not seem so unpleasant.

Her grip on her eating knife tightened as Sigimor moved to greet his uninvited guests, after hastily telling Somerled who the woman was and confirming Jolene's suspicions. The way Lady Barbara draped herself all over Sigimor as he helped her to a seat by the fire had Jolene clenching her teeth. When the woman kept hold of Sigimor's hands even after she was seated, Jolene slowly rose from her seat and walked toward them, barely aware of Fergus at her side.

"What ails her?" Jolene asked, both infuriated and dismayed by the woman's beauty.

"She says she and her traveling companions were set upon by thieves," Sigimor replied, studying his wife's furious expression with keen interest.

"In the melee, she hurt her ankle. Or her leg. She isnae being too clear."

The woman uttered an ear-piercing screech when Jolene flipped up her skirts, exposing her legs. Jolene looked for an injury, but saw little more than a few faint bruises on her right leg. Although she knew she was no expert, there was something about the bruises that roused her suspicions. They just did not look like the sort of injuries one would get from a fall or an attack upon one's person. A quick glance at the two men with her revealed only slightly disarrayed clothing and a few facial bruises. Jolene looked at Lady Barbara and knew, deep in her heart, some game was being played.

"What are ye doing, lass?" Sigimor asked calmly, idly wondering if he ought to relieve Jolene of her dagger.

"I was judging the extent of her wounds," Jolene replied and noticed that Barbara was very slow to cover her legs again. "If a bone had come through the skin, we would have to cut that piece off ere it rotted her whole leg." Her eyes narrowed as Barbara grabbed hold of Sigimor's hands again. "Might still need to cut off a piece or two."

"Ye can use my knife," said Fergus. "Tis bigger."

Sigimor hastily swallowed the urge to laugh. Ignoring their scowls, he ordered Jolene and Fergus to go help Old Nancy prepare some rooms for their guests. Although he was pleased by the jealousy his wife had revealed, he was a little uneasy as well. Barbara was trouble, always had been. He did not need any more trouble now, especially not in his marriage. Once Jolene was gone, he looked at Barbara and wondered how long he needed to be hospitable in order not to offend any of her powerful allies and family.

Chapter Fifteen

"Sigimor, what is that Englishwoman doing here?" Barbara demanded. "She held a dagger on me!"

"Actually, she was just holding one. She hadnae taken aim with it yet." Sigimor heard a faint choking sound at his side and realized Somerled and Liam had joined him, both men obviously trying hard not to laugh. "And that Englishwoman is my wife."

Barbara looked shocked, but Sigimor suddenly had doubts about the truth of that reaction. She pressed a hand to her fulsome breasts, but the gesture looked practiced, one used specifically to draw a man's gaze to her much-admired breasts. Although he was not sure how she could have discovered the fact, Sigimor felt certain that she already knew he was married. It was also curious that she was so close to Dubheidland when she had left Scarglas nearly a sennight ago.

"What possessed ye to marry a Sassenach?" she asked.

"That isnae really any concern of yours, is it?"

The flash of anger she was quick to hide was more like the Barbara he knew, and Sigimor relaxed a little. "Now, see if ye can tell me what happened more clearly, without all the wailing." He listened carefully to her tale, then looked at her cousin Donald. "Is that what ye recall?"

"Aye," Donald replied but added no details.

Realizing the man was not inclined to say any more, Sigimor studied him closely. He shared the looks that made Barbara such a beauty, the fine features, the rich blue eyes, and even the golden blond hair, but he was tall and slender. He looked almost sulky and, even though it could be because he had not shown well in the battle with the thieves, Sigimor felt it was something else souring his mood. Was he an unwilling cohort in some scheme of Barbara's?

Since she had shown an interest in him when she had been a guest of the MacFingals, Sigimor wondered if she was here to try to ensnare him. It seemed vain to think she would go to such trouble for him, especially as it could gain her no more than an adulterous tumble. He was already married and he still felt she had known that before her arrival. It was possible that Barbara did not see his marriage as permanent since his wife was English. There was some justification for the woman to think that as he suspected, the English courts and the English church would be willing to give an English-woman an annulment of any marriage made with a Scot. He quickly shook aside that thought, unwilling to linger on it.

"From what I saw, your injuries are nay so dire," he said. "Ye willnae need to rest here for long. I will fetch ye some drink. Twill be a wee while ere the rooms are readied for ye." Ignoring her stuttered attempts to hold his attention, Sigimor strode back to the head table, Liam and Somerled close on his heels.

"Who is that woman?" asked Somerled.

"Someone I kenned ten years ago," Sigimor replied as he grabbed three empty tankards and gave them each a fleeting wipe with a square of linen. "A foolish young mon's folly. She married a rich old mon who has recently died."

"And left her a rich widow?"

"I dinnae think so." Sigimor told him about the conversation he had had with the aging Lord MacLean two years ago. "I think he left her a verra poor widow."

"Ah, and so she seeks a new husband and has set her sights on you. Thought this wee game up to get herself under your roof."

"Ye dinnae believe her tale, either?"

"Nay, we dinnae have much trouble with thieves. And, the ones who have dared trouble this area from time to time wouldnae be so gentle with their chosen victims."

"Aye," agreed Liam. "They would have left those three with a lot worse than the wee love pats they are whining about, if they left them alive at all."

"'Tis just what I was thinking," Sigimor said as he filled the tankards with wine. "I am tempted to throw then out."

"Why dinnae ye?"

"The last I kenned, Lady Barbara had some verra powerful friends and kinsmen. Unless I find out otherwise, I dare not refuse her common hospitality. She would be quick to cry to them if I did. Aye, and she would make it sound far worse than simple rudeness. They arenae the sort ye wish to anger or offend."

"So we are stuck with the wench for a while," Somerled murmured. "Mayhap now that she kens ye are already married, she will quickly end this game and leave."

"That would please me," said Sigimor, "but I doubt that will happen. Truth is, I think she already kenned that I was married."

"Then why play this game at all? She can gain naught from it. Weel, nay unless ye break your own rules and decide adultery isnae such a great sin."

"That willnae happen. It certainly willnae happen with that bitch. She was weel used when I kenned her and, if all I have heard of her since then is true, 'tis a wonder she isnae bowlegged. Since neither of ye have a wife to shield ye from her tricks, I would advise ye to be wary."

"We arenae poor, but we arenae lairds and we dinnae hold any lands. Too poor a choice for the likes of her."

"That depends upon how desperate she is." He almost smiled at the identical looks of dismay the men wore. "Try to get close to her cousin Donald. Whate'er game is being played here doesnae sit weel with him. Although he has been her little pet for years, he isnae completely of her ilk. He may be the weak link. Something is afoot here and I cannae shake the feeling that more than getting some fool to marry her is behind all of this."

Once Liam and Somerled agreed, Sigimor took the wine to his unwanted guests. He responded curtly to all of Lady Barbara's attempts to engage him in conversation. It annoyed him when she made sly, flirtatious references to their past relationship. She seemed completely oblivious to the possibility that his memories of that time might

not be fond ones. The way she tried so hard to ignore Liam, and so often failed, was almost amusing.
Barbara might be eyeing him as her next husband,
but she was clearly unable to resist any handsome
man, and especially not one as handsome as Liam.
She seemed to have enough sense to know bedding
Liam could ruin her chance of becoming Lady of
Dubheidland, but Sigimor suspected even she was
not sure how long she could resist the temptation
Liam offered. If he was not so worried about what
trouble this woman could cause him, Sigimor knew
he would find her battle with her own licentious
greed extremely entertaining.

When Old Nancy arrived to say the rooms for
their guests were ready, Sigimor breathed a sigh of
relief. A heartbeat later, he found his arms full of
the voluptuous Barbara. He was impressed by how
quickly she had moved, even as he fought the urge
to drop her on the floor. As he conceded the vic-
tory to her this time and started to carry her to her
room, he noticed the scowls his kinsmen wore and
felt somewhat comforted. His family might not
have decided to fully accept Jolene, but this show
of disapproval for Barbara indicated that the seed
of acceptance had already been planted. Sigimor
felt confident that Jolene herself would be enough
to make it grow.

Once in the bedchamber assigned to Barbara,
Sigimor discovered that the woman was stronger
than she looked. As he set her down on the bed,
her grip had tightened around his neck, and he
had barely stopped himself from sprawling on top
of her. Now he stood next to the bed, her arms
around his neck like a noose, and wondered how
to get loose without hurting her. Sigimor held

himself as tautly as he could as he lifted his hands from the bed and grabbed her by the wrists.

"Let go of me, Barbara," he ordered, struggling to control his rising temper when she pulled herself up against him. "Now."

"So cold to me, Sigimor," she said. "Ye ne'er used to be. Dinnae ye remember all those times we were together?"

He stared at her beautiful face and briefly looked over her fulsome body. She had been a young man's dream, but he realized that dream had died a long time ago. Sigimor found that he could acknowledge her beauty, but was not moved by it in the slightest. Now he was all too aware of the rot beneath that fine skin. Even if he was a free man, he doubted he would be seduced by her, so completely unmoved did she leave him.

"I am married," he said and tightened his grasp on her wrists. She winced faintly, but did not let go of him.

"To that Sassenach? That bone-thin, black-haired child?"

" 'Ware, Barbara, I dinnae tolerate any insult to my wife."

"Ye ken as weel as I do that ye need not hold to this marriage. Either one of ye could have it annulled with ease simply because ye are a Scot and she is a Sassenach. Come, my braw knight, let me remind ye of what we once shared."

Sigimor knew she was about to kiss him and he was tempted to let her. He knew he would remain cold and that might pinch her vanity enough to make her give up this game. Then, just as her lips were a breath away from his, he saw her cast a swift, sly glance toward the door. He jerked his head back and tightened his grip on her wrists enough to make her gasp. Unfortunately, it was still not enough to make her let go and he inwardly cursed when Jolene stepped up next to him.

Jolene had a good idea that her husband was not a willing captive, but that only eased her jealousy a little. Some other time she might even be able to think back on the look of horror in his eyes and smile. Just now she was trying to decide which one of them she wanted to hurt—badly. She caught a glint of triumph in Barbara's expression and decided she would not give the woman the satisfaction.

"I thought it my duty to come and see if our guest was comfortable," Jolene said, proud of the calm tone of her voice. "I see you have taken care of settling her into her bed, husband."

"Aye, I just cannae seem to get loose," he said, seeing no sign that she believed him.

"Ah, I see. Easily taken care of."

She moved so quickly, Sigimor was not exactly sure what she did but it worked. Jolene's hand flicked toward Barbara and was back at her side in the blink of an eye. Barbara screeched and let go of him. There was even the glint of tears in the woman's eyes. Then she slipped her hand under her armpit and Sigimor almost smiled, knowing exactly where Jolene had struck and that it hurt.

"Shall I leave you to making sure that our guest is comfortable? Aye, I believe I shall," Jolene said, not waiting for an answer and heading for the door. "Do let me know if she needs her injuries seen to."

So sweet of voice, so polite, so absolutely furious, Sigimor mused as he watched Jolene leave. Her eyes had been nearly black. He was going to have to be very good at explaining what she had seen if he wanted to be slipping beneath the blankets with her tonight. Barbara was already stirring up trouble, he thought as he turned to look at her. The pretty little pout she wore only angered him more. Just how stupid did she think he was?

"Your wife hurt me, Sigimor," Barbara said, sniffing delicately. "That was cruel."

"That was weel deserved," he said.

"Sigimor! How can ye speak so harshly to me after all we shared?"

"We shared naught, m'lady, save for a few bouts of sweaty rutting." He watched her struggle to keep her temper under control, all the soft flirtatiousness in her expression rapidly disappearing. "If ye didnae have such powerful allies, kin and otherwise, I would have left ye to rot outside of my gates. Did ye think I had heard naught of ye since the day I found ye with that young Douglas lad atween your thighs? Ye are trouble, Lady Barbara. Ye stir it up where'er ye go. Weel, ye willnae stir it up here. Ye can stay until I decide ye are better or until I find out whether ye have any allies left or nay. Then ye will go." He started toward the door, but paused just inside it to add, "If ye hurt my wife, ye will wish ye had ne'er started this game." Sigimor headed down to the great hall, feeling a need for a strong drink before he faced Jolene.

"Did ye sort her out?" asked Liam as Sigimor entered the great hall and, upon reaching his seat, immediately poured himself an ale.

"Aye, the bitch is settled in her bedchamber and, if she has any wits at all, she will stay there until she finally leaves." Sigimor slouched in his seat and took a deep drink of ale. "We need to keep an ear to the ground more, mayhap e'en send some-one to the king's court more often."

"Why the sudden interest in such things?" asked Somerled.

"If I kenned where Barbara stood with her allies or e'en with her kinsmen, I might not be caught in this snare," Sigimor replied. "If she has cut them off or been cut off by them, I could kick her out. We have always been verra good at finding out a lot about one thing at a time, one enemy or possi-ble enemy or e'en a possible ally. I believe we must needs stop being so selective."

"Tis a thought. Considering how twisted and ever-changing things are, it might be a good way to stay safe *and* solvent."

"I assume from all this that the Lady Barbara has already tried to make trouble," Liam said.

"Tried and may have succeeded," replied Sigimor. "Once I get the backbone to go to bed, I will find out for certain."

"What did she do?" Liam's eyes widened with amused sympathy as Sigimor explained what had happened. "The woman wastes no time, does she? Are ye certain ye ought to leave Jolene alone to think about it for too long?"

Sigimor sighed. "Nay, but I will. I need to think about a few things myself ere I join my wife. Tis possible Barbara still seeks a husband. My having a wife doesnae seem to trouble her or deter her. That makes no sense."

"She could think that she could drive Jolene away. Jolene would go back to England then, wouldnae she."

"But she would still be my wife."

"Nay for verra long. Either one of ye could probably get the marriage annulled with ease. Jolene may not ken it now, but once back in England she would find out quick enough."

"Possibly. Barbara said much the same." Sigimor really hated to think of how easily Jolene could be shed of him if she chose to be. "I am surprised that Barbara would have any knowledge of such things, though. Yet, I cannae shake the feeling that there is more here than Barbara's need for a husband and her thinking me fool enough to step into her snare."

"Women like Barbara are verra vain. And, so many men have tumbled into her trap for so long, she probably cannae believe ye willnae do the same. She has fooled so many, 'tisnae surprising if she thinks we are all idiots."

"As I once was. Aye, there may be some justification for her thinking she can win this game."

"Ye havenae exactly explained what she once was to you," Somerled said. "I cannae recall ye mentioning her."

"That was when ye were off wandering the country trying to find out ways we might fill our coffers. Which ye did, thank ye verra much."

"My pleasure. Now, tell us all about Barbara. If we ken what she was, we might better understand why she thinks she has any chance at all of winning you as a husband."

Sigimor took a deep breath and very succinctly told them of what had happened between him and Barbara. He was pleasantly surprised to find that he was no longer so embarrassed by it all. It helped that he saw no pity or scorn in their faces, only a fleeting sympathy for the young fool he had been and anger. Sigimor suspected that both men probably had a similar tale which they kept to themselves.

"She may think she but needs to make a few amends for the past and ye will fall right back into her grasp," Somerled said. "I suspect she excuses the times ye turned her away after that as simply ye living up to your reputation as a mon who will have naught to do with married women."

"Ah, I hadnae considered that. Tis also evident that she doesnae expect me to hold to my wedding vows."

"The woman has probably kenned too many men who dinnae."

"True, true." Sigimor finished his drink and stood up. "This is getting me nowhere. I just cannae shake the feeling that there is something here I cannae see, something more than the obvious, but I simply cannae think what it would be."

"We will keep close to Donald as ye asked us to. We will also start looking for Harold in the morning." Somerled frowned. "Ye really believe he will come here, that he willnae give up the hunt and scurry home?"

Sigimor nodded. "Aye, I do. The mon's mind has settled on revenge now, I am sure of it. He has a need to punish Jolene for all he has suffered. Oh, he still toys with the idea of tightening his grasp on all he has stolen by wedding her and then silencing her, but there is much more to this hunt now. Much more. In truth, he should have stayed at Drumwich, held fast to it, and planned ways to catch her or thwart her when or if she returned to try and cause trouble for him. I think he kens he has made a serious mistake, but he blames her for it. I suspect he now grows desperate, and that makes him verra dangerous indeed."

"Weel, now we can hunt him," said Liam.

It was a pleasant thought and Sigimor held to it as he made his way to his bedchamber. He gave a soft sigh of relief when he found the door unbarred. Telling himself he had nothing to feel guilty about, he stepped boldly into the room and shut the door behind him. When he saw Jolene sitting on the thick sheepskin rug before the fireplace, brushing her hair, he relaxed a little. She might be angry, but she had not locked him out or gone to sleep elsewhere. Sigimor decided to see that as a good sign, as an indication that she was willing to hear what he had to say.

Jolene tensed as Sigimor walked over and sat down facing her. She did not look at him, but kept right on brushing her hair. From the moment she had left him with Barbara, she had gone over and over what she had seen in that room. He had not looked willing to be in the woman's arms, of that much she was certain. The problem was, a little voice in her head kept whispering that he had not looked willing *then*, but what about later? What about the next time? It was also hard to ignore the fact that he had taken a long time to come to her. How much of that had been spent with Lady Barbara?

When she finally looked at him, she caught him watching her brush her hair with a very familiar gleam in his eyes and she scowled at him. "Do not give me that look."

"What look?" he asked.

"That warm look. This is not a good time to be giving me warm looks, not after I saw—"

He held up his hand, pleased when she immediately fell silent. "Not when ye saw me in another woman's arms? I didnae want to be there, lass, and I think ye ken it."

"Are you trying to make me feel guilty for being angry?"

"Och, nay. If I had caught ye in a like situation with another mon, we would still be picking up pieces of him. Nay, ye can be angry, if only because I was idiot enough to get within ten feet of the woman, now or ten years ago. I got trapped into carrying her to her room and then she wouldnae let go of me. Stronger than I would have guessed her to be. Clung like a leech. I was puzzling o'er how to detach her without hurting her when ye walked in."

"You were about to kiss her, reluctant or not." Jolene clutched her brush tightly as she waited for his answer.

"Aye, I was." He grimaced when she paled. "She was being verra persistent, refused to accept that I could be cold to her. I had the passing thought that, if I let her kiss me, she would see that that coldness was no act." He removed her brush from her hand and took both of her hands into his. "I was completely unmoved by her, Jolene."

"But, she is so beautiful, all a man would want in face and form."

"She is certainly verra pleasing to the eye. I could see it and ye would think me a liar if I said elsewise. But, I could also see that there was naught but ugliness beneath that fair skin. Selfishness, vanity, greed, and an inability to understand or care how her actions might hurt others. She wants a husband and she thinks I am the same blind fool I was years ago. The woman is so vain, I am nay sure I can convince her otherwise."

"Then why not just send her away?" Jolene asked. "We both know her injuries are not e'en worthy of putting salve on them. I do not believe her tale of having been robbed is true."

"Neither do I, or Liam, or Somerled. I would like nothing more than to toss her out, right now, but I cannae. She has some verra powerful friends and kinsmen, or did. God alone kens what twisted tale she would give them if I threw her out, but I dare not chance it. I need to tread warily here. She isnae worth the trouble she could cause if she starts to cry about insults or abuse at my hands."

Jolene sighed and nodded. He was right. There was no doubt in Jolene's mind that Barbara wanted to cause trouble between her and Sigimor, but she could only succeed if they let her. On the other hand, if one gave her even the smallest reason to go crying to her allies and family, there could be blood spilled. She had to agree that the woman was not worth it.

"How long do you think we must endure her company to avoid giving insult to anyone?"

"A few days, nay more. As ye said, her injuries are minor, mere bruises. If I discover that she has lost her powerful allies, has been cast out by them, she will be sent off immediately. Tis odd, but, in a small way, some good may come out of this." Sigimor smiled at her exaggerated look of disbelief. "True. It made me realize that we need to keep ourselves better informed about who is allied with whom, who is feuding with whom, who is in favor, and who is not. All the things I have ignored until now, considered useless rumor and of no concern of mine."

Jolene nodded. "It can be good to know as much as possible about such things."

"Aye. Somerled and Liam agree. I fear it will mean sending one of the lads to court."

"Liam," Jolene said and smiled faintly. "He would be perfect if he is inclined to accept the chore. He is educated, can be most charming, and he is very handsome. If your court is like ours, his pretty face will be most welcome."

"By the women," he grumbled, but her suggestion had a great deal of merit.

"Despite all of the grumbling and complaining about him, Liam has a lot of male friends. Men do like him. And, do not discount the women as a source of valuable information. Tis true that some seem interested only in fashion and other womanly topics, but, not all. E'en the ones who seem to chatter and gossip about nothing can reveal the most interesting things."

Sigimor smiled at her. "Then Liam it is, if he is agreeable. And one other for those times Liam might wish a rest from it all." He tugged on her hands until she tumbled into his arms. "Now that everything is settled—"

"You are ready to go to bed," she finished for him.

"Actually, I was thinking of the rug before the fire at Scarglas, the one which is verra similar to this one."

"Sigimor," she whispered in shock, knowing he was thinking of what they had done on that rug, but her shock quickly changed into an eager willingness as he kissed her.

Jolene idly rubbed her cheek against Sigimor's chest, sleepily enjoying the last vestiges of the passion they had shared on the rug before the fire. She was not quite sure how they had gotten into bed, but was too happy and comfortable to puzzle over it for long. Sigimor made a soft rumbling noise that was not quite a snore and she smiled. The poor man had worn himself out. After all they had been through the past few days, she was a little surprised she was still awake. A few things still troubled her, however, refusing to let her mind rest.

Lady Barbara MacLean was one trouble that refused to be banished from her mind too quickly. Although Jolene did not doubt that the woman would like to snare Sigimor, Jolene felt there was more. Several people had told her that the woman had known Sigimor was married to an Englishwoman, that her well-played shock was just that— well played. The maids had been especially scornful. From what she had overheard the woman say to Sigimor while she clung to him like a limpet, Barbara also knew that the marriage could be easily annulled. The question was, how did she know? It was the lack of any clear, precise answer to that question that worried Jolene.

She decided she would have to discuss it with Sigimor and nearly smiled when she felt herself begin to relax. For a minute she feared she was being too weak, was too readily tossing all her troubles into his lap. Jolene quickly dismissed that fear. Although it was never spoken aloud, she knew Sigimor and the others were all aware of the fact that she would have released them even if they had declined to help her. They had a score to settle with Harold themselves. It was also not weak to want to share one's doubts or enlist help in finding answers. It was always better to have two people work on a problem. Finally, feeling sleep grab hold of her, Jolene promised herself she would speak with Sigimor in the morning about these troubling questions as soon as possible. She also promised herself that, powerful allies or not, if Lady Barbara MacLean did not keep her dainty white hands off Sigimor, she was going to hurt the woman.

Chapter Sixteen

Jolene neatly folded the shirt she had mended for young Fergus and looked around the great hall. It was nearly empty, only three young women from the village moving around cleaning the room. The men had finished their noon meal and rushed out to hunt for Harold, just as they had done after breaking their fast early in the morning. She ought to be pleased that Harold was nowhere to be found but, instead, it made her uneasy. After he had come so far, why would he give up now? There was the possibility that all the trouble he had suffered at Scarglas had made him give up, that he had headed back to Drumwich hoping to salvage what he could of his grand plans, but she could not make herself believe it. Everything inside her told her that he was out there, plotting, waiting for his chance. She shivered.

"Are ye cold, Jolene?" asked Fergus.

A little startled since she had not heard his approach, Jolene smiled at the youth. He was going to be as big and handsome as his brothers Sigimor and Somerled. He was also the only one, aside from the Camerons who had ridden with her from Drumwich, who had fully accepted her. She told herself it was early yet, that she had not even spent two full days in their company. And both days the men had spent little time at Dubheidland, for the hunt for Harold had begun immediately.

"Nay, I am not cold. I just had a dark thought, 'tis all," she said.

"About that whining lady upstairs?"

"Ah, nay, about Harold. I am troubled by the fact that he seems to have disappeared."

"They will find him and they will make him bleed."

Boys, she decided, were particularly bloodthirsty creatures. Jolene suspected Fergus said that to make her feel better, so she smiled as she handed him his newly mended shirt. He thanked her and ran off. Just like the rest of them, she thought, then scolded herself. They were gone because they were hunting down her enemy. It was ridiculous to feel as if she had been deserted. After so many days of being always in the company of others, she was just finding it difficult to be so alone.

The uncertainty of her own future made it even more difficult. If she knew she was going to stay at Dubheidland, was going to remain Sigimor's wife, she could start making a place for herself. There was certainly a lot she could do, such as planning some ways to ease the stark look of the place, the almost overwhelming feel of Dubheidland being solely a man's domain. Yet, she knew it might be unkind to add her own little touches to Dubheidland if she was going to leave and never return. Sigimor would certainly not want to see things that reminded him of her after she left him.

She turned her thoughts to Barbara and frowned.

The talk she had intended to have with Sigimor had not happened yet. The times she had been with him they had talked of the hunt for Harold or made love and gone to sleep. Yet, the question of how the woman had known so much still troubled Jolene. Since she could not speak with Sigimor, then she ought to speak to Barbara herself. There was a small chance that the woman would provide the answers Jolene needed.

One other question that needed answering was why the woman was still at Dubheidland. Sigimor avoided the woman as did most of his family. About the only company the woman enjoyed was that of the two men who had arrived with her and the occasional ill-tempered assistance of Old Nancy, who made no secret of her distaste for the woman. Barbara was comfortable and courteously given all she asked for, except Sigimor, but nothing else. Jolene began to wonder if the woman had decided to linger for that alone, yet, why would she unless she had no other choices.

Setting aside the mending, the one chore she had felt she could do without guilt, Jolene stood up and started out the great hall only to meet a scowling Old Nancy in the doorway. "Is something wrong?"

"Aside from having to wait hand and foot on that blond bitch?" Old Nancy asked.

"Aye, aside from that." Jolene was pleased to see some of the woman's anger begin to fade. "Lady Barbara *is* a nuisance, but I fear we have little choice but to endure her. At least for a little while longer."

"Aye, I ken it. Tis just the way she is constantly asking for things, as if I didnae have other work to do."

"What has she asked for now?"

"Some wine, bread and cheese. Why, I dinnae ken, as she had a full meal but a few hours ago. Told her that, if she didnae stop eating so much, we would be rolling her out of Dubheidland when it was time for her to leave." Old Nancy shook her head. "That woman has a vile, blasphemous tongue."

Jolene laughed and hugged the woman. Nan, as Jolene had decided to call her, was as blunt as any of the Cameron men. She had also been the one steadfast motherly figure in the men's lives, even though she was only ten years older than Sigimor. If she stayed with Sigimor, Jolene knew Nan would be both friend and ally.

"Poor Nan," she murmured as she stepped back. "If I was not afraid the woman would toss Sigimor to the floor and leap upon him, I would tell him to see to our unwelcome guest himself." She smiled when Nan laughed. "Howbeit, as I was about to go up to speak to the lady myself, I will take the tray of food and drink with me." She hooked her arm through Nan's and started toward the kitchens.

"Are ye sure, m'lady?" Nan asked even as, once in the kitchen, she fetched a tray and began to collect the things Barbara had asked for. "The woman has a poisonous tongue and she wants your husband. I dinnae like to think of what she might say to you, what lies she might whisper to ye."

Stopping herself from marveling yet again at the huge, well-appointed, and very clean kitchen that she would just love to put to use, Jolene looked at Nan. "Aye, I have a few questions I need answered."

"Now, now, she was just a lad's first lusting, eh?"

"Oh, not about her and Sigimor. I intended to

speak with Sigimor about this, but he has been too busy. Although I do not doubt that Barbara hoped to ensnare Sigimor, I have this feeling there is something more here."

"Weel, I am getting the feeling she has settled herself in for a long stay, as if she has no other place to go."

"So have I. Yet, she was married to such a rich man. Sigimor said the man once told him that she was so free with his coin, he would end up poor as dirt and that he had closed his purse to her. Still, that does not mean he did not leave her something when he died and, as mother to his heirs, she would have a home, would she not?"

"But she wouldnae be the lady of the keep if he gave the rule of the boys to some kinsmon."

"Oh. And, if that kinsman did not like her and her husband left her no money—"

"Then she becomes naught more than an unwanted poor relation. Mayhap, she has e'en been banished."

"Something to consider for, if her husband's family has banished her and suffered nothing for doing so, then 'tis safe to assume she no longer has all those powerful ties Sigimor worries about. It means we could send her away."

"Now there is a lovely thought. But, 'tisnae what ye were fretting o'er, is it?"

"Nay," replied Jolene. "It just puzzles me that she knew Sigimor had married an Englishwoman. According to those who saw her, she did a fine job of acting surprised, but it was just an act."

"Aye, aye, I have heard the same."

"Well, now I am certain of it. So, how did she know?"

"Gossip can move like a strong wind o'er this land," Nan said, but she frowned.

"Possibly." Jolene shook her head. "Nay, I do not think it is that simple. You see, she also knows that an annulment of this marriage could be easily had and the reasons why."

"An annulment? But, ye have consummated it, havenae ye?"

Jolene blushed. "Aye, but that would not matter in this case. I am the sister of an English earl and Sigimor is a Highland laird. There is also the fact that none of my kinsmen approved and there are many reasons why they should, e'en if I am three and twenty. The question here is—how did she know these things?"

"Tis a puzzle, but, if there is anything, weel, bad about it all, I am nay sure ye will get that one to confess it."

"Probably not, but there is no harm in trying." Jolene picked up the tray of food and drink and started out of the kitchen. "I suppose she has her pretty pets with her."

"Aye, the two men are there. Always are. That Donald isnae such a bad lad, but I dinnae like that mon Clyde. Just like the Lady Barbara, he is bonnie, but there is something nasty slithering about under that fair form."

And that was a chilling thought to have set in her head, Jolene thought as she headed toward Barbara's bedchamber. Since she agreed with Nan's opinion, however, it was impossible to shake it. There *was* something cold and nasty about Clyde. Jolene had the feeling he would do anything Barbara asked and, considering the type of woman she was, that was rather alarming.

"Aunt Jo," called Reynard as he skipped up to her just outside Barbara's door. "What are you doing?"

"Taking this food and drink to our guests," she replied.

"I will help."

Jolene opened her mouth to tell him not to, to send him away, but he was already rapping on the door. She told herself not to be so foolish. There was nothing these people could do to her or Reynard here inside Dubheidland and, if she thought the talk was becoming too rough, she would send the boy away then.

The moment Jolene walked into the bedchamber, she decided it would be better if Reynard left, but the child had already hurried over to see what Donald was doing. That man sat at a little table near the fire carving what looked to be a chess piece. He looked dismayed to see both her and Reynard, but the expression quickly faded, and he smiled at the boy. It was the faint smile upon Clyde's darkly handsome face that really worried Jolene, especially as it was matched by the one that curved Barbara's full lips.

"So, ye have finally condescended to visit with your guest," Barbara said as she sat up on the bed where she had been lounging while Clyde read to her.

"I have a few questions I would like to ask you," Jolene said as she set the tray on the table, frowning a litle at how quickly Clyde had moved, puttng himself right behind Donald and Reynard.

"About me and Sigimor? About what we once were to each other? What we could be again?"

"I know all I need to know about you two and your past. Sigimor told me."

Barbara chuckled as she donned her shoes. "And ye believed him? He is a mon, child. He lies."

The last of Jolene's concern about Barbara and Sigimor faded. The woman did not even know him. "Sigimor does not lie, m'lady. Not to me and not about you."

"Then what could ye possibly have to say to me?"

"I was curious as to how you knew that Sigimor was married and married to an Englishwoman. Also, how did you learn that such a marriage could be so easily annulled?" She decided that the brief look of surprise upon the woman's face was a compliment of sorts.

"But, I didnae ken it. Did ye nay see my surprise?"

"Nay, but many others did and called it an act. A very good one, but still just an act. You knew it all before you entered through the gates. Tis said that gossip travels very fast around here, but, I think, not that fast. So, how did you know?"

Barbara smiled and reached for the fur-lined cape draped over the end of her bed. "Why, Harold told me, didnae he?"

Jolene stared at the woman, all of her uneasiness, all of her doubts and fears, turning into a hard icy knot in her stomach. There was little joy to be found in this proof of her suspicions. It also explained one reason why this woman had not exerted herself to try and separate her and Sigimor. She had not needed to for Barbara had known that Jolene would soon be gone. The woman had not given up, she had simply been waiting for the impediment to her plans to be removed. Jolene took a deep breath and opened her mouth.

"I wouldnae scream, if I was ye," Barbara said,

pointing toward the men and Reynard as she moved to close the door.

Choking back the scream she had been about to let loose, Jolene looked at the men in horror. Clyde held Reynard close to his body, a gleaming knife held to the child's throat. Donald looked pale, his eyes gleaming with distress, but he made no move to help Reynard. Poor Reynard looked terrified, tears slipping down his cheeks, but he did not struggle and he made no sound.

"You are a mother," she said to Lady Barbara even as she held Reynard's gaze, trying to give him the strength to remain brave. "How can you allow a small child to be threatened like this?"

"Och, aye, I pushed out two puling little creatures," said Barbara. "'Twas the price I had to pay for a rich husband." She looked thoughtful for a moment. "Mayhap if someone held a knife to one of their throats, I might feel a twinge or two, but this one isnae mine, is he. Nay, he is some Sassenach's brat."

"Might I ask what will happen after you hand us over to Harold?"

"I will come back here and console poor Sigimor, the humiliated husband."

"And you expect him to believe that? To believe that I would risk my life and Reynard's by running away whilst the man who wants us dead is still out there?"

"He will when I tell him that ye have fled to join with your other kinsmen, the ones now hunting Harold."

Although she was pleased that her family might well have discovered Harold's crimes and now hunted him, the news also brought a chilling fear.

If it was true, she and Reynard were no longer of any use to Harold except as objects of revenge, as someone he could vent his fury on. She had nothing she could bargain with except the small chance that he might consider using them to save his own life. Depending upon how enraged he was over all he had lost, that might not be enough. Worse, Sigimor just might believe the woman.

Jolene quickly pushed that thought aside. Sigimor would come for her, would not believe this woman. If nothing else, he would feel it his duty to make sure that she and Reynard had reached her kinsmen safely. Jolene had to cling to the belief that Sigimor would come to her aid or she knew the fear clawing at her insides would overwhelm her.

"You place too much hope upon Sigimor believing you, especially when you showed him the folly of that ten years ago," Jolene said, pleased to hear no hint of her fear in her voice. "E'en now he thinks you are lying to him."

"If he does, then why has he allowed us to stay here?"

"Because you have a powerful family and powerful friends. He knows you could cause him a great deal of trouble and you simply are not worth it. But, I begin to think he is wrong. I think you have no more powerful friends or kinsmen. After all, if you did, and you truly wanted Sigimor, you would try and use them to get him for you. Or, get someone richer. You would not be forced to play such demeaning games if you had rich kin to go to."

"Pious fools, the lot of them!" Barbara snapped. "I did as they wanted, married that disgusting old mon and gave him his heir. And what is my reward? Naught! That old fool left me naught! I dinnae e'en have a roof o'er my head. Oh, the old fool left me a wee hovel, a pitiful place surrounded by sheep, and a pittance to survive on. Do my kinsmen help me? Nay! They have called me a whore, an embarrassment, a stain upon their name! They have all closed their doors to me! Oh, they will pay for that, mark my words. They *will* pay."

Jolene forced herself to remain calm as she watched Barbara rant, then fall into a sullen, brooding silence. If Barbara did manage to find some fool to marry her, she would undoubtedly try to use him to avenge her. In some ways, the woman was much like Harold. She obviously did not see that she had brought this all upon herself.

"And the money Harold has promised to pay for the two of ye will certainly help," Barbara said suddenly and smiled, her anger and dark mood disappearing with a disturbing suddenness.

"If you are putting your faith in Harold to keep his word, then you are a fool," said Jolene.

"The mon and I have an understanding. I give him what he wants and I get what I want—money and a clear path to Sigimor. What Harold is giving me will keep me quite comfortable until I can get Sigimor before a priest."

"The only way you will get Sigimor before a priest is if he is attending your funeral. And, if you are putting your trust in Harold, that is a distinct possibility."

"Oh, ye are so tiresome. Harold willnae betray us. We are already quite close. If he wasnae an Englishmon, I would consider him a good choice for a husband. He would certainly understand my need to avenge the insult I have suffered." She tied her cloak on and tugged the hood over her hair.

"We had best be on our way. I want to be back here by the time Sigimor returns."

"Just how do you plan to get out of here?"

"Why Clyde has found a bolthole. All keeps have them and Clyde is verra good at sniffing them out. Finds one where'er we go. Found Harold a good place to hide, too. I am sure it has amused him to ken that the Camerons are hunting him everywhere with no success."

Barbara went to the fireplace, turned a strange carving at the far edge of the mantel, and an opening in the thick stone wall slowly appeared. Clyde grabbed a torch from the wall sconce next to the fireplace, and, with his knife at Reynard's small back, nudged the boy ahead of him into the gloomy passageway. Smiling sweetly, Barbara waved Jolene to follow him. Knowing she had no choice, Jolene started toward the doorway set deep in the wall. She paused just inside, however, as Barbara grabbed a candle then frowned at Donald who had not made any move to join her.

"Weel? Come along," she ordered her cousin. "We are wasting time."

"Nay, I will stay here," said Donald, his eyes looking brilliant against his ashen face.

"Why?"

"Because this is as far as I will go in this."

"If ye betray me, Donald, ye will pay for it."

"Oh, aye, I ken it. I understand now exactly what ye are capable of, Cousin. Have no fear of that."

"Good, I mean it. If Sigimor asks ye where his wife has gone, ye had best say nothing. Swear it?"

"I swear it. If Sigimor asks me that, I willnae say a word. I will leave the lies to you. Ye are better at it."

"Weel, of course I am. Ye were ne'er as good as I am." Barbara turned to glare at Jolene. "Move. I cannae be gone too long."

Jolene cast one last look at Donald then headed down the passageway. A moment later she heard Barbara follow her. It was as dark and narrow as the one she had used to flee Drumwich and Harold. She thought it a little ironic to be taking a similar route right back into the danger she had escaped from.

Donald rose and shut the passageway, then rested his forehead against the cool stone. After a moment, he moved back to his seat by the table and returned to his carving. Barbara had gone too far this time. He would wait. The Camerons would return soon. He was confident one of them would stumble on the way to get him to tell them what he knew without his having to break his vow to Barbara. He just hoped he survived the confrontation. He was almost certain that Barbara would not survive the one she was headed toward.

"I think the mon has gone back to England," said Somerled as he tossed aside the cloth he had just used to dry himself off, and reached for his clean clothes.

Sigimor sighed as he rubbed his hair dry and glanced around at the men who had ridden with him today. They were all crowded into the large bathing shed he had had built a few years ago just for this purpose, the sudden arrival of nearly a score of filthy men all anxious to clean the mud off. Every one of them was waiting for his response to Somerled's words. The fact that they could find no sign of Harold and his men after two days did seem to imply that the man had finally given up.

"Nay," he said, "I dinnae think he has." He hung his drying cloth on one of the many hooks on the wall and started to get dressed. "He has gone to ground."

"Then we should have found him. We ken this land better than he does."

"Aye, but that doesnae mean he couldnae have stumbled upon a good hiding place. There are a lot about." He looked at his twin and shrugged. "I cannae explain it, but I am that certain that he is out there, and close."

"Had a vision, did ye, Sigimor?" called out his brother Ranulph.

Sigimor nodded in silent agreement as Tait and Nanty threw Ranulph into one of the many large vats used for bathing. "I just think that a mon who has been hunting us so hard, who rode away from and thus risks losing what he has already killed to gain, isnae going to tuck his tail between his legs and slink home now."

"Nay, probably not," Somerled agreed reluctantly as he started out of the shed beside Sigimor. "Tis just a wee bit humiliating that we cannae seem to find an enemy hiding on our own lands."

"I ken it." Sigimor felt himself tense as Fergus came running out of the keep. "What is it, lad?" he asked when the boy stumbled to a halt in front of him. Fergus's freckles stood out brilliantly against the linen-pale color of his face.

"They are gone!" Fergus grabbed Sigimor by the arm and tugged him toward the keep. "Jolene and Reynard are gone! They went to speak to that woman and now they are gone."

A chill entered Sigimor's veins. For a moment he could do no more than allow Fergus to pull him along. It was not until they were inside the keep and he saw an equally pale Old Nancy on the stairs that he gained some control of his shock.

"Are ye sure they are gone?" he asked her.

"Aye, m'laird," she replied. "Both her and the boy. Aye, as weel as Lady Barbara and one of her pretty pets, that mon Clyde. Her cousin is still here, but he willnae answer our questions."

Sigimor raced up the stairs and headed straight for Barbara's chambers. He could hear the others following him, but he did not wait for them to catch up. When he burst into Barbara's room, he looked around and felt that chill of fear grow even worse. The only one in the room was Donald. He sat at a table near the fire working on a small carving. Then, to Sigimor's confused astonishment, the young man smiled at him

"Tis about time ye got here," Donald said. "Ye are a wee bit late in returning."

"Where is my wife?" he demanded as Donald carefully set the piece he had been carving in the center of the table.

"Ah, now, I cannae answer *that* question."

"Ye will if ye wish to leave here in one piece."

"Oh, aye, I want that verra much. Verra much. Tis why I sit here. I but await ye to ask the right question."

Sigimor forced his anger down, as well as the sense of desperation he felt. Donald was not really defying him, he realized. In fact, he had the distinct feeling the young man was hoping he could help. There was a key to unlock the truth, but Sigimor was not in the mood for puzzles or in a state of mind to work one out. As Fergus, Old Nancy, and Somerled gathered around him, Sigimor took several slow, deep breaths to grasp at a thin thread of calm.

"Where has Lady Barbara gone?" he asked, his hand tightening on the hilt of his sword, but, to his surprise, the younger man smiled again.

"Now that is a question I *can* answer. I fear she has taken the Lady Jolene and the boy to this mon Harold." Donald pressed himself back in his seat as Sigimor took several steps toward him. "I told her it was wrong, e'en warned her against the mon."

"But ye did naught to stop her, did ye?"

"Nay. I thought I could change her mind right up until your wife and the boy entered the room. Once it all began, I suddenly realized that I couldnae trust in Barbara to e'en let me live, that there was a strong chance she would have Clyde cut my throat if I tried to stop her or betray her to you. Harold has promised her a veritable fortune. She truly believes he will honor his word and that she can then just slip back here to woo ye. They have gone to the catacombs."

Sigimor looked at Somerled when his brother cursed. "I thought they were sealed up."

"Liam and I recently opened them." Somerled shrugged. "Curiosity. They have been sealed since our father was a lad."

"But, how did Lady Barbara and Clyde leave without being seen? The church where those catacombs are is three miles away, at least."

Sigimor suddenly noticed how Donald kept playing with the little figure he had carved and cursed as he turned his gaze toward the matching figure on the corner of the fireplace. "I had forgotten about the bolthole." He looked back at Donald. "How long ago did Lady Barbara leave?"

"About two hours ago and on foot. M'laird!" Donald cried out when Sigimor started to leave.

Slowly, Sigimor turned to face the man again. "Do ye ken how badly I want to kill ye?"

"Aye, I think I do."

"Then why are ye still here?"

"I wait to take Barbara's body home," he replied softly.

Chapter Seventeen

Bile stung the back of Jolene's throat as she stared down at the bodies of Clyde and Lady Barbara, unable to look away. She had never seen anyone killed so quickly and coldly. Barbara had been blissfully unaware of her danger right up to the end. There had been an odd look upon Clyde's face in the heartbeat of time between his realizing that someone had stepped up behind him and having his throat cut. He had given Harold a look that could only be called admiring. In that last instant of life the man had done one good thing, however. He had shoved Reynard toward Jolene. She had caught her nephew and quickly cocooned him within her skirts to shield him from the sight of the abrupt execution.

When the two men who had done the killing started to drag the bodies away, she finally looked at Harold. "You will soon run out of allies if that is how you treat them."

"They sold you and the boy to me. Next they would have sold me to the Camerons," Harold said and shrugged.

"So you judged them guilty of a crime before they had e'en committed it?"

"The woman was determined to become the lady of that accursed keep no civilized tongue can pronounce the name of. She would have done anything to get Sir Sigimor to marry her. She betrayed him to me to be rid of you. To win his favor, she would have betrayed me." He scowled at the two bodies now thrown atop each other in the far corner of the large chamber. "It troubles me that that young cousin of hers did not come, too."

Jolene slowly rubbed the back of a faintly trembling Reynard and wondered if Donald had guessed what would happen, had somehow sensed the danger of dealing with Harold. "How disappointing for you."

"We will leave here as soon as it gets dark," he said, ignoring her sarcasm. "I have not yet decided what to do with you, but I think I can use the boy to buy me something. My life for his. Our kinsmen will be eager to get him back safe and alive. I fear you will not be so blessed." He looked around. "An excellent hiding place, is it not? That fellow Clyde found it. We have sat here snug, dry, and safe whilst the Camerons have exhausted themselves and their horses hunting for us."

"Clyde was duly impressed by your show of gratitude, I am certain." She looked around what was obviously the main burial chamber in what she suspected were some very old catacombs. "I wonder why Sigimor did not think to look here."

"Martin believes they have only recently been unsealed and after a very long time, too."

"M'lord," said Martin as he strode up to Harold, "I have a message from your kinsmen."

"We were not to make any contact with them until the morrow."

"They caught one of the men we had sent to watch them and gave it to him to deliver."

"Well, what is it then?"

"They ask for a meeting, m'lord. Your kinsman Sir Roger sends his greetings and requests that you or a man of your choosing meet with him on the morrow."

"Where and when?"

" 'Bout two miles south from here, at a clearing. One hour after dawn. Tis easy to find. But a few yards from here you can begin to see the top of an old peel tower. Head straight for that and you enter the clearing."

"How many men does he have?" Harold asked after frowning in thought for a moment.

"A score," replied Martin, "and two Scots. I think they might be MacFingals. They have the look of those bastards. They were the ones who caught our man."

Harold cursed and dragged his hand through his hair. "I must needs think on this. Is a reply requested?"

"Nay. Your reply will be if you come to the meeting."

Nodding, Harold suddenly glared at Jolene. "Take that sniveling brat and go sit down somewhere. I need to think."

More than happy to get away from Harold, Jolene picked Reynard up and sought a place to sit down. She moved away from the bodies of Barbara and her companion toward a large stone coffin set against the far wall. After a moment of thought, she sat down at the end of it, her back against the wall, putting herself and Reynard into the shadows. Jolene watched as Harold paced. She held Reynard close and hoped that whatever held Harold's attention so firmly did so for a long time.

Cousin Roger was close, she thought, and let the joy of that news wash over her. Jolene felt certain that would give Reynard a chance. With the opportunity to trade Reynard's life for his so close at hand, she was certain Harold would grab it. There was little chance he would hold to any agreement he might make, but at least Reynard would be taken out of the hands of his enemy. She was certain Roger would do what was needed to make Harold give him the boy.

She forced herself to ignore her own possible fate. Jolene knew that, if she let herself start wondering about what Harold might do to her, she would quickly lose her already tenuous control of the fear inside her. She needed to be brave for Reynard's sake, to try to remain calm, and that meant ignoring her place in Harold's dark plans. Sigimor would be looking for her soon, she told herself, and clutched at that hope like a shield against Harold and her own fears.

To keep herself from thinking on what she would soon face if she did not get away from Harold, she listened carefully to what was being said. Neither Martin nor Harold bothered to speak quietly and their voices carried well in the chamber. Harold's anger, she noticed, was no longer so well controlled.

"The boy will buy us our freedom, m'lord," said Martin.

"Aye, aye, but if I could get him back to Drumwich myself, there is still a chance I could gain control. The boy is the key to it all, Martin," Harold snapped when Martin shook his head.

"The only thing that boy is the key to now is our freedom. Sir Roger has a score of men with him. Since he also has two MacFingals with him, and they are not trying to steal his horses, that means he is being aided by the allies of the Camerons. They have brought him here to join with the Camerons against us. I am thinking that means Sir Roger knows everything and might well have some power behind him. Ransom the boy, for our freedom, for our lives, and, mayhap, for whatever coin the man is carrying."

"And then what? Where will we go?"

"France or some other country where we can sell our swords." Martin watched Harold pace some more. "And you might consider ransoming the woman as well."

"Never!" Harold yelled. "She is the reason we are in this mess! She has ruined everything and I want to make her pay for that. I want to make her suffer for it." He searched the chamber until he saw Jolene and glared at her. "You married that Scot."

"How did you discover that?" she asked.

"The priest. We followed you there," Harold replied, moving closer, clenching and unclenching his fists. "He told us after a little persuasion loosened his tongue. Aye, and he paid dearly for his part in that, as you will."

"You killed a priest?" Jolene was surprised that anything Harold did could still shock her, but this did.

"Nay. At least, he was not dead when we left him, although he was probably wishing he was."

"That priest is a Cameron, Harold," she said and heard Martin curse. "A cousin. You have just given them e'en more reason to hunt you down. You will probably be able to use Reynard to deal with Sir Roger, but the Camerons will hunt you all the way to the sea." Harold looked unmoved by her threat, but she noticed Martin narrow his eyes in thought.

"Why should that trouble me? They have been no threat thus far. They do naught but run from us, and hide."

"Aye, and have led you right to their gates, led you deep into their lands, amidst their allies and kinsmen."

Harold lunged at her, and, to her surprise, Martin grabbed him. For a few minutes the two men staggered around the chamber as Harold cursed and threatened Martin, but, despite the blows he took, Martin did not let go. Finally, Harold grew still. Martin slowly released him and stepped back. Harold drew his sword and held it on Martin so quickly, Jolene gasped. She put her hand to the back of Reynard's head and kept his face pressed against her, certain murder was about to be done. Either Martin had more confidence in his worth to Harold than she did, or, for his own reasons, he refused to draw a sword on the man, for he just stood there. Then she caught the glint of a knife's blade by his hip and realized the man held a knife in his hand. She knew Martin could deliver a mortal wound with that before Harold could make good use of his sword. All the men stood tensely, watching, and Jolene had the strong feeling that their loyalty lay more with Martin than with Harold.

"You would defend the little bitch?" Harold asked in a voice hoarse with fury.

"For now," replied Martin. "If naught else, she holds the boy and he must not be harmed."

Harold shuddered faintly and closed his eyes,

then slowly resheathed his sword. "I will deal with her later."

Martin nodded and his knife disappeared. "If you wish. You might also consider the possibility of using her to keep the Camerons from slaughtering us." There was the whisper of agreement from the other men in the chamber.

"The Camerons? They are no real threat. They have done nothing but run from us, have ne'er e'en tried to face us or fight us."

"Not yet." Martin watched Harold until the man began to frown, obviously considering Martin's words. "There were but six of them and they had her and the boy with them. It might have seemed cowardly to some that they did naught but elude us, but I did not see it thus. It was clever and the right choice of tactic. She is right. We are now deep in their lands, surrounded by his kinsmen and his allies. We are now the ones outnumbered, the ones hiding from the hunters."

Jolene looked around at the men in the chamber who all watched Harold closely. It was very clear to see that they all agreed with Martin and waited to see if Harold would as well. They understood that they had been caught in an ever tightening net and they wanted out of it. She strongly suspected that, if Harold did not begin to show that he had more interest in getting out of the trap alive than in revenge, he would find himself without any swords to call to his aid. Jolene smothered the sudden hope that a rebellion in the ranks could offer her a chance to escape, but she still watched closely for one.

"And, I suppose you have some plan?" Harold asked, mockery weighting every word.

"Aye, I do," replied Martin, ignoring the taunt. "We use the boy to get the English swords sheathed and we use her to get us safely out of this cursed country." Martin sighed and rubbed a hand over his face. "She is Sir Sigimor's wife. If naught else, honor will demand that he do whate'er he must to protect her and keep her alive. Between ransoming the boy to the English and her to the Scots, we may yet come out of this tangle with a heavy purse. At least we have a chance of coming out of this alive. Study this as I do; the only other choice I see is that we try to at least make it a little difficult for them to slaughter us."

A faint sound plucked at Jolene's attention, but she fought to ignore it. What was happening between Martin and Harold was too important to miss. Her fate was in the balance here. She knew Harold needed to make her pay for all he had lost, for the failure of all his plots, but, if Martin convinced him that she could be of use to them, her chance of survival rose. She silently prayed for Harold to heed Martin's advice, to hold her as a shield between them and the Camerons until they could reach a port and flee to France. The thought of spending days as Harold's captive was a chilling one, but she would be alive, and she knew that Sigimor would come after her.

Sigimor gently lowered to the ground the body of the man he had just killed and then scowled at the old church. Beneath the slowly crumbling building was Jolene. She had been in Harold's hands for an hour, maybe even longer. The thought of what that man might have already done to her had his stomach twisted in knots. It took all of his will-power, and the occasional watchful presence of Liam, to stop himself from simply racing down to the burial chambers screaming for Harold's blood.

From the moment Fergus had told him Jolene was gone, he had felt cold with fear, a fear for her. Even more so, a fear of losing her, of not being able to save her. It was almost impossible to keep his mind from conjuring up grim images of what Harold had said he would do to her. He kept hearing the man speak of his plans for her. Logic told him that Harold could not accomplish much in the time he had had, but Sigimor was not having much success at remaining logical at the moment. It also only took an instant to kill someone, his mind kept whispering to him.

"The guards are all cleared away, inside and out," said Liam as he stepped up next to Sigimor.

"Aye," said Somerled as he moved to stand on Sigimor's other side. "Those two Scots fled for the hills, didnae e'en warn these men."

"No honor amongst thieves," murmured Tait, crouching by the body of the man Sigimor had killed and studying him closely. "Hired swords, I think. If we can get the ones below cornered or surrounded, they might well surrender."

"How do we get in?" Sigimor asked, knowing that concentrating on the battle ahead of them was the only thing keeping him sane.

"Three ways," replied Liam. "There were guards at the opening of only two so I think we can safely assume they dinnae ken about the third."

"Mayhap one of those swift-footed Scots was supposed to guard it."

"Nay. They had been set out to watch for us,

probably to warn Harold if our search drew too close to them. When we headed straight here, moving with some stealth, they realized that we were nay longer searching and decided the game was lost. Decided to leave the Sassenachs to their fate and save their own necks. Our plan?"

"Tell me where the entrances are and where ye think Harold will have set up his little refuge."

Sigimor closed his eyes and listened carefully, relaxing a little when Liam and Somerled both said there was only one chamber below where Harold and his men could camp in any comfort. After a moment's thought, he began to disperse the nearly thirty men with him, seven through each entrance and the rest to stay above and make sure none of Harold's men escaped, as well as to stand guard at their backs. They decided on how much time would be needed for each group to get into position and Sigimor chose a signal to annouce the attack. Nanty stayed above with the guards, Somerled took six men to the main entrance inside the church, Liam took six more to the hidden inside entrance, and Sigimor took six to the outside entrance only feet away from the man he had killed.

Moving through the passageway was slow work and Sigimor cursed the dark every step of the way. Then a faint light began to pierce the dark and he smiled. Harold was near and it took every scrap of control he had to keep moving slowly. His well-trained men needed no signal to press close to the wall as the sound of voices reached them. Inching along until he reached the end of the passage, Sigimor chanced a peek inside. He counted six men, and Harold and the man he was standing with, a man Sigimor recalled from Drumwich called Martin.

Just as he was about to pull back into the full shadows, Sigimor heard a soft sniff. He glanced to the right and nearly gave himself away with an abrupt cry of joy. Jolene sat on the floor barely two feet away. She was set snug in the corner made by the wall of the chamber and a large stone coffin, holding Reynard in her lap, and watching Harold closely. Sigimor quickly pressed himself back into the shadow and closed his eyes, feeling nearly weak-kneed with relief. Jolene did not appear to even have a bruise.

"Your idea has some merit," Harold said. "I must think about it."

"What is there to think about?"

"I need to think of a way to do as you say, but keep hold of Jolene."

Martin swore. "That woman isnae worth dying for!"

"I do not intend to die for her."

Sigimor gave the signal to attack, smiling with satisfaction as his soft blackbird's call brought two swift echoes. He quickly left the passage, immediately positioning himself in front of Jolene. He watched with pleasure and pride as twenty other Camerons suddenly appeared, encircling Harold and his men. Grim-faced and with swords drawn, they made a fine sight, he decided. When Harold's startled gaze settled on his, Sigimor smiled at the man.

"I fear your intentions are for naught, Harold," Sigimor said. "Ye are going to die. Right here. Right now."

It pleased Sigimor when Harold suddenly screamed in fury and drew his sword. He had been hoping the man would not want to surrender. Moving away from Jolene, and sensing one of his men quickly taking his place to shield her, Sigimor stepped up to meet Harold's challenge before the man recovered his senses and withdrew it.

Jolene kept a wriggling Reynard's face pressed against her and flinched at the sound of sword meeting sword echoing through the stone chamber. She watched her husband and Harold for only a moment before she felt calm banish the chill of fear. Harold was good, but Sigimor was much better. Harold *was* going to die. Right here. Right now.

She looked around to see what else was happening. Martin and two of the other men had surrendered immediately. They stood unarmed near Liam watching the fight. Four others had made the mistake of drawing their swords. Two were already dead and, although she was no expert on fighting, she felt sure the other two soon would be. The Camerons had met these attacks one on one, but Harold's men were obviously outmatched.

Just as she turned her gaze back to Sigimor, the fight ended. Harold moved awkwardly, leaving an opening, and Sigimor took swift advantage, burying his sword deep in the man's chest. The way Harold died so quickly, barely gasping as the blade entered his body, told Jolene that it had probably been a clean thrust to the heart. The end of the other two men's lives was very nearly as abrupt and silent. She watched while Sigimor cleaned his blade on Harold's elaborately embroidered jupon and then resheathed it. Sigimor looked at her, then nodded when she smiled at him and turned his attention to Martin and the last of Harold's men.

"Since my woman is unharmed, I feel a wee bit merciful," Sigimor said. "Get out. Dinnae pause to rob the dead, dinnae linger to e'en water your horses until ye are far off my lands. Keep running until ye are out of Scotland. My good mood could fade. Ranulph, lead them out so that our men set outside dinnae kill them. Tait, Gilbert, ye follow and if they e'en twitch, kill them."

This was Sigimor the warrior, Jolene thought as she listened to his cold, hard voice ring through the room. He even said the word mercy in a tone that offered none. Knowing the men Harold had placed outside were probably dead and having seen how easily and coldly he had killed Harold, Jolene suspected she ought to be feeling nervous. In many ways this man was a Sigimor she did not know, a man she had never met before. Instead, she felt only pride, in him and herself, for he was hers. She smiled at him again when he crouched in front of her and gently, tenderly, stroked her cheek with the very hand that, moments before, had wielded a deadly sword. It was hard to subdue the fierce urge to throw herself into his arms and kiss him.

"Ye arenae hurt?" he asked.

"Nay, Martin was trying to convince Harold that I would be very useful in dealing with you. Martin wanted to get out of this alive. At least he got what he wanted." She glanced toward the wall where the bodies of Barbara and Clyde lay. "I fear Lady Barbara and her companion did not."

Sigimor winced as he saw the bodies, and quietly signaled his men to take them out. "Donald wants them, to take them home."

"I had the feeling he had guessed how dealing with Harold might end."

"Yet, he did naught to help you."

"He did help you, though, did he not?"

"Aye, after I guessed the right question to ask. Ye can smile at that?"

She smiled as Tait took Reynard from her and left with the boy. "Now, aye," she replied. "I heard how very carefully he worded his promise to Barbara and thought it was done apurpose. I do not blame him for not helping as we were taken away. He was in some danger himself, I believe."

Sigimor nodded and helped her to her feet. He pulled her into his arms and held her for a moment, simply breathing in the scent of her hair. Slowly, the last of his fear for her faded away. Keeping an arm around her shoulders, he led her out of the chamber, grabbing a torch to light their way and leaving a few of his men to clear away the bodies and collect anything of value.

Jolene wrapped her arm around his waist and pressed herself close to his side as they walked. She told him all that had happened since she and Reynard had walked into Barbara's bedchamber. The only thing she held back was the news that, not very far away, was her cousin Roger. His presence meant a decision would soon have to be made, and, for the moment, she just wanted to savor being safe, free, and back with Sigimor.

"Oh, your cousin William, the priest, was the one who told Harold about our marriage," she said as they stepped out of the passage and both paused for a deep breath of fresh air. "Harold said that he had to persuade the man to do so and that he beat him near to death afterward. He did not linger to see if the poor man actually did die."

"I will get a few men and go to him," said Gilbert. "If needed, we can take the man to Scarglas and let Fiona and Mab tend to his injuries. They will soon put him back on his feet."

"Good lad," Sigimor said and sighed as Gilbert

hurried off. "I wouldnae be surprised if there are a few more along Harold's route who suffered at his hands, but there is naught we can do about it."

"Nay," agreed Jolene. "Harold did have a skill at leaving a bloody trail where'er he went. Someone should have killed him years ago. There was ne'er any proof, though, and he was high enough born to make that be very important."

"Aye, the poor mon can get hanged on naught but a suspicion. The rich mon needs to be caught with a bloody hand and e'en then he may ne'er pay for his crime." He set Jolene up on his horse and mounted behind her. "I still feel a wee bit merciful, so I will let Donald stay the night and toss him out in the morning."

"You are a true saint, husband," she said and exchanged a grin with him.

She snuggled back against him as he started to ride, placing her hands on his arms. It was a little hard to believe it was all over, that Harold was no longer a threat. It had not been that long since she had fled Drumwich, but the weight of that threat had made the time go by so much more slowly. He was no longer a constant shadow at her back, a knife held at Reynard's throat, or the one who might actually be able to make her wish for death.

There was a new shadow, however, but she refused to study it just yet. Roger and the need to make a choice lurked at the edges of the happiness she felt right now. She had until the dawn. For a few hours more she would pretend all was well.

Chapter Eighteen

Breathing deeply of the soft scent of lavender rising from her hot bath did little to ease the tension in Jolene. She had succeeded in ignoring what now faced her for as long as she could. It had insisted upon intruding into her mind for most of the time since returning from what was now Harold's grave, and all her attempts to push such thoughts away had caused her to be a little distracted. She was certain Sigimor had noticed that, but he seemed to accept that it was just a result of the things that had happened while she was a captive.

This was her last night with him, she thought, and fought the urge to weep. There really was no other choice for her. Reynard was a child, his needs greater than a man's or hers. She had sworn to her dying brother that she would care for his child. It could hardly be called caring if she simply handed him to someone to take back to Drumwich for her and never looked back.

A part of her urged her to speak to Sigimor about it, to tell him of Roger and the meeting, but she ignored it. She was afraid he could convince her to stay with him, to turn her back on her vow, her duty, and little Reynard. Even worse, she was afraid he might not even try.

Stepping out of her bath, she rubbed herself dry. When she picked up the delicate night shift Fiona had given her, she had to swallow another welling up of tears. She would never see Fiona again, either. Never see Fergus's freckled face. Never hear Old Nancy tell one of the huge Cameron men that he was acting like a child. Never see any of the Camerons or the MacFingals.

And never feel the joy of Sigimor's kiss, she thought, and had to sit down on the bed. Jolene took several minutes to beat down her sense of overwhelming grief. Sigimor would see it, would sense it, if she did not conquer it. It could be dealt with later. She could weep later. In truth, she would have year upon empty year to indulge herself with weeping for all she had lost.

When she felt a little more in control, she donned the night shift. Tonight she was going to soak herself in memories. She was going to exhaust herself and Sigimor, make love until they could not move. Jolene had a few thoughts on what she wanted to do. It made her blush even to think of them, but she would not allow modesty to halt her tonight. That wild, sensuous woman inside her, the one who would burst free when Sigimor made love to her, was going to be in full control tonight.

Standing before the fire, she brushed her hair dry and waited. This was the sight she wanted Sigimor to keep in his mind after she was gone. Jolene knew he would be angry, his pride lacerated, but at some time in the future, he might be able to think of her with some kindness. When he did, she wanted him to remember her standing here, waiting to make love to him.

Sigimor stepped into the room and slowly closed the door behind him. The way Jolene looked made him catch his breath. He had sensed something troubling her since their return from the church, but she had said nothing. He decided she had been shocked by the killing of Barbara and Clyde, that such cold cruelty had left its mark, but he was not entirely satisfied with that answer. It was almost as if she was keeping something from him, but he could not think of anything she would have to keep secret.

Moving toward her as she smiled at him, he decided he could puzzle over it tomorrow. The way his blood was heating up and his body hardening, he would not have the wit to remember his own name soon. He took the brush from her hands, pulled her into his arms and kissed her. There was the hint of desperation in her kiss, but he decided that was because she had faced death today. Such a thing always gave a person a greed for the joys of living.

When he stepped back and began to remove his clothes, she put her hands on his and took over the chore. Sigimor gritted his teeth as her soft hands brushed against his skin. She took every chance she could to caress him as she removed his clothes and he was not sure how much of that game he could endure.

Jolene knelt by his feet to unlace his boots. Once he was completely naked, she eluded his attempt to pull her into his arms as she stood up. She pressed her lips to the hollow at his throat as she stroked his big, strong body, trying to memorize every ridge and hollow. Ever so slowly she began to kiss her way down his body, occasionally using her tongue to soothe whatever small sting she may have inflicted with a small love bite here and there. The way he was beginning to breathe hard told her he was enjoying her attention as much as she was enjoying the giving of it.

A soft grunt escaped him as she ignored what jutted out from between his legs and began to kiss her way down one leg and slowly up the other. As she nipped and kissed his inner thighs, she curled her fingers around his erection and gently stroked him. He cursed softly and she smiled against his thigh. It had been one of her little dreams to pleasure him in the way he had pleasured her several times, and now she knew he wanted that as well.

"Lass, ye are about to make me crazed," Sigimor said.

"Mayhap that is my intention," she murmured against his taut stomach as she drew a circle around his navel with her tongue.

"Then ye are succeeding beyond your wildest dreams."

"Ah, husband, you have no idea what my wildest dreams are like."

He was about to respond to that, when she licked the tip of his staff and the first word of his comment came out as a squeak. Sigimor threaded his fingers through her hair, and groaned softly as she began to make love to him with her mouth. The feel of her warm, soft lips and the heated strokes of her tongue were making him blind with need. He struggled to rein in his passion, determined to enjoy this pleasure for as long as he could. Then she took him into her mouth, and he felt that control begin to shatter.

Although he desperately wanted to savor the way she was making him feel, Sigimor finally had to put a stop to it. He was too close to release and he needed to be inside her. Pushing her down on the rug, he stripped off her night shift. He kissed her with all the hunger he felt and slipped his hand between her legs. To his surprise, and relief, she was already hot and wet. The flattery he tried to whisper in her ear came out as a soft growl as he joined their bodies. As her tight heat surrounded him and her lithe body rose up to meet his, he decided there was no need to talk, or think, just let passion rule them.

"Wife," he managed to say after he had finally roused himself from a sated stupor and carried her to their bed, collapsing at her side, "do ye mean to kill me?"

"Only with pleasure," she said, curling up next to him and stroking his stomach.

"Hah! I could make your eyes roll back in your head if I wanted to."

"A challenge, is it?"

Feeling newly invigorated, Sigimor pushed her onto her back and crouched over her. "A challenge indeed. I bet I can make ye get too weak to lift a finger ere ye could put me in such a state."

"Oh, nay, I think not."

"Are ye sure ye want to accept this challenge, wife?"

"Are you sure you can handle defeat?"

"I have no intention of losing."

"Neither do I."

Sigimor opened one eye and noticed the fire was burning low, then groaned and closed his eye when

Jolene wagged a finger in his face. "I concede," he said.

"Tis about time," said Jolene from where she was sprawled on her back at his side and let her hand fall to her side.

It was an effort to do so, but he curled an arm around her shoulders and pulled her against his side. "I think we best limit these challenges, wife," he said, then yawned.

"It might be wise."

"I *would* like to live to a ripe old age." He smiled sleepily when she laughed.

Jolene soon felt his body grow lax. A moment later he made that odd little sound that was not quite a snore. It was a strange thing to make her want to cry, she thought, as she eased out of his arms to sit by his side.

Her body felt sated and pleased, but her heart ached with sorrow. He was everything she had ever wanted in a husband and she had to leave him. Glancing toward the window, she knew she could not even stay here and watch him sleep for a while. It was going to require a great deal of stealth to get out of Dubheidland unseen and stealth could be very time consuming. There was also a long walk ahead of her. She looked back at Sigimor and struggled against the urge to kiss him, afraid that might make him stir.

Wincing a little at the various little aches in her body, she cautiously got out of bed. Never taking her eyes from him, she got dressed and collected her small sack of belongings from under the bed where she had hidden it earlier. For a moment, she just stood there, unable to take that first step, but she forced thoughts of Reynard and promises made to the fore of her mind. As silently as she was able, she let herself out of the room.

Collecting Reynard was relatively easy. He slept near the door in the room with several other boys who slept like the dead. She wrapped him up in his blanket, grabbed his little sack of clothes and hurried out of the room.

Slipping into the room Barbara had used, she set the still-sleeping Reynard down on the bed and dressed him. He was just starting to wake up when she began to put him in a blanket sling she then hefted onto her back and secured around her chest. Out of the corner of her eye she caught his eyes widening slightly when he looked around and realized where they were.

"Hush, m'love," she whispered. "There is no danger. We are going to go and visit someone."

"Who?"

"Cousin Roger."

"Oh. I like Cousin Roger."

"He likes you too." She picked up their small sacks in one hand and moved to the fireplace to open up the passageway.

"Why are we going this way?"

Grabbing a torch in her free hand, she replied, "Because it is very early and I do not want to disturb everyone. They are all very tired after saving us yesterday."

He fell silent and she slipped into the passage. The lie she had just told was a small added weight to the guilt she was already feeling. She pushed aside all thought of guilt, lies, a peacefully sleeping husband who would wake to find himself alone, and how her grief was growing deeper and deeper with every step she took on the journey that would take her away from Dubheidland. There was a long walk ahead of her and, if only to be sure she did not get lost, she had to concentrate on the journey alone.

It was a little later than an hour after dawn when Jolene stepped into the clearing where Roger was supposed to be waiting. For a moment she feared he had already given up and left, but then, one by one men appeared from the surrounding trees. She looked for Roger and smiled when she saw him. He looked absolutely stunned, but a moment later he was hugging her.

With an admirable efficiency a fire was made, Reynard was tended to, and Jolene found herself seated on a folded blanket before the fire sipping wine. She told Roger all about Harold's death and he told her all he had done since hearing of Peter's murder. When he told her that he had been appointed Reynard's guardian, that his wife was already at Drumwich waiting for the boy, she was stunned. She finished her wine, stood up, and stared in the direction of Dubheidland.

"I hope you are pleased," said Roger as he moved to stand beside her.

"Very pleased," she replied. "It is all exactly as I wanted it to be."

"About this husband I have heard you now have. It will be possible to get an annulment, you know." He frowned when she shook her head.

"I am going back," she said, and, despite the fact that she would have to leave Reynard, she felt the hard knot of grief she had suffered since yesterday begin to unravel.

"Go back to Sir Sigimor? But, Jolene, he is a Scot."

"Aye, a big, rough, redheaded Scot. He is my husband." She suddenly smiled, with joy and at her own idiocy. "And I love him."

"Ah, well," Roger dragged a hand through his hair, "after all you have been through you may be mistaken in your feelings. Some time back at Drumwich and you will see that this is not the marriage for you." He cursed softly when she shook her head again. "Does he love you?"

"Perhaps. He gets jealous and is very possessive."

"Most men are, but it doesn't have to mean much."

"He is always seeing to my comfort and will not stand for any insult to me."

"As any gentleman should."

"Oh, Sigimor is not really much of a gentleman."

"There, you see, a woman of your blood should have a true gentleman as her husband."

"He talks with me, about a lot of things, and he listens to what I have to say."

"Jolene—"

"If I ask him, he will explain himself to me. He tries to understand my moods and will ask me the why of them."

"He is a Scot!"

"He is as at ease with me as he is with his brothers and he laughs with me."

"He sounds like a good friend, but—"

Jolene looked at her cousin and even though she blushed, she whispered, "And the passion is hot and fierce and he holds me in his arms all through the night." She was a little surprised when Roger blushed, too.

"You really intend to go back?"

"Aye, I have to go back to him. I love him, although it may be a while before I tell him so. I think he could come to love me, may already do so in some ways. It does not matter. I have to go back to him. Even if he does not love me now, he is still the only husband I want."

"But, what about Reynard?"

Jolene looked at her nephew as he came to stand with them. "Reynard, you are going to have to be a brave little man. I am going to go back to Dubheidland to live with Sigimor and you are going home to live with Cousin Roger and Cousin Emma."

"No, I don' like that."

She crouched in front of him and kissed his cheek. "I do not want to leave you, my sweet boy, but I must. I have a husband now. I have to be with him, but you have to be in England."

"Is it because I am an heir?"

"Aye, you are an heir, you are an earl and a baron and there are a lot of people depending on you to be there, to grow up and be their lord. Sigimor is a lord and he needs me to watch out for him. That is what a wife does."

She pulled him into her arms as he cried. It was hard not to cry with him, but she knew she had to stay calm. She just kept repeating what she had already said. After a few minutes he sniffled and walked over to be with the other men. She rose and looked at Roger.

"This is going to hurt," she whispered.

"Of course it will," he said as he took her into his arms.

"I wish I could be two people so that I could be with him and with Sigimor."

"That is what we all wish sometimes."

"I am going to cry a little bit, but, if Reynard comes near, let me know so I can stop."

Roger laughed softly and held her in his arms as she cried softly. He rubbed her back and stared off in the direction she had done as she had spoken of her husband. Slowly his eyes widened as, from out of the shadows of the forest, men appeared. A glance all around him revealed that his men were tense and ready to fight if the need arose. Reynard looked at the men now surrounding them, smiled, and waved at one, but that sign of recognition did not make Roger relax just yet. One of these large redheaded men was undoubtedly Jolene's husband, but not one of the men looked particularly friendly.

Chapter Nineteen

"Jolene!"

By the time Sigimor's enraged bellow had finished echoing through the halls, he was out of bed and almost fully dressed. Liam and Nanty stumbled into the room, half-dressed, half-asleep, and holding their swords as Sigimor reached for his boots. The way they looked around for a threat, then scowled at him, would have amused him at any other time. So would have the sight of the growing number of his family, equally disheveled, sleepy, and armed, crowding the hall behind the two men. At the moment, however, nothing could amuse him.

"What ails ye, mon?" snapped Liam. "Have ye raised the alarum o'er naught?"

"Jolene is gone," Sigimor said as he finished lacing his boots and reaching for his sword.

"What did ye say to make her leave?"

"Why do ye think I made her leave? Mayhap someone took her."

Liam shook his head. "Nay, that didnae happen."

"How can ye be so certain?"

"Ye are still alive."

A telling point, Sigimor mused, although he would crawl naked through glass shards before he would say so. "I believe she is heading back to England, taking the wee lad back to Drumwich."

"Alone? I would have thought she had more sense than that."

She did, but Sigimor's conviction that she was headed for Drumwich did not waver. He was now certain that all her soft flatteries and greedy passion last night had not been the sign that she had settled to being his wife as he had thought. She had been saying farewell. If she thought he would allow that to stand, she was in for a surprise. He had finally found his mate and he simply refused to believe that Jolene would not fall in with Fate's plan.

He also refused to believe she had left without a firm plan of action. Although she might mumble clever excuses when she went the wrong way, Jolene knew she had no sense of direction. If she did not take anyone with her to lead her, then she knew someone was near and at a place she *could* get to. Jolene was meeting someone and returning to England with him.

For a brief moment, he was seared with a fierce jealousy, then calmed himself. If Jolene had a man in England whom she loved, she would never have married him. That much he was sure of. That she might be joining up with some English ally Harold had mentioned was, however, a strong possibility. It would explain the feeling he had had that Jolene was distracted after her rescue, that she was keeping something secret from him. Unfortunately, he had let passion divert him. The thought that

Jolene had used the passion they shared for just that purpose angered and hurt him more than he cared to think about. He shook the thought aside and started out the door, pleased by the way everyone hastily moved out of his path.

"What are ye planning to do?" Liam asked.

"Go fetch my wife back," replied Sigimor.

"Nay alone ye arenae."

Sigimor watched his large family scatter, racing to their chambers to prepare to ride with him. He considered ignoring them and starting on his way immediately, then inwardly shrugged. It would make an impressive show if he arrived at Jolene's rendezvous with a goodly force of men. If some ally or kinsman of hers had been chasing Harold, he would undoubtedly have fighting men with him. Sigimor went to the great hall to break his fast as he waited for the others. He would not wait long, however. He was willing to chase his wife all the way to the gates of Drumwich, but that did not mean he wanted to.

When Sigimor finally rode out of Dubheidland, he had to wonder if anyone was left to watch over the keep. A careful look over the men revealed that his twin and Ranulph had stayed behind, but the other ten brothers residing at Dubheidland were with him, including Fergus the Last. At a quick guess, he felt there were about a dozen of his cousins with him as well, and, of course, Nanty. When he did reach his wife, Sigimor realized there would be little privacy available to them. Whatever needed to be said would have to wait until they returned to Dubheidland. There was a reckoning due with his little wife and he was not going to indulge in it in front of half his kinsmen.

Pain formed a tight knot in his chest. That only

added to his anger. He had been so intent upon making Jolene succumb to him in body, mind, and heart, he had not truly realized how fully he himself had succumbed to her. All of his well thought out plans to lead the dance had failed miserably. His only hope of avoiding humiliation now was to make sure Jolene joined him in this confusing state of mind and heart, one that seemed to consist of equal parts of bliss and torment. Someone should have warned him about love, he thought crossly.

Sigimor startled himself so thoroughly with that thought, he jerked hard on his reins causing his horse to rear slightly and then move sideways. He quickly calmed his mount and ignored the startled and curious looks of his kinsmen. For a moment, he tried to scorn the thought that had skipped through his mind, but it refused to be pushed aside, settling in hard as the truth was wont to do.

He loved Jolene. Somehow she had wrapped her little fingers around his heart while he had been distracted with thoughts of finding a comfortable mate and keeping her safe. As he had sought to tie her to him with passion, she had captured him in a far more complicated and complete way. He had been so caught up with the thought that she was his mate, that she felt *right*, that he had not really considered why that was. Nor had he given much thought as to why Jolene could make him, an experienced man of two and thirty, tremble and sweat like some untried boy. Now that *that* word had lodged itself in his mind, he understood it all. He loved Jolene. He loved a tiny, dark-haired Englishwoman who did not tremble before his anger, who would never blindly obey him, probably not even under threat of dire torture, and who was as impertinent as his sister Ilsa. Sigimor would not be surprised if God and the Fates were rolling about their celestial realms convulsed with laughter.

There was, of course, only one solution to this problem. She would have to love him back. It had been his plan all along to make her love him, but it had been a plan based mostly upon his opinion that a wife *should* love her husband. He had decided it would be a nice boon, one that would make his life easier. Now it was a necessity, something as vital to him as water.

She did care for him, he told himself. Sigimor did not think pride or vanity prompted that belief. He could not believe a woman could give so freely and fiercely of her passion unless she *did* care for the man she was with. Surely, even he could nurture that until caring became love. He could continue to keep her passion stirred up hot and fierce, but that had apparently not yet succeeded in completely capturing her heart. Sweet words, compliments, and tokens of affection might help, but he had little skill in the ways of a proper wooing, he mused, fixing his gaze on Liam. It would choke his pride to ask advice, but Sigimor knew of none other as well versed in wooing as Liam.

"Why are ye staring at me?" asked Liam when he noticed Sigimor's steady gaze.

"Weel, we are all following ye, aye?" Sigimor shrugged. "Just wondering if ye really ken where ye are leading us."

"Tis a verra clear trail I follow. Jolene is obviously giving the wee lad bread to gnaw on and he is dropping near as much as he is eating as far as I can see."

Glancing down at a piece of bread Liam pointed

to, Sigimor grunted. "I suspicion the wee lad likes to see the birds come after it," he said, nodding toward a point a few yards ahead where several blackbirds poked at something on the ground.

"Aye, that would interest the boy." Liam smiled faintly at Sigimor. "I dinnae think that was the reason ye were staring at me, though. Ye have ne'er questioned how I followed a trail before."

"Ye havenae been following my wife before."

"Ah, of course, save for that one time she got caught by Harold," Liam muttered. He nudged his horse to a slightly faster pace, then rolled his eyes when Sigimor kept close by his side. "I sent Nanty ahead to see if he could espy this meeting ye think she has gone to."

"Good." Sigimor inwardly cursed, annoyed that he had been so caught up in his own thoughts he had not noticed that or suggested it himself.

"If ye have something to say or ask, just do it. Tis clear something is gnawing at ye."

"Could it be that my wife ran away?"

Liam grimaced. "I dinnae think she *ran away*, nay as ye seem to mean it. I think we all forgot the laddie's place in all of this. He is the laird of Drumwich, her dead brother's only heir. The mon who wanted the lad dead, wanted to steal all that was rightfully Reynard's, is dead. There isnae any need for the lad to hide away in Scotland now, is there? In truth, it could cost him dearly."

Sigimor muttered a curse. In some ways, Liam was right. Although he had never truly forgotten who and what Reynard was, he had given little thought on what must happen after Harold had been defeated. It was too easy to see Reynard as just a bairn, not the lord of an English castle. Once or twice he had considered what might need to be done once the threat to the boy was gone, but only in vague, fleeting ways. He had made no plans for that future. Worse, he had not discussed that future with Jolene. He had become so concerned with making her completely his, he had ignored her responsibility to the boy, and her vow to her dying brother to care for his son. That had been a serious error and he was not sure how to rectify it.

Stupidly, he had ignored the fact that a hard choice awaited Jolene once Harold was defeated. She had had the care of Reynard since his birth and the bond between the two was clear to see. Although she would not be accepted as his guardian since she was a woman, that did not mean she would simply walk away from him. In his heart, Sigimor knew he may have realized all of that. It would explain some of the fierce need he had felt to try and bind her to him in any and every way he could. He had been trying to weight the scales in his favor for when the time to choose came. What Sigimor feared now was that she had made her choice and it was not him.

He closed his eyes as a searing pain swept over him. His future rose up before him as a bleak, lonely stretch of years. Despite the horde of kinsmen he would always be surrounded with, he knew he would be fighting that sense of cold emptiness for the rest of his life.

"Sigimor?"

"Aye?" Sigimor stared blindly at the trees as they rode past. "She has to stay with the lad."

"Weel, mayhap. She certainly needs to make some hard choices."

"She has made them."

"Ye cannae be certain of that."

"Nay? If she meant to stay with me, why did she

creep away? Why didnae she tell me she was to meet someone, ask me to go with her to settle the future of the child?"

Liam softly cursed. "I dinnae ken. Mayhap she didnae want to have ye about because ye would tempt her to stay. Who can say what was in her mind and heart when she realized it was time to make a choice? She sore loved her brother, saw him cruelly murdered, and made him a vow as he lay dying in pain. She loves that wee lad, has had much of the raising of him, and was willing to do anything to keep him safe. She has a husband, a mon who must stay in Scotland whilst all that belongs to Reynard is in England."

"And she doesnae love me." Sigimor hoped he did not sound too pathetic as he spoke that bitter truth.

"Ah, weel, who can say? She cares for ye." Liam held up his hand to silence Sigimor's protest. "A lass like that wouldnae have let ye cozen her into marriage and into your bed unless she had some feeling for ye. And, she wouldnae have slipped away like this, either. She would have looked ye in the eye and said it was time for her to return to Drumwich with Reynard. If she didnae have some caring for ye, she wouldnae have avoided that confrontation. Nay, she did it this way because she feared ye could sway her from what she sees as her duty, as the fulfilling of a deathbed vow to a beloved brother."

They both reined to a halt as they saw Nanty riding toward them, and Sigimor thought about what Liam had said. Jolene was no coward yet this secretive flight carried the taint of cowardice. There was also the night of passion they had shared to con-

sider. There had been the air of greedy desperation to it all. He had thought it was because she
had faced death, but now wondered if it had all
been born of a need to try and grasp a fistful of
memories. What need would she have of those unless she cared for him, unless it was only duty that
forced her from his side? It was a somewhat comforting thought, but it did not help him solve his
problem. She had chosen the boy and Sigimor was
not confident that confronting her now would alter
that choice. It could well only add to his pain, and,
perhaps, hers as well.

There had to be a better way, he thought a little
desperately. Somehow there had to be a solution
that would satisfy her duty to the boy yet keep her
at his side. As Nanty reined in before them, however, Sigimor knew he was not going to be given
the chance to think of one. The confrontation was
upon him.

"She has met with some Sassenachs just beyond
the edge of this wood," Nanty announced.

"How many?" asked Sigimor, more than willing
to fight to get his wife back, but not sure he would
be given that option. Even he knew that slaughtering her kinsmen would not be a good way to woo
his wife.

"A score or so. All weel armed, but no threat to
Jolene and the boy."

"So, allies or kinsmen?"

"Kinsmen. At least a few are. There is a similar-
ity of looks to a few. That black hair."

"That must have been what she learned from
Harold whilst he held her captive. It would also explain the desperate action he took. He kenned that
his kinsmen had finally learned what was happen-

ing at Drumwich and had come to Jolene's aid. Harold's chance to tighten his grip on Drumwich had slipped away."

Nanty nodded. "He had no time left to make her his wife, to give them a tougher knot to untie. All that was left to him was a ransom, her and Reynard's life for his, or to silence the one witness to his crimes that others might actually listen to."

"Can we reach them unseen?"

"Aye, if we are careful. We could encircle them, too. They are in a clearing with trees all about them. Howbeit, I believe they have two of your kinsmen from Scarglas with them. I couldnae get close enough to see which ones."

"Giving them safe escort, aye?"

"Aye. So, ye cannae attack them."

"Tempting as that may be, I think it might displease my wife," Sigimor drawled, causing both Liam and Nanty to grin. "Are they readying themselves to leave?"

"Nay," replied Nanty. "They seem to be resting and talking."

Sigimor could see that everyone awaited orders from him as to what they should do next, but he was suddenly unsure. It would appear that Jolene had made her choice, duty and love for Reynard and Drumwich over staying with him. Was it fair or right for him to interfere in that? Worse, if he did try to interfere, was he simply opening himself up to a greater and more wounding humiliation than he had suffered at Barbara's soft hands? Not many of his kinsmen knew about that embarrassment, the few he had had to tell keeping it quiet, but there would be over a score of them to witness this one.

Pride told him to say Jolene had made her

choice and then go home and forget her. All the rest of him told him there was little chance he would ever forget her. Since he understood her dilemma, he knew he would not even be able to turn his pain into a cleansing fury. Then, suddenly, he knew that, if he turned back now, he would forever wonder if he had cast aside a chance, turned aside from the opportunity to change her mind and bring her back to Dubheidland. Although the threat of a well-witnessed rejection loomed, he knew he could not live with that doubt.

Taking a deep breath to strengthen his resolve, he began to give orders to his men. With Nanty's help, he sent his men in different directions that would stealthily bring them up close to the meeting place in a neat circle. He gave them strict orders not to attack, not to harm anyone unless pressed to save their own lives. Sigimor had no wish to try and retrieve his wife over the corpses of her kinsmen. Soon he was left with only Liam, the two of them riding forward to the spot where Sigimor felt confident they would close that circle of Camerons tightly around Jolene and her allies.

"She may have been planning to return," said Liam.

"Nay, she wouldnae have been so sly and secretive if she didnae intend to return to England with these men," replied Sigimor. "If all she planned to do was hand Reynard into their care, she would have told me about them, would have e'en asked if they could come to Dubheidland."

"Ye dinnae seem verra angry about this any more."

"Oh, I am angry, but I ken 'tis both useless and unfair. I closed my eyes to this, didnae think on what would happen—what must happen—once

Harold was dealt with. Plans should have been made, discussed, and settled. Aye, she should have spoken to me, but, by my silence, I may have led her to believe I didnae want to hear it. And she was right to think so. I didnae. As ye say, 'tis a fair hard choice for the lass to make."

"Aye. Tis hard enough for any lass to leave her family if 'tis a close one. Jolene has to leave her country, too. Leave it for a place that hasnae been too welcoming."

"And leave the wee lad she has raised since his birth. Reynard is as a son to her in many ways. She has attempted to keep the lad from seeing her as his mother, but has it worked? Has she convinced her own heart of it? He is but a wee bairn who has just lost his father. Can he let her leave him as weel? Can she resist any pleas he might make? Nay, this isnae a simple matter of choosing the child or the husband. And, I am nay sure I want her to come with me if 'tis naught but a sense of duty, of honoring vows made."

"Oh, I suspicion it would be more than that if she walked away from that bairn."

"Mayhap, but would it be enough to keep her from regretting it later? Enough to keep the pain of leaving the boy from festering until it becomes a hard anger or resentment against me?"

"Ah, there is that to consider. Weel, ye shall just have to tell her that ye love her."

"Why should I be telling her that?"

"Why shouldnae ye? Tis the truth."

"I have ne'er said so." Sigimor was not sure why he was so inclined to deny it, except that he found it a little unsettling that Liam could recognize a feeling inside him that he himself had only just acknowledged. He also wondered how such a nearly pretty man could so skillfully produce such a rude and scornful sound. "She is my wife. Naught else matters."

"It does if ye want to hold her fast at your side and have her pleased to be there."

"She *was* pleased to be there. I kept her and the lad safe, saw to her earthly needs, and bedded her until her eyes crossed."

"Weel, what more can a lass ask for? Her eyes crossed, eh? Tis an odd image that should be alarming yet is strangely intriguing. Then again, are ye sure ye are doing it right? Mayhap—"

"Mayhap ye best cease emptying that bucket of mockery o'er my head. Leastwise, if ye plan on reaching your next saint's day. Of course I was doing it right. I may nay have wooed and rutted my way through half the lasses in the land as ye have, but I am nay without some skill. The lass burns hot for me."

"Aye, ye will get no argument on that. Twas easy to see. Howbeit, ye cannae tie a lass to your side with only that, Cousin. Any lass with wit—and we both ken that Jolene has more than her share— kens that a mon's passion can be a fleeting thing, with no depth or true feeling to it. Ye need to let her ken that she has a place in your heart, in your life, nay just in your bed."

Sigimor knew Liam was right, but he still felt a need to defend himself. "She has said naught."

"She was a highborn Sassenach virgin who took ye, a Scot, to husband," Liam said. "That says a great deal. And, ye arenae the one who must give up something. Jolene must give up Reynard and her home, her land of birth. There needs to be more than the delight of the bedchamber to make her do that. Ye need to woo her."

"Weel, 'tis a wee bit late for that," Sigimor whispered as they drew near the clearing where Jolene met with the Englishmen.

"Tis ne'er too late. She is still within reach. Give the lass a few sweet words."

"In front of two score men or more?"

"They would carry more weight if spoken so openly, witnessed by so many."

There was a lot of truth to that, but Sigimor knew he would be hard pressed to take that good advice. He was not a mon skilled in sweet words or speaking openly about what he felt. Jolene should understand that. Sigimor felt the knot in his chest tighten as he and Liam took their places in the circle of Camerons now formed around Jolene and the Englishmen. He had one last chance to keep his wife, but only if he could woo her with soft, sweet words of love—a skill he had never obtained.

He looked at Jolene and all thought of wooing fled his mind. She was in the arms of another man, a tall, handsome man. The man had black hair which meant he could be a cousin, but Harold had also been a cousin and that blood tie had not stopped the man from lusting after her. It had not proven any true obstacle to marriage, either. Sigimor felt jealousy rear up and blind him to all but the need to tear her out of that man's arms.

"Soft words, Cousin," murmured Liam as he watched Sigimor dismount.

"I willnae yell at her."

Liam sighed. "Ye said we werenae supposed to kill any of the Sassenachs."

"I willnae kill him. I will just break his arms."

Chapter Twenty

"We have company, Jolene."

Jolene pulled away from Roger's tense body and looked around. Her eyes widened as she saw how completely they had been encircled by Camerons. They were all scowling at her, even young Fergus. Just as she realized they could not know that Roger was her cousin, that the embrace they saw was totally innocent, she saw Sigimor. Despite the fierce scowl upon his face, she felt her heart skip in her chest, signaling her pleasure at the mere sight of him.

"Is that man your husband?" asked Roger as he watched Sigimor dismount and start toward them.

"Aye, that is Sir Sigimor Cameron, laird of Dubheidland."

"He looks like an enraged bull."

Watching the way Sigimor approached them, Jolene had to agree with her cousin. Sigimor's head was lowered slightly, his broad shoulders were hunched up, and he was stamping toward them with his hands clenched into fists. A quick look at the Camerons and the two MacFingals revealed that they were obviously anticipating a fight. She quickly moved to stand facing Sigimor, her body planted squarely between him and Roger.

"Move aside, wife," Sigimor said as he stopped in front of her.

"Nay, you cannot hit Roger. He is my cousin."

"I begin to think your cousins are too friendly by half."

Jolene realized Sigimor was jealous and almost gasped. She quickly hid her surprise, and delight, knowing he would not appreciate her acknowledging it. It did, however, give her hope that she had made the right decision.

"Roger was comforting me, nothing more. He is a wedded man." She ignored Sigimor's raised brow that indicated he did not see that as reason enough to trust the man. "Harold knew Roger and his men were chasing him," she began.

"Something ye neglected to tell me. Could ye nay have taken a wee rest in your greed for me during the night to mention that ye had more kinsmen slinking about the countryside?"

"Sigimor!" Jolene could feel the heat of a blush all over her face. She glared at the MacFingals who hooted with laughter, but it had no effect upon them, so she turned her glare on Sigimor. "There is no need to be so . . . to be so *rude!*"

"Rude? Seems to me rude is loving a mon until he cannae move, then creeping away from his bed ere the sun rises to meet with a score of men in the woods."

"If you do not cease speaking of such things, I will have Roger hit you."

"Go ahead then. I was of a mind to break his arms when I first saw him holding ye, but I could find a wee bit of pleasure in just pounding him into the mud. I am still of a mood to bruise someone."

Jolene gaped at her husband, then looked at her cousin. "Are you not going to say anything?"

Roger shrugged. "While I understand what you did, Jolene, I fear I also understand him. If my Emma had done the like to me, I would not be in a very good humor, either."

"Men! You are all alike. You—" Jolene gasped in shock when Reynard suddenly appeared and kicked Sigimor in the shin. "Reynard! Why did you do that?"

"Because he is a mean man!" Reynard said, struggling slightly in Roger's grasp and glaring tearfully at Sigimor, who idly rubbed his abused shin. "He is going to steal you from me. I want to kick his arse!"

Sigimor studied the child, taking careful note of the tears and the fury. He then looked at Jolene. There was such a look of pain and sorrow in her eyes, he had to fight the urge to comfort her. Either he had misjudged the situation, and her, or she had changed her mind about what she had to do somewhen between leaving his bed and meeting with her cousin. He felt a little guilty about how good that possibility made him feel when he looked back at Reynard. The boy was little more than a bairn, yet he was being asked to accept so much loss and change. A quick look at the expression upon Roger's face, however, told Sigimor that the child would be well comforted.

"I think the three of us need to talk," Sigimor said, then turned to his men. "Best ye be at ease," he told them, "as this may take a wee while. No fighting with the Sassenachs." He caught the way the two MacFingals eyed Nanty and Liam, and added, "Or with those two fools." He crouched down in front of Reynard. "Now, my lad, ye have a chance to say a goodly Godspeed to your friends ere ye part. I think ye ought to be making the best of it."

"Nanty, too?" Reynard asked in a trembling voice.

"Aye, my wee mon, Nanty, too."

"I want to keep my friends."

"Ye will. Ye can ne'er lose good friends, laddie. Aye, they may nay be close at hand, but ye cannae lose them. If ye e'er have the need of them, they will be there for ye. Now, go and say your fare-thee-weels." He stood up as the boy ran to Nanty and looked at Jolene. "Come, we will talk." He started toward the far corner of the clearing.

"He is so arrogant," Jolene muttered.

Glancing around as he took Jolene by the arm and followed Sigimor, Roger said, "From what you have told me of his life, he has had to be. It could not have been easy to find himself laird of this lot at a young age, most of them no more than boys. A man cannot keep a tight rein on this lot by being gentle and sweet or by sitting them down for a pleasant talk." He nodded to where Nanty and Liam were exchanging taunts with the MacFingals. "There is a wild spirit in these Camerons. Good men all, I am certain, but not quite tamed, I think."

Her cousin was a perceptive man, Jolene decided. "Nay, not quite tamed, but, aye, all very good men." She frowned at Sigimor who stood watching them, his arms crossed over his chest. "Of course, a few of them might be improved by a few hard knocks offside the head." She ignored Roger's soft laughter as she faced Sigimor, crossing her arms over her chest, and giving him a frown to equal his.

"Start with what ye learned from the late and unlamented Harold," Sigimor ordered.

"He knew Roger was hard on his heels and suspected his crimes were no longer secret," Jolene replied. "Whilst he held me, one of his men arrived to say Roger wanted to meet with him, where, and when."

"Meet with him?" Sigimor looked at Roger. "Ye had doubts about his guilt?"

"Nay," replied Roger, "but he was my blood kin. I felt it only right that he hear the accusations against him and be allowed to respond to them."

"His response would have been to try and kill ye and all your men."

Roger nodded. "I have ne'er trusted him and was prepared for treachery. Once I dealt with him, I intended to find you for Old Thomas told me who Jolene and Reynard had fled with."

"Ye had no fear of all the grand allies Harold claimed as his?"

"Nay, for I have grander ones. Harold ne'er considered me more than a minor baron, my holding small, and my wife but the daughter of a knight. He ne'er looked further and that was his folly. My wife's line winds all the way to the king and she is much loved by near all of them. My mother's line is nearly as rich in blood and power. I quickly gained the right to be guardian to Reynard from the king himself. I requested it the moment one of Peter's servants arrived to tell me what was happening at Drumwich, but hours after Peter's death. I arrived at Drumwich but a day after Harold left to hunt you down."

"So close. Of course, if we had waited, me and my men would have been rotting on the gallows when ye rode in." Sigimor saw Jolene pale and nodded, silently pleased at her reaction to that image. "Harold didnae ken ye were named guardian, did he?"

"Nay, 'tis why I wished to parley. I felt he should know he had already lost all chance of holding Drumwich, that there was no gain to be had in hurting Jolene or Reynard. Then I was to take him to the king for judging."

"Will it cause trouble when your king hears that Harold met with justice here?"

Roger shook his head. "Nay. Though few doubted his guilt, there was no blood on his sword, so to speak. He would have been judged, but it would have been a complicated matter. Harold's allies may not have been equal to mine, but they are powerful enough that the king would have had to tread a very delicate path. He will be relieved to be excused from that dance. Few will argue with your right to kill the man. He threatened you and yours and he took your wife. As Reynard's guardian, I am the only one who can say why Reynard was here and, e'en as I set out, I began to spread the tale that it was of no consequence. Nay, this trouble has ended here."

Sigimor nodded, then looked at Jolene. "Ye didnae come here just to give the lad into his arms, did ye. Ye didnae ken that he was named guardian, either. So, ye crept away from your lawful husband like a cowardly thief. Ye didnae think I might like to ken that I was about to lose my wife?"

Jolene inwardly grimaced. The cowardly remark stung, but she accepted it as her due, for she had been just that. She had not wanted to face him squarely and tell him her plans. She had feared he could make her stay when duty forced her to leave and equally afraid that he would not even try to make her stay. A part of her had hoped he would chase her down as he had, but she had not thought it would change what she had to do. Instead, she had changed her mind, had realized she could not leave him. It was not something she wished to discuss now, however, in front of so many men.

"I intended to send you word when I reached Drumwich," she said.

"Och, how kind of ye." He grunted with satisfaction when she winced. "Just what did ye plan to do about me, about our marriage? Our weel consummated, priestly blessed marriage?"

"Well, since I am the daughter of an English earl and you are a Scottish lord, and we had gained permission from none of my kinsmen, or my king—"

"Ye would have our marriage annulled. Aye, I have heard how that would work many times. Did ye ne'er consider that, e'en now, ye might be carrying my bairn? That an annulment would mark that child a bastard?"

Not until Sigimor had mentioned it, but Jolene was not about to confess to that. "I would have waited to be sure there was no child ere I acted on it." She wondered why he looked so ill-pleased by her words.

Sigimor wanted to shake her until her bones rattled, even though he knew he could never bring himself to cause her any harm. Every word she spoke struck him like a knotted whip on bare flesh. He was not quite sure what he wanted her to say, but it was not this calm recitation of her plans to cast him aside. She had not even given him any true indication that she had changed her mind. He and Jolene needed to have a serious talk, perhaps even a rousing argument or two to clear the air between them. However, he glanced around at all the men in the clearing, his and Roger's, and knew this was not the place for such a talk. The problem was, he needed to know what she had decided. He rubbed

his chin as he tried to think of a way to ask if she intended to stay with him without exposing his own
confused and intense emotions.

"Jolene was but saying her farewells when you
arrived," Roger said, ignoring the sharp nudge of
Jolene's elbow in his side. "The king will not be
pleased that an English heiress was lost to a Scottish
lord, but I will swear it was approved by her brother
as I believe it would have been. After all, you have
saved the lives of his sister and his only child, his
heir. I will hold her lands in trust save for one small
keep in Scotland left to her by a maternal aunt.
That you can openly claim." He smiled briefly at
the surprise Sigimor was unable to hide. "Ere the
king can devise a way to confiscate her fortune, I
will send her goods and dowry to you by the same
route I myself came here—passed safely from one
of your friends or kinsmen to another. Or, if you
prefer, I could send it to her Scottish keep and you
may send men there to collect it."

Although Sigimor had suspected that Jolene
was well dowered, he had not anticipated gaining
any of it. This was a great boon he would be a fool
to ignore. He also saw that a discussion with Roger
concerning her dowry was a good way to avoid a
discussion with her. She was returning to Dubheidland with him. That was enough for now.

"I think we need to talk ere ye leave," he said to
Roger and waved Liam to his side. "If we can find
aught to write with, this lad is an excellent scribe
with a neat and readable hand." When Roger nodded, Sigimor looked at Jolene. "We will talk when
we return to Dubheidland unless ye wish us to air
all our thoughts before this lot." When she shook
her head, he nodded and went to join Liam and
Roger.

Jolene watched the three men gather something to write with then sit together on some large stones at the opposite side of the clearing. She briefly brooded over how her dowry had so firmly caught her husband's attention, then soundly scolded herself for such foolishness. Sigimor's surpise had been heartfelt. He may not have married her out of love, but he certainly had not married her for gain. She also knew he would make good use of the riches she brought him. With so many kinsmen to provide for, there was a lot of good he could do. Jolene was also sure that each child they might be blessed with would be carefully provided for. One could not ask for a fairer use of her dowry. Harold and many another man would have just enriched themselves.

She turned her thoughts to what Sigimor might wish to talk about once they returned to Dubheidland. There would probably be a lecture to endure. Considering his tendency to refer to their passionate, private moments, she hoped the lecture would be private. It was appalling enough that Roger probably thought her some rabid succubus by now, as did most of his men, and anyone else within listening distance when Sigimor had first spoken to her and Roger. Jolene simply could not think of what he might wish to talk about, and did not want to. It would be easy to find herself hoping for, or even foolishly expecting, some words of affection. It would then break her heart if none were forthcoming and she would only have herself to blame.

A heavy sigh escaped her as she watched Fergus and Reynard walk toward her. Fergus still looked angry with her, an expression that made him look even more like Sigimor. Reynard looked lost and hurt which stirred to life her own grief. When he ran to her, she caught him up in her arms and held him close for a moment. When he rode away with Roger, she would see him rarely, if at all, and it made her heart clench with the pain of the loss.

It was such a difficult choice, yet she knew she had made the right one. Roger and Emma would give Reynard all the love and direction he needed. They also had the power to keep him and his heritage safe until he was of an age to take the reins. Although it galled her to admit it, Reynard and Drumwich needed a man to care for them and the only one she wanted could never rule over an English earldom, nor would he wish to.

"I need you to come home with me," muttered Reynard as Jolene sat down on the ground and he crawled into her lap.

"She cannae," said Fergus as he sat down facing them. "She is a wife now. Sigimor's wife. Wives have to stay with their husbands." He scowled at her. "She just forgot that law for a wee bit."

"Mayhap I could stay too," said Reynard.

"Weel, we wouldnae mind that, but ye cannae. Ye are a laird. Ye have to go to Drumwich and be an earl."

"Don' wanna be an earl."

"Ye dinnae have much choice. Tis what ye were born to be. Tis what your fither wanted for ye. Ye are an heir. Tis a great responsibility. Most of us dinnae e'er get to be an heir. Tis a thing to be proud of."

When Reynard looked at her, Jolene nodded. "Your father would expect you to do your best to care for his lands and his people. They are now your lands and your people. Roger and Emma will come to Drumwich to stay with you. They will love you and teach you how to be a good earl, one to make your father proud."

"You cannot love me anymore?"

She kissed his cheek and stroked his hair. "I will always love you. I just cannot be with you. Howbeit, ne'er forget that your aunt loves you most dearly and will always hold you in her heart."

"I cannot lose your love just like Sig'mor says I cannot lose a good friend."

"Exactly like that. And, if you e'er have a need for me, I will be there for you. Always."

Jolene held her nephew close as he sighed and tried to rub the tears from his face. It was almost painful to hold back her own tears, but she fought to do so. She did not know how much Reynard understood, but she did know it was best to remain calm as she tried to explain matters. Glancing toward Liam, Roger, and Sigimor, she hoped they would soon finish their business. It was going to break her heart to ride away from Reynard, but she knew the parting had to come soon. Her grief and her tears could not be tethered for much longer.

"Ye will care weel for the boy, aye?" Sigimor asked Roger as he rolled up one of the marriage agreements they had both signed and handed it to Liam.

"Aye," replied Roger. "Emma and I have not been blessed with children, though we dearly wanted a child. Reynard will be our child. My wife is already at Drumwich waiting for him. And, as a Gerard, 'tis my duty to see that the boy grows to do the name proud and care well for the family seat."

"And that he willnae hate his aunt for leaving him like this?" Sigimor asked quietly as he watched Jolene hug Reynard.

"Never. He will never be allowed to forget all she did for him, all she risked, or how she loved him. Or what the Camerons did for him. You will have one English border holding that will not be hot for Scottish blood."

"And if ye have a bairn of your own?"

"We have been wed for ten years, since she was but fifteen and I seventeen, and my seed has ne'er taken root. We were content, but I know my wife is most eager to be a mother to that little boy."

"Ye are both still young. Ye may yet have a bairn. Sometimes I think 'tis just that the seed is weak or the lass has but one or two bairns within her. This bonnie fool's parents," he nodded toward Liam, "were wed near to twenty years ere they had him whilst my father spawned fifteen of us. That old fool MacFingal is my uncle and he has bred an army. Liam's mother was sister to both men but she had only two bairns late in life." Sigimor stood up as Roger did and clapped the man on the shoulder. "There is nay kenning God's plan for us."

"True. I do not think I will tell my wife your opinion, however. It might be cruel to stir her hopes."

"Aye. Tis best if she has accepted it all. Liam's mother was slow to accept the lack of a bairn. Verra slow."

Roger smiled faintly as he asked, "How slow?"

"Took her near to twenty years to give up trying." He nodded when Roger's eyes widened. "Fate's a capricious thing."

"It would seem so. But, do not worry o'er Reynard. I loved Peter as a brother." Roger looked toward

Reynard. "It will be very easy indeed to love his child. And, my wife has a very big heart."

Sigimor sighed heavily as he looked at Jolene. "So does the lass and 'tis sure to be broken o'er this parting. Aye, especially since she must ken that there is little chance she will see the lad again."

"Mayhap not. Yet, that holding you now own is not so very far from the border. If we are not at war, the occasional visit might be arranged. Tis something we can both think about."

"True. I willnae promise her that until we have a sound plan, however. Best if we let each of them grow accustomed to the parting, too, or this grief will be felt after each visit." He looked at Roger. "Ye say she had already decided to return to Dubheidland?"

"She had. That decision was made not long after she joined me here. In all honesty, I tried most vigorously to change her mind." Roger met Sigimor's scowl with a grin. "She is a rich prize and the king will not be pleased to have lost the chance to arrange a marriage for her. I was awarded the guardianship of Reynard, but my king hesitated to put Jolene into my care. He likes to award loyal men with orphaned heiresses for brides and there are not so very many of them."

"Are ye *sure* your king willnae be crying foul and trying to get her back?"

"Quite sure. If he seems to even consider that, I will tell him that she has been well bedded by her Highland lord and is already breeding." Roger gave Sigimor an apologetic smile. "No Englishman would want her now."

"Aye, they ken they wouldnae bear up weel under the comparisons sure to be made." He ignored

Roger's stuttered protest and started toward Jolene. "Best I get the lass home and start working on that bairn. Wouldnae want anyone to be able to cry ye a liar."

"How kind of you," Roger muttered as he scowled at a grinning Liam, then followed Sigimor.

Jolene saw Sigimor and Roger start across the clearing toward her and Reynard. She set Reynard on his feet and stood up. It surprised her a little when Fergus immediately moved to stand close by her side. She wondered if he thought to put himself between her and Sigimor's anger or was boldly reminding Roger of the Camerons' claim to her, then decided it was probably a little bit of both.

A quick look around the clearing revealed that the rest of the Camerons were already at their horses and gathering behind her, all of them keeping a close eye on Roger and his men. Catching her glance, several of Sigimor's kinsmen grinned and winked at her. They all considered her one of them, she realized. This united display of possessiveness comforted her in some ways. She was not sure if she was truly needed, and she had no idea exactly what her husband felt for her, but she was obviously considered one of their clan now, part of their family.

Sigimor collected her sack of belongings and a horse for her as she exchanged a few words with Roger. He had her sign a few papers, including one that said she had willingly accepted her brother's choice of husband for her. It was a lie, but she did not hesitate to put her name to it. Not only would it make things much easier for Roger, especially if the king was annoyed by the marriage, but Jolene felt her brother would have approved.

Then she said her farewells to Reynard. His lip

trembled and his eyes shone with tears, but he did not cry or fret. She was so proud of him. Peter would have been, too, she thought and had to swallow a sudden welling up of a still raw grief. Giving her nephew one final kiss, she placed him in Roger's arms. There was sympathy in her cousin's eyes, but also a hint of possessiveness in the way he held Reynard. He would love the boy and raise him to be a fine and honorable man. Jolene found some comfort in that.

After Sigimor said farewell to Roger and the boy, he helped her mount her horse, then led them all on the way back to Dubheidland. Jolene glanced back only once to see Roger comforting Reynard. She quickly fixed her gaze in the direction of Dubheidland, beating down the urge to rush to the child's side and comfort him herself. She would accept this parting with a dignity that would make her ancestors proud. Gerards were strong, stout of heart and mind, and able to accept the blows life and Fate dealt them with fortitude.

Chapter Twenty-one

She had cried all the way home, bawled, sniffled, and wailed like a baby. Sigimor had finally taken her up before him on his horse, muttering that she was sure to fall out of her saddle and crack her head open. By the time they had reached Dubheidland, she had wept herself into a stupor and had had to be tucked into bed like a child. Jolene shook her head, thoroughly disgusted with herself. So much for dignity and fortitude.

Removing the cool, damp cloth she had placed over her eyes, she studied them in the looking glass. They did not look quite as red and swollen as they had when she had first woken up. The lavender water had helped soothe and heal the damage a few hours of sleep had not. Her deep wallow in grief had left her feeling slightly bruised all over, however. The only good she could find in such a complete loss of control was that she had avoided a confrontation with Sigimor.

Then again, she mused as she took one last look at her gown to be certain it was hanging correctly and fully laced, that confrontation might still be ahead of her. It all depended upon how angry Sigimor was over what she had done. For one brief moment she considered claiming a headache or something similar, and forgoing the evening meal in the great hall.

"Nay," she said as she started out of her bedchamber, "this is no time for cowardice."

As Jolene made her way to the great hall, she stiffened her spine by reminding herself that she had chosen this man. She had turned away from her family, her home, and her country for him with no assurance that she would ever see any of them again. Surely that was enough to soothe any insult or bruised pride caused by the way she had left him. He might have the right to be annoyed over the risk she took in going off alone, but that was all.

Pausing in front of the entrance to the great hall, Jolene admitted to herself that his anger over her leaving was not what truly made her reluctant to face him. She feared he would not understand what her choice meant, or, if he did, not acknowledge it. It was the possibility that everything would return to what it had been, a marriage where he treated her with respect and kindness and gave her passion, but not much else, that made her hesitate to confront him. She needed so much more from the man. It was the chance, the blind hope, of obtaining that *more* that had made her decide to stay with him. If he did not see her choice as the declaration it was or did not want to, she feared she would begin to think she had made a very bad choice indeed.

The touch of a hand upon her arm startled her out of her thoughts and she looked to see Fergus beside her. There was a look of wary concern in his eyes and his grip upon her arm was firm. Jolene realized he was wondering if she was going to try and slip away again. She then realized that Sigimor may also have gained that wariness because of how she had left him. If so, the man's pride would be badly lashed each time he suffered that doubt. It was a consequence she had not considered.

"Ye still look a wee bit wan and bruised," said Fergus.

"I feel a little wan and bruised, but I shall recover," she replied, allowing him to lead her toward her seat at Sigimor's side.

"Your cousin will care for Reynard verra weel. He will have a family and be back in the home he was born in."

"True, and, if I knew I could see him there whene'er I wished, I would not grieve so, but it will pass. Better that I gave him up of my own free will to a man I trust to love and care for him, than have him taken from me by the king and court to be given to someone of their choosing. Tis most fortunate that Roger was both my choice and the king's."

Sigimor watched his youngest brother bring Jolene to his side. She looked more delicate than she ever had before. He had a suspicion that her somewhat alarming descent into blind grief had not solely been because of the loss of the boy, but also because of the loss of her brother. There was a very good chance that she had never really, properly grieved for Peter since she had immediately been caught up in the fight against Harold and the need to protect Reynard. Once certain she was not going to make herself ill, he had left her to her grief, but that had meant he had had no chance to ease his anger. It was still a hard knot in his chest. Seeing how wan she was, he was not sure she could endure any airing of his grievances yet and he felt that knot in his chest tighten.

A quick glance at his kinsmen as Jolene took her seat told Sigimor they would not approve of him unleashing his anger on her. They all wore expressions of concern and sympathy as they looked at her. The looks they gave him were ones of warning. Jolene had obviously won a place in their hearts at some point over the past few days. Although that was a very good thing, the fact that it made them think they had some say in how he acted with his wife was not. Their interest in Jolene's welfare and their involvement in chasing her down also meant whatever happened between him and his wife now would probably not be the private matter he wished it to be.

He sipped his ale and watched her eat. It pleased him to see that her appetite had not fled, but the wary looks she cast his way now and again told him that his anger was probably easy to see. Sigimor hoped the uncertainty he felt was not, however. When he saw annoyance begin to reveal itself in her expression, he actually felt relieved. That was something he could deal with. Her growing anger also put some color into her cheeks, making her look less frail.

"Are you just going to brood then?" Jolene finally asked, unable to endure his silent staring any longer.

"I am nay brooding," he replied with a calm that he could see only annoyed her more.

"You just sit there, all silent and staring at me. If it is not brooding, then 'tis sulking."

"Mayhap I am but wondering if ye will try to

sneak away again. Ah, but, nay," he said quickly, silencing whatever she had opened her mouth to say, "ye like to save such sneaking about until after ye have wrung your poor mon's body dry and left him in a blind, happy stupor."

Sigimor almost smiled at the deep blush that colored her cheeks. She was stuttering and bouncing slightly in her seat she was so angry. This was good. This he could respond to easily, even in front of his kinsmen, some who looked as if they were thinking of gagging him. He was not about to stop now, however, not when she was working herself up into such a nice rage. There was a chance to clear the air now and he intended to take full advantage of it.

He helped himself to another bowl of thick rabbit stew. "Now that I think on it, I best eat a wee bit more. If ye have any sly plots twisting about in your head, I will need all my strength tonight. At least then I might be able to recover from your greedy use of me ere ye get yourself too far away. Or thoroughly lost." His eyes widened slightly at the curse she spat as she leapt to her feet, thinking that he was going to have to have a word with his kinsmen about watching their language. "Leaving the table so soon? Dinnae ye think ye ought to eat some more? The way ye try to keep a mon from guessing what trick ye are about to play requires strength, ye ken."

"You are the most impossible man I have e'er met. Arrogant, rude—"

"If I have so many faults, why did ye come back here then?"

"Because I am insane, kissed by the moon, and have lost whate'er wits I was e'er blessed with. There is no other explanation for why I should love such a contrary, dull-witted oaf!" Realizing what she had just said, Jolene gave a muted scream, grabbed the bowl of stew Sigimor had just set in front of him, and tipped it over his head. "Oh! Curse you, now look what you have made me do! I used to have manners!"

Sigimor blinked the dripping stew from his eyelids and watched as his wife fled the hall. He was pleased that she turned toward the stairs to the bedchambers and not the doors leading out of the keep. Of course, he might find the door to his bedchamber barred firmly against him, he thought as Old Nancy and Fergus tried to clean the stew out of his hair and off his face. A quick scowl at Old Nancy and Fergus did nothing to dim their grins, but he decided to ignore that impudence for now. He had to decide what to do next.

"Are ye really intending to just keep sitting there?" asked Somerled, poorly suppressed laughter trembling in his voice.

"It might be wise, e'en safer," Sigimor replied as he waved away Old Nancy and Fergus. "There are a lot of sharp weapons in my bedchamber." He suddenly grinned as the words she had said finally settled firmly into his heart and mind. "She loves me."

"Aye, and she may be right to question her sanity in doing so. She also called ye a contrary, dull-witted oaf and many of us may be inclined to agree with her if ye dinnae go after her. Quickly."

"Ye have changed your mind about her, havenae ye? Ye werenae pleased with my marriage nay so verra long ago."

"I have no love for the English and it grated that ye would marry one, e'en though she seemed a good lass. I also didnae like the reasons *why* ye married her—for her protection and the lust ye felt. It wasnae long ere I thought there was more there, but both of ye seemed unable or unwilling to see that for yourselves. Weel, now I have been proven right. Wheesht, I kenned it for certain when she returned with ye. She gave up a lot to stay with ye."

"Aye, she did," Sigimor said as he stood up, sighing faintly as he heard bits of his stew hit the floor. "I need to wash and change first. I dinnae want to get rabbit stew all over my wife and my bed linen." He ignored the groans of his family as he strode toward the door.

"Ye should woo the lass," called Somerled.

"Give her some sweet words," yelled Liam.

"Aye, aye," Sigimor said, giving them a negligent wave of his hand as he started out of the great hall. "And just where do ye think that will lead us, aye? I will be borrowing some of your clothes, Somerled," he called over his shoulder, then, as soon as he felt no one could see him, he raced up the stairs, taking them two at a time.

Jolene stared at Sigimor as he entered their bedchamber and wondered why she had not bolted the door. For a moment she was hurt over how long it had taken him to come to her, but then she noticed that he had changed his clothes and his hair was damp. Recalling why he would have to clean himself, she returned to staring out the window, hoping to hide the blush staining her cheeks.

She felt him come up behind her and tensed. In a moment of anger she had bared her soul, not only to him, but to everyone else crowded into the great hall. Had there been the moment of tenderness she had always envisioned? The soft exchange of love words and vows of devotion? Nay, she had called him names and dumped his stew on his head. Jolene wondered how long she would have to hide in her bedchamber before that humiliating incident was forgotten. She inwardly grimaced, suspecting she would still hear it mentioned when she was old and gray. Accept it, Jolene, she told herself ruefully, it will probably be the first tale told at your funeral feast.

When Sigimor reached around and placed his hands over hers where they rested upon the stone sill of the window, she frowned. She could feel the warmth of him all along her back. A tendril of heat began to curl through her body and she nearly cursed. He could stir her passion even when she was sunk in embarrassment and wanted to beat him about the head with a club. Jolene could only hope he did not know how completely ensnared she was, despite her declaration of love.

Sigimor pressed a kiss to the top of her head and struggled to think of something to say. To his dismay, he heard himself say, "So, ye love me, aye?" He could almost hear his entire family groan in disgust.

Jolene seriously considered turning around and punching her beloved husband right in his handsome nose. Then she sighed. She had said it. Loud and clear. There was no sense in denying it. If nothing else, she thought crossly, there were plenty of witnesses he could ask for verification.

"Aye, that is what I said," she replied. "That is why I am here instead of riding back to Drumwich with Reynard and Roger."

It surprised him that she admitted it so freely, did not try to take the words back since she was so angry with him. There was a sadness in her voice,

however, as if she wished it were not true. Sigimor
supposed he could understand that. Her love for
him had cost her dearly and he had given her little
in return save for passion and, concerning that,
Liam was right. Jolene had the wit to know that a
man's passion could be a very shallow thing, built
upon no more than a need to rut. She was also too
innocent to be able to discern the difference between meaningless rutting and the passion they
shared. It was not something he could explain to
her, either. He might not be the sweet-tongued
courtier Liam was, but even he knew it would not
be wise to tell his wife that he knew the difference
between true passion and empty ruttings because
he had indulged in a fair bit of the latter. Especially
not when she had just confessed to loving him.

He knew he had to say something. He could not
continue to stand there like an idiot, reveling in
the fact that she loved him. Sweet words, he told
himself, and grimaced. Search through his mind
though he did, Sigimor could find nothing there
except awkward, common flatteries. He needed to
make love to her, he decided. With passion heating his blood, he was sure he could find a few of
those sweet love words she needed to hear. He slid
his hands up her arms until he grasped her shoulders, then turned her around until she faced him.

"If ye love me, why did ye leave?" he asked as he
began to unlace her gown, pleased when she offered no resistance except for a frown.

Jolene watched him remove her clothes. A
dozen evasive replies crowded her head, but she
pushed them all aside. She had just turned her
back on her family, her home, and her country for
this man. It was past time for the truth. Perhaps if
he knew exactly what was going on in her mind

and heart, he would give her some hint of what was going on in his. At the very least, she might discover how hard she would have to work to gain what she so desperately needed—his love.

"I thought I could do it, could honor my vow to Peter to care for Reynard. I did not want to go, but it was not until I faced the choice full on that I realized I *could not* go. I suppose you intend to take me to bed now," she said when he tossed aside the last of her clothing.

"Aye, I do," he replied as he began to shed his own clothes.

She watched him, feeling her desire stir with each piece of clothing he removed. He was such a fine-looking man, big, strong, and very, very virile, she mused as he tossed aside the last of his clothing revealing that he was more than ready to indulge the passion they shared. Jolene supposed she ought to feel flattered that she could stir his desire so, and she did, but it was no longer enough for her. She was not sure it had ever been. She knew she would never turn from it, but she ached for the heart of him. In truth, she feared that even this glorious passion would begin to wane if they did not become bonded to each other in some other, deeper way. Just the thought of that made her cling to him as he carried her to their bed.

"Ah, wife, ye are so beautiful," he murmured against her mouth, and then he kissed her.

Jolene wrapped her arms around his neck and gave herself over to his kiss, to the feel of his body pressed close to hers. She would not hide her feelings from him anymore. She would love him so well that, one day, he would wake to find that he loved her back. It was, perhaps, a fool's dream, but she would cling to it for now.

"I wasnae pleased to wake and find ye had left me," Sigimor said as he kissed his way to her breasts. "I intended to hunt ye down all the way to the gates of Drumwich if need be, to get back what ye stole from me."

Gasping softly as he licked the hardened tips of her breasts, Jolene struggled to speak clearly. "I stole nothing from you."

"Aye, ye did." He leisurely suckled at each breast, then raised his head to study the results with satisfaction. "Ye took these pale beauties from me, walked away with these sweet rosy nipples that give me so much pleasure."

"I am very sorry I could not leave them upon your pillow for you to enjoy at your leisure." Jolene suspected the breathless huskiness of her voice dimmed the sharp sarcasm of her words.

Sigimor briefly grinned against her skin as he kissed his way down to her smooth, taut stomach. Her sharp tongue was one of the things he loved about her, but he did not think he would admit to that. He placed his hand over her stomach, envisioning it swelling with his child.

"And this fine white belly within which my seed may have already taken root." He kissed her stomach and felt the faint tremor that went through her. "I will probably have the night sweats for a long time just thinking of how close a Cameron came to being born in England." He sat up and stroked her legs. "And ye would have deprived me of the pleasure of these bonnie legs. Sleek and strong like some lad's, but all woman in shape and softness."

He spent several minutes honoring her slim thighs with kisses and strokes of his tongue. The soft sounds of pleasure she made caressed his ears like the sweetest of music. She always made him feel as if he was the greatest lover ever born. When her hips shifted on the bed in blind invitation, he slid one hand up the inside of her thigh and watched her as he intimately stroked her. She was hot and wet and the feel of her strained his control over his own needs. He would not be able to play this game much longer.

"Ah, but one of the greatest thefts of all was taking this sweetness away."

Jolene cried out in delight, with a hint of shock she had yet to overcome, when he replaced his tormenting fingers with his mouth. It was a wicked delight, one she wished she had the control to enjoy for a long time, but she knew she was already lost to restraint. His flattery was an earthy sort, but it had fired her passion. A skilled courtier would probably decry such words as too rough, too blunt, too common, but they were sweet music to her ears.

When she felt her release close at hand, she cried out for him, but he ignored her, sending her tumbling into pleasure's abyss with his mouth. Jolene was still trembling from the strength of her release as he kissed his way back up her body. She felt her desire heighten yet again as he slowly joined their bodies and closed her eyes against the sweetness of it. How could he make her feel this way, how could he make love to her so tenderly, she wondered, if he did not love her? They were questions she dared not linger on for too long for fear of giving herself false hope.

She realized he was not moving, and opened her eyes. He held himself slightly above her body by resting his weight on his forearms and stared down at her. There was something in the way he was looking at her that made her tremble from the strength of the emotion that swept over her.

"Sigimor?" she whispered, sliding her hands down his side until she clasped his lean hips.

"Ye were going to steal this away from me, too," he said as he began to move within her, his pace slow, almost lazy. "Ye gave no thought to how I would miss this silken heat." He touched his forehead to hers, bewitched by the way her eyes turned the color of a fierce Highland storm when her passion ran hot. "Or that ye would leave this poor mon cold, alone, cursed to endlessly ache for this sweet haven. Aye, abandon him to the torment of waking in the night trembling with the need to feel this tight fire enclose him, but kenning he would ne'er enjoy such pleasure again."

The way he was rubbing against that blindly lustful part of her every time he moved was making it difficult to think clearly, but Jolene struggled to keep her mind fixed upon his words. "But, I came back—"

"Aye, so ye did." Knowing his control was rapidly slipping away, and sensing that Jolene's passion was swiftly climbing to its peak, Sigimor increased his pace. "Tis a good thing, too. For when I woke to find ye had left me, I kenned that, along with all these other treasures ye had stolen from me, ye had taken what no mon can live without."

"What?" She wondered how he could keep talking, but also prayed that he would not falter now.

"His heart and soul, my beauty. Aye, ye had fled with the verra heart and soul of me." He brushed his lips over hers and whispered, "Aye, for I do love ye, my Jo, my wife, my soul mate."

Jolene felt herself shatter. She wrapped her body even more tightly around his as he praised her, then groaned out her name as he found his own release. It was a long time before she roused herself from the stupor caused by the intensity of their lovemaking, an intensity caused by his words as much as his skillful touch. By the time he had briskly cleaned each of them off with a damp cloth and crawled back into bed, she felt able to talk again. When he reached for her, she swiftly moved to sprawl on top of him, squirming faintly in delight over the feel of his big, strong body. She kissed his proud nose and smiled at him.

"So, you love me, do you?" She nearly laughed at the way he sighed and rolled his eyes.

"I suspicion ye wish to talk about it now, aye?"

"Just a little. When? When did you know?"

"When did ye ken it?" he countered.

"Ah, well, I knew it not long after we were married, but I tried to ignore it."

"Because of Reynard and your vow to your brother."

Jolene nodded and idly traced the intricate pattern of the design encircling his strong arms. "It was very important to me to fulfill that vow. And, I felt Reynard's needs had to take precedence over all else, for he is but a small child. I crept away as I did because I feared you could too easily turn me from what I saw as my solemn duty. It was not until I faced Roger, was confronted with all that leaving would mean, that I knew I could not do it, not even though I was still so painfully uncertain of what you might feel for me. I could see that, by giving Reynard into Roger's excellent care, I was already fulfilling my duty and honoring my vow. Leaving would no longer be a matter of honor, but an act of cowardice, of fleeing the chance of being hurt because I could not win your heart."

"Ye won it from the moment ye stepped up to the bars of my cell at Drumwich. I just didnae see it clear. List your faults as I might," he ignored her gasp of outrage, "I couldnae silence the voice in my head that kept saying *mine*. Ye were English, dark of hair, and so wee I feared I could crush ye if I tried loving ye, but none of that stopped me from feeling that ye were, weel, right, the one I had been waiting for. My mate."

She had to kiss him for that, then tried to hug him with her whole body. "I wish you had said something. It might have saved us both a hurt."

"It sounded foolish. I didnae give ye love words because I didnae think that was what ailed me. Nay, not until I thought ye had left me. S'truth, I think the knowledge had begun to settle in when Harold grabbed ye and I nearly lost ye to him, but ye slipped away ere I had accepted it." He slid his hands down her slim back and idly caressed her taut little backside. "But, now I have given ye the sweet words everyone says a lass needs and ye have given me some, and so all is weel, aye?"

He looked so relieved, she almost laughed. This was not a man who would constantly stroke her with flatteries and love words, but she did not care. Now that he had told her that he loved her, she knew she would be able to see it in his every action, feel it in his every kiss. It had been there from the beginning, but without the words, she had not been able to trust her own judgment. There would probably be long stretches of time between each such declaration, but she knew she would now hear the words every time he scolded her for not taking care of herself, or each time he made love to her. Of course, Jolene mused, there was no need to tell him that.

"Aye, but a lass can feel uncertain from time to time, can need some reassurance," she murmured.

Sigimor held her face between his hands, kissed her nose, then held her gaze with his. "Heed me, my sly Sassenach wife, ye are my mate. I love ye. There. I have said it twice now. Ye are the better half of me. Ye are my comfort, my joy, my pride, my reason for facing each day and getting on with the business of life. Ne'er doubt your importance to me or I will be placing a few sharp slaps on this bonnie bum of yours."

"Oh, Sigimor, I do love you so, you sweet-tongued devil."

"Always," he said in a soft serious voice. "Ye forgot to say always."

"Aye, my braw laddie, always. Always and forever. Until the sun forgets to rise in the morning," she whispered and the kiss he gave her told her all she needed to hear in reply.

Epilogue

Scottish border—3 years later

Smiling at the baby seated on her lap, Jolene then looked at her cousin Roger. "He is a beautiful child, Roger. Plump, healthy, and happy." She glanced toward Emma who sat on the floor before the fireplace laughing at the antics of Reynard, his half-siblings, and his cousins. "Emma fair shines with joy."

Roger immediately picked up his son when the boy reached out to him. "We both see little Peter as something of a miracle. Nearly as astonishing as you giving Sigimor twin daughters." He winked at her. "Black-haired daughters, too."

"There was quite a bit of astonishment all round when they arrived. With so many uncles, real and honorary, I fear they are in danger of becoming quite spoiled." Jolene smoothed her hand over her slightly rounded stomach. "This one will be a boy."

"Do you think your husband was disappointed not to get his heir?"

She looked at Sigimor who also sat near the fire allowing his daughter Bridie to climb all over him, then looked back at Roger. "Does he look disappointed?" she asked and smiled when Roger laughed. "Nay. As he says, he already has more heirs than any man needs. I know *you* are pleased to have an heir, but I suspect you would have been equally as pleased with a daughter."

"Aye." Roger kissed the top of his sleepy son's head. "Your husband predicted this you know." He nodded at her look of surprise and told her all Sigimor had said at the clearing that day almost three years ago and smiled when she laughed. "I thought it all nonsense myself. Yet when I brought Reynard to Emma, she took him into her arms, and became content. So, too, when we took in Peter's other children. Then her sister and her husband died and her two children came to live with us. Emma had a houseful of children and became very content indeed."

"She had children to love and care for."

"Aye, and that sadness I sometimes sensed in her disappeared. She had the family she had always wanted."

"And then there was little Peter."

"And then there was this wondrous gift from God."

Jolene looked at Reynard, now almost six. It had taken so long to arrange this reunion with the boy on her Scottish lands, lands now being run very competently by Somerled. Her pregnancy and then Emma's had caused several delays. She began to think that had been for the best. Reynard had been happy to see her, but no more than that. It had taken only a few moments for her to see that Emma had become his mother in his heart and mind, and Roger his father. He also had a bounty of children to play with. Although it was a litle sad to see that she had become of less importance to the child and that Peter was only a pleasant but fading memory now, Jolene knew it was for the best.

"Emma loves him," Roger said quietly, "as do I."

"I know. Tis easy to see. He is happy as only a child who knows he is loved can be. Have I thanked you yet for naming your child after my brother? It was good of you to honor him so."

"Emma insisted. When we were sure she was with child, I found myself telling her what your husband had said. Emma was most impressed with such reasoning." Roger exchanged a quick grin with Jolene. "She believed in it. She then decided that, grievous and tragic though Peter's death was, it set us on this path which has given us such joy. Emma wanted to honor him for that. Ah, someone has been hurt."

Jolene looked at her daughter Allason who was held securely in her father's arms as he sat down next to her. Allason's big green eyes held a mournful look and she was pouting slightly. Sigimor was trying very hard not to look amused. He was an excellent father, loving yet firm when he needed to be, but she did think he found too much amusement in his daughters's occasional naughtiness.

"Mama, I have a ouch," Allason said, holding out her arm and pointing to a very faint red spot.

After kissing the spot, Jolene asked, "How did that happen, my love?"

"I felled when I picked up the stool. It was heavy."

"Why did you pick up the stool?"

"To hit Reynard o'er the head 'cause he wasnae list'nen to me."

Ignoring the badly smothered laughter of Roger, Jolene lectured her pretty daughter about controlling her temper and not hitting people. She then had a brief argument with Allason about apologizing to Reynard, for Allason felt it was unnecesary since she had not hit him. When, after heaving a martyred sigh, Allason went to apologize to Reynard, Jolene frowned at Roger and Sigimor who looked far too amused. She was just about to lecture the men, too, when she realized they were now watching the children. One look told Jolene there was about to be more trouble. Reynard was looking very lordly, Allason looked furious, Bridie stood by her sister looking equally as furious, and Emma looked as if she was terrified she would start laughing. Jolene sympathized. Laughing at the wrong time was a danger a parent was constantly faced with.

"I have seen that look before," murmured Roger, smiling at Sigimor. "It looks very similar to the one you wore three years ago when you arrived at my camp to retrieve your wife. You looked much like an enraged bull. It sits rather oddly on your delicate, beautiful little girls, but 'tis the same look."

Sigimor grinned, kissed Jolene on the cheek, and started to return to his children. "Be at ease, wife. I will see to it."

Jolene watched as Sigimor crouched by his daughters, putting an arm around each little girl. Both began to talk to him as was their habit and it always astonished her that he seemed to be able to sort through the babble. Just looking at Sigimor with their daughters made Jolene feel warm, and so content she felt close to tears. She turned her attention back to Roger and caught him smiling at her.

"You are happy and very much in love, I think," he said.

"Oh, aye, very much so."

"And your husband is very much in love with you and those angel-faced little devils of yours."

"Aye, and although he is a little rough and will ne'er possess a courtier's skill with sweet words, I know I am loved. You know how hard it was for me to make that choice between two lives, between child and man, but I have no regrets. There lingered only a concern for Reynard, for how my choice affected him, but all of those concerns are now laid to rest. We are both just where we should be."

Roger nodded. "Well, I had best get this boy to his nurse."

A few moments after Roger left her, Sigimor returned to her side. He sat down next to her on the high-backed bench and draped his arm around her shoulders. Smiling faintly, she snuggled closer to him.

"Peace reigns," he said, idly stroking her arm. "Allason didnae think Reynard was accepting her reluctant apology with the reverence it was due and Bridie concurred." He grinned briefly when she chuckled, then placed his hand over her stomach. "Do ye feel weel?"

"Very well. I could not delay this visit any longer, Sigimor. Despite the letters exchanged, there was still a concern within me about Reynard. I needed to see him, to see his happiness. My choice that day was as important to him as it was to me."

"And do ye still feel ye made the right choice?" he asked quietly.

Jolene smiled at him and lightly stroked his cheek. "I speak of choice, but that day, when I faced leaving you, I knew there was no choice for me. I had to stay with you. It hurt to part from Reynard and this visit has fully healed that wound. I just needed to know that I had made the right choice for him as well and now I see that I did."

He pressed a kiss on her forehead. "And the right choice for ye was me."

"Aye, husband, the right choice for me was you and it will always be you. As I am the right choice for you."

"Och, aye, lass. Was, is, and will always be. I kenned that the moment I saw ye. In truth, I set out to conquer ye most thoroughly."

"You did that, husband. Most thoroughly indeed."

He nodded. "Good. I like to win."

Sigimor smiled and savored the sound of her laughter. He had his mate. He had two daughters who would probably turn his hair white and another child was on the way. Life was good. He just needed one little thing to make this moment perfect and he tightened his hold on his wife, the match he had waited so long for.

"Always, wife," he said and waited.

"Always, husband."

He nodded. Life was very good indeed.

ABOUT THE AUTHOR

Hannah Howell is an award-winning author who lives with her family in Massachusetts. She is the author of eighteen Zebra historical romances and is currently working on a new Highland historical romance, which will be published in December 2005. Hannah loves hearing from readers and you may write to her c/o Zebra Books. Please include a self-addressed stamped envelope if you wish a response.

Please turn the page for an exciting sneak peek of
Hannah Howell's newest historical romance
HIGHLAND CHAMPION
coming in December 2005!

Scotland, Spring 1475

What was an angel doing standing next to Brother Matthew? Liam thought as he peered through his lashes at the couple frowning down at him. And why could he not fully open his eyes? Then the pain hit and he groaned. Brother Matthew and the angel bent closer.

"Do ye think he will live?" asked Brother Matthew.

"Aye," replied the angel, "though I suspicion he will wish he hadnae for a wee while."

Strange that an angel should possess a voice that made a man think of firelit bedchambers, soft un-clothed skin, and thick furs, Liam mused. He tried to lift his hand, but the pain of even the smallest movement proved too much to bear. He felt as if he had been trampled by a horse. Mayhap several horses. Very large horses.

"He is a bonnie lad," said the angel as she gently smoothed one small, soft hand over Liam's forehead.

"How can ye tell that he is bonnie? He looks as if

someone staked him to the ground and rode over him with a herd of horses."

Brother Matthew and he had always thought alike in many ways, Liam recalled. He was one of the few men Liam had missed after leaving the monastery. He now missed the touch of the angel's soft hand. For the brief time it had brushed against his forehead, it had felt as if that light touch had smoothed away some of his pain.

"Aye, he does that," replied the angel. "And, yet, one can still see that he is tall, lean, and weel formed."

"Ye shouldnae be noticing such things!"

"Wheesht, Cousin, I am nay blind."

"Mayhap not, but 'tis still wrong. And, he isnae at his best now, ye ken."

"Och, nay, that is for certain. Howbeit, I am thinking that his best is verra good, aye? Mayhap as good as our cousin Payton, do ye think?"

Brother Matthew made a very scornful noise. "Better. Truth tell, 'tis why I ne'er believed he would stay with us."

Why should his appearance make someone think him a bad choice for the religious life? Liam did not think that was a particularly fair judgment, but could not seem to give voice to that opinion. Despite the pain he was in, his thoughts were clear enough. He just seemed to be unable to voice them, or make any movement to indicate that he heard these figures discussing him. Even though he could look at them through his lashes, his eyes were obviously not opening enough to let them know he was awake.

"Ye dinnae think he had a true calling?" asked the angel.

"Nay," Brother Matthew replied. "Oh, he liked the learning weel enough, was verra quick and bright, but we could only teach him so much here. We are but a small monastery, nay a rich one, and nay a great teaching place. I think, too, that he found this place too quiet, too peaceful. He missed his family. I have met his kinsmen and I can understand. A large, loud, somewhat, weel, untamed lot of men they are. The learning offered to him eased that restlessness in Liam for a while, but it wasnae enough in the end. The quiet routine, the sameness of the days began to wear upon his spirit, I think."

Liam was a little surprised at how well his old friend knew and understood him. He had been restless, still was in some ways. The quiet of the monastery, the rigid schedule of the monastic life had begun to press in upon him and feel more smothering than comforting. He *had* missed his family. For a moment he was actually glad that he seemed unable to speak for he feared he would be asking for them now like some forlorn child.

"Tis hard," said the angel. "I was most surprised that ye settled into the life so verra weel. But, ye have a true, deep calling, dinnae ye?"

"Aye, I do," Brother Matthew replied softly. "I did e'en as a child. But, ne'er think I dinnae miss all of ye, Keira. I did and do most painfully at times, but there is a brotherhood here, a family of sorts. Yet, I will probably visit again soon. I have begun to spend a great deal of time wondering how the bairns have grown, if everyone is still hale and strong, and many another such thing. Letters dinnae tell all."

"Nay, they dinnae." Keira sighed. "I have missed them all, too, and I have been gone for but a six-month."

Keira, Liam repeated the name in his mind. A fine name. He tried to move his arm despite the pain and felt a twinge of panic when it would not respond to his command. When he realized he was bound to the bed, his unease grew even stronger. Why would they do that to him? Why did they not wish him to move? Were his injuries so dire? Was he wrong to think he had been given aid? Had he actually been made a prisoner? Even as those questions spun through his mind, he fought past his pain enough to tug against his bonds. A groan escaped him as that pain quickly and fiercely swept through his body from head to toe. He stilled when a pair of small, soft hands touched him, one upon his forehead and one upon his chest.

"I think he begins to wake, Cousin," Keira said. "Hush, sir. Be at peace."

"Tied," Liam hissed the word out from between tightly gritted teeth, the pain caused by speaking that one small word telling him that his face had undoubtedly taken a severe beating.

"Why?"

"To keep ye still, Liam," Brother Matthew replied. "Keira doesnae think anything is broken save for your right leg, but ye were thrashing about so much it worried us some."

"Aye," agreed Keira. "Ye were beat near to death, sir. Tis best if ye remain verra still so as not to add to your injuries or pain. Are ye in much pain?"

Liam muttered a fierce curse at what he considered a very stupid question. He heard Brother Matthew gasp in shock. To his surprise, he heard Keira laugh softly.

"Twas indeed a foolish question," she said, laughter still tinting her sultry voice. "Ye dinnae seem to have a spot upon ye that isnae brilliant with bruising. Aye, and your right leg was broken. Tis a verra clean break and I have set it. After three days there is still no sign of poison in the wound or in the blood, so it should heal verra weel."

"Liam, 'tis Brother Matthew. Keira and I have brought ye to the wee cottage at the edge of the monastery's lands. The brothers wouldnae allow her to tend to your wounds within the monastery, I fear." He sighed. "They werenae too happy with her presence e'en though she was weel hidden away in the guest quarters. Brother Paul was particularly agitated."

"Agitated?" muttered Keira. "Cousin Elspeth would say he—"

"Aye," Brother Matthew hastily interrupted, "I ken what our cousin Elspeth would say. I think she has lived too long amongst those unruly Armstrongs. She has gained far too free a tongue for a proper lady."

Keira made a rude noise. "My, but ye have become verra pious, Cousin."

"Of course I have. I am a monk. We are trained to be pious. Now, I can help ye give Liam some potion or change his bandages, if ye wish, but then I must return to the monastery."

"Ah, weel then, best see if he needs to relieve himself," Keira said. "I will just step outside so that ye can see to that. Now that he is waking, 'tis best, I think. I shall just run up to the monastery's garden and collect a few herbs. I shall be but a few moments."

"What do ye mean *now* that he is waking?" demanded Brother Matthew, but then he grunted with irritation when the only reply he got was the door closing behind Keira as she hurried away. "Wretched wee lass."

"Cousin?" Liam asked, realizing that not only was his throat injured, but his jaw and mouth as well.

"Cousin? Oh, aye, the lass is my cousin. One of a vast horde of cousins, if truth be told. A Murray, ye ken."

"Kirkcaldy?"

"Tis what I am, aye. Her grandmother was one, too. Now, I do fear that nay matter how gentle I am, this is going to hurt."

It did. Liam was sure he screamed at one point, and that only increased his pain. He welcomed the blackness when it swept over him, as he suspected the continuously apologizing Brother Matthew did.

"Oh, dear, he looks a wee bit paler," Keira said as she set the herbs she had collected down on a table and moved to stand at the side of the small bed Liam was tied to.

"He still suffers a great deal of pain, and I fear I added to it," said Brother Matthew.

"Ye couldnae help it, Cousin. He is better, nay doubt about it, but such injuries will be slow to heal. There truly isnae a part of this mon that isnae hurt. Tis a true miracle that only his leg was broken."

"Are ye certain that he was only beaten? Or that he was e'en beaten at all?"

"Aye, Cousin, he *was* beaten. I have nay doubt about that, but he could have been tossed off that hill, too. Some of these injuries could be from the rocky slope his body would have fallen down and the equally rocky ground he landed on. I dinnae suppose he was able to tell ye what happened to him, was he?"

"Och, nay. Nay. He spoke but a word or two, then made a pitiful cry and has been like this e'er since." Brother Matthew shook his head. "I wish I could understand this. Who would do such a terrible thing to the mon? I ken I havenae seen that much of the mon o'er the years since he left here, but he really wasnae the sort of mon to make enemies. Certainly nay such vicious ones."

Keira idly tested the strength of the bonds that held Liam still upon the bed and carefully studied the man. "I suspect jealousy is a problem he must often deal with."

Brother Matthew frowned at his cousin. She seemed far too interested in Liam Cameron, revealing more than just a healer's interest in a patient. A healer surely did not need to touch her patient's hair as often as Keira did Liam's thick, dark copper hair. Liam was certainly not looking his best, might well have lost a little of his beauty due to this vicious beating, but there was clearly enough allure left in his battered body and face to draw Keira's interest.

He tried to see Keira as a woman grown, not simply as a cousin he had played with as a child. His eyes widened slightly as he began to see that his cousin was no teasing child now, but a very attractive woman. She was small and slight, yet womanly, for her breasts were well shaped and full and her hips were pleasingly curved. Her hair was a rich, shining black, and hung in a thick braid to well past her tiny waist. That hair made her fair skin look even purer, a soft milk white with the blush of good health. Keira's oval face held a delicate beauty, her nose being small and straight, a hint of strength revealed in her small chin, and her cheekbones being high and finely shaped. What caught everyone's interest was her eyes. Set beneath gently arced black brows, and trimmed with thick, long lashes, were a pair of deep green eyes. Those wide eyes bespoke innocence, but their depths held all the womanly mystery that could so intrigue a man. He was a little startled to realize that her mouth, slightly wide and full of lip, held the same contradictions. Her smile could be the epitome of sweet innocence, but Brother Matthew suddenly knew men of the world would quickly see the sensuality there as well. He suddenly feared it had been a serious error in judgment on his part to allow her to tend to a man like Liam Cameron.

"Ye have a rather fierce look upon your face, Cousin," Keira said as she moved to begin preparing more salve for Liam's injuries. "He willnae die, I promise ye. He will just be a verra long time in healing."

"I believe ye. Tis just that, weel, one thing Liam did find hard to abide about the monastic life was, weel, was . . ."

"No lasses to smile at." She grinned at the severe frown he gave her for it sat so ill upon his boyishly handsome face.

"I think, just as with our cousin Payton, this mon has a way with the lasses. Aye, and he need do nay more than smile at them."

"I dinnae think he e'en needs to smile," grumbled Brother Matthew.

"Nay, probably not. Come, Cousin, dinnae look so troubled. He is no danger to me now, is he? Aye, and e'en when he is healed enough to smile again, he can only be a danger to me if I wish him to be. Ye cannae think that, with the kinsmen I have, I havenae been verra weel taught in the ways of men." She glanced toward Liam. "Is he a bad mon, then? A vile, heartless seducer of innocents?"

Brother Matthew sighed. "Nay, I would ne'er believe such a thing of him."

"Then there is naught to fret o'er, is there. Tis best if we worry o'er our many other troubles. They are of more importance than whether or nay I can resist the sweet smiles of a bonnie lad. I have been here nigh on two months now, Cousin. There has been nary a sign of my enemy so I think, soon, I must try to get home to Donncoill."

"I ken it. I am fair surprised none of your kinsmen have come round. Tis odd that they wouldnae start to wonder on how long ye have stayed at a monastery, or e'en why the monks would allow it."

"Tisnae so verra unusual for guests, male or female, to linger in the guest quarters, and I paid weel for the privilege."

She smiled and patted his arm when he flushed with embarrassment over that hard truth. "It has been worth it. I needed to hide and mend my wounds, needed to o'ercome my grief and fear, and needed to be certain that, when I did go home, I wasnae leading that murderous bastard Rauf to the gates of Donncoill."

"Your family would protect ye, Keira. They would feel it their duty, their right, and willnae be pleased that ye denied them."

Keira winced. "I ken it, but I will deal with it. I also had to decide what to do. Duncan pulled a vow from me and I had to think hard on how to fulfill it, and how much it might cost me to do so."

"I ken it willnae be easy. Rauf is cunning and vicious. Yet, ye swore to your husband ye would see to it that his people didnae suffer under Rauf's rule if he failed to win the battle that night. He failed. He died that night, Keira, so your vow is much akin to one made at a mon's deathbed. Ye have to do all ye can to fulfill it." He kissed her cheek and started for the door. "I will see ye in the morning. Sleep weel."

"Ye, too, Cousin."

The moment he was gone, Keira sighed and sat down in the little chair next to Liam Cameron's bed. Her cousin made it all sound so simple. She dearly wished it was. The vow she had made to her poor, ill-fated husband weighed heavily on her mind and heart. So did the fates of the people of Ardgleann. Duncan had cared deeply for his people, a mixed lot of gentle and somewhat odd souls. It distressed her to think of how they must be suffering under Rauf's rule. She prayed for them every night, but she could not fully dispel the guilt she felt over running away. Although some of what Duncan had asked of her did not seem right, the people of Ardgleann could no longer wait for her to debate the moral complexities of it all, however. It was time, far past time, to do something.

She idly bathed Liam with a soft cloth and cool water. He did not really have a fever, but it seemed to make him rest more quietly. He was a strong man and she felt certain he would continue to recover. When he would be able to tend to himself, she had better have decided what to do about Ardgleann and Rauf. Once she knew why Liam had been hurt and was certain that no enemy hunted him still, she would leave him in the care of the monks and face her own destiny.

Keira felt an immediate pang at the thought of leaving the man and almost laughed at the absurdity of it. He was a mass of bruises and had barely said three words in as many days. She supposed that she felt some odd bond with him because she had been the one to find him. In truth, she had been drawn to him by a strange blend of dreams and compulsion. It had been a little frightening for, although similar experiences had occurred in the past, she had never seen things so clearly or felt as strongly. Even now she could not shake the feeling that there was more to it all than helping him recover from his injuries.

"Foolishness," she muttered and shook her head as she patted him dry with a soft rag.

Perhaps she should send word to his people, she thought as she began to make a hearty broth to feed to him when he woke again. From what her cousin had told her, Sir Liam's kinsmen were more than capable of protecting him. Keira quickly discarded the idea for the same reason she had given her cousin when he had suggested sending for the Camerons. Sir Liam might not want that, might be reluctant to pull his family into whatever trouble he had gotten himself into. She could sympathize for, she, too, hesitated to involve her family in her own troubles.

That, too, was foolish, she suspected. She had done nothing wrong, had not caused the trouble or invited the danger. If one of her family was in such trouble, she would be ready and eager to ride to their side. Which is why they would hesitate to tell her about it, she suddenly thought and briefly grinned. It was instinctive to try to keep a loved one safe, she decided. When her family found out the truth, they would be angry, perhaps a little offended or hurt, but they would understand for they would know in their hearts that they would have done the very same thing.

And, she told herself as she sat down at the small table near the fire, if this man was as close to his family as her cousin implied, he would do the same. The last time she had seen her cousin Gillyanne, she had heard a few tales about the Camerons. Even though the tales had been told to amuse everyone, they had revealed that the Camerons were probably as close a family as her own. There was also Sir

Liam's manly pride to consider. It would undoubtedly bristle at the implication that he could not take care of himself. No, Keira decided, it was not a good idea to send for his people without his permission.

After a meal of bread, cheese, and cold venison, Keira took a hasty bath. She then settled herself upon a pallet made up near the fire. Keira stared into the flames and waited for sleep to come. She hated this time of the night, hated the silence, hated the fact that sleep was so slow to come, leaving her alone in the silence with her memories. Try as she might, she could not shake free of the grip of those dark memories. She could only suppress them for a while.

Duncan had been a good man, passingly handsome, and gentle. She had not loved him and she still felt guilty about that, even though it was hardly her fault. At nearly two-and-twenty, however, she had decided she could wait no longer for some great, passionate love to stroll her way. She had wanted children and a home of her own. Although she loved her family deeply, she had begun to feel an increasing need to spread her wings, to walk her own path. Marriage did not usually free a woman, but all her instincts had told her that Duncan would never try to master her. He had wanted a true partner and, knowing how rare that was, she had accepted him when he had asked her to be his bride.

She could still recall the doubts of her family, especially those of her grandmother Lady Maldie and her cousin Gillyanne. Their special gifts had told them that she did not love the man she was about to marry. They had sensed her unease, one she could not explain even to herself. Keira was not sure it was a good thing that they had not pressed her on that, then roundly scolded herself. They had respected her choice, and it had been *her* choice.

Why she had felt uneasy from the moment she had accepted Duncan's proposal of marriage was still a puzzle to her. Keira had smothered that unease and married him. Within hours of marrying him, the first hint of trouble between them had begun and within days of reaching Ardgleann the trouble with Rauf had begun. She had thought that explained all those odd feelings she had suffered, the reluctance and the wariness, but now she was not so sure. Every instinct she had told her that the puzzle was not solved yet.

Just as she began to relax, welcoming the comfort of sleep, a harsh cry from Sir Liam startled her. Keira hurried to his side to find him straining against his bonds, muttering furious curses at enemies only he could see. She stroked his forehead and spoke softly to him, telling him over and over where he was, who cared for him now, and that he was safe. It surprised her a little when he quickly grew calm again.

"Jolene?" he whispered.

Keira wondered why hearing him speak another woman's name should irritate her as much as it did. "Nay, Keira," she said as she placed her hand over his to try to stop him from tugging against his bonds.

"Keira," he repeated and grasped her hand in his. "Aye. Keira. Black hair. Confused me. Thought I was home. At Dubheidland."

"Ah. She is your healer?" Keira tried to wriggle her hand free of his grasp, but he would not release her, so she sat down in the chair at his bedside.

"Sig'mor's wife. Lady of Dubheidland. Thought I was home."

"So ye said. I can give ye something to ease the pain, if ye wish it."

"Nay. Thought I was caught again."

She could see that it pained him to speak, but could not resist asking, "Do ye remember what happened to you?"

"Caught. Beaten. Thrown away. Ye found me?"

"Aye, me and my cousin Brother Matthew."

"Good. Safe here."

"Aye, ye will be." She tried yet again to wriggle her hand free of his, but failed.

"Stay." He heaved a sigh. "Please. Stay."

Keira inwardly cursed the weakness that caused her to heed that plea. She carefully shifted her seat closer to the bed so that she could sit more comfortably as she waited for him to release her hand. After a few moments of silence, she wondered if he had gone back to sleep, but his grip upon her hand remained firm. To her surprise, he began to stroke the back of her hand with his thumb. The warmth that gesture stirred within her was a little alarming, but she could not bring herself to stop him.

This was not good, Keira thought. The light brush of a man's thumb over her hand should not make her feel warm. True, it was a very nice hand, the fingers long and elegant, but it was too benign a caress to stir any interest. Or, it should be. She looked at his battered face and sighed. To all the troubles she already had, she realized she now had to add one more. A man she did not know, a man whose face was so bruised and swollen it would probably give a child the night terrors, could stir her blood with the simple stroke of his thumb.